Christmas
with the
Railway Girls

isie Thomas was born and brought up in Manchester,
ich provides the location for her Railway Girls novels.
e loves writing stories with strong female characters, set
imes when women needed determination and vision to
ke their mark. The Railway Girls series is inspired by
r great-aunt Jessie, who worked as a railway clerk during
e First World War.

Maisie now lives on the beautiful North Wales coast
th her railway enthusiast husband, Kevin, and their two
cue cats. They often enjoy holidays chugging up and
wn the UK's heritage steam railways.

Also by Maisie Thomas

The Railway Girls
Secrets of the Railway Girls
The Railway Girls in Love

Christmas
with the
Railway Girls

MAISIE THOMAS

PENGUIN BOOKS

PENGUIN BOOKS

UK | USA | Canada | Ireland | Australia
India | New Zealand | South Africa

Penguin Books is part of the Penguin Random House group
of companies whose addresses can be found at
global.penguinrandomhouse.com

Published by Penguin Books in 2021
001

Typeset in 10.75/13.5 pt Palatino LT Std by
Integra Software Services Pvt. Ltd, Pondicherry

Printed and bound in Great Britain by Clays Ltd, Elcograf S.p.A.

The authorised representative in the EEA is Penguin Random House
Ireland, Morrison Chambers, 32 Nassau Street, Dublin D02 YH68

A CIP catalogue record for this book is available from
the British Library

ISBN: 978–1–78746–790-3

www.greenpenguin.co.uk

MIX
Paper from
responsible sources
FSC® C018179

Penguin Random House is committed to a
sustainable future for our business, our readers
and our planet. This book is made from Forest
Stewardship Council® certified paper.

Acknowledgements

Special thanks to my editor, Jennie Rothwell, whose commitment to this series and to the individual characters helped make this a better book.

Many thanks to Catherine Boardman, Zoe Morton, Jane Cable, Jen Gilroy, Beverley Hopper and Jenny over the road for their support.

I am grateful to Kevin for devising the near miss in the marshalling yard and for answering various random questions.

And a huge thank you to everyone who read the first three Railway Girls books. It's because of you that I was asked to come back and write three more.

CHAPTER ONE

Late June, 1941

Cordelia stood at the foot of the tall pole, looking up at the pair of railway signals jutting out high above her. It used to be scary to climb a ladder that was vertical rather than one propped up at an angle, but she was used to it now and didn't think twice about settling her knapsack on her back, grasping the sides of the ladder and placing her foot on the bottom rung. Some signals weren't all that high off the ground. It was simply a matter of their being visible to the train driver. These two signals were at least twenty feet up, because of the water tank beside the permanent way that would have obscured the train driver's view if the signals were lower.

She climbed to the top. If there was more than one signal, she always began at the top and worked down. As she stepped from the ladder onto the wooden platform, she felt the usual little swirling sensation in the pit of her stomach, but after all these months of experience in her job as a lamp-woman, it lasted only a moment. It was another cool day. Last week had been gloriously hot, but the end of June looked set to be significantly less warm. Beneath overcast skies, Cordelia removed the lamp from the signal arrangement, cleaned it and put it back in position before swinging herself back onto the ladder to climb down to the platform beneath.

The upper signal was for the main line, the lower for the branch line. How proud she had been when she had learned

1

that. The feeling of becoming good at her job above and beyond simply going through the motions of the endless cleaning and putting back of lamps, the feeling of actually understanding the workings of the railway, had made her rock on her heels with satisfaction. But who was there to share her small triumph? Not Kenneth. He didn't like her working on the railway. He would have infinitely preferred her to join the Women's Voluntary Service or take on a role in the Citizens Advice Bureau, like her friends had.

She couldn't tell her friends either – not *those* friends, her old, long-established friends, with whom she had for years played bridge, learned flower arranging and attended matinée performances at the theatre. Those ladies were similar to herself, married to well-to-do professional men and living in smart houses, with at the very least a daily help, if not a live-in maid. These friends did their bit for the war effort dressed in the green of the WVS – the whole uniform, mark you, not just the hat or the jacket with which less well-off women had to make do – while for her war work, Cordelia wore sturdy dungarees and a headscarf – though, she acknowledged with a smile, her headscarves were pure silk.

She had new friends now. My goodness, what an eye-opener that had been. Whoever would have imagined before the war that Mrs Kenneth Masters, Mrs thoroughly middle-class Kenneth Masters, would make friends with women from lower down the social scale? They weren't superficial friendships either. She truly valued, even loved, her circle of railway friends, especially Dot, dear, working-class Dot, whose big heart and common sense Cordelia treasured.

It was thanks to Miss Emery that the group had got together in the first place. She was the assistant welfare supervisor with responsibility for women and girls of all grades. On Cordelia's first day on the railways, Miss Emery had given the newcomers a piece of advice that had – well, Cordelia couldn't speak for the others, but from her own point of view, it had changed her life, if that didn't sound too dramatic. It all came down to class distinctions. Take her and Dot. As Dot had rightly pointed out, in normal circumstances she would have been Cordelia's charwoman, beating her rugs and scrubbing her kitchen floor. But Miss Emery's advice had been to set aside disparities in class and become friends. Cordelia had hidden her initial shock at the very idea. Fortunately for her, she had had the good sense to appreciate that Miss Emery wouldn't have suggested such an extraordinary thing without a solid reason and she had soon found that the assistant welfare supervisor was right.

Cordelia had grown fond of the younger girls who made up the bulk of their group, Mabel, Joan, Alison, Colette and Persephone, who were all in their twenties; she had also developed a real rapport with Dot, who, like herself, was in her forties, married and a mother, though Dot had two grandchildren as well. In recent weeks, their group had opened its arms to welcome newcomer Margaret, whom Joan knew from when the two of them had worked at Ingleby's before the war.

If anybody (namely Kenneth) had ever doubted the sincerity and depth of the railway girls' friendship, Cordelia believed that a certain event at the beginning of the month had proved it beyond doubt. This was when she and Dot had had the honour of being mothers of the bride to Joan. There had been four mothers of the bride altogether, the other two being Joan's then landlady, Mrs Cooper, and her fellow lodger, Mrs Grayson, who had an unhappy past involving a dead baby and an errant husband.

Joan and Bob's wedding had been a touching and emotional occasion, but the reception that followed had been

3

even more special because, following a water leak in the church hall where the reception had been due to take place, Joan's friends had mucked in and put together a fresh reception with all the trimmings in the station buffet, to the delight and astonishment of the happy couple, from whom the disaster of the water leak had been kept secret. Cordelia had been proud to be involved. It was one of the best days she had had, if not the very best day, since war had been declared.

She was due to meet up with her friends in the buffet after work this evening and it was going to be one of those special times when they were all present, something that didn't happen often because of shift patterns and compulsory overtime. Warmth radiated through her as she thought of the tickets she was going to hand out.

She climbed down the ladder to the ground and set off at a brisk pace for her next set of lamps. Sometimes, she worked in the yards outside Victoria Station, removing, cleaning and replacing the sidelights and tail lights on the wagons. Other times, like this week, she walked the line, cleaning the lamps along an allocated stretch of the permanent way. That brought another smile to her lips. To the rest of the population, it was the railway track, but she, being in the know, called it the permanent way. Just another tiny piece of knowledge that, added to all the others, made her feel professional, a feeling she very much enjoyed. She had married in 1920, and since then her life had revolved entirely around the home, which was only to be expected of a family such as theirs – but how wonderful it was now to have a life and a purpose outside the home.

Her job was menial, according to Kenneth.

'People of our sort don't work with their hands.'

If she was honest, Cordelia had felt somewhat taken aback when she'd discovered what her war work on the railways was going to involve, but she had hidden that response, just as she had hidden her initial response to Miss Emery's advice, and afterwards she was grateful that she had, on both counts.

'It's a novelty for now,' Kenneth had told their friends, speaking with the confidence of a gentleman whose well-bred wife would never contradict him in public. 'When Cordelia gets tired of it, there are plenty of more suitable roles in which she will be far more useful.'

Cordelia felt extremely useful where she was, thank you very much. Her job might involve working with her hands and it might not be the most intellectually stimulating task, but, crikey, one thing you could never say about it was that it wasn't useful. Keeping the lamps clean so they could shine clearly helped to keep the trains running and helped keep the railways safe. Her job as a lampwoman might not seem like much on the face of it, but her contribution to the war effort was, in its own small way, to help keep the country's essential transport system moving. Britain couldn't manage without its railways. How else could they have sent hundreds of thousands of children to safety at the outbreak of war? How else could thousands upon thousands of soldiers rescued from Dunkirk have been dispersed speedily throughout the country? How else were food, fuel, munitions and troops to be moved around efficiently? The way Cordelia saw it, the railways were every bit as important as the army, the navy and the air force.

She realised she had thrown back her shoulders as she walked to the next set of signals. Quite right too. She was proud of her job and proud, too, of the work done by each of her friends. Dot was a parcels porter, working on the trains, Joan a station porter, assisting passengers on Victoria Station itself. Persephone was also based at Victoria Station for her work as a ticket collector, though her chums sometimes joked that she had the additional job of giving men's spirits a bit of a boost by being so beautiful. Margaret worked in the engine sheds, cleaning the locomotives, while Alison and Colette both had clerical positions in nearby Hunts Bank. The only other member of their group who worked outdoors on the permanent way was Mabel, who belonged to a gang of lengthmen, whose job was to shore up the ballast beneath the railway sleepers, the eight-foot-long wooden planks on which the tracks lay. The difference between Mabel and Cordelia was that whereas Cordelia sometimes worked in the yards and sidings belonging to Victoria Station, Mabel was out on the permanent way every single day come rain or shine.

Cordelia gradually made her way down the line, covering today's portion of this week's section. A week's work was around a hundred and fifty lamps, including those on level crossings. When she finished for the day, she walked up the slope onto a station platform. While she waited to catch the next train into Manchester Victoria, she nipped into the Ladies to spend a penny – though she didn't actually put a penny in the slot to unlock the lavatory door. One distinctly annoying aspect of working on the railways was the shocking scarcity of facilities for female employees, most notably the lack of lavatories. Women railway workers were obliged to use the same facilities as the women passengers, which was fine up to a point, but many of them drew the line at paying for the privilege. Not to worry, though, as a cleverly bent nail could undo the lock if you knew precisely how to manoeuvre it. Although it irked her that the London, Midland and Scottish Railway hadn't seen fit to make proper provision for its many women workers, it didn't sit well with Cordelia, maybe because she was married to a solicitor, to cheat LMS out of its pennies, so she made up for it by putting half a crown a week into the

Red Cross box. She was the local collector, both around where she lived and also in the lamp sheds, for the Red Cross's successful Penny a Week Fund, which bought comforts for the troops.

Standing in front of the mirror over the pair of basins, Cordelia removed her green silk headscarf and checked her clip-on earrings were still in place: she wasn't dressed without her earrings. Then she delved in her knapsack for her comb, powder compact and lipstick. Wearing dungarees was no reason not to look her best. Shaking out her scarf, she folded it in half into a triangle, laid it over her head and tied it at the back of her neck, beneath her hair, careful not to disturb the stuffed stocking around which her hair was rolled, making it sit just above shoulder-length.

She used to wear her hair shorter and fashionably shingled when she was in her thirties, but as she had drawn, oh horror, ever closer to her fortieth birthday, she had grown her hair because she felt it was her last chance to have a bit of length. Then the dreaded age had hit her and she had discovered that being forty didn't feel different to any age starting with a thirty and she had ended up keeping it longer.

She went onto the platform just as the train came into view, white clouds puffing from the funnel. As the train ran alongside the platform, the white clouds stopped appearing and there was a hissing noise, then the brakes shrieked and some of the doors were thrown open even before a deep clunking sound signalled that the mighty vehicle had come to a halt.

The train was packed, which was par for the course at this time of day. Cordelia squeezed aboard, holding her knapsack close to her body so as not to bash anyone with it. She edged into a corner, giving a general smile to the passengers who had somehow made room for her, and pretended not to notice the glances that came her way. She was well aware of the disparity between her workmanlike dungarees and her air of well-bred elegance. She liked the contrast. She was proud of it. It showed what she was made of.

Cordelia Masters – lampwoman.

CHAPTER TWO

When the train pulled into Manchester Victoria, Cordelia was more or less carried off it by the press of bodies. At the end of the platform, she passed through the ticket barrier, exchanging a smile – there was no time for more – with Mr Thirkle as passengers thrust their tickets at him, then she was on the concourse, from where she headed by a route unknown to the travelling public to the station's array of workshops and sheds.

In the lamp shed, she logged her day's work, then disappeared into the glorified cupboard that served as the women's cloakroom, where she got changed, then emerged wearing a linen dress with padded shoulders beneath a lightweight edge-to-edge coat, together with gloves that flared slightly at the wrists, gauntlet-style, and a simple pale pink felt hat with a trim of deep magenta. Not everyone wore hats any more, but Cordelia always did. In the lamp room, no one looked twice at her transformation, though the first few times it had happened, heads had turned and everyone had gawped, to use a word Cordelia had picked up from Dot.

She returned to the station, where the concourse was crowded. Above their heads, the large clock hanging from the gantry told Cordelia she was in good time for meeting up with her friends. A porter made his way carefully through the mass of people, pulling a flatbed trolley loaded with suitcases, parcels and sacks, with a second trolley linked on behind.

Cordelia threaded her way towards the buffet, which was one of a group of buildings within the station, each of which was tiled in pale yellow on its exterior walls. Inside, she joined a short queue, pleased to see that her friends had already arrived and were crushed around a table. If the buffet wasn't too busy, they would push two tables together, but it wasn't fair to do that when there were lots of customers.

Cordelia's gaze went first to Dot Green, the dear lady who had unwittingly taught her that friendship between the classes was perfectly possible. Dot wore her coat over her porter's uniform so as to hide the latter from the eyes of the general public. If she didn't do this, she wouldn't be allowed to take the weight off her feet in the buffet. Dot's faithful old coat had perished a few weeks ago during that terrible raid at the beginning of June, when it was used to help smother an incendiary, so Cordelia had given Dot a coat of her own that she'd had since before the war, a loose-fitting navy garment with wide lapels and big patch pockets.

'Please don't be offended,' Cordelia had said when she offered it. 'I have my wine-coloured coat that I love, so you wouldn't be depriving me. In fact, the only way in which you'll deprive me is if you refuse me the pleasure of giving this coat to my dear, brave friend.'

To Cordelia's delight, Dot had accepted. Cordelia would never have revealed to their friends where Dot's new coat had come from, but Dot had no such reservations. When their young friends had admired it and asked where she had got it – the question on everyone's lips these days, since the introduction of clothes rationing – she'd had no hesitation in proudly declaring she was wearing Cordelia's cast-off.

'It puts me in mind of my auntie Aggie,' Dot had told them with a chuckle. 'She never had sixpence to scratch herself with, but when my cousin Lorna got wed, Auntie Aggie wore the best coat any of us had ever seen.'

'Did she make it?' asked Alison.

'Nay, love. She piked off to the poshest part of Parrs Wood and bought it there.'

'How could she afford it?' asked Mabel.

'Because she got it from a jumble sale,' Dot had laughed. 'Posh folk pass on posh things.' She'd reached across and squeezed Cordelia's arm. 'Like my friend here.'

Arriving at the front of the queue, Cordelia ordered a cup of tea from Mrs Jessop, exchanging a few pleasantries as it was poured, then she went over to her friends, who had saved her a seat.

'This is the first time I've seen you this week,' Alison said to her. 'Have you been working in the yard?'

'No, I've been out walking the line, though this week it isn't exactly glorious summer weather to be doing so.'

'But overcast skies mean less likelihood of air raids,' Persephone pointed out and the others nodded. There hadn't been as many raids in recent weeks, though there had still been enough to make everyone feel they hadn't had enough sleep.

'Please let's talk about something other than the war,' said Joan. Then she laughed. 'That's a tall order these days. Everything relates back to the war.'

'Are you and Bob settled happily in your new home?' Margaret asked her, adding, 'Well, I suppose it's not so new now.'

Joan's smile warmed her blue eyes. 'Everything's fine and we're very lucky to have our own sitting room. Not that we have it entirely to ourselves. Young Jimmy often knocks. He loves having Bob in the house.'

'He must miss his dad,' Mabel said sympathetically.

11

'We had Bob's mum and dad over for tea on Sunday and Bob and his dad ended up taking Jimmy to the park to play cricket.'

'I bet Sheila gave our Jimmy a clip round the ear for that,' said Dot. 'I hope he didn't put the mockers on your afternoon. The trouble is there are so many lads now in need of a father's guiding hand, thanks to this war. There – Joan said everything related back to the war, and she's right.'

Cordelia nodded. 'But it isn't all bad. Look at us. We wouldn't have one another, but for the war. And it isn't just that we're friends. Our lives are becoming intertwined – especially in your case, Joan. Your mother-in-law is the foreman of Mabel's gang of lengthmen, and your landlady is Dot's daughter-in-law.'

'Don't forget Mrs Cooper,' Mabel added. 'Joan's cleaner is her old landlady.'

This was followed by a short silence and there was emotion in the glances they all exchanged, because a further connection within their group was that Mrs Cooper was the mother of lovely, vibrant Lizzie, a railway girl like themselves, who had been killed in an air raid last year. A further connection was that Joan had subsequently been moved into Lizzie's old job as a station porter.

Cordelia reached for her handbag. 'I have something for you all – the tickets for the War Weapons Week dance in July.'

It was gratifying to see the others looking pleased and interested. Cordelia was one of the organisers of the dance. There were many such fundraising events these days. Not just dances but whist drives, raffles and beat-the-clock crossword evenings. Even an unpretentious jumble sale that raised just a couple of pounds made a difference.

Cordelia handed round the tickets. One each for Persephone and Margaret, who didn't have boyfriends.

'If you need another, let me know, but don't worry about coming alone, because you'll be with all of us. Two for you, Dot, and let me know if you want tickets for your daughters-in-law. Two for Joan – and I hope you'll rope in all of Bob's family. Two for Mabel, though I know you can't say at this stage if Harry can come.'

'Even if he can't,' said Mabel, 'I'll still pay for the ticket.'

'That's good of you.' Cordelia smiled at her. 'Two for Colette.'

'Thank you,' said Colette, taking them.

It was especially pleasing to know that Colette would be able to come. Tony, her husband, had kept her wrapped in cotton wool until fairly recently and the poor girl had hardly had any social life. While it was entirely laudable that Tony wanted to keep her safe in these uncertain times, it was better that she was now able to spend a meaningful amount of time with her friends.

'And last but not least, Alison, these are for you and Paul. Tell me, does your sister have a boyfriend?'

'Yes, but he's away in the army.'

'Never mind. I hope you'll also invite your parents and your sister to the dance.'

Alison laughed. 'You're in the wrong job. You should be a door-to-door salesman.'

'I'm determined to make this fundraiser a huge success,' said Cordelia. 'Most of my Penny a Week people are coming, and my husband is under orders to sell tickets to everybody in his law firm.'

'Have you had any luck talking him round so that your Emily can come home?' asked Dot.

Cordelia drew in a breath. Realising she was going to sigh, she stopped herself. Unhappiness quivered inside her, but she didn't let it show. It wasn't the done thing to put your feelings on display. But, oh, how she ached to have her daughter home again.

'He wants to keep her safe.' She deliberately kept her tone light. 'No one can blame him for that.'

'He's trying to be a good father,' said Mabel.

'I know,' Cordelia agreed, 'and I completely understand. I don't want Emily to be in danger any more than he does, but ... '

'But you miss her and you want her at home with you,' said Dot. 'We all understand. Heaven knows, I remember the anguish when our Jimmy and Jenny were evacuated when war was declared – and then the overwhelming joy when they came home again because of the Phoney War. But ever since then, there's been the worry and guilt of having them here during the air raids. It's complicated. You can't bear to be parted from your children, but at the same time you want to keep them safe.'

Cordelia's heartbeat quickened, but once more she concealed it beneath her usual air of calm. 'I know. Emily's safety matters more than anything.'

Even so ... Was it wrong of her? Was she being selfish? The fact was she would willingly live with any amount of anguish if only she could have her daughter home again.

Colette looked at the tickets in her hand. It would be lovely to spend an evening out dancing with her friends. Tony had never been a great one for socialising, but he had turned over a new leaf earlier this year and now always came with her when she called on dear Mrs Cooper. Colette was enormously fond of Mrs Cooper – and Mrs Grayson, too, of course. Such warm-hearted ladies and so hospitable. They were delighted to welcome Tony, and not just because he helped out in the vegetable garden and around the house.

If only they knew.

14

Mabel gave Colette a nudge. 'Don't forget to put those tickets in your bag. You don't want to lose them.'

With a smile, Colette reached down and picked up her handbag. It was cream leather with a padded handle and a metal clip. It was the last present Mother had given her and Colette treasured it.

Mabel leaned her head towards Colette's. 'I've been trying to persuade Mrs Cooper to come to the dance.'

'She is coming, but only to sell raffle tickets.'

'I know, and it's such a shame. I can appreciate that it would be difficult for Mrs Grayson to come. It's too big an occasion for her – not like Joan's wedding. But Mrs Cooper ought to join in the fun with the rest of us.'

'It's kind of you,' said Colette, 'but I think she's made up her mind.'

'Don't say that. I was hoping to rope you in to help me twist her arm.'

Colette hesitated. Should she tell Mabel what Mrs Cooper had quietly confided in her? The date of the War Weapons Week dance would have been her twentieth wedding anniversary.

'I shan't feel like dancing and the last thing I want to do is spoil the occasion for others,' she had said. 'I'll be happier on my own selling raffle tickets. That'll keep me busy.'

Knowing how much Mabel cared for Mrs Cooper, Colette was tempted to tell her, but then held back. It was up to Mrs Cooper to decide whom she told.

'Honestly,' said Colette, 'just leave her be.'

'If you say so.' Mabel sat up straight and glanced round at the others. 'Oh, you're talking about that again, are you?'

Colette picked up the thread of the conversation, which had moved from the dance to another current subject, one that she didn't want to join in with. There was something about it that made her uncomfortable, which was unfortunate to say the least, because it was a topic that seemed to be under discussion all over the place at the moment. It was about a trial that had been in the papers for days. A soldier had come home on leave unexpectedly and caught his wife with her bags packed, about to leave the house with her new boyfriend. The soldier had knocked seven bells out of the other chap and put him in a coma. Canteen gossip in Hunts Bank had been firmly on the side of the wronged husband so far and one or two girls who were known to go gadding about in their husbands' absence, instead of stopping at home as decent wives should, had found themselves on the receiving end of some arched eyebrows and snooty looks.

Everyone else seemed caught up in the story as evidence emerged piece by piece at the soldier's trial, but Colette disliked hearing about it. She hated the thought of people peering inside somebody else's marriage as if – as if gossip was all it was good for.

'Have you heard the latest?' Alison asked. 'In the early edition of the *Evening News*, it said the wife's mother and sister stood up in court and swore that the husband had been knocking her about for years.'

'How horrible,' said Persephone.

'Marking her where it wouldn't show,' Alison added.

'Eh, that's nasty.' Dot pulled a face. 'It just goes to show. No one knows what goes on behind closed doors.'

'Here comes Tony,' said Joan.

Colette turned to smile at him. For about a year after she had made friends with the other railway girls, Tony had whisked her straight home at the end of the day, meaning that she had seldom been able to meet up with the others in the buffet. But in the spring of this year, at the same time as he had started coming with her to Mrs Cooper's, he had started letting her come to the buffet, something she was grateful for. He still collected her so that they could go home together, but instead of standing at the door while she hastily gathered her things, now he came over to the table to say a quick how-do.

He was a good-looking man with hazel eyes and brown hair that he slicked back with Brylcreem. His build was slim and he had a narrow face with a somewhat pointed chin. His job with the water board meant he was exempt from being called up. It wasn't easy for a healthy young man to have to stick in a reserved occupation and Tony was sensitive to ignorant comments that were sometimes levelled at him by people who didn't know any better.

'Evening, ladies,' he said, arriving at their table. He politely raised his trilby to them all.

'Look.' Colette took the tickets from her bag to show him. 'Here are our dance tickets for War Weapons Week.'

'Jolly good,' said Tony.

'I'm pleased the two of you are able to come,' said Cordelia.

'We wouldn't miss it for anything – would we, darling?' said Tony. 'Are you ready? If we hurry, we'll catch the half-past bus.'

Getting up, Colette said her goodbyes and Tony ushered her out of the buffet, one hand at the back of her waist to guide her. That was one of the first things she had liked about him, the way he squired her. It had made her feel cared for. For an only child whose father had died, leaving her and her mother in a frightful financial pickle, and whose mother had leaned on her even though she was young, feeling cared about had made all the difference.

They went home to their small end-of-terrace house in Seymour Grove. Colette had learned always to refer to it as an end-of-terrace as Tony didn't like to hear it called a terraced house. Living in an end-of-terrace meant they had a side passage, which, in Tony's eyes, made them a cut above.

As they walked into the house, Colette went to fetch Tony's slippers before taking off her hat and jacket and putting on her own slippers. Then she made Tony a cup of tea. While he drank it, she ran upstairs to get changed. In the bottom drawer of her dressing table, she kept a duster and she quickly ran it over the dressing table, moving aside the glass tray with her hairpins and comb, then cleaning the mirror, the top of the chest of drawers and the bed frame. Tony liked the house to be spick and span, but he didn't want her doing housework at the end of the working day, so the simplest thing was to do a spot of dusting without his knowing.

Downstairs once more, Colette entered the parlour, took the dance tickets from her bag and propped them up on the mantelpiece. A little smile pulled at her lips. There was something exciting and full of promise about displaying invitations on the mantelpiece.

'What are you doing?' asked Tony.

She turned, wanting him to share the moment, share the small pleasure. 'Just putting the tickets here.'

'If you must,' said Tony. 'I have to say, I wasn't impressed with your friend Mrs Masters.'

Colette was bewildered. What had Cordelia done? 'She only said she's glad we're attending the dance.'

'I don't mean today. I mean when she asked us in the first place.'

'That was ages ago.' When? April? May?

'What has when got to do with it? It's the manner in which she did it that I object to. She invited us in front of other people – as if a man could say no in a situation like that.'

'I thought you wanted to go.'

'That isn't the point. She should have mentioned it to you, then you could have asked me privately and I could have decided one way or the other. I don't appreciate being manipulated.'

'I'm sorry, Tony.'

'It's because her husband's a solicitor. She thinks all you girls should dance to her tune.'

Colette waited, but he didn't say anything else, so she said, 'I'll go and start the tea, shall I?'

Tony stood up and kissed her forehead. 'That was a good cup of tea. Thank you. I'll polish the shoes, then read the paper while you're cooking. What are we having?'

'Sausages.'

'Sausages? Good show.'

'Oatmeal and herb sausages. I'm sorry. I should have said that in the first place.'

'Well, never mind. I know what a lucky man I am. I'd better put extra elbow grease into the polishing to work up an appetite.'

Tony took the shoes into the side passage, smoking as he polished. Colette had already stirred the oatmeal into boiling water that morning before work. Now she poured the mixture over the herbs and onion and carefully cracked open an egg to beat. By the time she had added breadcrumbs and was shaping her sausages, Tony was settled comfortably in the parlour, reading the paper.

'This is disgraceful!' he exclaimed.

Colette flinched, then froze.

'Sorry – did I make you jump?' Tony had appeared in the kitchen doorway.

'What's disgraceful?' Colette asked.

'This.' Tony shook the newspaper. 'This trial. You know, the soldier who laid out the wife's fancy man. It turns out he's been beating her all through their marriage.'

'Yes, I heard.'

'Disgraceful. Hitting a woman – it's inhumane. I'd never lay a finger on you. You know that, don't you?'

'Yes, Tony.'

'I know I've said it before, but it's worth repeating for your own good. It's important that you realise how bad things are for other women, so you can appreciate what you've got – and what you've got, my darling, is a husband who would never raise a hand to you.'

'I know.'

Yes, she did know. It was the one thing she never doubted. But there was more than one way to hit a woman. You didn't have to slap her or thump her. There were other ways to beat her down.

No one knows what goes on behind closed doors.

CHAPTER THREE

Alison looked over her shoulder to make sure her bedroom door was shut, then she knelt on the floor to open the drawer at the bottom of her hanging cupboard, where she kept her woollies. On top was a cherry-coloured knitted jumper with a round neck and short sleeves that she had reworked from an old cardy, unravelling the wool and washing it to remove the kinks before her sister Lydia helped her wind it into new balls, ready to be knitted up. Some girls, no matter how ingenious they were, hated making do, adding a lace collar here or a bit of braid there to refresh a garment and try to make it look like new, but Alison loved it. It meant she could be patriotic *and* save up to get married both at the same time.

She delved underneath the woollies to where a sheet of old newspaper lined the bottom of the drawer to deter moths. Here, tucked away, where she could only see them if she deliberately dug them out, was her final pair of brand-new silk stockings. Maybe it was daft of her to hide them away. If you knew where something was, it wasn't truly hidden, was it? But she kept the stockings here on the out-of-sight, out-of-mind principle, meaning she would be less likely to squander them. They were intended to be her wedding stockings.

Reaching behind her for her handbag, she took out the pair of tickets Cordelia had given her earlier. She popped them next to the stockings and closed the drawer. It felt sneaky putting the tickets there, but it was the only place she could guarantee they wouldn't come to light. Lydia had always rifled through Alison's things in search of something to borrow whenever the fancy took her, so it was important to hide the tickets right away.

As she sat back on her heels, Alison felt her heart beat faster than usual. Was it wrong of her to keep the dance secret from her family? If they knew, Dad would immediately offer to purchase tickets and Mum would probably want her friends to buy some too. It would end up like a charabanc trip. Alison couldn't permit that. She needed to keep the dance to herself. Just her and Paul. A special occasion with no mothers or well-wishers watching like hawks to see if Paul was finally going to go down on one knee could be – had to be, please, had to be – the right time for him to propose.

Oh, please, it had to be. She had waited so long, her hopes rising every birthday and Christmas, every Valentine's Day, only to be dashed yet again. The trouble was that everyone knew Paul was going to ask her to marry him, so it was no wonder he hadn't done it yet. What self-respecting man wanted to feel he was part of a peep show? Paul would want the proposal to be memorable for romantic reasons, not because a dozen women had leaped out squealing 'Congratulations!' before Alison had had a chance to say yes.

The War Weapons Week fundraiser would provide him with the opportunity he had been awaiting for so long – and Alison would be delighted to be taken by surprise. Even the thought of it called forth a smile that she couldn't contain. She pictured a beautiful summer's evening and Paul taking her outside for a breath of air, using that as his moment to pop the question. Then again, the dance was to take place at the splendid Claremont Hotel. Alison had never been there, but Cordelia had described it. The ballroom was on the ground floor.

'Up above,' Cordelia had said, 'imagine a huge hole in the ceiling. Up there, around the hole, is the restaurant, where diners who are seated next to the balcony can look down on the dance floor. Hanging from the dining-room and ballroom ceilings are chandeliers, of course, and from the topmost ceiling in the hotel, all the way down as far as the balcony level, hangs the largest and most wonderful chandelier of all, with thousands of crystals, right above the ballroom.'

'It sounds beautiful,' Alison had whispered, entranced.

'It is.'

Paul might ask her to marry him right there in the ballroom, and later they could hold their wedding reception at the Claremont. Could Dad afford that? Well, why not? He'd had long enough to save up. Alison felt all fluttery inside. Was she going to get engaged beneath the twinkling crystals of the Claremont's famous chandelier? Or would Paul prefer a private corner? Maybe he would ask the bandleader to play 'Begin the Beguine', which was the first piece of music they had ever danced to. It wouldn't do any harm to slip the title into the conversation. Alison was always careful not to drop hints about getting engaged. She had too much pride for that. But this wouldn't count as a hint, would it? Just a little memory-jogger.

She had a length of silver braid that she'd been hoarding. Now was the time to use it to trim her apricot-coloured dress. She would wear Granny's crystal beads and matching drop earrings, which would catch the light prettily. She would make herself look as lovely as she could for Paul.

The door opened and Lydia leaned in, hanging on the doorknob.

'Mum says are you coming down? Tea's on the table.' Lydia walked in, trying to peer over Alison's shoulder. 'What have you got there?'

'Nothing.' Alison took her cherry-red top out of the cupboard. 'I thought I'd wear this tonight.'

'Yes, do. It suits you.'

Alison laid the top on the bed and followed Lydia downstairs. Mum was dressed in her WVS uniform, ready for her shift on the mobile canteen. Alison had done first-aid training last year at the same time as Joan, Mabel and poor Lizzie, but they all lived to the south of Manchester while she lived to the north, so she had never had the chance to do her first-aid duty alongside her friends, though she was proud to feel she was helping in her own area, the place where she'd grown up and where she and Paul would spend the rest of their lives.

Dad was a builder and he had always taken care of their house. He joked that the girls had a choice between a fancy wedding and an extra room on the back of their matrimonial homes, but he was a softy and Alison secretly thought she might end up with both. After all, weddings weren't that big these days. She and Paul were due to start their married lives living with Paul's widowed mum. Alison had always got on well with her and had none of the fears you sometimes heard about – two women sharing a kitchen, that sort of thing. As for the rivalry between the young wife and the mother-in-law, you could forget that right away. Alison and Mrs Dunaway were great friends and they both adored Paul. Three definitely wasn't going to be a crowd. It was going to be cosy, loving and good-natured.

What more could a girl ask for?

There wasn't as much bustle on Saturday mornings in the corridors of Hunts Bank. Alison made her way towards the suite of offices where she worked as a wages clerk for the various railway works. It was a responsible job that called for concentration and there had been a time when she had despaired of getting to grips with all the piecework rates, but she was confident these days. If only Miss Evans, that old dragon from school, could see her now!

For some reason, half the clerks started and finished fifteen minutes earlier than the rest, but the early starters didn't account for the level of noise as Alison approached her office. Colette appeared in the doorway and looked up and down the corridor. Seeing Alison, she hurried to meet her.

Alison was fond of Colette. She was the friend whom the group knew the least well, thanks to Tony's overprotectiveness. He seemed to have outgrown that now, thank goodness, and had even joined Colette in her weekly visits to Mrs Cooper's house, where Joan had lodged until she got married and where Mabel still lived, and where Dot, Cordelia and Persephone were frequent visitors. Apparently, Mrs Cooper and Mrs Grayson had encouraged Margaret to drop in when she felt like it too. That was one thing Alison didn't like about her group of friends all living in various parts of the south of Manchester. She couldn't just pop round to Wilton Close when the fancy took her. Sometimes it made her feel left out. Not that she would ever say so, because she knew perfectly well that she was valued within the group every bit as much as the others. Even so, she couldn't help feeling miffed sometimes.

There was another reason Alison liked Colette. She had exactly what Alison dreamed of: a happy marriage with a devoted husband. She even had a home of her own. Alison had no qualms whatsoever about moving in with Paul's mum, but Colette had never had to share a home. In Alison's admiring eyes, she led a charmed life.

Smiling, Alison went to meet her. Was that a flicker of anxiety in Colette's eyes? She was a pretty girl in a quiet sort of way. She really ought to make more of herself. A dash of the red lipstick that had become the height of fashion because Hitler was said to hate it would work wonders on her, highlighting her fair complexion and blue eyes and possibly even adding a touch of richness to her buttermilk-blonde hair. Instead, Colette favoured just a touch of light pink lipstick, which was a rotten shame in Alison's opinion.

'Morning, Colette.' Alison linked arms with her friend as they headed for the office. 'Are you the welcoming committee?'

Colette stopped and turned to her. 'Milly Horrocks is engaged.'

'So that's what all that silly shrieking is about.' Alison forced herself to sound casual, but her heart bumped. 'Good for her.'

Honestly, they must put something in the tea in the wages section. It was a hotbed for romance and engagements. There was a joke going round that if you wanted to fall pregnant, you needed to work in the typing pool, and if you wanted a ring on your finger, wages was the place to be. Alison had lost track of the number of her colleagues who had got engaged – or maybe she had been too embarrassed to keep a tally. It wasn't fair. Weddings were ten a penny these days, but Paul had still to ask her. How much longer would he keep her waiting?

Then she pulled herself together. Cordelia's dance was going to provide the perfect backdrop, an essential part of that backdrop being the absence of Mum, Mrs Dunaway and all the neighbours. Paul would never get a better opportunity than this to pop the question without squirming because all eyes were on him.

Alison hoisted her smile into position and locked it there. 'Lucky her. How exciting.'

And how humiliating to think that Colette had felt the need to meet her outside the office to warn her. But she mustn't show her humiliation. Goodness, if she could manage to be thrilled for Joan when she got engaged, she could certainly do it for Milly Horrocks. And she *had* been thrilled for Joan, she truly had, once the shock had worn off. Joan was a good friend who had gone through a tough time after the death of the sister she had been so close to. If anyone deserved a happy ending, she did. Alison believed that unreservedly and she had been proud to be one of Joan's bridesmaids. But still, it had been rather a blow when Joan and Bob had got engaged before her and Paul.

She gave Colette's arm a squeeze before dropping it as they entered the office so that she could make her way straight to the crowd of excited girls clustered around Miss Horrocks. Alison eased through to the front.

'Congratulations. How wonderful.'

Mrs Ford, one of the supervisors, clapped her hands.

'That's enough, thank you, everyone. I'm sure we're all very pleased for Miss Horrocks, but it's time to settle down to work.'

The group dispersed. Alison popped her hat into the deep drawer at the bottom of her desk and hung her jacket over the back of her chair. Most of the girls hung up their jackets and coats on the hatstands, but not Alison. Her jacket would keep its shape better for spending her working hours on the back of her seat. This was a rather fetching bolero jacket she had made from a lightweight wool dress she had bought at the market and cut down, using the pattern that had been used for the boleros worn by Joan's bridesmaids.

Alison was soon absorbed in her work. It didn't matter how much you had on your mind. As a wages clerk, she couldn't afford to let an error slide through. They all had to concentrate extra hard in the first half of the week because that was when all the information, simply masses of it, arrived, and then they had to carry on working extra hard in the second half of the week, because slacking could lead to mistakes.

The clerks who did the wages for the staff who worked on the stations or on the trains had it easy. Alison's job was to calculate the wages for staff in the railway works, including those who worked for small companies employed by LMS to fulfil contracts, and this was far trickier. She had to keep abreast of all the piecework rates for the different jobs, which was jolly fiddly. Honestly, the sum of three farthings should be abolished and all amounts should be rounded up to the next penny. On top of all that, there was the War Wage and overtime. Oh crikey. Alison had spent most of her very first day in a blind panic, but now she was proud of being reliable and efficient.

Joan had hated being a clerk before she became a station porter. She had told Alison that clerking hadn't felt like real war work, but Alison had never had any such reservations. She had always pictured herself working in an office until she got married. Of course, this being wartime, she wouldn't be required to leave her position upon marriage. She had been sorry about that to start with, because all she wanted was to be Paul's wife, looking after him and their home, but over her months in the wages office, she had developed a new, modern, distinctly pleasing image of herself – the wartime wife, working hard by day, then hurrying home to be with her husband.

At the end of the morning, those who had started fifteen minutes earlier tidied their desks. Alison got up and went over to Milly Horrocks. It was important to be seen to do the right thing, the gracious thing. She hadn't always been gracious when other girls had got engaged and she dreaded getting a reputation for being a bit of a cat.

'I didn't have the chance to congratulate you properly earlier.' She seized Miss Horrocks' hand. 'Let's see.'

'Bert's serving overseas. He proposed in a letter, so I haven't got a ring yet.'

Well, that was something. God, what a bitch she was. Her cheeks burned as shame coursed through her. Sometimes she was so jealous of girls with rings on their fingers that she could hardly breathe. The smallest disappointment of the other girl, like Miss Horrocks' now, felt to Alison like a kind of triumph, albeit a bitter one. She hadn't always been horrid. It was something that had sneaked up on her while she'd waited for Paul to go down on one knee.

She would change when she got engaged. She would be a better person, the girl she was meant to be.

CHAPTER FOUR

Cordelia paid for Kenneth's cigarettes, then opened the packet and tipped them into her handbag before handing the empty packet over the counter to the tobacconist. Salvage was an intrinsic part of everyone's life these days, especially women's, as housewives were encouraged again and again to save paper, cartons, jam jars and tin cans, as well as patriotically hand over their saucepans to help build aeroplanes.

Cordelia walked home, thinking about the War Weapons Week dance. The band was booked and the committee was gathering raffle prizes. It was the sort of thing she excelled at. As the wife of a prosperous solicitor, she had sat on many a committee before the war, organising everything from flower shows and musical evenings to Poppy Days and fundraising for the Seamen's Mission. But there was something extra – extra special? No, that wasn't right. Extra important? Extra urgent? – about organising this dance. This war wasn't just happening to the servicemen far away. It was happening here too, to the families left behind. It meant air raids and barrage balloons, shortages and evacuation, all accompanied by a sharp sense of what they were fighting for and how best they could support their troops.

Cordelia often worked on Saturdays, but she had today off. Off? She shook her head as she walked along Edge Lane with its smart houses in their gardens lining either side. All over the kingdom, women who worked flat out in all kinds of jobs, including those that belonged to men who had been called up, used their so-called 'time off' to look after their homes and families, do the shopping, which often as not meant standing in endless queues, as well as doing shifts in soup kitchens and rest centres and spending nights fire-watching and afternoons digging for victory in gardens and allotments. There was barely any such thing as time off, which was why the meetings in the buffet were so precious. Cordelia felt closer to her railway friends than she ever had to the ladies she had always associated with in her capacity as Mrs Kenneth Masters. She had the extraordinary feeling that she was experiencing real friendship for the first time.

She walked in through their gateway, empty of its metal gate with fancy swirls on top, which had been taken away to be melted down. Steps ran up to the red front door, above which was a half-moon-shaped stained-glass window beside a handsome bay window, with another bay window above it. She had moved in here as a bride. It had two reception rooms, three bedrooms and full indoor plumbing. Very swish. Cordelia's parents had been fairly well off, but they had still had to walk down the garden to use the lavatory.

'Three bedrooms, and two of them doubles. It's a house built for a family – two boys in the second double, a little girl in the single.'

That was what Mother had said when she had toured the house shortly before Cordelia's wedding day. She had employed a bright, encouraging voice, as if nothing was wrong. Maybe by that time she had convinced herself that nothing was.

Cordelia let herself in. The house was empty – in more ways than one. No Kenneth, because he was out at a meeting about the staging of a pretend invasion in the middle of

Manchester towards the end of October. No Emily – and no hope of Emily. Now that the possibility of her return had finally been dashed, Cordelia realised how deeply it had sustained her. Emily hadn't just been away at boarding school. She had lived away from home in the holidays as well since the war began, Kenneth having arranged for her to stay with his godmother, Lady Appleton, in Herefordshire. Now it seemed that Lady Appleton was to have the pleasure of Emily's company for the duration.

'For the duration.'

Those words were uttered so often in relation to so many things. The rationing of food for the duration; clothes coupons for the duration. Perfectly ordinary things like paper clips and trowels vanishing off the shelves in the stationer's and the ironmonger's and none to be had 'for the duration'.

Children living away from home for the duration.

Wretched duration. It would be so much easier to cope with if they only knew how long it was going to last – which was probably an unpatriotic thought to entertain and she should know better.

Cordelia pulled herself together. She put away the shopping and settled down to write her letters. One of the advantages of being a husband was that you handed over all letter-writing and card-sending duties to your wife, which meant that Cordelia had had the dubious pleasure of corresponding with Adelaide Masters since 1920.

Dear Mrs Masters, she wrote. She had always called her mother-in-law by her formal title. She had never been invited to address her as 'Mother'. She knew Adelaide didn't care for her – no, that was a bit strong. Didn't approve of her. That was more like it.

'Too young' had been Adelaide's instant assessment when she was introduced to her son's fiancée.

Young? Yes, she'd been young, but only in years, not in her heart. The Great War had robbed her of her youth.

Oh, Kit, darling Kit, her one true love, her soulmate. It was as if her life had started the day they met, as if everything that had gone before had been preparation and waiting.

Father hadn't liked Kit.

'Not good enough. Not our sort.'

After Kit had marched off to war in the autumn of 1914, beaming with pride and excitement in his Pals battalion, Cordelia had written to him every day, though his replies had to be sent care of her old school friend for fear of Father finding out. Father did find out and then Cordelia asked Kit to write to her care of a post office two miles away.

Then his letters had stopped coming. It was like that sometimes and she had tried not to worry. On occasion, she wouldn't hear for a while and then she would receive several letters all at once. But then the silence had continued and Cordelia had dug her nails into her palms, her suffering all the harder to bear because she couldn't share it with anyone. Her old school friend had gone off to drive ambulances, but Father wouldn't hear of it for his daughter.

'What do you care about the war? All you want is to find that man and marry him on the sly,' he had exclaimed.

Kit had been dead for months before she found out. Sweethearts didn't get telegrams. It was the wives or parents who were informed. Kit's widowed mother lived twenty miles away, though it might as well have been a thousand since, although she knew of Cordelia's existence, she didn't know where she lived. It wasn't until Kit's brother came home on leave towards the end of the war, with Cordelia's letters to Kit in his knapsack, that Cordelia was told.

Eventually, somehow, she had ended up marrying Kenneth. Her parents had pushed her into it and she had been too heartbroken, too desperate, to resist.

'I shall say this to you once, Cordelia, and then I'll never say it again,' her father had said to her on the eve of her wedding. 'It would be sinful of you ever to give a certain person another thought. Do I make myself clear? Do I make your duty clear?'

Cordelia and Kit. Kit and Cordelia. Kit was short for Christopher. Mrs Christopher Franklin. That was whom she had dreamed of being. She had had to force herself to pair her name with this new one, trying to make it feel right and natural. Cordelia and Kenneth – never Ken, always Kenneth. Mrs Kenneth Masters.

'Such a good name for you,' Miss Vernon from the Ladies' Circle had told her years ago in a flutter of admiration. 'Mrs Masters – so efficient, so organised, always on top of everything.'

And that was who she had been ever since, the efficient Mrs Masters, calm and composed, with a gravity that must have gratified Kenneth's well-wishers, because it showed he hadn't had his head turned by a pretty young thing with nothing between her ears.

Dear Mrs Masters. Cordelia looked at the empty page, then proceeded to fill it with details of the forthcoming dance – fill being the operative word. She wrote from edge to edge, leaving no margins, so as not to waste the paper.

Her reward for sending the duty letter to her mother-in-law was to write a letter to Emily. Writing to Emily was one of the pleasures of her life and she was never stuck for what to say. She ended every letter *Much love from both of us* and signed herself *Mummy and Daddy*, with kisses.

Afterwards, she prepared a meal. Kenneth would have eaten his main meal at the British Restaurant, so a high tea was all that was called for. A vegetable roll would do, made with potato pastry, which was half flour and half mashed potato. She could prepare it now and pop it in the oven when Kenneth got home.

Before the war, Cordelia had had a daily cook, who arrived mid-morning every day, and a daily help, who had seen to all the housework and didn't leave until the evening's washing-up was done and the table had been laid for breakfast. Breakfast was the only meal for which Cordelia had been responsible in those days, but when war broke out, the cook went off to live with her sister in Lytham St Annes, and the help, eyes gleaming at the prospect of higher wages, had disappeared into the munitions.

Now Cordelia had a woman who came in to clean twice a week and that was all. She would have loved to offer a cleaning position to Mrs Cooper, who a few weeks ago had set up a little business called Magic Mop, but no matter how wonderful it would be to help her friend by giving her work, it would also be problematic to turn a friend into an employee, even a servant, some would say. She couldn't bear to jeopardise her relationship with Mrs Cooper. It was bad enough that she was obliged to inspect the house in Wilton Close once a month on behalf of the owners to make sure Mrs Cooper was taking proper care of it.

It was funny how she had changed. Before the war, she wouldn't have thought twice about watching over someone's housekeeper. Heavens, before the war she would probably have run her finger along the tops of the doors to make sure they had been dusted and would have torn the housekeeper off a strip if her fingertip had come away dirty.

But not now, not with Mrs Cooper, whom she liked – cared for, even. The only way in which she had felt able to support Mrs Cooper's venture had been to purchase some hours of Magic Mop spread over a number of weeks to help Joan as she embarked upon married life. It felt good to support her friends. She just hoped they didn't view her as Lady Bountiful.

That was another thing. She had never before worried about how other people viewed her. She hadn't needed to. As the spouse of Mr Kenneth Masters, she knew precisely what was expected of her. She had been a top-hole wife in that respect.

But it did concern her now how her new friends perceived her. Nothing was going to stop her being reserved and serious, because it was too deeply ingrained, but did her friends realise that, as cool as she was on the surface, underneath she felt warm towards them?

The last time she had wanted to be liked, actively wanted and needed to be liked, had been when she met Kit. Goodness, what a thought. The moment of self-knowledge made her breath catch in her throat – and then came the sound of the front door opening and she quickly wiped her hands and went to greet Kenneth.

He was full of the plans for the simulated attack.

'We're going to have a group of chaps who'll pretend to be fifth columnists,' he told her over their meal. 'They're going to disrupt the traffic and attempt to take over the BBC building.'

'Should you be telling me this?' Cordelia asked. 'Isn't it a secret?'

'Not as such. Well, don't go telling all and sundry, obviously. Closer to the time it will be widely publicised. We don't want the public panicking, thinking it's the real thing. Everyone will be warned to carry their gas masks and ID cards, both of which they ought to be carrying anyway, of course, though some are getting a bit lax about their gas masks these days, I'm sorry to say.'

'The Lost Property at Victoria is full of them, apparently,' Cordelia murmured.

'We're going to have flashbangs and even some dive-bombing planes – without the bombs, of course,' Kenneth said with uncharacteristic enthusiasm and Cordelia glanced at him in surprise. Why, he looked quite boyish in that moment, with a brightness in his eyes and excitement in his tone. Then the doorbell rang and the enthusiasm vanished, replaced by a crisp annoyance. 'Who's that at this time?'

'I'll answer it,' said Cordelia.

'No, I will.'

Kenneth rose from the table, dropping his linen napkin beside his plate. Cordelia put another piece of vegetable roll in her mouth. Potato pastry was said to be nutritious.

'Emily!' Kenneth exclaimed.

Emily! Cordelia threw down her knife and fork at the same moment as she leaped up from her chair. Emily! She rushed into the hall and there, oh, there on the front step, with a suitcase at her feet, was Emily, looking travel-rumpled and tired, but stubborn.

'I've come home. I've taken my School Cert and I'm not going to do my Higher, no matter what you say, Daddy. I'm fifteen and old enough to decide for myself. I want to do my bit for the war and I want to do it here, not stuck out in the back of beyond, so don't try to send me back, because I won't go.'

Cordelia still couldn't believe it. Emily had come home. There had been an argument during the evening between Emily and Kenneth – and precisely how and when had Emily grown up sufficiently to argue with her father? Cordelia had been left baffled and dismayed. Yes, Emily shouldn't have come home, but – she was here. Surely they

37

could leave the arguments until after they had celebrated? Even if Kenneth wanted to pack her off back to Herefordshire on the first available train, surely he should want to smother her in hugs and kisses first?

'What's happened to our little girl?' Kenneth asked with a heavy sigh in bed.

'She's grown up.'

Kenneth snorted. 'She's fifteen.'

'Most girls her age would have left school at fourteen and been at work for a whole year.'

'Are you taking her side against me, her father?'

'Of course not. It isn't a question of sides. Can't you be happy that she's home? We haven't seen her for such a long time.'

'Unlike you, I don't have the luxury of putting my feelings first. I have to do what's best for our daughter.'

'So do I. Maybe what's best is accepting that she isn't a child any longer.'

'She's *fifteen*, for pity's sake.'

'And if she were twenty-five, you'd still feel as protective as you do now. She'll always be your darling daughter. But there's more than one kind of danger.'

'What d'you mean?'

'It isn't just bombs falling from the sky. It's what might happen if you send her back to Herefordshire. What if she left there again? She wouldn't risk coming back here a second time.'

'I won't be held to ransom by a child.' The tightness in Kenneth's voice made it sound as if his jaw was clamped rigid.

'Let her stay,' Cordelia whispered. 'Set as many conditions as you like. She's a clever girl – she'll see reason.'

'You're giving in to her.'

Emotion welled up inside Cordelia, but her tone was measured as she said, 'If I'm giving in to anything, Kenneth, it's the pure delight of seeing her again. I know that if she stays, if you permit her to stay,' she added as a sop to his authority, 'you and I shall both spend the rest of the war worried sick about her, and if anything should happen to her, I for one will never forgive myself, *but* ... '

Didn't Kenneth feel that *but* as well? *But* I love her so much ... *But* I've missed her every single day ... *But* I can't think of anything better than having her at home and my heart will crack clean in two if you send her away again.

'Please, Kenneth,' Cordelia whispered.

Cordelia looked at Emily as they walked together along Edge Lane and her heart nearly burst with pride. Her daughter was beautiful. Well, all mothers thought that, didn't they? But in Emily's case, it really was true. She had a heart-shaped face with a dainty chin. Her eyes were cornflower blue and her brown hair had a natural curl. Cordelia had been born with brown hair, but it had become steadily lighter all through her childhood and she had watched Emily's hair closely, waiting for it to do the same, but it never had.

Emily was wearing the short-sleeved, light green dress with white collar and cuffs together with the dark green cardigan that made up her school's Sunday uniform in the summer term, although her school boater was no more.

'We all chucked them in the river on the last day of exams,' Emily had blithely announced as she got ready for church that morning.

'I suggest you don't mention that to your father,' Cordelia had replied drily, 'not if you want him to think you're grown-up enough to have a say in where you live.'

Emily had pretended to pout, then smiled disarmingly. 'You'll let me borrow one of your hats, won't you? I saw a really pretty pink one with magenta trim in the cloakroom. I quite fancy it.'

'So do I. You may have my grey and be thankful.'

The church service had been a wonderful experience. Cordelia had paid not one iota of attention to the vicar because she was too busy soaking up all the interested glances that came her family's way. Now, as she often did on a Saturday or Sunday afternoon, she was walking along to Wilton Close – but this time she was taking her darling daughter with her. She couldn't wait for her friends to meet Emily.

'Tell me again, Mummy,' said Emily. 'Who are these ladies I'm going to meet?'

'We're going to the Morgans' house. Do you remember them? They've moved to North Wales for the duration and friends of mine live in their house now. You know about them from my letters. There's Mrs Cooper and Mrs Grayson. Mrs Cooper's daughter, Lizzie, died, so be careful what you say, darling.'

'And Mrs Grayson is a marvellous cook, who can whip up a first-class dinner from dried egg and a pair of old boots. They were pretend mothers of the bride, same as you were.'

'And you'll meet the fourth mother of the bride as well – Mrs Dot Green. There's also a girl called Mabel living in the house, but I don't think she'll be there. Another friend, Mrs Colette Naylor, and her husband call on Mrs Cooper each weekend. Mr Naylor does odd jobs and helps in the garden. I know they're going to see Mr Naylor's parents today, so presumably they visited Mrs Cooper yesterday.'

When they arrived at the house, Mrs Cooper opened the door to them.

'I hope you won't mind that I've brought an unexpected guest with me, Mrs Cooper.' Suddenly not caring about the rule that required you to keep your hands to yourself, Cordelia slipped an arm around Emily's slender shoulders. How wonderful to touch her daughter! 'This young lady is my daughter, Emily. Emily, this is Mrs Cooper, who is the Morgans' housekeeper.'

Mrs Cooper gasped. 'Well! What a surprise. Come in, come in.' She called over her shoulder, 'You'll never guess who Mrs Masters has brought with her.'

Emily shook hands, murmuring, 'Pleased to meet you.'

'And I'm delighted to meet you too,' Mrs Cooper enthused. 'Come through and meet Mrs Grayson and Mrs Green.'

They entered the front room, which, in spite of the William Morris wallpaper and dark blue curtains, was a bright room, thanks to the large bay window. Mrs Grayson sat in her usual armchair, beside which was her knitting basket. Dot, in her simple Sunday best of a soft pink blouse and a cream knitted cardy with a Peter Pan collar and dainty puffs at the shoulders, looked first at Emily, her hazel eyes widening, then at Cordelia, and her smile of understanding melted Cordelia's heart.

'Don't tell me this is your Emily,' said Dot.

'I know.' Cordelia laughed. 'I can hardly believe it myself.'

She performed the introductions and Emily smiled pleasantly and shook hands.

'Did Mr Masters arrange for Emily to come home without telling you?' Dot asked. 'As a surprise, like.'

'No.' Cordelia gazed at her daughter. She ought to be annoyed, but it was impossible. 'This young lady made the decision all by herself. She arrived yesterday.'

'How long shall you be staying?' Mrs Grayson asked Emily.

'I'm not here just on a visit,' said Emily. 'I've come home for good. Mummy approves, don't you?' She looked at Cordelia.

'I'm not sure that I approve exactly, but I'm certainly very happy to have you back, Emily.' Cordelia glanced at Dot. 'I know, I know. This is where I start living with worry and guilt for the rest of the war.'

'It'll be worth it,' said Dot.

'Did you have a good journey?' Mrs Cooper asked Emily.

'Well, I don't like to complain, obviously … ' Emily began.

Dot laughed. 'Feel free, love. You're among friends here.'

'There's very little you could tell Mrs Green about the difficulties of rail travel,' said Mrs Grayson. 'She works on the railway as a parcels porter.'

'It was rather dire,' said Emily. 'I had a seat to start with, but I gave it up to an old lady and then I stood for the rest of the way. I upended my suitcase and sat on that, but it was rather suffocating being surrounded by all those people on their feet, so I stood up again. And the train kept stopping for no apparent reason.'

'Giving way to troop trains or freight,' said Dot. 'It happens all the time, chick.'

'Even when it did go, a lot of the time it travelled so slowly,' Emily went on with a touch of drama. 'There was a lady somewhere in the crowd who cried every time it slowed down because she was convinced it meant there was an air raid.'

'They removed the speed limit earlier this year – in daytime, anyway,' said Dot.

'That's what the guard tried to tell her,' said Emily, 'but it didn't make any odds.'

'The poor thing,' said Mrs Cooper. 'I hope you had something to eat if it was a long journey.'

'I tried to get a bite when I changed at Crewe, but the queue was too long.'

'There's more to it than that, though, isn't there, Emily?' said Cordelia. She couldn't say her daughter's name often enough. Emily, Emily, Emily: it was the best word in the whole world.

'*Mummy.*' Emily dealt her a meaningful stare.

'Darling, you turned up out of the blue and you've let people down. Don't you think you should be honest about what you've done?'

Emily pressed her lips together, but then a smile broke through. She had been an expert pouter from an early age, but she rarely had the sulks.

'What Mummy means is it's the grown-up thing to do. I had a big lecture from Daddy this morning all about being grown-up. The reason I'm here is because I – well, I ran away, in a manner of speaking.'

'You ran away?' There was shock in Mrs Cooper's voice and on the faces of the other two.

'Auntie Flora would never have let me go if she'd known.'

'Auntie Flora is what Emily calls her father's godmother, whom she's been living with when she hasn't been away at school,' Cordelia explained.

'I told her I was staying with a school friend for a few days,' said Emily, 'which is why I turned up with next to no luggage. But at least I brought my ration book,' she added virtuously.

'Emily will be writing a long letter of apology to Auntie Flora later today,' said Cordelia, 'and so will I.'

'It wasn't your fault, Mummy,' said Emily.

'When you're a mum yourself, chick,' said Dot, 'you'll learn that you feel responsible for owt your children do.'

'Out?' Emily frowned.

'Everything,' Cordelia said quietly. 'It's colloquial.'

43

Emily turned to Mrs Cooper. 'To answer your question, the reason I needed something to eat at Crewe was because I didn't have a sandwich with me because I couldn't tell Auntie Flora or Cook I was going on a long journey.'

'You poor child,' said Mrs Grayson. 'You must have been starving hungry when you arrived home.'

'Reet clemmed, as my dear old mam would have said,' smiled Dot.

'I think it's time to put the kettle on,' said Mrs Grayson, getting up. 'I've made a walnut cake, which was no mean feat, I don't mind telling you, with no eggs or fat to put in it.'

Mrs Cooper stood up as well. 'I'll come and help you.'

When they left the room, Cordelia's heart swelled as Dot turned to her. She knew that Dot of all people understood exactly how much Emily's return meant.

'Well, Cordelia, what can I say? Your Emily's a bonny lass and I know how happy you are to have her back.' Dot smiled at Emily. 'You might have taken the law into your own hands, chick, but I've never seen your mum with that light in her eyes before.'

A feeling of warmth radiated through Cordelia. This afternoon, showing off her daughter to her friends, was all she could have hoped for.

Later, as they walked home, she was as eager to hear Emily's praise for her friends as she had been for them to get to know Emily.

'What did you think of the ladies?' she asked and when Emily didn't immediately answer, she glanced sideways and was puzzled by the expression on Emily's pretty face. It looked almost as if her face had frozen. 'Emily? Did you like Mrs Cooper? She liked you.'

Emily hesitated, then said in a rush, 'I was a bit surprised, to be honest. She's rather lower class, isn't she?'

'Emily!'

44

'Well, she is. She wasn't what I would have expected of the Morgans' housekeeper. Have they come down in the world?'

'They chose an honest and good-hearted person as their housekeeper – on my personal recommendation, I might add.'

'Why would you know someone like that in the first place?' asked Emily. 'She's beneath you. And as for that Mrs Green, with her "reet clemmed" and her "owt" and calling me "chick". Honestly! And she called you Cordelia – and you let her. I never heard anything like it in my life. How could you, Mummy? How *could* you?'

CHAPTER FIVE

Colette was in a quandary. What should she wear to the dance? Cordelia told the group not to worry about it.

'Admittedly, there will be plenty of couples in formal evening dress, but there'll also be women in their best frocks. What matters is that everyone is supporting War Weapons Week.'

Margaret said openly that even if she wasn't required to wear an evening gown, she still didn't think she had anything smart enough.

'I lost all my togs when our house was hit. Since then I've been more interested in getting together some everyday clothes than dressy things.'

'You can't fool us,' Alison teased. 'We've all seen you turn up for work in the engine shed, decked out in beaded velvet with a chiffon wrap.'

'Oh, that old thing,' Margaret replied airily. 'I don't call that special. Seriously, though, I really don't possess anything good enough.'

'Don't fret,' said Mabel. 'I'll lend you something.'

'Or I will,' Persephone added and Margaret smiled at them both.

'What are you going to wear, Joan?' Dot asked.

Mabel slipped an arm around Joan's shoulders. 'Don't ask daft questions, Dot. She's going to get out her wedding dress – aren't you, Joan? We bridesmaids practically had to rip it off her back to get her to change into her going-away dress.'

Joan laughed. 'I loved every minute of being dressed as a bride.'

'I suppose you've returned the dress to Margaret's friend,' said Cordelia.

'No, actually. She joined the Wrens and she asked Margaret to look after the dress and pass it on to someone in need. Now I'll keep it until someone else needs it.'

'That was good of her,' said Dot. 'What about you, Colette? You're keeping quiet. Are you going to wear your lovely blue dress?'

'I'm not sure,' Colette replied.

'I think you should, love,' said Dot. 'It's perfect on you.'

It was a nice compliment, but Colette's lips felt tight, as if they were refusing to smile. She never knew what to think about that dress. She had made it herself last year, her eye immediately drawn to a wonderful fabric the colour of bluebells in Ingleby's drapery department. She had fallen in love at first sight with the colour and had taken pleasure in choosing a flattering pattern with a semi-fitted, short-sleeved bodice and a gently flared knee-length skirt.

How proud she had been the first time she wore it. That had been to church on a Sunday and afterwards a couple of ladies had admired it, which Colette had particularly appreciated because they were ladies with whom she had never exchanged more than a polite nod before. Tony had smiled at the compliments and that had made her feel even better.

But when they got home, Tony frowned.

'Is something the matter?' Colette had asked.

He pressed his lips together, shaking his head, as if he didn't want to say anything. 'I don't like to say it, but it's for your own good. That colour – that blue ... '

'Mrs Pemberton and her friend liked it. They said it suits me.'

'Darling, they were being polite.'

'They didn't have to say anything. They've never spoken to me before.'

'They felt sorry for you. I don't like the thought of people pitying my wife. That colour does you no favours, Colette. I'm telling you for your own good. You understand that, don't you? It doesn't suit you at all.'

Colette had taken off her once lovely dress and hung it up, all her delight squashed. She didn't want to wear it after that, but of course she had to. It was her best dress and you couldn't leave a best dress to hang unwanted in the wardrobe. That would be wasteful. Waste was always wrong, but even more so in wartime. She had taken to wearing it under her coat so nobody would see it and she wouldn't let Tony down. On a couple of occasions she had been obliged to wear it for others to see, once when the friends had gone to Mrs Cooper's for tea on what would have been Lizzie's eighteenth birthday last October, and again as her bridesmaid's dress at Joan's wedding. She had felt very iffy about that, but honestly, it was her best dress and the occasion demanded it.

And Tony had told her she looked beautiful, which had been confusing, though oh so wonderful. Had he meant it? Had he changed his mind? Was he just being kind? She would have liked to know the answer, but she couldn't ask.

Now here she was again, agonising over whether to wear the bluebell-coloured dress. For a mad moment, she pictured herself buying something new, but it would be a shocking waste of clothing coupons, but also Tony wouldn't want her to buy something second-hand. Could she ask Mabel or Persephone … ? But Tony would be displeased and besides, she was shorter than they were and fuller in the bust and hips.

So it had to be either the blue or else something notice-ably less dressy – and the occasion called for something special. She didn't want to look out of place.

And Tony *had* told her she looked beautiful in it.

When the day of the dance came round, anticipation made Colette feel all fluttery inside. Her reservations about her dress had melted away. How could she have been such a silly? She was going to have a wonderful evening with her friends in beautiful surroundings. It was the kind of thing you talked about for years afterwards.

She had the Saturday off work, which, as well as making the day feel even more special, helped make up for the dis-turbed couple of hours caused by last night's air raid, although as she cleaned the house and queued up outside the butcher's, Colette had to smile to herself, because those two activities were anything but special. In the afternoon, she pressed Tony's shirt and trousers, taking extra care to get the turn-ups just so. Turn-ups weren't allowed on new clothes any longer, because they were a waste of fabric.

At last it was time to get ready. How handsome Tony looked in his double-breasted jacket – they weren't being made any more either – and his best tie. He had polished his black leather lace-ups until they gleamed. He had pol-ished Colette's shoes too, though not to the same extent. He never polished hers to a high shine, so there was no danger of her shoes reflecting what was up her skirt.

Colette dressed and applied a little make-up. She had never worn much because of being fair-skinned. Mother had warned her against looking painted. She wore her hair with an off-centre parting and a wisp of a fringe, and only slightly waved, unlike the curls and sculptured waves that most girls had these days. It was the same style she'd had when she was a shy eighteen-year-old, desperate to go in for a modern style. She was twenty-three now. A couple of years ago, she had tried a fuller style that called for a handful of curlers, but Tony hadn't liked it and she had changed back.

'Are you ready?' asked Tony. 'It's time to go.'

The evening was still light as they made their way into town. As they walked along the road to the Claremont Hotel, a taxi overtook them. It pulled up outside the Claremont and Harry Knatchbull emerged, dressed in his RAF uniform. He turned to offer his hand first to Mabel and then to Mrs Cooper. Having assisted them from the vehicle, he paid the driver.

Mabel caught sight of Colette and waved. Then she pointed to the hotel steps.

'Red carpet!' she called.

There was a scallop-edged awning above the steps as well.

'Isn't it all lovely?' said Colette as she and Tony arrived. The awning was dark blue, its underneath covered in silver stars.

Mabel laughed. 'And this is only what they've done with the front steps!'

'Let's see what delights await us inside.' Harry offered an arm each to Mabel and Mrs Cooper, adding with a cheeky wink, 'Come on, girls.'

Mrs Cooper swatted his arm before she linked hers with it. 'I'm not a girl, you daft ha'p'orth.'

Colette and Tony followed them up the steps into the lofty, pillared foyer, with its gleaming woodwork, handsome armchairs and massive flower arrangements. People were milling about and Cordelia broke free from a group and came over to greet them, looking elegant in a full-length evening gown that rippled as she moved. Mabel was in a proper evening dress too, and Persephone was bound to be in a long dress – and so was Margaret because she had borrowed something from one of them. But Joan, Dot and Alison would definitely be wearing knee-length and there were plenty of day dresses to be seen, made more formal by jewellery or elbow-length gloves or sparkly aigrettes worn in the hair.

'Is your Emily here tonight?' Mrs Cooper asked Cordelia.

Cordelia looked round the foyer. 'She's over there with her father.' She smiled at Mabel and Colette. 'I'll make sure I introduce her.'

'She's a pretty girl,' said Mabel, looking across the room.

'Your table awaits,' Cordelia told Mrs Cooper, 'if you're absolutely sure you're happy to spend the night selling raffle tickets.'

'Of course I'm sure,' said Mrs Cooper. 'It's a small thing to do to help our boys.'

'Hear, hear,' Mabel agreed. 'And you won't be on your own all the time, because us girls will pop in and out to sit with you. Here come Alison and Paul. Alison, what a gorgeous dress. What do you call that colour?'

'Apricot,' said Alison, clearly delighted when all eyes turned in her direction.

She wasn't, as Colette had expected, in a day dress, but wore a full-length evening gown with short sleeves, trimmed at the sweetheart neckline, cuffs and the swirling hem with silver braid that gave off tiny twinkles when it caught the light. Her jewellery twinkled too. How pretty she looked. Alison wasn't a beauty like Persephone. Colette thought she was more what magazines called the girl-next-door type, but tonight she looked truly lovely. Colette's heart warmed towards her. She looked radiant.

Cordelia led Mrs Cooper to the table where the raffle tickets would be sold. It was close to the entrance to the ballroom. The double doors stood open, surrounded by an archway of red, white and blue rosettes. Guests started strolling towards the doors, pausing to buy tickets from Mrs Cooper.

Joan and Bob arrived in a group with Dot and her husband and two young women, one a brunette with rather sharp features, the other a blonde with flawless make-up and perfectly styled hair.

'Evening, all,' said Dot. 'We've brought us daughters-in-law along – Sheila and Pammy.'

'How do you do?' said Mabel. She smiled at Sheila. 'I think you're Jimmy's mother, aren't you? We love hearing about his escapades.'

Colette couldn't help admiring Mabel's social grace. She had beautiful manners, but it was more than that. She had confidence too, the ability to make conversation with anyone at all. Persephone was the same. Colette wished she possessed the same ability, but at heart she had always been shy.

'We'd best go into the ballroom,' said Dot. 'We can't hang about out here if we mean to sit together.'

'That won't be a problem,' said Alison. 'Cordelia has reserved two tables next to one another for all of us.'

'Three tables, actually,' said Joan, standing close to her new husband. 'Bob's family is coming too.'

'Why don't the rest of you go in and I'll lend Mrs Cooper a hand,' Mabel suggested. 'She's got a queue building up.'

Dot laughed. 'We queue up for everything else these days, so we might as well queue up for raffle tickets an' all.'

In the end, Mabel, Joan and Colette all helped sell tickets while Harry, Bob and Tony chatted with one another. Gradually, the foyer cleared of guests. Music spilled out of the ballroom and Colette hummed along to the waltz.

'You need to get in there and start dancing,' said Mrs Cooper. 'You mustn't spend all night out here with me.'

Harry, Bob and Tony strolled across to the table, Tony with a cigarette between his fingers. Joan joined Bob and took his hand. In the ballroom doorway, beneath the patriotic archway, Bob paused and dropped a kiss on her cheek, taking her in a ballroom hold and waltzing her onto the floor.

'They're such a delightful couple.' Mrs Cooper stood up. 'I'm just going to take this money to the office for safekeeping before I sell the next batch.' She disappeared across the foyer.

'Talking of delightful couples … ' Harry took Mabel's hand and placed it in the crook of his arm, leading her towards the ballroom. He too paused in the doorway, looking deep into her eyes. 'You're the most beautiful girl here.'

And in they went. Colette sighed softly. Mabel must feel like a princess.

Tony looked round for an ashtray. He stubbed out his cigarette and offered Colette his arm.

'Our turn.'

He stopped under the archway and Colette's heart swelled as he turned to her. He bent his head and she rose slightly on her toes.

'I've told you before. That dress really doesn't do you any favours.'

Colette's eyes widened. She fell back on her heels. The sensation felt as though she had been dropped from a great height. As Tony turned to lead her into the ballroom, something made her glance back – and she looked straight into the shocked face of Mrs Cooper.

What a glorious evening. Alison had seen on the others' faces how much they admired her dress and that meant a lot to her, along with all the compliments she received. She was completely open about her dress not being anywhere

53

near new and she lapped up all the praise that came her way when she explained how she had sewn on the silver braid herself.

'That's a clever lass you've got there,' Dot told Paul, and it was all Alison could do not to beam her head off. She couldn't help thinking that if Dot had saved her comment for an hour or two, she might have had the chance to say, 'That's a clever fiancée you've got there.' Was tonight the night? Oh, it had to be, it simply had to.

As the dance ended and everyone clapped, the master of ceremonies took to the stage to welcome everybody and encourage them to contribute as much as they could.

'We've come up with plenty of ways to part you from your cash, ladies and gentlemen. There's the raffle, with tickets on sale outside the ballroom, and for the sum of five shillings, you can choose a favourite melody from the song-book on the table in front of the stage and the band will play it during the evening.'

Alison's heart bumped against her ribs. Would Paul pay for 'Begin the Beguine'? She couldn't take any chances. She would have to find a moment to request it herself – and if Paul should ask for it too, all well and good. Would the band play it sooner if two people requested it?

'We guarantee to play all the requested pieces,' went on the MC, 'even if it means we have to carry on dancing until breakfast time – and we're charging ten bob for breakfast,' he quipped, allowing a moment for chuckles and scattered clapping. 'There will also be a couple of gentlemen's excuse-me dances. Gentlemen, if you wish to dance with a lady, you must pay a shilling for the privilege. And now, ladies and gentlemen, take your partners, please, for a foxtrot.'

As the music started and couples took to the floor, Paul was in the middle of a cigarette, so Alison knew she would have to sit this one out. She didn't mind. There was something about sitting together while others danced that made her feel she and Paul looked like an established couple. New couples danced every dance, desperate to stay in each other's arms, but she and Paul didn't need to gaze constantly into one another's eyes to know how deep their love went.

Cordelia slipped into the seat beside Alison's. 'It seems to have got off to a good start.'

'You can relax and enjoy it now,' said Alison.

Cordelia laughed. 'I shan't relax until it's over.'

Alison looked round the crowded ballroom. 'It's wonderful to see so many people here. You must be very pleased.'

'I am,' Cordelia agreed, 'and I'm delighted that all the Hubbles are here and that Dot brought her daughters-in-law. What about your parents and your sister? Do they have something else on tonight?'

'Um, yes. It's such a shame they couldn't come.'

Paul chose that moment to come to life. 'My mum could have come. She'd have enjoyed it.'

Alison took what remained of his cigarette and stubbed it out, smiling beguilingly. 'Why don't you ask Margaret to dance? She's here on her own.'

Paul got to his feet amiably and went to Margaret at the adjacent table. A moment later, he led her onto the floor. As they disappeared among the dancers, Alison excused herself and made her way towards the stage. In front of it, to one side, a bow-tied gentleman sat behind a table with a music book in front of him. He started to offer it to Alison, but she didn't so much as glance at it.

'Please may I have "Begin the Beguine"?'

'You certainly may.' He made a note of it while Alison waited for a breathless moment lest he remark that she was the second person to ask for it, but all he said was, 'That's five shillings, please.'

She handed over two half-crowns.

'Cheers,' said the man. 'Cheap at half the price.'

She smiled back at him. It certainly would be if it helped get Paul across the line. Weaving her way back to the table, she had to press her lips together to prevent a dazzling pre-engagement beam from bursting through and eclipsing the light from the chandeliers.

As the music ended, Paul escorted Margaret back to her seat and Alison stood up.

'My turn,' she said.

She kept Paul on the floor for the next couple of dances and then a ladies' excuse-me was announced. A waltz started and almost at once Alison felt a light tap on her shoulder. Paul stopped dancing and Alison just had time to see a pretty blonde girl in a green day dress before Paul whisked her away in his arms. Alison laughed good-naturedly. When other girls excused you so they could dance with your boyfriend, it meant he was good-looking and light on his feet, two reasons why she was so proud of him. Looking round, she chose a well-dressed lady to excuse and waltzed with the lady's distinguished-looking husband until someone else excused her.

When the music was coming to an end, Alison excused Paul's current partner so she could end the dance in his arms.

'Now that everyone is in the mood for excusing,' the MC said into the microphone, 'let's continue with a gentlemen's excuse-me – but remember, gentlemen, it'll cost you one shilling each time.'

There was laughter and some of the men jingled the change in their pockets. Paul swung Alison into the quick-step, but it was only moments before he was excused. Alison found herself being passed from partner to partner.

Mr Green danced with her and so did Harry and Bob. She glimpsed Paul with the fair-haired girl in the green dress, then with an older lady, then Mabel, but after that she didn't catch sight of him again.

At the end, the MC announced, 'We'll give you a couple of minutes to find your correct partners and then the next dance will be a slow foxtrot.'

Alison thanked her partner and returned to her table. Mabel was about to sit down when Harry dashed to hold her seat for her. He sat beside her, shunting his chair close to hers and resting his arm along the back of her chair. He leaned towards her and it looked as if he might kiss her, but he simply murmured in her ear and Mabel looked delighted with whatever he said.

But they weren't the sort of couple to embarrass their companions by canoodling in public and a moment later, Mabel hailed Paul as he approached.

'You were a busy bee on the dance floor. I'm sure you were with a different partner every time I saw you – well, apart from that girl in green. Do you know her?'

'Never seen her before in my life.' Paul sat down, patting his pockets in search of cigarettes.

'I just wondered because I thought I saw you dancing with her twice.'

'Did I? I wouldn't know.' Paul smiled. 'I was too busy doing my duty and pouring my shillings into the weapons fund.'

Alison drew a deep breath of pure pride. Paul was generous, though he wasn't foolish. He would never overspend. She loved that quip about doing his duty, too. It was the sort of off-the-cuff thing Harry Knatchbull would say and she had long admired Harry's charm.

'Don't get too comfy,' she said to Paul. 'Let's go and make sure Mrs Cooper is all right.'

They got up and she linked arms with him as they headed for the double doors into the foyer, where Mrs Cooper had a short queue in front of her table.

'Do you need a hand?' Alison asked, willing her to decline.

'I'm managing fine, thank you, dear. You two run along and enjoy yourselves.'

Alison deliberately didn't glance at Paul as she took a step, just one step, further into the foyer. There were comfortable-looking armchairs in groups with coffee tables in the middle, and around the walls were tables for two, illuminated by candlelight. Perfect for a proposal. She took another step. Just enough to prompt Paul to seize the initiative.

'Well, if we're not needed here,' said Paul and escorted her back to the ballroom. She could have crowned him.

Then she relaxed. Had he sensed her little plan? She didn't want to be obvious. Goodness, hadn't she spent ages cursing their respective mothers for dropping hints like bricks? It was important to leave Paul to do this in his own way. Much more romantic and special.

The dance continued. Alison danced with Paul and also with Bob and Harry. Dot's husband breathed beery fumes but proved to be surprisingly light on his feet. Dot was a nifty dancer as well and when there was a short break from ballroom dancing in favour of old-time sequence dancing, she and Mr Green partnered one another in the veleta to tremendous applause.

As midnight approached, the railway friends and their partners were sitting around their tables, enjoying a breather.

'And now for our next requested song,' said the MC. 'It's "Begin the Beguine". Take your partners, please.'

Alison was on her feet so fast she knocked the table and the others leaned forwards to steady their drinks. She held out her hand to Paul.

'I've been summoned,' he joked to the others before leading her onto the floor.

'And to make the dance more interesting,' went on the MC, 'this will be a ladies' excuse-me.'

Drat! That was the very last thing Alison wanted, but she refused to let her smile slip.

When she felt a tap on her shoulder and heard a voice saying, 'Excuse me,' she turned her head to say, 'I'm sorry, but this is a special tune for us,' and the girl nodded and went to excuse someone else.

'You shouldn't refuse to be excused,' said Paul.

'Don't you want us to have our special dance?'

'Of course I do.'

'Excuse me.'

Alison looked round. It was the fair-haired girl in green.

'Sorry,' she said, 'but we want this dance together.'

'You shouldn't stand up during the excuse-me, then,' said the girl.

And somehow – somehow – Alison was no longer in Paul's arms. The girl in the green dress had usurped her rightful place. Paul and the girl whirled away, leaving Alison staring after them.

CHAPTER SIX

Cordelia had been assigned to the marshalling yard for two weeks. This was where locomotives, wagons and coaches were taken when they needed to be put onto different tracks on the permanent way. Cordelia had explained it to Kenneth by comparing it to taking a canal boat through a series of locks to get from one part of the canal to another.

'Except that the canal locks are there to accommodate different levels of water,' Kenneth had pointed out pedantically, 'and the canal boat stays in the same stretch of water, whereas the purpose of the marshalling yard is to move wagons and so forth from one track to another, using the points.'

As she moved between the wagons, Cordelia was constantly aware of the importance of paying attention. The marshalling yard wasn't the safest place in the world and accidents happened. She was equally safety-conscious when she was out walking the line. No lampman or woman could afford to miss their step when climbing up to or down from a gantry.

This week, her job was to clean the tail lights and sidelights on numerous brake wagons.

'And that's all you do all day?' Emily asked at the table on Monday evening. 'Don't you get fearfully bored?'

Kenneth gave a bark of laughter. 'Good question, Emily. Don't imagine you're the first to ask.'

'As a matter of fact, it isn't boring, Emily darling – as hard as that might be to believe.' Cordelia felt like glaring at Kenneth but refrained. 'I admit I prefer walking the line because of being out and about in the fresh air.'

'Except when it's pouring with rain,' Emily put in.

'In poor weather, it's even more important to ensure the lamps are clean and visible.' Dear heaven, how school-mistressy she sounded. Cordelia softened the words with a smile. 'Obviously, I'm capable of doing a job that calls for more intellectual ability, but that's beside the point – isn't it, Kenneth?'

He nodded. 'In wartime everyone has to pull together and do the work that's handed to them.'

'And do it to the very best of their ability,' Cordelia added.

'Feeling bored would be unpatriotic,' said Emily with the wisdom of her fifteen years, and Cordelia and Kenneth exchanged indulgent smiles. 'Maybe I should get a job on the railways, then I'd be doing real war work. No offence, Daddy, but working as an office junior in your law practice wouldn't exactly be crucial work.'

'There's no need to decide just yet,' said Kenneth. 'After all, the school year hasn't ended.'

'But everyone's allowed to finish early after they've done their School Cert,' said Emily. 'It's not as though I'm playing truant.'

'A neat little money-spinner for the school,' Kenneth remarked wryly, 'letting the exam girls leave early, though their fathers are still required to pay fees until the last day. The point is, Emily, that you don't need to find work quite yet.'

Cordelia said nothing, but she was thrilled to hear Emily apparently preferring the idea of a railway job. Since she had returned from Herefordshire, a discreet tug of war had developed between Cordelia and Kenneth over where Emily might work. Kenneth naturally wanted his daughter to take a clerical post in his firm.

'It makes sense,' was his view. 'The war won't last for ever and a clerk can always find work. If she ends up in some sort of wartime role, she'll lose her job when peace is declared and have to start all over again. Not only that but she'll find herself in competition with all the other girls who've been doing war jobs.'

That was all true and Cordelia could see his point. Even so, wouldn't it be wonderful if Emily worked on the railways and became part of her group of friends? There was another reason too. Cordelia was anxious for Emily to discover for herself that people from all walks of life were every bit as likeable as the middle-class sort among whom she had grown up. It had shocked Cordelia that her own daughter should have taken against Dot and Mrs Cooper both on a personal level and for their friendship with her mother. Worse, Emily had said she didn't trust the friendship. She thought Dot and Mrs Cooper were in it for what they could get. Two working-class women getting chummy with a lady from the professional middle class – as far as Emily was concerned, they must think they had it made.

At first, Cordelia had spoken up in spirited defence of her friends, but that had backfired when Kenneth had got involved.

'Mummy has become fond of these women,' he said in what Cordelia thought of as his pontificating voice, 'and I'm afraid you'll have to learn to accept it.'

The mulish look on Emily's pretty face showed what she thought of that.

'War makes for strange bedfellows,' Kenneth went on. 'That's how you must think of it.'

'Is that how you think of it, Daddy?' Emily asked.

'That's quite enough of that, thank you,' Cordelia interjected, 'from both of you.' She kept her voice light. It would be a mistake to sound defensive.

62

Was it wrong of her not to give Emily a lecture on accepting people for themselves instead of judging them according to their position in the world? But then, even though it had broken her heart to send Emily away to boarding school as Kenneth had insisted, hadn't she been happy and grateful for Emily to enjoy the best of everything all her life? A sound education, well-brought-up friends, music and dancing lessons ... the list went on. Emily had benefited from every advantage, the more so through being an only child, and she had only ever mixed with nicely spoken, educated girls. It had seemed so natural and appropriate before the war, but now ...

Cordelia longed for her daughter's eyes to be opened as her own had been, but she couldn't force it to happen by laying down the law. She needed Emily to learn for herself – and what better way than by becoming a railway girl? So Emily's remark about 'real war work' made Cordelia's heart pitter-patter with happiness.

It also eased the feeling of guilt that had been plaguing her whenever she was in Dot's company. It had been perfectly beastly knowing that her own daughter despised and resented her dear friend's use of her first name. In turn, she felt disloyal to Dot and Mrs Cooper because she hadn't given Emily a severe talking-to, but now she was glad she hadn't. If Emily came to work on the railways, she would find herself mixing with girls and women from all kinds of backgrounds. It would do her good – a dose of reality after the privileged and refined atmosphere in which she had been brought up.

Cordelia felt buoyed up as she went to work the next day. She changed into her dungarees in the walk-in cupboard as usual and set off for the marshalling yard in the company of a few others.

'Look at those clouds,' said Glenys. She was quite new on the lamps. She was a young mum whose mother-in-law took care of her little ones so she could do her bit. 'I'd much rather have a spot of sun.'

Mrs Haughtrey laughed. She was an older woman with nearly forty years as an unblocker in the sewers under her belt before the war had given her the chance to find work above ground. 'When you've been here longer, love, you'll learn that all you want is for it to be dry.'

'Aye, that's true enough,' said Mr Winton. His weather-beaten face was testament to his many years in this job. He was a likeable fellow, who Cordelia rather suspected couldn't afford to retire.

They were all given their allocation of wagons and they separated to work in different parts of the yard. Cordelia was near the head of one of the inclines. Wagons were brought up and gravity did the rest, sending the wagons downhill through a series of points so that they joined the correct track and therefore the correct train at the bottom. As Cordelia made her way along her first line of wagons, she was scrupulous about keeping close to them and not stepping towards the lines of track that fed wagons towards the slope.

What job might Emily be put into, should she join the railways? With her education and general knowledge, she would be certain to pass the written tests in English, maths and geography. Moreover, she was a healthy girl who had been captain of both lacrosse and tennis, so she would pass the medical with flying colours. There were so many different jobs on the railways, not just the station jobs that everyone thought of, like porter and ticket collector. The railways employed crane drivers, motor drivers, bridge painters, engine cleaners, level-crossing keepers, to name but a handful. They employed an army of clerks too, but Cordelia sincerely hoped Emily wouldn't be put into an office. She wanted her daughter to widen her horizons. There would be ample time for office work after the war.

Cordelia was accustomed to the noises around her, but the moment she heard a loud yell of 'Watch out!' her senses jumped to attention and she spun round to see what was happening, sucking in a sharp breath of shock. On the face of it, nothing out of the ordinary was happening. A line of wagons had just begun trundling down the incline, the same as happened numerous times every day, but the man at the top was bellowing down the slope, 'Out of the way! Get out of the way!' and another man was running hell for leather down the incline.

Cordelia ran to the top of the incline and watched in horror as the wagons, picking up speed, headed down the same track as one that already had wagons on it at the bottom – wagons where Mr Winton was working. He was – yes, he was standing in between two of them. Cordelia's mouth went dry. If the moving wagons bashed into the stationary line, Mr Winton would be killed, no doubt about it.

'Dear heaven.' Mrs Haughtrey had appeared beside her. 'Someone has sent them wagons down the wrong track.'

Both women cupped their hands round their mouths, shouting, 'Mr Winton! Mr Winton! Watch out!'

And, miraculously, Mr Winton did. He jerked round, froze – then leaped for his life seconds before the travelling wagons hit those standing there, smashing them together before the whole line of them shunted along.

Mrs Haughtrey threw her arms around Cordelia and hugged her and Cordelia hugged her back, and never mind that she had been trained from infancy to keep her hands to herself. Then, along with several others, they ran down the incline towards Mr Winton, who was gaping at the wagons, probably unable to take in what had just happened.

Yet within minutes everyone was sent back to their work. They weren't allowed to stand around, discussing what had happened, boggling at Mr Winton's escape and generally coming to terms with the near catastrophe. The person who had messed up the points would be dealt with and everyone else had their jobs to do.

Cordelia returned to her line of wagons, feeling shaken but extra alert. The memory of those wagons heading down the incline remained with her all day. She wished it was a buffet evening so that she could talk about it with her friends and get it out of her system.

As it was, she wasn't able to discuss it until she got home.

'Good grief,' said Kenneth. 'And you saw it happen?'

'But the man was all right, wasn't he?' asked Emily.

'Yes, darling,' said Cordelia. 'He was.'

'By the skin of his teeth,' said Kenneth. 'He could just as easily have been crushed. That settles it. Emily, when the time comes, you shall work in my office. No daughter of mine is working in a railway job after this.'

'Kenneth—' Cordelia began.

He held up his hand. 'I'm well aware that there are plenty of safe jobs on the railways, but who's to say Emily would be given one of them? No, Cordelia. My mind is made up. Emily is categorically not going to apply to the railways.'

Last Sunday, the day following the War Weapons Week dance, Colette hadn't visited Mrs Cooper and Mrs Grayson. Tony had told Mrs Cooper not to expect them. Colette could understand that after spending all Saturday evening with her railway friends, Tony wouldn't wish to spend Sunday afternoon with them too, but she had felt disappointed on her own account. Before the dance took place, she couldn't imagine anything more enjoyable than talking about it the next day – but that had been before. Afterwards, she had felt quite different.

What was she going to do this coming weekend? If she made an excuse not to go to Mrs Cooper's, Tony wouldn't mind in the slightest. He only came to keep an eye on her. But if she cried off this weekend, what about the following weekend? The problem would still exist. Would she feel she had to put off her visit again? But if she did, there was the danger that their weekly visits to Wilton Close would drop out of their regular routine – and the moment that happened, Tony wouldn't let her reinstate them. She knew that for certain. He was so much cleverer than she was. Everyone thought he was so amenable, but really he was in charge of everything. It had taken enormous determination on Colette's part to make those early visits to Mrs Cooper. Even Tony hadn't been able to object to her calling on a recently bereaved mother.

But then Mrs Cooper's solitary household had expanded to include first Mrs Grayson and then Joan, though by then Colette's visits were a settled thing and it was too late for Tony to withdraw permission. After that, poor Mrs Cooper had been bombed out and she and her lodgers had upped sticks and moved to Wilton Close, where Mabel had joined them. Tony hadn't liked it, but what could he do? Colette had relished her little bit of weekly freedom with the friends who were so dear to her.

Then it had turned out that Tony could do something about it. Of course. She should have known. It had been stupid of her to enjoy her Wilton Close visits, stupid of her to rely on them. Tony hadn't stopped her going. It was too much of a settled arrangement and Tony cared what people thought of him, even though caring about it could make him angry.

Instead, he had started coming with her. When he had announced this intention, her insides had shrivelled, but she'd had to ask Mrs Cooper if it was all right for Tony to accompany her; she'd had to make the offer of odd jobs and a spot of gardening; and she'd had to smile and look pleased when the offer was accepted and everyone told her how lucky she was to have such a helpful, caring husband.

No one knows what goes on behind closed doors.

But it wasn't 'no one' any longer, was it? Mrs Cooper had overheard the words Tony had uttered beneath the red, white and blue archway at the dance. Colette had seen her face – the widened eyes, the parted lips. Shame had flooded through her. Someone knew. Someone *knew.* Oh, she had wanted to sink through the floor. It had ruined the evening for her. It had even eclipsed what Tony had said – until he started on her when they arrived home.

'Did you enjoy yourself?' he had asked.

There had been a small lurching sensation beneath her ribs. What answer did he require? When in doubt, apologise.

'I'm sorry I wore this dress. I thought – I thought you liked it.'

Tony's eyebrows had climbed up his forehead.

A flutter of panic. 'You said you did. At Joan's wedding, you said you did.'

'That was because Mrs Green admired it. She was being kind – and so was I. Decent people don't say nasty things in public. We were sparing your feelings. You were foolish if you didn't appreciate that. You know what I think of that dress, of that colour. God knows, I've told you enough times.'

Tony lifted his hand and she flinched. Tony had smiled and frowned at the same time, as if her reaction was idiotic – and it was, of course, because he had never raised a hand to her, not once. She knew that. He would never physically hurt her. If there was one thing she knew, she knew that.

Tony brushed her cheek with the backs of his fingers, a lingering touch, a caress. 'Silly girl.' His voice was a caress too. 'Silly girl, not knowing when people are just being polite. It's a good job you've got me to take care of you, isn't it?' He looked at her, his smile never faltering. 'Isn't it?'

She had nodded. 'Yes.'

They had been married for five years. She had been a bride at eighteen, not much more than a girl. Her mother had been so pleased and proud on her wedding day – and so relieved to know that her precious only child was going to be looked after.

Some months afterwards, Mother had told Colette about the cancer. She had found the original lump when Colette had first been going out with Tony.

'That's why I was keen for you to get together with him – well, and also because he's a good catch, of course. I could tell he was right for you, Colette dear – and he is, isn't he?'

And she had said, 'Yes.' Of course.

It was what everybody thought. Tony Naylor was the perfect husband. And in many ways he was, he honestly was. He was a good provider and while he didn't have the looks of a matinée idol, he was handsome in a sensitive kind of way. And he worshipped the ground she walked on. All her friends told her she had landed on her feet. All her friends?

Oh yes, she had had friends in those days, though some-how they had grown apart, but that was only natural, wasn't it, when a girl got married? She didn't expect to be out and about with her friends any longer. Her life now centred on her home and her husband. Certainly that was the way it had happened for Colette. She had missed her friends, though she'd refrained from saying so, not wanting to seem disloyal to her husband. Tony had approved of her domestic instincts, of the way she gradually lost touch with her former life. Had he done more than approve? Had he engineered it? Or was she wicked to wonder?

That was why she had been so grateful when the war started and she could apply to do war work. She longed for female companionship, for a life outside her own four walls. She had imagined being shunted into a munitions factory, but instead the lady at the labour exchange had given her an application form for the railways. Once she had filled it in and posted it, there was nothing Tony could do to stop it. He'd discouraged her from sitting the necessary tests, telling her there was no point as she wouldn't pass.

'I have to sit them,' she'd protested, her eyes full of tears and her heart thudding. 'I'll get into trouble with the labour exchange if I don't – and then who knows what job they'll make me do.'

She'd apologised for applying. Later, she apologised for passing the tests. Tony, meanwhile, had hammered away at her in bed every night, eager to get her pregnant so she could resign even before she started.

Then, on her first day, she had suffered the excruciating humiliation of being accompanied by her husband so that he could lay down the law and require that his wife be given a ladylike job in an office. To this day, Colette had no idea whether his request had resulted in her being yanked out of a job as a ticket collector or a bridge painter or a boilermaker's assistant, or whether she had been down to do a clerical job anyway.

The new friends she had made through her railway post meant the world to her and she would be for ever grateful to Miss Emery for urging them on their first day to stick together. It wasn't just Dot and Mabel and the others who worked on the railways whom Colette appreciated, but their wider circle – Mrs Cooper and Mrs Grayson and, to a lesser extent, Miss Brown and Mrs Mitchell from Darley Court, where Persephone lived. Meeting up with the others in the buffet and visiting Mrs Cooper at weekends had given Colette a sense of companionship and belonging – a very different sort of belonging to the one Tony made her feel.

At first, there had been a sense of fear too, fear that the others wouldn't take to her because she was shy or that they might drop her because she wasn't available anything like as often as she ought to be. But they had taken to her and they hadn't dropped her. Far from it. They had warmly welcomed her whenever Tony let her spend a little time with them in the buffet.

Now she was seeing far more of them than previously, which she loved – but it had led to her current situation. Mrs Cooper had heard. She had *heard*. And how was Colette ever to face her again?

She would have to. It was either that or give up the friendship. Quite apart from how much it would hurt her to do so, precisely how would she explain it to the others? No, she must go to Wilton Close as usual this weekend and she'd have to put a brave face on it. Perhaps Mrs Cooper hadn't heard after all – but Colette knew she had. It would be awkward for both of them. Colette took comfort from the certainty that Mrs Cooper would be far too embarrassed to refer to it in any way.

But she did.

For once, Colette and Tony were the only visitors. Mabel had gone over to Darley Court to see Mrs Mitchell, who was her father's cousin, so the only ones in the house were the Naylors, Mrs Cooper and Mrs Grayson. When Tony removed his jacket to go outside and tackle some gardening, Mrs Grayson went with him to show him which vegetables to dig up.

Colette immediately launched into a story of something that had happened at work. She felt horribly self-conscious. She was a quiet person by nature, not a prattler.

The moment she paused for breath, Mrs Cooper said softly, 'That's how it's to be, is it? We're going to pretend nowt happened.'

'I don't know what you mean.' Damn her fair colouring, which made a blush so much more obvious.

Mrs Cooper smiled sadly. 'I think you do know, love. You can't blame me for feeling concerned.'

In that moment, Colette wanted nothing more than to hurl herself into Mrs Cooper's arms and cling to her for dear life, but she lifted her chin and pushed her shoulders back.

'I don't know what you think you heard,' she began.

'I know exactly what I heard and so do you,' Mrs Cooper said gently.

'He was joking. It wasn't a good joke, but he was joking.'

'Oh, aye? Jokes a lot, does he?'

Tears sprang to Colette's eyes. 'Mrs Cooper – please stop. Just stop.'

'Eh, chuck, don't cry. I don't want to make you cry.'

Colette sniffed and dabbed her eyes; they mustn't look pink or swollen when Tony came back. She forced a laugh. 'It was a bad joke, that's all. I'm sorry you had to hear it.'

Mrs Cooper nodded. 'If you say so. There's just one thing that worries me. Are you telling me that this is the first and only time your Tony has made a bad joke?'

CHAPTER SEVEN

After the bitter blow of no proposal at the War Weapons Week dance, Alison had struggled to maintain her composure all through the following week, repeatedly reminding herself that she was the only one who knew why she had attached the sparkly silver braid to her dress and why she had worn the special jewellery. As far as her friends were concerned, she had simply been dressing for the occasion. They had no idea that the occasion was meant to have been her engagement.

Honestly, she felt like giving Paul a good shake. That was how *she* felt – all shaken up inside. It made her feel twitchy and out of sorts, but she had to keep smiling. That was how she presented herself to the world – smiling, happy, confident – because she *was* confident, she honestly was. She and Paul were made for each other and they were destined to get married and grow old together. She had no doubt in her mind about that whatsoever, the same way that there was no doubt in Mum's mind or Mrs Dunaway's or in the mind of anyone you cared to name who was acquainted with her and Paul. Paul knew it too.

Was that the problem? Did knowing that his proposal was going to be accepted make Paul feel he could take his time over popping the question? Was he building up to the perfect proposal? But what better venue could there be than a dance at the Claremont? Maybe he would end up asking her over a bag of chips. Now that really would take her by surprise – well, no, not now that she'd thought of it.

But it would surprise everybody else and maybe that was what he was aiming for, which would be entirely understandable when you thought of Mum's hopeful glances every time Paul brought her home, and his mum was just as bad. But she couldn't be vexed with them. The three of them were going to have such a wonderful time organising the wedding together. A shiver of pure joy rippled through her. She couldn't wait.

She spent Sunday afternoon with Paul while he played cricket. Lydia sat outside in a deckchair, giggling with her friends, but Alison preferred to do her stint in the clubhouse, helping to make the tea. That was what the married women did. All right, so she didn't have a ring on her finger, but everyone knew she was as good as engaged. She smiled to herself as she spread fish paste on bread for sandwiches. If Paul became the team captain one day, organising the cricket teas would be her responsibility.

After the match, the men got changed and there was talk of going to the pub. Alison quite liked it when Paul went to the pub because it meant she could have a little groan with the other wives, but she preferred it when he didn't, because that showed what a devoted couple they were.

Paul did go to the pub, but he could only have stayed long enough for a swift half because he turned up at Alison's not long after she got there, which she wouldn't normally have expected and it made her feel special. That was one of the wonderful things about their relationship. No matter how long they had been together, the gloss never wore off.

They sat in the front parlour, the traditional place for couples who were courting strong, but when Alison made a move to snuggle up, Paul pushed himself to his feet and stood on the rug, hands on hips. He frowned, then he smiled, but it was a distant sort of smile, as if his thoughts were miles away.

Then he – oh my goodness, he dropped down as if – as if—

Alison's heart thudded. After all those times when she had planned and hoped ... and now he really and truly had caught her by surprise—

But instead of dropping onto one knee, he landed on the sofa. He sat right up close beside her and caught her hands in his.

'You're such a wonderful girl, Allie. You know that, don't you? You know how much you mean to me?'

She laughed, a nervous reaction. 'Yes, of course. You mean the world to me too.'

'I know.' Paul shook his head, once, twice. He closed his eyes. 'I know.'

He pressed his mouth to hers. It wasn't a long kiss, but it was intense and it left Alison with stars in her eyes. Paul didn't pull away. He rested his forehead against hers, his breath soft on her face.

'We're meant to be together,' he said.

It was Alison's turn to whisper, 'I know.' When Paul said nothing more, she added, 'I've always known.'

Paul moved his forehead away and Alison started to lift her face for another kiss, but Paul kissed her forehead and then drew her into a huge cuddle, not a soft, cosy one, but a deep, ardent one that rang with passion and commitment. Alison wriggled to get as close as she could and clung to him.

'Let's go back to the Claremont,' said Paul, his voice a rumble as Alison's ear pressed into his chest. 'I'll take you there for dinner and you can wear your beautiful dress again.'

'I'd love that.'

'Good. Then that's what we'll do.'

Alison's body relaxed and her pulse steadied as a feeling of the deepest satisfaction poured through her. *Now* she understood. Proposals weren't about taking the girl by surprise. They were about setting the scene and building up to the perfect moment. They were about two people thinking and feeling as one. Paul was going to ask her to be his wife when they had dinner at the Claremont. She knew it more certainly and completely than she had ever known anything, but just when she'd expected fireworks of excitement to burst and fizz inside her, what she experienced was the deepest possible confidence – no, more than confidence. Utter serenity.

It was going to happen. It really was going to happen. She knew it.

Utter serenity.

It was the start of Cordelia's second week in the marshalling yard. It began as usual with getting changed into her dungarees and silk headscarf, then her duties were assigned.

'Oh, and you'll have a new girl to look after. She's being given the grand tour at the moment. I'll point her in your direction when that's finished.'

A new girl. Cordelia would enjoy showing her the ropes, but she couldn't help feeling a pang of disappointment at the thought that Emily was destined for Kenneth's stuffy office. It would have meant so much to have her daughter working alongside her. Even if they had been miles apart in completely different railway jobs, she would still have loved it. Cordelia was more than satisfied with her own position as a railway employee, but if Emily could have enjoyed the same status, she would have burst with pride.

She hadn't been at work long when she was approached by a girl in her twenties, dressed in slacks and wearing her fair hair scooped away from her face with a hairband.

'Mrs Masters? I've been told to report to you. My name's Sarah Jackson. I'm the new lampman.'

'Yes, they tell everyone that,' said Cordelia, looking up from what she was doing. 'Personally, I call myself a lamp-woman.' She smiled to show she wasn't giving a lecture. 'I'll show you what to do and then I'll watch you while you have a go. It isn't a difficult job, but don't let that fool you into thinking that it isn't important. Nothing matters more than safety.'

Sarah wriggled her shoulders in a theatrical shudder. 'Yes, I heard about that near miss last week.'

'That happened because someone made a mistake with the points and it could have had a nasty ending,' Cordelia agreed. 'There are two things you need to remember in this job. One: no matter where you are, whether you're here in the marshalling yard or out walking the line, always be aware of your surroundings and what's going on around you. And two: if you make a mistake, own up to it. There's a form you have to fill in, called a number one. Remember those two things and pay attention when you're handling the lamps, and you won't go far wrong.'

Cordelia enjoyed watching over Sarah and guiding her through her first day and it provided her with something different to talk about at home in the evening. She was gratified when Emily sat up straighter, looking interested.

'If you're being asked to train new recruits, perhaps that means you're going to be made a supervisor or something like that.'

Cordelia smiled wryly. 'If everyone who shepherded a new person became a supervisor, there'd be an awful lot of supervisors. New lampmen and -women have to be trained properly. It isn't a difficult job in itself, but it is an essential one. The safety of the railways depends upon it.'

'It wasn't very dependable last week when those wagons went down the wrong track,' Kenneth remarked.

Honestly, he was like a dog with a bone. Cordelia disliked being made to feel she had to defend the marshalling yard. If only Kenneth would be more sympathetic and open-minded about her job – if he would be more respectful – she would be more open with him about how dangerous a place the marshalling yard could be, as well as being import-ant and fascinating. Kenneth's dislike of her job put her on the defensive. Previously, she had promised herself that she would never allow his attitude to sway her, but now that Emily was here, lapping up every word, Cordelia felt resent-ment stirring. She didn't want to be made to look small in front of her daughter.

'I think we all know your opinion on last week's inci-dent,' she said a trifle sharply. 'If working alongside me this week helps the new girl stay out of harm's way in the future, then I'll consider it a job well done on my part.'

'Well said, Mummy.' Emily smiled at her. 'The new girl is lucky to have you to train her.'

'Thank you, Emily.' Cordelia spoke quietly, but pleasure sang loudly inside her. 'I'm going to the knitting circle at St Clement's this evening. Would you like to come with me?'

Emily wrinkled her nose. 'I don't remember the last time I did any knitting.'

'Then it's high time you started again, not least because of clothes rationing. Moreover, there are plenty of people to knit for these days, with so many losing everything in the air raids.'

'The raids seem to be easing off now,' Kenneth observed.

'Don't say that, Daddy,' cried Emily, 'or you might jinx it.'

Cordelia laughed. Emily might have been brought up in a serious and sedate household, but nothing had ever quenched her bubbly spirit. There was a formal studio portrait of her in their sitting room, but Cordelia's favourite picture of her was in the dining room. It was a holiday snap, a happy moment captured by chance, showing Emily laughing as she pushed her hair away from her face during a breezy day on the beach. Kenneth and his mother had declared the photo far too informal for public display, but to Cordelia, this showed the real Emily.

She had an ulterior motive for asking Emily to accompany her to St Clement's. Mrs Cooper and Mrs Grayson were both going to be there and she wanted Emily to get to know them, and if Emily's knitting was rusty, then who better than Mrs Grayson to give her an impromptu lesson? Mrs Grayson was an expert knitter. When she had lived in her own house, before she became Mrs Cooper's lodger, she had smothered everything with her knitting – cushion covers, lampshade covers, patchwork quilts, mats on the dressing table – but now she devoted her talent to providing clothes and baby blankets for those in need.

Not so long ago, Mrs Grayson had done all her knitting at home in Wilton Close and others had delivered it to St Clement's for her, but these days she attended the knitting evenings in person, accompanied by Mrs Cooper. The sessions took place in the church hall, St Clement's Church being one of the places Mrs Grayson was now able to walk to without panicking.

When Cordelia and Emily arrived, they crept through the hall, where the Home Guard was being given a talk about gas attacks, and went into a side room where women of assorted ages were already busy with their needles. Mrs Cooper saw them and smiled a welcome, her fingers never faltering.

'Oh,' said Emily. She smiled across the room, then turned to Cordelia and murmured, 'Do we have to sit with them?'

Something inside Cordelia froze. 'Yes, we do. They're my friends and I should like you to get to know them. Come and say good evening and then you can go and greet other people you know. You may sit with someone else, if you like – to start with. We shall be here for two hours and I expect you to spend at least one hour with me *and my friends.*' She altered her tone a fraction to show that argument wouldn't be tolerated.

To Cordelia's relief, Emily took it on the chin. She gave her mother a genuine smile.

'All right, Mummy. You can trust me to do the polite.'

Emily more than did the polite. She was charm itself and Cordelia's pride in her soared, enabling her, for now at least, to set aside her concerns about Emily's dislike of hobnobbing with the lower classes.

Miss Travers approached their table. She was Cordelia's hairdresser and she did Mrs Grayson's hair as well.

'I'm sorry, Mrs Grayson,' she said, 'but I shan't be able to do your trim tomorrow. My assistant's little boy has caught chickenpox, so she has to stay at home to look after him, and I'll be on my own in the salon and won't be able to come round to do your hair.'

'I'd walk with you to the salon,' said Mrs Cooper, 'but I'm booked up all day with cleaning jobs.'

'Cleaning?' squeaked Emily.

'Mrs Cooper runs her own business,' said Cordelia.

'That makes it sound very grand,' laughed Mrs Cooper. 'There's only me.'

'The business is called Magic Mop,' Cordelia told Emily.

'Mabel thought up the name,' said Mrs Cooper, 'and Miss Persephone liked it at once.'

'The Honourable Persephone Trehearn-Hobbs,' Cordelia murmured for Emily's benefit, adding, when Emily turned startled eyes towards her, 'Oh, we get all sorts working on the railways, Honourables and all.' The devil in her was tempted to add, 'So put that in your pipe and smoke it, dear daughter,' but she contented herself with thinking it.

'Anyroad, I can't come with you to the salon,' Mrs Cooper said to Mrs Grayson. 'What a shame. I know how you look forward to having your hair done.'

An idea struck Cordelia and she blurted it out before she could change her mind. 'Emily isn't doing anything particular tomorrow, are you, darling? I'm sure you wouldn't mind accompanying Mrs Grayson to her appointment and waiting for her, would you?'

It was soon settled. Cordelia placed her foot on top of Emily's and pressed gently to warn her against asking questions and Emily took the hint.

On the way home, Cordelia explained about Mrs Grayson's situation.

'She had a bad time years ago and it affected her deeply. She ended up not being able to leave the house.'

'Why not?'

'Because it was the only place she felt safe. Her little boy died and I gather her husband and his parents weren't exactly supportive. By the time her grief started to lift, she found she couldn't bear to go out.'

'Her grief was a pit,' said Emily, 'and she couldn't climb out of it.'

'That's a good way of expressing it.'

'But she can go out now,' Emily observed, 'because she was at the knitting circle.'

'She can go to certain places as long as someone goes with her. But normally, you see, the hairdresser visits her in Wilton Close. Mrs Grayson has never been to the salon.'

Emily nodded. 'I'll take her. Don't worry.'

'Thank you for understanding, darling.'

'Of course I understand. I'm not a child any longer.'

*

When they got home, Kenneth was standing in the hall, hanging up at the end of a telephone call.

'Graham Finnegan's wife has gone into labour, so he'll be spending the night pacing up and down the corridor outside the maternity ward. I've been asked to fill in for him. Make me a flask, will you?'

'Of course,' said Cordelia.

'And bring my shoes. Good evening, was it, Emily? Did you remember how to knit?'

'It's like riding a bicycle. You never forget.'

Cordelia went to fill the kettle, leaving the door open so she could listen.

'How would you like a day out in Chester tomorrow?' Kenneth asked Emily. 'I'm going on business. You could look round the shops.'

'Oh,' Emily said brightly, then, in a different voice, 'Oh. Sorry, Daddy. I'd love to, but no can do. I've got to take Mrs Grayson to the hairdresser's.'

'Mrs Grayson? Oh – her.'

'Somebody has to take her because—'

'I know all about Mrs Grayson, thank you, Emily.' Kenneth sounded put out.

Cordelia stepped into the kitchen doorway and looked down the hall. 'Emily has been most understanding about Mrs Grayson's difficulty.'

'Well, if she's agreed to do something, obviously she has to do it,' said Kenneth.

'There'll be other times when you can take her out,' said Cordelia, going to the stove. The kettle was starting to sing.

'When I'm working for you,' said Emily, 'you can take me out as much as you like.'

'I most certainly can't. If I visit a client, I don't take my staff with me, and certainly not the office junior. Is my flask ready, Cordelia? I need to get my skates on.'

When he had gone, Emily looked forlorn. Did she feel cheated of a day out or was she realising that working for Daddy wasn't going to be a picnic?

'I'm proud of you for not trying to wriggle out of taking Mrs Grayson,' said Cordelia.

'It's like Daddy said. When you agree to do something, you jolly well do it.'

Cordelia would far rather she had said something like, 'She's a dear lady and I want to help her,' but at least she had spoken graciously. That was something. Might it be the start of Emily developing a real regard for Mrs Grayson, followed by Mrs Cooper and Dot? Oh, how Cordelia hoped so. It warmed her heart to picture it.

She couldn't help but tell her friends about Emily's good deed the following evening in the buffet.

'Emily accompanied Mrs Grayson to the hairdresser's today.'

Oh, the relief of being able to say something open and honest about Emily. Ever since her daughter had arrived home unexpectedly, Cordelia's friends had been asking after Emily and generally taking an interest, especially Dot, who understood how dearly Cordelia had missed Emily all the time she had lived away from home. But every time anyone had mentioned Emily, Cordelia had experienced a tiny tremor of shame at the memory of what Emily had said after she had met Mrs Cooper, Dot and Mrs Grayson at Wilton Close.

But she didn't need to feel shame on this occasion, did she? Emily had done Mrs Grayson a kindness today and Cordelia wanted her friends to know.

'Eh, she sounds like a good lass,' Dot commented warmly.

'She is,' said Cordelia.

It was true. Emily was good at heart. She just needed to remove those snobby blinkers that her rigid upbringing and expensive schooling had given her. Going out with Mrs Grayson today was the first step towards that – surely.

Cordelia couldn't wait to get home and talk to Emily, though if she was hoping that Emily might have undergone a dramatic revelation in the middle of her outing, she was doomed to disappointment.

'It was fine,' said Emily. 'I took a book to read while she had her hair done.'

'And you saw her safely home afterwards?'

'No, I dumped her in the middle of Wilbraham Road. Of course I saw her home, Mummy. She invited me in for tea and cake by way of a thank you.'

'That was sweet of her.'

'I didn't accept. I said I had to get home.'

Oh well. It had been foolish to hope for more. But it was a first step.

Kenneth came home and they all sat down to their meal together.

'How was your day?' Cordelia asked.

'Fine, fine. The client listened – they don't always – so no worries on that score.'

'How was the journey?'

Kenneth put down his knife and fork. 'Not too bad going, but coming back the trains were crowded. Do you know, passengers were using the first-class carriage without having first-class tickets.'

'If the train was packed,' said Cordelia, 'it's understandable.'

'Understandable? Is that what they teach you at LMS? That the riff-raff can occupy first class?'

Emily chuckled. 'Sorry, Daddy, I shouldn't laugh, but Mummy's right. If the train is packed solid, what do you expect people to do? They're hardly going to suffocate to death in the crush when there are seats going begging in first class.'

'Good Lord,' said Kenneth. 'That's remarkably socialist of you, Emily.'

'It isn't socialist,' said Cordelia. 'It's common sense.'

'Exactly,' said Emily. 'Common sense. Don't accuse me of socialism. Mummy's the socialist if anyone is. She's the one with the lower-class friends, not me.'

CHAPTER EIGHT

'Friday at last,' said Miss Horrocks. 'I thought the weekend would never come.'

Alison looked at her colleague's reflection in the mirror above the line of basins. They were washing their hands and tidying their hair at the end of the morning's work.

'Of course,' one of the others said to Miss Horrocks. 'Your chap's on leave, isn't he?'

'He should arrive sometime this evening. I can't wait,' said Miss Horrocks, her eyes shining. 'We're going to choose my ring tomorrow.'

Miss Simpson put her hand behind her ear. 'I'm sorry, I didn't quite catch that. Did somebody say "ring"? Or did they say "engagement ring"?'

'Idiot,' laughed Miss Horrocks, her cheeks pink with delight.

Alison turned to her with a smile. She could afford to smile at the likes of Milly Horrocks because it wouldn't be long before she was wearing her own engagement ring.

'Good for you,' said Alison. 'I hope you find one you love.'

Miss Horrocks' face fell, but only for a moment. 'Bert hasn't got much money. I hope we find a nice ring he can afford.'

'Of course you shall,' Miss Simpson said stoutly. 'It's the sentiment that counts, not how flashy the stone is.'

'Miss Simpson's right,' Alison said reassuringly, but inside she was working out how long Paul had had to save up. Her own stone would be the size of half a brick, at this rate. Was this the reason Paul had taken so long to propose – because he wanted the best ring? That would make sense, though quite honestly Alison would have been happy with a novelty ring out of a Christmas cracker. All she longed for was to be officially engaged.

'Are you going out with your boyfriend over the weekend?' Miss Simpson asked Alison.

Alison's heart beat a little faster. She wished she could say he was taking her to the Claremont tomorrow, but that wasn't happening until Saturday of next week. It was a kindness to Milly Horrocks in a way. If Alison's Claremont dinner and proposal had taken place tomorrow, then she and Miss Horrocks would both have come to work on Monday wearing their new rings, and Alison's was certain to be much better.

The thought made her give a laugh of pure excitement, which she then needed to justify.

'I'm seeing him later on, actually, though he doesn't know it yet. I'm finishing at half two today because I've got to go to the dentist.'

'Poor you,' sympathised Miss Simpson.

'Loose filling,' said Alison. 'I'll be glad to get it seen to.'

'And it won't be worth trailing all the way back here afterwards, I don't suppose,' Miss Horrocks said with a smile.

Suddenly, Alison was dying to confide. 'Paul works shifts, so I know he'll be at home, and Friday is his mother's afternoon for doing tea and buns at the Mother and Baby Club.'

'So you thought you'd drop in and surprise him,' finished Miss Simpson. 'Lucky him.'

Alison laughed. Lucky him – and lucky her, too. They were the happiest couple she knew of. Happier than Joan and Bob? Yes, because no matter how strong the Hubbles' marriage undoubtedly was, they had gone through a dreadful time when Joan had been torn between Bob and another man – her late sister's boyfriend, no less. Alison and Paul had never had to face anything of that kind. Neither did they have to cope with being separated most of the time, as so many couples did these days, including Mabel and Harry, and also Lydia and Alec. Having Paul at home in a reserved occupation was a great blessing, not just because it kept him relatively safe, but also because it provided him with ample opportunities to propose. Alison didn't want to be mean, but she quite liked it that her sister's boyfriend was far away. It was important that, as the elder sister, she got married first.

She went to the dentist, then took herself off for a walk around what used to be the park, but was now turned over to allotments, while the numbness wore off. Finally, it was time to go to Paul's. She stopped at the corner to check her face in her compact mirror. There was no swelling and her mouth felt normal and more than capable of responding to Paul's attentions when she told him she'd been to the dentist and he offered to kiss it better.

She walked down the road, blissfully aware that in the not too distant future this would be her way home from work. Once they were married, Paul would sometimes finish work at the same time as she did and he would collect her from outside Hunts Bank or from the buffet, like Tony Naylor always collected Colette. How long would she continue working before she fell pregnant? You sometimes heard girls talking about wanting 'to have some time together' before they started a family, but Alison didn't feel the need for that. She had looked forward to marriage for a long time and she couldn't wait to submerge herself in it, babies and all. Life was going to be wonderful.

She arrived outside Paul's house and walked up the side path to the kitchen door, stifling a giggle at the thought of catching him unawares and seeing his surprise turn to delight. In his mum's absence, they could indulge in some heavy petting. Her skin tingled in anticipation.

The back door was unlocked, as it always was when someone was at home. Alison opened it silently and slipped inside. Though old, Mrs Dunaway's kitchen was neat and clean. A fresh pie sat on the table, covered by a fly net, and the scent of pastry, apple and ginger hung in the air.

Alison removed her hat and jacket and put her handbag and gas-mask box on one of the kitchen chairs. Then she opened the door to the narrow hallway. The door to the parlour was shut. Was Paul in there? Dozing, perhaps, after a long shift? He worked hard. His life would improve ever such a lot when, as well as his mother, he had a wife to take care of him. He would wonder why on earth he hadn't got married sooner.

Alison crept to the parlour door, catching her lower lip beneath her teeth as she concentrated on turning the door-knob without a sound. Slowly she opened the door, revealing the glass-fronted cabinet that housed Mrs Duna-way's 'for best' tea service. The door opened a little further. There was one of the armchairs and the hearthrug ... the tiled fireplace with the mirror above the mantelpiece—

In the reflection, Alison could see Paul's head and shoulders, his face lowered as he – as he—

Her hand fell from the doorknob, but the door kept opening. Now it revealed the utterly impossible sight of Paul, her Paul, her future husband, kissing someone else. A girl with fair hair. A huge cry filled the room and since Alison's mouth was wide open when it ended, presumably it must have come from her. Paul and the girl jumped apart, staring at her, their eyes wide. The girl was wearing a green dress – no, she wasn't, she was in yellow. But in that first moment, Alison's eyes had shown her a green dress and that was exactly how she knew who the girl was.

The excuse-me-dance girl.

'I'm sorry … I'm so sorry.' Paul said it over and over again until Alison thought it would drive her mad. 'I'm so sorry.'

The girl had left in a flurry of blushes and tousled hair, clutching her jacket in one hand and her bag in the other. She was pretty in spite of how horrified she looked. Paul had let her out of the front door. Had the neighbours witnessed her departure? Were they wondering who she was and why she looked upset? Had they spotted Alison arriving five minutes earlier?

Alison's brain had turned to sludge. She didn't know what to think, what to believe. Paul, *her* Paul, had been caught kissing another girl in his mother's parlour.

'I'm sorry,' he said again, his slumped shoulders and repetitive swallowing making him look harried and utterly miserable.

'Stop saying that.' Should it have come out as a great roar of hurt, anger and fear? All that emerged from Alison's lips was a croak. She could hardly breathe. Had the dentist's anaesthetic given her this terrible dream?

'We never meant anything to happen,' Paul whispered. He sank into the armchair that had once been his late father's and which his mum had insisted should be his when he became the man of the house. He hunched forwards, not looking at Alison, his elbows on his knees and his head bent.

'She was at the dance,' said Alison.

'Yes.' That was all he said. He still wouldn't meet her eyes.

Alison waited, then finally insisted, 'Talk to me. Tell me what this is about. I don't understand.'

She sat on the sofa – she had to. Her body was trembling. Even her bones vibrated in distress.

Paul lifted his head, but when she expected him to look at her, he turned his face away, scrubbing his mouth with the splayed fingers of one hand. Shouldn't he be on his knees in front of her, gazing into her eyes, begging for forgiveness? But he wouldn't even look at her. The knots in Alison's belly tightened.

'Look at me,' she said in a low voice.

At last, he turned his face to hers. He rubbed the back of his neck and took a deep, shaky breath. Alison felt a flicker of anger. He had no right to be upset when she was the one who had been hurt.

'I never intended anything to happen,' he said.

'And just to make sure it didn't,' Alison said bitterly, 'you invited that girl round to your house.' She had to draw a breath before she could ask, 'How long has it been going on?'

'I met her at the dance. That was the first time I ever saw her, I swear. If you knew how hard I've fought against this ... '

'Really? And has that girl fought against it too?'

'Don't call her "that girl". She has a name. Katie. She's called Katie.'

'I don't care what she's called. I just – I can't believe ... ' It felt as though her throat had cracked open. Tears poured from her eyes.

Now, at last, Paul came to her. He sat beside her, pulling her close, kissing her hair. She melted into his arms, clinging and gasping for breath as the tears flooded out.

'I'm sorry,' he murmured. 'I know I keep saying it, but it's true. I can't bear to hurt you.'

'Then *why*?' Alison tipped her head back to look up at him.

'It was madness, sheer madness. I'm so sorry. At the dance ... I can't explain it.'

Alison sniffed and he gave her his handkerchief. She mopped her face.

'I can explain it,' she said, her voice thick with tears. 'She threw herself at you. She was determined to get you.'

'Don't say that. Katie is as upset by this as I am.'

'What about me? Aren't I allowed to be upset?'

Paul threw back his head and huffed out a long breath, then he brought his face back to her. 'You poor darling. I'm so sorry. I never wanted to hurt you. This is appalling. I don't know how it happened. I wish I'd never set eyes on her.'

Hope fluttered inside Alison's chest. 'D'you mean that?'

'Of course I do. Allie, you mean the world to me. You know that.'

'Then how *could* you?'

'I told you, I don't know. It just happened. It's not as though I went out that night intending to look for another girl.'

'I should hope not!' Alison reined in the surge of emotion. 'It's bad enough that you – you liked this other girl.' If he dared tell her to use Katie's name, she would spit in his eye. 'But ... but she was *here*, in your house. That didn't just *happen*. It was arranged. It was on purpose. If I hadn't ... ' Her throat clogged with pain and she pressed her knuckles to her mouth. She tried again. 'If I ... Has she been here before?'

'God, no. Of course not.' Paul sounded shocked by the suggestion.

'Well, that's something, I suppose.'

As hurt and desperate as she was, here was something to hang on to. She could barely string a sentence together, but she needed to get through this somehow and bring Paul back to her. This wasn't the sort of thing that happened to *them*. It happened to other people, other couples. It had happened to Cynthia and Angus from the local G & S society when Angus had gone off with that girl from the Lyon's tea shop. It had happened to Mark and Sybil from the tennis club when Sybil had fallen madly in love with the man who came to paint the lines and Mark wouldn't take her back afterwards.

These disasters happened to other people – not to her and Paul. They were the perfect couple, utterly devoted, and everyone knew they were going to get married. Everybody, simply everybody knew it. Alison had built her entire life around it. And now—

How could this possibly have happened to her, to *them*? It was unbelievable. If she hadn't seen that girl with her own eyes, she would never have believed it. In fact, even having seen the girl, she still struggled to accept it, to make sense of it. It couldn't be happening. That was her over-riding sensation. It couldn't be happening.

'Don't look like that.' Paul caught her hand and pressed it to his lips, his cheek. 'I'm sorry. Please let's put it behind us. Think how long we've been together. I should never have jeopardised it. I've – I've been feeling so guilty. I can't stand it a moment longer.'

As he spoke, Alison nodded along, hope rising once more.

'Oh, Paul.'

'I know, I know. You don't have to say a word. I'm sorry, I'm sorry, I'm sorry.' He spoke into her hair, his arms around her once again. 'I never meant to let you down. I can't bear to see the hurt in your eyes. God, what a mess. I'm sorry, I'm sorry.'

CHAPTER NINE

'It's been more than a week now since the last air raid,' said Colette's mother-in-law. 'Not since the early hours of Thursday last week. I hardly dare talk about it in case it tempts fate.'

'I know what you mean, Mother,' Colette agreed.

It was Saturday morning and the two of them had come to town to do some shopping. In her heart of hearts, Colette didn't like having to call her mother-in-law 'Mother' because that had been what she had called her own mother, but on her wedding day, Tony's father had said, 'Welcome to the family, Colette. We are Father and Mother to you now,' and it would have been churlish to object, not to mention downright impossible. Tony's father, though he had never been anything but polite to her, had a rather stiff manner that brought out her compliance.

Besides, Mother – her real mother – had said brightly, 'You've got two mothers now, dear. Fancy that!'

Later, after Mother died, Colette had tentatively suggested to Tony, 'Do you think your mother would mind if I called her something other than "Mother" now?'

'That's a bit extreme, isn't it, darling? Is it the grief talking? That's only natural, but I don't think it's a good idea. My parents have always been Father and Mother.'

Tony's mother was such a sweet and gentle person that Colette was sure she wouldn't have minded, but maybe Tony's father wouldn't have liked it. He was a bit of a stickler and liked things to be just so. Besides, it didn't really matter, did it? It was only a name.

Although she called her mother-in-law 'Mother' out loud, in her head Colette thought of her as …

Bunty! It never ceased to amaze her that her mother-in-law's name was Bunty. A less appropriate name would be impossible to imagine. Bunty sounded all jolly hockey sticks. A woman called Bunty ought to be tweed-clad and sturdily corseted. She should sit on umpteen committees and be the area organiser of the WVS.

Bunty Naylor was a small woman, on the plump side, her salt-and-pepper hair worn neatly. She was quiet, the sort of wife who looked up to her husband and accepted that it was his place to make all the decisions.

'Lucky her,' Colette's mother had said bitterly. 'At least she has the sort of husband who'll never let her down.'

Unlike Colette's father, and the debts he'd left behind him when he died; debts that had reduced Colette and her mother to a state of shock, shame and downright terror.

'Where would you like to go first?' Colette asked now.

'Ingleby's,' said Bunty. 'I need some new needles.'

They walked down Market Street, past all the large shop windows criss-crossed with anti-blast tape.

'My friend Joan used to work here before the war,' Colette said as they came to Ingleby's and went inside.

'I've always thought how lovely it must be to work in a nice shop.'

Colette felt a flicker of surprise. She had never thought of Bunty as anything but a housewife. 'She wasn't on the shop floor. She worked in one of the sewing rooms, making clothes.'

'Clever girl,' said Bunty and Colette felt a little glow of pleasure to hear her friend being praised.

'Hello there.'

About to exclaim 'Dot!', Colette remembered just in time to be formal. The railway friends were scrupulous about how they addressed one another in public. She turned to her mother-in-law.

'Mother, this is Mrs Green, who works on the railways. And this is my mother-in-law, Mrs Naylor.'

'How do,' said Dot in her friendly way.

'Pleased to meet you,' said Bunty. 'Do you work in the office with Colette?'

'Nay, love. I work on the trains. I'm a parcels porter. It's my job to make sure things get delivered to the right stations.'

'That's a big responsibility,' said Bunty.

'You get used to it,' said Dot. 'What brings you here this fine day?'

'Needles,' said Bunty.

'Good luck.' Dot glanced round at the shelves and displays, which were nothing like as full as they had been before the war. 'You never know what the shops will run out of next these days.'

The three of them approached the counter and Bunty asked for needles.

'Certainly, madam,' said the black-clad assistant. 'Which size?'

'I was hoping to get one of those packets with a selection.'

'I'm sorry, madam. We aren't allowed to sell those packets any longer. We sell needles individually by size.'

'I hope you aren't about to say, "There's a war on, you know," are you?' There was a smile in Bunty's voice.

The assistant smiled back. 'Ingleby's trains its staff never to say that, madam.'

'Quite right an' all,' put in Dot. 'It's jolly annoying.'

Bunty selected a needle, then the assistant asked, 'May I show you anything else, madam?'

'Yes, please. Do you have a tray cloth I could embroider?'

'Of course, madam. This way, please.'

Dot nudged Colette. 'Eh, she's a lovely lady, your ma-in-law.'

'She's always been kind to me.'

'A friendly sort.' Dot's gaze was on Bunty as she walked off with the assistant. 'Chatty, a sense of humour. I like that. Bubbly.'

Bubbly? *Bubbly*? Bunty Naylor? Colette had never heard anything so bizarre in her life. Bunty was quiet to the point of self-effacing.

'Wouldn't say boo to a goose, that one,' Colette's mother had said of Bunty. 'But then if you've got the right sort of husband, he'll say boo for you.'

Poor Mother. She had never really recovered from what Dad had lumbered them with.

'I wonder which department Margaret was in when she worked here,' said Dot, but Colette was hardly listening.

She managed to say, 'I'm not sure,' but all she could think about was the astonishing idea of Bunty being described as bubbly, especially by somebody like Dot, whom Colette had always seen as a shrewd judge of character.

Colette spent the next hour or so watching her mother-in-law with new eyes as they went round the shops. Bunty was definitely chattier than normal. Colette had never seen her like this – or had she? It was a puzzle. Perhaps she had, but without really noticing, because she was so accustomed to thinking of Bunty as being quiet. Was she, Colette, really so lacking in the power of observation? Surely not. Colette would be the very last person to blow her own trumpet, but she knew herself to be sensitive to others. Being quiet and shy herself provided her with ample opportunity to be aware of others.

So why had she never seen this side of her mother-in-law before? She thought back over the times she and Tony had gone to his parents' house and the occasions when Father and Bunty had visited them. At their house there had been Sunday dinners, when Bunty had looked anxious until Father had complimented her on the roast. Well, Colette knew how that felt. Father had high standards and it was important not to let him down. Colette was the same with Tony; she didn't want to disappoint him. There had been Christmas afternoons spent quietly playing cards. Back in the early spring, before Tony had started coming to Wilton Close with her, Colette had spent a wet Sunday afternoon playing cards with Mrs Cooper, Mrs Grayson and Mabel and it had come as a revelation to her just how uproarious whist could be. It had never been like that at Father's house. Not that Colette would ever have said so to anybody, not even Tony – especially not Tony – but Father was something of a stick-in-the-mud.

If anybody had asked her before today, Colette would have said Bunty was a stick-in-the-mud too. Well, she wouldn't have said so out loud, of course, but she would have thought it. Bunty was exactly the right sort of wife for Father. He expected everything to be just so and Bunty ran their home and their joint lives that way.

But look at her now, smiling as she admired a baby in the bus queue. Previously, Colette had thought she and Bunty were two of a kind, quiet and reserved, but now she wasn't so sure.

They arrived back at Father's house, where the two Naylor couples were to have their dinner together. Bunty removed her coat and hat and went straight through to the kitchen to put the kettle on. Colette followed. Through the window, Father and Tony could be seen repairing part of the roof of the garden shed.

Colette opened the back door and went out to say hello.

'How's it coming along?' she asked.

'Almost done,' said Tony.

'Has Mother put the kettle on?' asked Father.

Colette glanced round, realising that Bunty hadn't followed her outside. She returned to the kitchen to find Bunty already in her apron, just standing up again after lighting the oven.

'I got everything ready before I went out,' she said. 'It only needs to heat through for half an hour.'

'You're so efficient.' Colette smiled at Bunty, expecting an answering smile, but Bunty had gone back to being her usual quiet self and her eyes, which had been bright earlier on, were now – 'guarded' was the word that sprang to mind, but where on earth had that come from? Guarded? Ridiculous! What did Bunty have to feel guarded about?

Presently, the four of them sat down to Bunty's vegetable bake with potato topping. Father tasted his and frowned.

'I was hoping for more flavour,' he remarked.

'Would you like some HP Sauce?' Bunty scurried to fetch it.

Father shook a dollop onto the side of his plate, tried another mouthful and nodded. Bunty's shoulders relaxed. A tiny frown tugged at Colette's forehead. She smoothed it away.

'Did you find what you needed in the shops?' Father asked.

Colette waited for her to list her purchases and mention meeting Dot, but she didn't. All she said was, 'Yes, thank you,' and then dropped her gaze to her plate. She had gone right back to being the quiet little mouse. What had happened to the bright, pleasant woman from earlier on?

A hot feeling expanded inside Colette's chest. The bright, pleasant woman had come home. That's what had happened. She had come home and turned back into the near-silent mouse.

Oh my goodness. Was that the explanation? Had Bunty been ground down over the years until all that remained was a quiet little shadow? An obedient shadow? Was Father a bully?

The hot sensation in Colette's chest turned in an instant to ice. Was that where Tony got it from? From his father? Was Tony in the process of grinding *her* down? In years to come, would she too be nothing more than a near-silent, obedient shadow?

Was she halfway to becoming that already?

Alison had been told off during the morning for making a silly mistake. Ordinarily she would have been furious and humiliated at being shown up in front of the other girls in the office, but today it barely signified. She had hardly slept last night and was exhausted but at the same time painfully alert. How she had survived yesterday evening, she didn't know. At home she had carried on as normal, giving no sign of the terrible upset she had endured. She was too ashamed to tell her mother or Lydia. Paul had had a fling with another girl – no one must ever know.

It was a mercy she and Lydia didn't share a bedroom, because Alison had huffed and sighed and turned over and back again all night long, unable to find comfort. There was a dark churning sensation in the pit of her stomach. She had never known distress like it, not even when Granny had died. It felt as if her life had been hurled to the ground to smash into tiny pieces. In all the time she and Paul had been going out together, she had never, not once, had any reason to doubt him or their relationship. Yes, he was taking his time about proposing, but there were reasons for that. Alison had always felt supremely confident about them as a couple.

Among the girls at church, the girls she used to go to school with, the girls at the tennis club, there had been disappointments and broken hearts, every single one of which had reinforced Alison's confidence in her own romance. Other people's relationships might wobble or break down, but she and Paul would be together for ever. Alison carried the knowledge in her bloodstream and her bone marrow, and she was deeply proud of it.

Secretly she had even sneered at relationships that floundered, knowing that she and Paul were above that kind of trouble, but now it turned out that they were as vulnerable as anyone. Her mouth was dry, her chest tight; she was ashamed and afraid.

Katie Green-Dress had set her cap at Paul and he had strayed. No one must ever find out. How could he let her down like that? He was desperately sorry, of course, but how could he have let it happen in the first place? Did he realise the damage he had done? Yes, he had come back to her, but the experience had dealt a devastating blow to her confidence. It would take her a long time to get over this.

In the meantime, how should she behave? Forgive him unreservedly? After all, they were going to get married, so there mustn't be any ill-feeling. Or should she twist the knife and give him a taste of the pain he had inflicted on her? It would only be what he deserved. Might it be a good idea to do that, just to make sure he never did anything so stupid ever again? Or would outright forgiveness make him worship her for ever?

Her Saturday half-day at work dragged to an end. Alison tidied her desk and handed in the papers that had to be locked away. As she got up to leave, her gaze fell on the desk where Miss Horrocks normally sat. Was Miss

Horrocks in the jeweller's right this minute, poring over a velvet-lined tray of rings? Jealousy squeezed Alison's ribs so hard she could barely breathe. Imagine envying Milly Horrocks. She had never envied another girl. She had never had reason to. When you were half of the perfect couple, you felt sorry for other girls in a way, because you held the ultimate happiness in your hands and they didn't.

Alison slipped on her jacket and hat before going to the Ladies to check her face. Did she look as wrecked as she felt?

'Late night, was it?' asked a voice behind her.

Alison looked round, startled, feeling caught out.

'I only meant you look a bit tired,' said the girl. Then a look of curiosity entered her eyes. 'Why? What did you think I meant?'

'Nothing. As you say – late night.'

Grabbing her things, Alison marched out, head held high. Her heart thumped. She hurried along the corridor and ran downstairs, deliberately trailing her hand lightly along the bannister rail because that would make her look less like she was running for her life.

Others were leaving at the same time. A man was holding the door open to let several girls through. They laughed as they went.

'You'll stand there all day if you're not careful,' one of them said.

She picked up her pace and tacked onto the end of the group, saying a quick 'Thanks' as she passed the obliging man. Emerging from the deep porch, she went down a couple of steps – and there, over the road, was Paul, waiting for her. She almost burst into tears of pure relief. He was smoking – nervous, perhaps? He jolly well deserved to be. He took one final drag, then chucked the cigarette onto the pavement and ground it beneath his heel before crossing the road.

Perhaps she should have waited and let him come to her, but she flew to meet him, holding on to her hat so she could reach up to kiss his cheek. She slid her hand through his arm as he guided her to the pavement.

There, Alison stopped and gazed up at him. She was overjoyed that he had come to meet her. It was exactly what she had needed and she longed to tell him so, but Paul looked serious – and quite right too, since he had a lot of apologising still to do, so maybe now wasn't the right time for her to gush and be grateful. He had undoubtedly got a speech all prepared. Alison's muscles relaxed and her breathing felt easy and natural as some of her old confidence slid back into place, giving her strength.

'We have to talk,' said Paul.

'Yes, we do,' she agreed. She didn't want to hear the sordid details about Katie. What she wanted was reassurance and renewed promises. She would gladly listen to that until the cows came home.

'Where shall we go?' Paul made it sound as if the bomb-damaged city centre was full of parkland and pretty grottoes.

Alison didn't want to waste time searching for somewhere suitable. She plumped for the nearest, most obvious place, steering Paul towards the station. As they walked in, the noise of a train pulling in sounded around the huge building, rising high over their heads and echoing throughout the station's arched canopy. It was tempting to suggest a cup of tea and a sandwich in the buffet because she had barely been able to swallow her breakfast, but this conversation wasn't one that could be held in public.

'If we get platform tickets, there's a bench near this end of the Southport platform, close to the ticket barrier. Passengers don't normally sit there because there are other

benches along the platform which are much more convenient for the train. I know someone who sometimes sits there
with a friend.'

Was she babbling? She made herself shut up. Her nerves
were jumping. Paul, by contrast, wasn't saying a word. It
was funny how nerves affected people in different ways.

Paul bought tickets from the machine and they went to
the barrier. The ticket collector, with his peaked cap and
gleaming buttons, was someone she didn't know, thank
goodness. Breathing in the combined scents of steam and
smoke, Alison led Paul to the bench and they sat down.
Considering they were in a mainline station on a busy
Saturday, this was a surprisingly private spot.

While Paul stared along the railway track as if mesmer-
ised, Alison came to a decision.

'What happened yesterday was vile and it'll take me a
long time to stop being upset, but I want you to know that
I'm not going to play silly beggars. I'm not going to punish
you. You made it clear yesterday how desperately sorry you
are and I'm not going to drag things out by going on and on
about it. What matters now is that we concentrate on our
future. You've hurt me deeply, but what I want, what I need
more than anything, is for things to go back to the way they
were, the way they ought to be.'

She gazed at Paul's profile, expecting him to turn to her,
his eyes filled with warmth and sorrow and maybe even a
few tears, but his gaze remained fixed on the permanent
way. He must feel distraught at having treated her so badly,
as well as being riddled with shame. Should she be pleased
by that? Some girls would be, in her position, but Alison
found she wasn't one of them. Yes, she had been hurt in a
way that would take a long time to heal, but what she
wanted more than anything was for the two of them to
cling together through this difficult time.

Paul turned his face to hers. He didn't angle his body towards her, just turned his head, and yes, his eyes were full of sorrow – more than sorrow. Anguish. He shook his head.

'I'm so sorry.'

'I know,' she answered softly.

'No – you don't. Damn and blast, what a mess. I can't begin to tell you how sorry I am.'

'You made a big mistake—' Alison began.

'But I didn't.' At last, Paul swung round to face her properly. 'I didn't. Katie and me – we're meant to be together.'

Instead of beating, Alison's heart hovered, then delivered a single great clang. 'No, you're not. Yesterday you said how sorry you were for what you'd done.'

'I *was* sorry – I am sorry. I've never felt more sorry or more guilty in my life. I can't bear to hurt you, but … '

'But?' Alison went cold inside, every instinct screaming at her not to ask the question.

'But … Katie and I – we love each other.'

'*No* … ' A wave of dizziness struck Alison as dread streaked through her. 'You said you wanted to put it behind us.'

'I know and I'm sorry. I've been feeling so horribly guilty ever since the night of the dance. I've lived with it for two whole weeks. Yesterday, when you walked in on us, I couldn't stand it any longer and I thought that giving Katie up was the answer.'

'What are you saying? Yesterday I thought you regretted meeting her. You called what had happened madness. That was what you said: madness.'

'Love at first sight might be a kind of madness.'

'Love at … ? *Oh*.' Alison shook her head in denial. 'Don't be ridiculous. It couldn't have been. A sudden attraction, that's what it was. It's this girl, this Katie. She set her sights

105

on you and she was determined to get you and – and I suppose that was flattering, but it doesn't *mean* anything. It isn't real. What you and I have, that's real, that's lasting. This – this business with Katie is a flirtation.'

'No, it isn't. I know how mad it sounds, but when she tapped your shoulder in the excuse-me dance and our eyes met and then I held her and started to dance, I knew, I just knew, and so did she.'

'Yesterday you couldn't stop apologising. You wanted us to put it behind us.'

'That was the guilt talking. Listen to me, Alison. It's over. I'm sorry. I'm sorrier than I can say, but it's over.'

Alison's mouth opened but no words came out.

'I'm sorry I misled you yesterday,' Paul went on, 'but I felt so rotten and for a moment I thought I could give her up … but I can't. This past fortnight has been so hard … going behind your back, knowing I shouldn't deceive you but not being able to help myself.'

Panic flushed through Alison's body. Her pulse was hammering. She couldn't believe this; she *wouldn't* believe it. 'I know you want us to stay together. Why else would you have planned the dinner at the Claremont?'

'Oh, that.' Paul sounded almost dismissive. 'I did that out of guilt, if I'm honest. I wasn't honest to start with – with myself, I mean. I tried hard to do the right thing, the decent thing, to stay with you. That's why I booked the Claremont, because staying with you was the right thing to do.'

'Then … ?'

'I know it's wrong of me to leave you. I desperately don't want to let you down. I've put Katie through hell these past two weeks, blowing hot and cold and agonising over what to do, because a decent man would never walk out on his girl. But in the end—'

'In the end, you found you weren't as decent as all that,' Alison said bitterly. 'I can't believe you're doing this to me. Have you any idea how much stuff I've got in my bottom drawer? All those things I've collected, ready for when I'm married.' Despair swept through her. Her 'bottom drawer' had grown steadily, occupying the bottom of her wardrobe as well as boxes on the top and one of Mum's kitchen cupboards. Gathering together all those household items – receiving them as birthday presents too – had given her so much pleasure, but now – now … 'Don't you love me any more?'

'Allie, I'll always love you,' said Paul, but just when hope flickered in her heart, he added, 'but she is the love of my life.'

CHAPTER TEN

The next few days were a nightmare for Alison. Telling her parents and Lydia, trying to convince them of something she could barely believe herself, was just frightful. As much as she needed their sympathy and understanding, somehow their kindness made everything worse and their outrage seemed excessive, because she herself was too shocked for outrage. Maybe it would come later, but just now she was grief-stricken.

Yes, grief-stricken. It was a bereavement of sorts, but a bitter, jagged-edged one because Paul had chosen to leave her. He hadn't skidded on his motorcycle, hit a tree and died on impact. He had chosen to leave her, *chosen* to. Another girl had come along and dazzled him and he had tossed good old faithful Alison on the scrapheap.

Oh, it was unbearable. It was impossible. If Paul had come to her and begged her to take him back, she would have done. Maybe she shouldn't have, but she would have done, even after everything he had said.

I'll always love you, but she is the love of my life.

You couldn't fight back against that, could you? To hear those words from your future husband! But he was no longer that, was he?

Alison didn't attend church on Sunday.

'You mustn't breathe a word to anyone, anyone at all,' she insisted, extracting promises from Mum and Lydia before they left the house.

'I can't answer for what I'll do if I clap eyes on him,' growled her father.

'Dad, you mustn't. Please,' Alison begged. God, wasn't everything bad enough without the world knowing about it?

Mum gave Dad a hefty nudge and he said, 'Well, all right then, but I'm doing this for you, Alison, not because it's what I want.'

But it turned out later that the promises of secrecy had been for nothing, because Paul's mum, in floods of tears, had told anyone who would listen.

'Poor Mrs Dunaway can't believe it,' Mum reported. 'She's stunned to think her lad would do that to you.'

'Do you think I should go and see her?' asked Alison.

'Best not,' said Dad. 'You don't want to bump into Paul.'

But she did want to, oh, she did. That was the trouble. Even after everything he had said, even though that other girl, that boyfriend-stealer, was the love of his life and you couldn't fight back against that, Alison still wanted to bump into him. Her heart yearned for him and her skin was hungry for his touch. She loved him. She needed him. She needed their future life.

But Paul didn't want her.

Would he realise he had made the worst mistake of his life? Would he come back?

I'll always love you, but she is the love of my life.

Mum let her have the day off sick on Monday, but on Tuesday she insisted Alison must return to work.

'This is wartime and you have a job to do. Besides, the longer you're off, the more people will be aware of it and the more questions you'll face when you go back. I know it's hard—'

'Hard?' Alison exclaimed on a fresh wave of distress. 'That doesn't begin to describe it.'

But Mum wouldn't let her duck out of it, so she had to go. She thought of playing truant, but what would she do all day? At least in the office, she'd have something to keep her busy.

Wouldn't you know it, the first thing that happened as she entered Hunts Bank was Colette running to catch her up.

'I'm glad to see you back,' said Colette. 'How are you feeling today?'

'Better, thanks.'

'What was the matter?' Miss Simpson asked, falling in beside them.

Alison pretended to glance at her wristwatch. 'We'd better get a move on.'

She put on a spurt, not caring if she left the others behind, then put on a brave face as she entered the office, but it very nearly crumbled when Milly Horrocks made a beeline for her, holding out her left hand for inspection.

'Lovely.' Alison's vision blurred as she bent her head briefly over the ring. 'Congratulations.'

'Thanks.' Miss Horrocks laughed. 'I've had it since Saturday and I'm still excited.'

Alison didn't find it easy to concentrate on her work, but hers wasn't the sort of job where you could let your mind wander. Her brain seemed to be divided down the middle. One side juggled with piecework prices, the War Wage and overtime, while the other side resounded with shock and anguish. Astonishment, too, that she could go through the motions of her ordinary, everyday life when her world had shattered into a million pieces.

She was supposed to go to the buffet that evening, but she couldn't face it. All she wanted was to run home and hide away, but if she simply failed to turn up, her friends would be concerned and might come looking for her tomorrow and that would be unendurable. It was a confounded nuisance, but she would have to pop over to the buffet and write a message in the notebook they used for organising their meetings, and which they kept under the counter. Actually, maybe it wasn't such a nuisance, as it would give her something to do during her dinner break.

Accordingly, she later headed for the station, where the concourse was packed, probably because of late-running passenger trains that had had to give way to troop trains or freight. That was the usual reason. As she threaded her way between the groups of passengers, breathing in cigarette smoke and Californian Poppy, picking her way around suitcases and shopping bags, Alison felt a burst of anger. All these damn people getting in her way! Didn't they know how insignificant they were compared to the pain and the – yes, the fear she had to cope with? Everything in her life had changed and she kept having to hold her breath so as not to gasp in terror.

'Make way, please, ladies and gents,' called a familiar voice and Alison groaned inwardly. 'Coming through.'

Ducking her head, Alison tried to get out of the way, but the crowd around her obligingly melted away to make room for the procession of two flatbed trolleys loaded with parcels and boxes, the first of them being manoeuvred by Dot.

'Hello there,' Dot said cheerfully. 'I can't stop, but would you like to tag along for a minute? I assume this is your dinner hour.'

'Yes, but—'

'Come on, then. I've only got to deliver this trolley to the parcels office. I haven't got to unload it.' Dot glanced over her shoulder at the spotty young porter who was bringing up the rear with the second trolley. 'That's the job of young feller-me-lad here.'

All Alison wanted was to be alone and she felt like marching off in the opposite direction, but she found herself walking alongside Dot's trolley. Dot and her young colleague disappeared into the parcels office – 'office' being a modest name for a huge sorting area – and Alison hovered outside until Dot reappeared. She had removed her peaked cap and exchanged her uniform jacket for a cardy that, judging by its size, belonged to a somewhat larger lady.

'Ta-da,' Dot sang. 'What a transformation, eh? Now we can go in the buffet for a barm cake and a cuppa.'

'No, really, I'm not hungry – though I do need to pop into the buffet.' Why on earth had she tagged along with Dot? 'I need to write a message in the book.'

'Good. Then you can come and sit with me while I grab a bite to eat.'

'Honestly, Dot, I don't feel like company.'

'I can see that.' Dot looked straight at her. As kind as they were, Dot's hazel eyes were the sort that missed nothing.

Alison glanced away. 'I don't know what you mean.'

'Come on, love. I'm not as green as I am cabbage-looking. You look like death warmed up.'

'I – I was off sick yesterday.'

'Oh aye? If one of my lads looked like that, I'd keep him at home longer than one day. If your mam has sent you back to work, I don't think you're poorly, so what is it, chick? You can tell me.'

And suddenly that was exactly what Alison wanted – needed – to do. She admired Dot and liked her enormously; loved her, even. She was warm-hearted and sensible and funny. More than once, in the days when Alison had expected to move in with Paul's mum, she had thought what a lovely mother-in-law Dot must be.

'Let's see if we can bag a quiet corner in the buffet, shall we, eh?' Dot suggested, linking arms.

Alison pulled away slightly, not withdrawing from Dot but shying away from the idea of the buffet. 'Too public.'

Dot didn't bat an eyelid. 'Fair enough. There's a bench near the barrier on—'

'No!' If she never set foot again on the Southport platform, it would be too soon.

'All right.' This time Dot sounded as if she was choosing her words with care. 'It's not glamorous, but we'll nip round the side of the parcels office. If nowt else, it'll be private. Best foot forward.'

Dot gave her no time to object, but whisked her off round a couple of corners. Was she really going to open her heart here, beside a grimy wall?

'You wanted private,' said Dot. 'This is private. Summat bad has happened.' It wasn't a question.

Alison nodded, pain squeezing the inside of her throat. Pressure built up behind her eyes.

'Eh, lass.' Dot moved closer and gave her a hug.

For a moment Alison accepted the embrace, wanting to sink into it and feel safe, but she made herself pull free.

'Don't be kind to me,' she whispered, 'or I'll howl the place down.'

'All right.' Suddenly Dot was all business. 'Tell me what's happened.'

'It's Paul. He's – he's met another girl. He's left me. Please don't say he'll regret it and come back, because he won't.'

That was what Mum and Lydia kept saying, words that Alison had lapped up at first, but they were dangerous words because they gave her hope – and Paul had made it clear there was none.

I'll always love you, but she is the love of my life.

'He's made that crystal clear,' Alison added, trying to be strong, though she was trembling.

'Oh, Alison, oh my lovely lass. I'm that sorry. I know how much you … well, never mind. What a shock for you.'

'That's one way of putting it. It's my whole life, Dot. It's gone up in smoke.'

'I know, chick, I know. You must be reeling. I can hardly believe it myself. It's not five minutes since Cordelia's War Weapons Week dance and there were nowt then to suggest owt was wrong.'

'That was when it happened. He met her at the dance.'

'And he's already decided to go off with her, permanent like, and give up everything he had with you?'

Alison nodded. 'She bagged him for an excuse-me dance and that was all it took. Never mind me. Never mind how long we've been together. He danced with her and that was that. Goodbye, Alison.'

'It's a terrible thing to lose a person you love,' Dot said quietly. 'All you can do is face each day as it comes.'

'That's easy for you to say.'

'Maybe not as easy as you think, love. I'll tell you this. You've done the right thing in coming to work. Keeping busy, carrying on as normal, that's what will get you through – and you will get through. However impossible it seems just now, you will come through it.'

'You make it sound like the war.'

'It is a war. It's your personal war. I know you've got your mam and your sister, but I'll always be here if you need to talk or just sob your heart out. You're one of my lasses, you are, and I care about you.'

'Oh, Dot.' Alison smeared tears away with the back of her hand. 'Thank you.'

'And it's not just me. I know I can speak for the whole group when I say we all care about you. They will all want to support you. Why not come to the buffet tonight after all?'

'No. Absolutely not. You're going, aren't you? You'll let them know for me, and the ones that aren't there this evening, please make sure they know as well. I don't want to have to tell them.'

She lifted her chin, but something inside her crumpled as shame overtook her. Her friends had all expected her engagement – she had led them to expect it. Her throat bobbed and her face felt hot, even her eyes felt hot, as humiliation consumed her. Then panic sent her heart beating faster. What if Dot told everyone – and then Paul came back to her? She would have endured the public humiliation for nothing.

But he wasn't going to come back, was he?

I'll always love you, but she is the love of my life.

'Oh, Dot,' she said and walked into her friend's outstretched arms.

It was Thursday morning. Her friends would all know by now, thought Alison, and that included Mrs Cooper and Mrs Grayson. Dot would have made sure that the ones who hadn't gone to the buffet on Tuesday evening would have been told on Wednesday. God, and didn't that make it sound like a piece of juicy gossip to be passed around. Nausea rolled in Alison's stomach and her lips twisted. She hated to think of others talking about her behind her back, no matter how kind and concerned they were. Not long ago, up until last Friday, in fact, she had relished the idea of being talked about. She used to imagine the girls with whom she did first-aid duty and the girls from the church choir, not to mention complete strangers in the dance hall, murmuring to one another about how good she and Paul looked together, how they were so obviously made for one another.

115

Alison had been avoiding Colette in Hunts Bank. Colette seemed to understand this and wasn't hovering around her, which was a mercy. Just imagine if her colleagues started to realise she had personal problems – the prospect made her shudder, because at that point it really would become a piece of gossip. She didn't know which she dreaded more, the gossip or the pity. Oh, when she remembered how she had pitied other girls whose boyfriends had let them down! The pity she'd felt for them had been accompanied by confidence in her own solid relationship with Paul.

But hadn't what she'd felt then been more than confidence? Hadn't it been … self-satisfaction? Alison closed her eyes as she held in a groan. She had been knocked well and truly off her high horse now, hadn't she? Oh heavens, had others perceived the extent of her confidence? Might there be those who would feel she deserved to be jilted, to be taken down several pegs? Surely no one would be that catty? But in her heart, Alison knew that if she had observed that level of confidence, of self-satisfaction, of … of arrogance in another girl, and that girl had then been dumped by her boyfriend, she would have felt she deserved it. What a hypocrite she was. She couldn't bear to think of others being catty about her, but she knew she was a bit of a cat herself.

When she left work that evening, she saw Joan watching for her from across the road. For half a second, she was thrown back in time to that uplifting moment when she had seen Paul standing in that spot, waiting for her to appear when she had finished work last Saturday.

Although she felt like bursting into tears and running to Joan for comfort, she raised her chin and plastered a smile on her face before she crossed the road. The smile felt ghastly and frozen, but at least it was a smile.

'What brings you here?' she asked, daring Joan to show sympathy.

Joan looked a trifle taken aback – well, maybe Alison had sounded a bit sharp – before she said, 'Just wanted a quick word. Just the two of us.'

Alison waited until the crowd of office workers who had clocked off at the same time as she had started to thin out. To make up for her abruptness, she linked arms with Joan and they walked slowly up the road.

'When I felt absolutely desperate and heartbroken after Letitia died,' said Joan, 'I didn't want to see anyone.'

Alison felt a spurt of resentment. What had Letitia got to do with anything? *She* was the one in distress now; she was the one who was heartbroken.

'I wanted to hide away,' said Joan.

Alison fought past her self-centred reaction and realised what Joan was saying. 'I know how that feels.'

'And if that's honestly the right thing for you, then that's what you must do. The point is, I thought it was the right thing for me, but it wasn't. What I needed was to be with my friends. Sometimes I just sat there in the buffet and never uttered a word, but I had my friends around me and that was what counted.'

'I remember.'

'I'm not trying to push you into anything,' said Joan, 'but we all care about you and we won't pry. We'll just be there, chatting away as usual, and you can join in or not, as the mood takes you. I know that's the way it'll be, because that's what it was like for me after Letitia died, and that's what we'll all do for you now, if you'll let us. I hope you will. I hope you'll find it as supportive as I did.'

'We'll see.' Alison wasn't ready to commit herself, but the way Joan squeezed her arm said that Joan was pleased with her response. 'I appreciate your taking the trouble.'

Joan gave a little shrug. 'I know what it was like for me. Look, I don't want to be pushy, but Margaret, Mabel and Persephone are going to the flicks tomorrow after work. You could go too. You never know. You might be able to lose yourself in a film for a while.'

'I don't know.'

'Whatever suits you,' said Joan. 'It was only a thought.'

That wasn't what Alison had expected her to say. She had expected to be pressed into going – pressure that she would have resisted. But Joan's easy-come, easy-go response made her consider it.

'Maybe,' she said. 'We'll see.'

After all, she had nothing else to do, not tomorrow, and not for the rest of her life.

CHAPTER ELEVEN

Cordelia felt shocked and deeply distressed on Alison's behalf. The poor girl must be heartbroken.

'It came as a bolt from the blue,' Dot had said when she told the rest of them. Kenneth would undoubtedly have sneered at the use of such dramatic vocabulary, but as she so often did, Dot had hit the nail on the head, capturing not just the suddenness of what had happened to Alison but also its force.

Inevitably, it brought Kit to mind and Cordelia relived her own heartbreak, the years melting away as she remembered the anguish stabbing her in the heart. She quickly subdued the feeling. She shouldn't be thinking of herself now; she should concentrate on Alison. Besides, hadn't she promised herself after Emily's birth that she wouldn't think of Kit any longer? He was in the past. Emily was her present and her future.

Mabel, Margaret and Persephone had arranged to go to the pictures on Friday afternoon after work and Alison had been invited to go with them. Would she? Cordelia hoped so. It might do her good. Nothing was going to make her feel better, but at least it might provide a distraction.

Cordelia, too, was going out this Friday night. Kenneth was taking her and Emily for dinner and then to the theatre to see *The Importance of Being Earnest*, which was one of Cordelia's favourite plays and she was looking forward to sharing it with her daughter. Even better – and she hoped it wasn't selfish of her to be looking forward to this when

Alison was in such despair – she had planned things in such a way that Emily would spend a little time with her mother's younger friends. Cordelia had introduced Emily to them at the War Weapons Week dance, of course, but that had been a brief courtesy and Emily hadn't had the chance to get to know them – now she would. Cordelia felt a little thrill of anticipation. Her plan had actually sprung out of something Emily had suggested.

'Why don't I come to Victoria Station and meet you, Mummy? I'll bring your evening dress for you to change into. It'll save you rushing home to get ready. Then we can toddle along and drag Daddy out of his office. I know he always keeps a set of evening togs there.'

'Maybe it wasn't such a good idea to have both dinner and the theatre at the end of a working day,' Kenneth had remarked. 'It's going to be rather a rush.'

'It'll be worth it,' Cordelia said, not wanting him to change their plans. Nights out with Kenneth were usually work-related. 'When was the last time we had a night out as a family?'

'The War Weapons Week dance,' Kenneth replied promptly.

'You know what I mean,' said Cordelia.

'That wasn't exactly a night out for Mummy,' said Emily. 'She spent most of it seeing to things and making sure there weren't any problems. Don't worry, Mummy. We'll make sure the theatre night is special and we'll both spoil you – won't we, Daddy?'

How thoughtful Emily was, though Cordelia was aware that what would really make her feel happy and spoiled wasn't going to be dinner and the play, but taking Emily into the buffet beforehand. She wanted to show Emily off and she also wanted Emily to like the younger members of her group of friends.

On Friday, Emily met her beside the station's war memorial, carrying a bag containing her evening things. Colette had kindly arranged for her to get changed in an office belonging to one of the secretaries in Hunts Bank. Emily helped her into her evening ensemble of a beaded collarless jacket and black velvet skirt with silver shoes.

Then they went into the Ladies for Cordelia to touch up her make-up and do her hair. She unclipped her daytime pearl earrings, replacing them with smoky topaz ones and the matching pendant.

Lastly, Emily brought out of the bag a small box that contained a glittery aigrette with a froth of dainty feathers. Cordelia was about to fasten it into her hair when she changed her mind and held it out to Emily.

'Would you like to wear it?' she offered and the sight of her daughter's delight was all the reward she needed.

'May I? I'd love to.'

'I think you're old enough. Here, let me.'

They stood together before the mirror, Emily unashamedly gazing at herself while Cordelia tried the aigrette in a couple of places, holding it in position as she looked at her daughter's reflection.

'I know,' said Cordelia. 'We'll leave your hair on that side just as it is, and on this side we'll use the aigrette to scoop it back and up a little. There. What d'you think?'

'Oh *yes*,' Emily enthused. 'That looks sophisticated, doesn't it?'

Cordelia laughed. 'Don't be in such a hurry to grow up. But yes, it does,' she added, placing her hands on Emily's shoulders from behind and admiring their joint reflection. Something caught at her heart, a mixture of pride and wonder. Goodness, but Emily was lovely. If she was this pretty at fifteen, how beautiful would she be at twenty?

Emily reached up and touched the fingers that rested on one of her shoulders. 'Thank you.'

'We've got a bit of time before we need to go to Daddy's office,' said Cordelia, as if this had just occurred to her. 'Let's pop over to the buffet. I know my friends will be there and,' she added as a master stroke, 'you can show off your sophisticated hairdo.'

They returned to Victoria. The concourse was busy with men and women heading home from work. In an hour or so, it would be busy again with people catching the 'funk express', as it was called, which people caught so that they could spend their nights at a safe distance from Manchester. Cowards.

But Cordelia didn't give two hoots about those people right now. At this moment, this special moment, with her daughter by her side, she walked proudly beneath the station canopy, where a huge clock with Roman numerals hung from one of the gantries. On one side of the concourse there was the departure board in its wooden frame, and on the other was the long line of ticket-office windows set within a handsome sweep of gleaming wood panelling, and all around were passengers, some in a hurry, others smoking or reading newspapers while they waited – and all of them, every single one, or so it felt to Cordelia, was looking at her and her daughter in admiration. She and Emily weren't the only ones in evening dress. Others in evening attire had come into town on the train and were now heading for the taxi rank. But as far as Cordelia was concerned, she and Emily were the ones to stand out in the crowd because of the glow of happy excitement that had been shining from Emily since Cordelia had fastened the aigrette in her hair. Such a small thing to do – and such a wonderful result.

They entered the buffet, where their evening clothes caused yet more heads to turn. Cordelia's gaze immediately found the table around which her friends had squeezed. She turned briefly to the counter to acknowledge Mrs Jessop, who, although she was busy serving, gave her a smile and a little wave.

Cordelia led Emily to where her friends were smiling a welcome that she knew was for Emily's benefit.

'Dot,' said Cordelia, 'I wasn't expecting to see you.'

'When I knew you were fetching your Emily here, how could I stay away? We've saved seats for you. You sit here next to me, chick.' Dot smiled at Emily and patted the chair beside her.

'Thank you,' Emily murmured and sat down.

Although she was pleased by Dot's kindness to her daughter, Cordelia knew it was important to divert Emily's attention towards the others. She wanted Emily to like them.

'In case you don't remember all the names from the dance,' said Cordelia, 'here we have Margaret ... Mabel ... Alison ... and Persephone. I'm sure it's quite in order for you to use their first names, Emily, as they aren't that much older than you.'

'Please, yes, first names all round,' said Persephone.

They chatted for a while. The girls made a fuss of Emily, admiring her dress and her hair, which of course made Emily blossom. Cordelia felt relief sweep through her – and then heat tingled in her cheeks as shame bit into her. Was she really so desperate for Emily to like these girls? Well, yes, frankly. Emily had already taken against Dot and Mrs Cooper. It would be a huge blow if she found a reason to dislike the rest as well. But what reason could she have for that? None, surely. These girls were young and friendly and – Cordelia was forced to drop her gaze as shame coursed through her once more – they weren't working class like Dot. Persephone was out of the social top drawer and Mabel the moneyed top drawer. Alison came from a family of builders, who two or three generations ago were probably working class through and through, but now, after a couple of generations of indoor plumbing and educated children, were comfortably lower middle class. As for Margaret, she was a fairly new member of the group and she hadn't shared much about herself so far, but her family home, which had suffered a severe battering in an air raid last year, leading to Margaret and her father having to move out, had been one of those tall houses opposite Alexandra Park and they were nice properties on the whole.

Emily would be comfortable in the presence of these girls – wouldn't she? Of course she would. She was bound to be.

'We must keep an eye on the time.' Cordelia consulted the clock on the wall above the buffet's fireplace. 'We don't want to be late.'

'Is your dad collecting you from here?' Dot asked Emily.

'No, we're going to his office,' Emily replied.

'It isn't far,' said Cordelia. 'Rosemount Place, off Market Street. In fact, we really should be going.'

'I'm sorry you couldn't have stopped for longer, lass,' Dot said to Emily. 'It's been good seeing you again.'

'Thank you.' Emily was politeness itself, though she stopped short of returning the compliment.

Saying their goodbyes, Cordelia and Emily set off for Rosemount Place, where the row of smart buildings with black front doors was lined with sandbags. Mr Hathersage, who had been the senior clerk here since before Kenneth joined the firm and who must be well into his sixties now, made a discreet fuss of them while they waited for Kenneth to finish getting changed. When he appeared, dressed in his black evening suit with his wing-collared shirt, black satin bow tie and silk handkerchief peeping from his top pocket, Cordelia felt a certain satisfaction. It was agreeable to have a distinguished-looking, well-dressed husband. The three of them made a good-looking family.

'Tell Emily how grown-up she looks,' she murmured to Kenneth.

When they were seated in the restaurant and had placed their orders, Cordelia sipped her wine.

'Look at me,' said Kenneth, 'accompanied by two beautiful ladies. You look very grown-up tonight, Emily. I'm proud of you.'

Emily beamed. 'It's going to be a wonderful evening, isn't it – even if it did start in the station buffet.'

Cordelia felt as if alarm bells were going off all around her, but she didn't bat an eyelid. 'It's not the most glamorous venue, I grant you, but it has a pleasant atmosphere and I thought you'd like to say hello to some of my friends. It's only polite, since you met them at the dance.'

'I was pleased to see them,' said Emily, 'though I wish Mrs Green hadn't been there. I'll never be anything but civil to her, Mummy, you know that, but you also know I'm not comfortable with her. But I like the others,' she added brightly, 'though I can't get over you calling them your friends. You're much too old for them.'

'Emily,' said Kenneth, but as reprimands went, it was singularly ineffective because there was laughter in his voice.

'It's true,' Emily said indignantly. 'I'll tell you what I think. I think they're out for what they can get.'

'That's preposterous,' Cordelia exclaimed.

'Is it?' asked Emily. 'Daddy told me he was called upon to help Mrs Green when she was in the soup.'

'Did he?' Cordelia gave Kenneth a look.

'I didn't explain the nature of the soup,' he replied.

'It was a serious incident, Emily,' said Cordelia. 'Anyway, I thought we were talking about the girls, not Mrs Green.' She felt like bashing Kenneth on the nose with her spoon.

'The same goes for them,' said Emily. 'One of them wanted advice about a change of surname, didn't she? Who better to ask than the wife of a solicitor, who can get the advice free, gratis and for nothing?'

'That's enough, Emily,' said Cordelia. She wanted to say – oh, she wanted to say a hundred things, but if she did, it would cast a dark cloud over their special evening.

'I'm sorry, Mummy.' Emily was instantly contrite. 'I didn't mean to hurt your feelings, but it makes me hopping mad to think that they're using you.'

CHAPTER TWELVE

A whole week had passed since Colette's revelation about her mother-in-law and herself. For the first few days, she had walked around in what she thought must be a state of shock. Her skin felt numb and prickly at the same time and she felt distanced from the world around her. Was she really destined to end up a silent shadow of a creature, like Bunty? Was Bunty truly only able to be her real self when she was well away from her husband? The more Colette thought about it, the more it came home to her that in Father's presence, Bunty didn't speak unless spoken to.

No one knows what goes on behind closed doors.

When in doubt, apologise. That was what Colette had learned to do with Tony. Had Bunty, years ago, learned the same rule with Father? Was 'when in doubt, apologise' one step along the path to silence? How long had Colette been married before it had become an integral part of her behaviour? It had just seemed like keeping the peace, smoothing things over. It was a wife's job to make life as easy and as regulated as possible for her husband. Everyone knew that. A woman who neglected to do so would be condemned as a poor excuse for a wife.

Colette had tried her best all along to be a good wife, to please Tony and make him happy. She had fallen in with his wishes in countless small ways. Was that her being a good wife – or was it her giving in? If she hadn't given in, that would have made her a bad wife – wouldn't it? Besides, it couldn't be called giving in when you agreed to buy salted bacon instead of unsalted, or lime marmalade instead of orange. It wasn't giving in to use lemon-scented polish instead of lavender, and to hang up her apron in the cupboard under the stairs instead of on the back of the kitchen door. Those things weren't giving in. They were just ... going along with Tony's preferences. That was what a good wife did; the same way, when her husband didn't like her new hairstyle, she changed it back again. It wasn't worth the disapproving looks to keep it the new way.

Did that make her a doormat? She didn't think so, she honestly didn't think so. In her own way, she was sensible and capable. Goodness knows, she'd had to be sensible and capable after Dad had died and Mother went to pieces. She'd had to deal with the bank manager and he'd told her how well she was coping. 'You're doing splendidly in a sticky situation, Miss Davis.' That was what he had said, and he'd said it again, with feeling, after he'd met Mother.

So she wasn't stupid or useless, even though Tony sometimes made her feel she was. Not that he meant to, of course. He was just setting her straight.

'I'm telling you this for your own good.'

And she had never doubted it ... until now. Did she doubt it now? Was Tony helping her, being a good husband, taking an interest in the small details of their life together? Or was he – as bizarre as it sounded – exercising control over her in a hundred minute ways? Put like that, it sounded completely ridiculous and a wave of relief washed over her. Of course he wasn't controlling her. What a word to use about your own husband. Honestly!

But ... had Bunty spent the early years of her marriage trying to accommodate Father's wishes and preferences? Had she believed she was being a good wife? Was that the way it started? Had that marked the beginning of her descent into the safety of near silence?

It was hard to comprehend. Bad marriages weren't supposed to be like this. They were supposed to involve drink, infidelity, violence.

'I've never laid a finger on you.' How many times had Tony said that? 'I never have and I never will.'

Was it normal to be grateful to your husband for not hitting you? Was it normal for him to make you feel you had to be grateful?

Colette wrestled with her thoughts all week, at the same time feeling guilty for being preoccupied with herself when things were so awful for Alison. Word had got out at work about Paul going off with another girl.

'One of the ladies in the typing pool goes to our church,' Alison had announced in the buffet, her brown eyes dull with pain, 'and she told people in the office. It's been just frightful. Some girls have stopped me to say how sorry they are.'

'They're trying to be kind—' said Persephone, but Alison cut her off.

'And then there are the ones who stop talking when I walk into the room,' Alison went on, 'and then there are all those sympathetic looks that come my way.'

'Sympathy is preferable to being the subject of gossip,' said Cordelia.

'Is it?' Alison asked sharply. 'I don't want to be the object of anybody's pity, thank you.'

Alison had to leave the buffet earlier than normal because her first-aid group was having a training session that evening. When she left, the others all looked at one another.

'She sounds so angry,' said Margaret.

'I expect that's her way of keeping herself strong,' said Dot. Dear Dot, she could always be relied upon to understand.

A mad idea appeared in Colette's head. What if she confided in Dot? What if she told her about Bunty and not being hit by Tony and 'when in doubt, apologise'? Would Dot help her to sort out the thoughts crowding inside her head? Would Dot help her to understand?

But it was only a mad idea. She could never tell anybody. Mother had always said you shouldn't wash your dirty linen in public.

But there was someone who already knew, wasn't there?

Could she – dare she ask for help? And – help to do what, exactly?

Before Tony accompanied her to Mrs Cooper's that Sunday, Colette was in a state of agitation, but she was careful to hide it. Even so, there were some things that couldn't be concealed.

'You look peaky,' said Tony before he tucked into the chicken she had roasted and served with roast potatoes and peas. The best of the meat was on Tony's plate. Mother had taught her that. The husband always got the best of the meat.

'Peaky? Do I?' Did she sound guilty? 'I'm fine.'

'Are you certain? We needn't go out this afternoon if you don't feel up to it.'

'I'm fine, honestly.'

'If you're sure.' Was he trying to talk her out of going?

Colette forced a smile. 'I'm sure, but thank you for noticing.'

'Noticing what? You *are* off colour, aren't you? That settles it. We needn't go.'

'Oh, please let's. There's nothing wrong with me. "Noticing" was the wrong word. I should have thanked you for caring or for paying attention.'

'It's my job to pay attention,' said Tony. 'I watch over you all the time.'

A frisson of alarm passed through her – or was she being stupid? 'So we can go to Mrs Cooper's?' she asked.

'We'll see.'

Colette knew from experience not to argue with 'We'll see.' Not that she had ever really argued as such. On previous occasions, she had risen to the bait in other ways. She had tried to persuade him, though the persuasion had often ended up as pleading. Tony had liked that. There had been one occasion when she was pleading and a smile had touched his face and she had thought, *He's enjoying this,* and she had felt diminished.

After their meal, Colette washed up and tidied the kitchen while Tony had a cup of tea. The moment she sat down, he stood up.

'I thought you wanted to go to Mrs Cooper's.' He sat down again. 'We don't have to if you'd rather not.'

Colette jumped up. 'Of course I want to go. I mean, yes, please, let's go. I thought you weren't ready yet. That's why I sat down.'

'Why wouldn't I be ready? We always go at this time.' Tony laughed indulgently. 'What a good thing you've got me to take care of you. You'd drive any other man mad – wouldn't you?'

'Yes, Tony.'

When they reached Wilton Close, Tony took off his jacket and went outside to clip the hedge, leaving Colette with the two ladies of the house.

'It's just us today,' said Mrs Grayson. 'Mabel is playing the piano at a children's party.'

'Are you expecting Mrs Masters and Emily?' Colette asked.

'No,' said Mrs Cooper. 'We don't see so much of Mrs Masters now that her Emily is at home, but that's understandable, I suppose, though it's a shame for us.'

Colette experienced a flutter of anticipation, but there was fear mixed in with it and her palms felt damp. With no Mabel present and no visitors expected, all she had to do was wait for Mrs Grayson to go and put the kettle on, after which she would take Tony's tea outside to him and have a little chat ... and Colette would be alone with Mrs Cooper.

Could she? Did she dare?

'Are you telling me that this is the first and only time your Tony has made a bad joke?' That was what Mrs Cooper had asked her – an invitation, surely, to open her heart. Did she dare?

'I'll make the tea.' Mrs Grayson stood up. 'I made some of my ginger biscuits this week.'

As she left the room, Colette's mouth was so dry that she had to work up some saliva before her tongue could move. At last she was able to speak and she said – she said ...

'Are you getting plenty of cleaning work, Mrs Cooper?'

'Enough to keep ticking over, thank you for asking. Mind you, when I started up – and that makes it sound like it was years ago, but it was only in the spring – I offered a special service for all the extra cleaning that's needed following an air raid, but now the raids seem to be easing off, touch wood, so I'm trying to get ordinary work these days.'

'Offices always need cleaners,' Colette suggested.

'Aye, chuck, but they want you at either six in the morning or seven at night, which doesn't fit in with me being the housekeeper here and having my lasses to look after.' Mrs Cooper laughed. 'Hark at me. I say "my lasses", but it's just Mabel these days.'

'You must miss Joan.'

'Sometimes I wish she was still here, but my wish for that isn't as big as my wish for her to be happily married and living with her Bob. D'you mind if I ask you summat?'

Was Mrs Cooper about to raise the subject of Tony? The hairs on the back of Colette's neck stood up, but wasn't this what she wanted? Unable to speak, she moved her hand to indicate assent.

'What do you think of Margaret?' asked Mrs Cooper.

'Margaret?'

'Yes. Do you like her?'

Colette struggled to accommodate the unexpected subject. 'She's likeable. She's a good listener.' A quiet person herself, Colette always noticed who were the talkers and who were the listeners.

'Do the others like her? What I mean is, it can't be easy joining a group of friends.'

'We all get on with her.'

'That's good to know. Do you think she and Mabel get along?'

'As far as I know.'

'Me and Mrs Grayson like Margaret. We liked her the very first time she came here, after she lent Joan the wedding dress. Joan had to go out later that evening and Margaret stayed to help us with some sewing, which was very good-natured of her.'

Mrs Grayson came in with the tray and Colette got up to close the door behind her, cursing herself for losing the chance to confide. How could she have been so stupid – so frightened? Mrs Cooper was her friend, and in this matter, she was the only friend Colette had.

As she went home with Tony, Colette vowed that she would definitely talk to Mrs Cooper next Sunday, but the thought of waiting a whole week made her heart feel like a lump of lead inside her chest and the days dragged by.

Her resolve didn't waver, though, and knowing how badly she needed Mrs Cooper's support made it all the more important to her to help Alison through her heartbreak. Alison looked as though she was wasting away. She'd gone thin and her cheekbones were sharply defined.

'Are you eating?' Colette asked when the two of them were sent to the stationery cupboard.

'I don't have much appetite. I walk around in my dinner break. I don't want to see anybody. Actually, it's the other way round. I don't want anybody to see me. I hate to feel I'm being stared at.'

'I tell you what. Let's eat together in the canteen.'

'I told you. I hate being looked at.'

'We'll bag one of the small tables in the corner and you can sit with your back to the room.' Colette seized the pack of carbon paper from Alison's hands. 'I'm not giving this back until you say yes.'

Alison smiled, more of an almost smile than a real one, but it was good to see all the same.

Later, they carried trays with vegetable rissoles and cups of tea to the table in the furthest corner.

'We can talk about something else if you'd rather,' said Colette, 'but if you want to tell me how you are, how you *really* are, I'm happy to listen.'

Alison raised her eyebrows. 'It's not like you to be so ... '

'So what?'

'I don't know. Forthright, I suppose. You're normally the timid one.'

Just imagine if she said, 'Last Sunday I missed out on the chance to tell Mrs Cooper how miserable and desperate I am at home. I don't want you to miss the chance to talk if you need to.'

Instead, all she said was, 'I want to help if I can. I know there's nothing I can actually do, but I want to be a good friend.'

After a moment, Alison said, 'Thank you. I appreciate that.' She looked away, as if gazing into the distance. When her head swung back again, she looked at Colette with a kind of fierceness. 'You're so lucky. You've got everything – a husband, a home, a *future*. That's what I've realised. I haven't just lost Paul and our relationship. I've lost my whole future.' Her voice dropped to a whisper so quiet that Colette was practically lip-reading when Alison said, 'It's *terrifying*.'

'Oh, Alison.' Colette started to reach across to press her hand, but Alison dropped both hands into her lap.

'I've lost the rest of my life,' she went on, and now her brown eyes were the grey-brown of dead leaves. 'I had it all mapped out and now it's gone, vanished, and I've never been more scared in my whole life.'

'Father's invited us round for dinner on Sunday,' said Tony.

'What about going to Mrs Cooper's?' The words popped out before Colette had time to think.

Tony's eyes hardened. 'I hope you aren't suggesting that visiting those old biddies is more important than seeing family.'

'Of course not. I only meant ... ' How could she excuse it? 'I only meant they'll be expecting us.'

'I'm sure your friend Mabel will pass on a message to say we can't come.'

'Yes,' Colette whispered. Her shoulders slumped, but then she rallied. 'We could go to Wilton Close on Saturday instead. If it's inconvenient for you, I – I could go on my own.'

'Don't be silly. How would that look? We go together or not at all.'

'Can we? Go on Saturday?'

Tony smiled. It made him look pleased with himself. 'We'll see.'

And that was that. The dreaded 'We'll see.' Colette said nothing. They were in the parlour. She was sewing and Tony was due to go out fire-watching in a quarter of an hour. She set aside her sewing and got up to prepare his flask. It was better to do it before he issued a reminder.

Tony made no decree about Wilton Close before he went out, but Colette didn't really expect him to. He said nothing the next morning over breakfast and it wouldn't be right to ask him when a sleepless night was to be followed shortly by a day's work. He didn't mention it that evening either. Had he forgotten?

Colette plucked up the courage to ask.

Tony looked surprised. 'I thought you didn't want to go.'

She stopped herself from saying 'Of course I do,' which might have sounded pushy or exasperated. Instead she said, 'I'd like to.'

'Only I said "We'll see" and you haven't mentioned it since, so I thought you didn't want to. I thought I was doing you a favour.'

'I'd like us to go,' Colette said, eyes downcast.

'We don't have to. I've been thinking about what we could do instead.'

That was a trap. If she said she wanted to go to Mrs Cooper's, Tony would take offence; but if she embraced the idea of their doing something together, it would be a nail in the coffin of the Wilton Close visits.

When in doubt, apologise.

'I'm sorry. This is my fault for not making myself clear in the first place. You're right, it would be lovely to do something together, but would you mind awfully if we did it another time? Then we could look forward to it properly. Mrs Cooper does rely on our visits, you know. She appreciates the company and you're such a help to her. I'm sorry I've made a muddle of things.'

'You've been a foolish girl,' Tony said kindly.

'I know. I'm sorry.'

'So you do want to go to Mrs Cooper's after all?'

'Yes, please.'

Tony nodded, as if assessing the possibilities. He smiled. Then he turned away from her. He actually turned away.

She dared to say, 'So can we go … please?'

'We'll see.'

Colette lay awake for ages on Friday night, not moving a muscle for fear of disturbing Tony. She was too wound up to sleep. They were going to Wilton Close. Oh, thank heaven. At last she dozed off and was dimly aware of her body snuggling down, only to be brought sharply awake by the sound of the siren.

She stumbled out of bed, Tony doing the same on the other side, both of them pulling on the clothes that Colette laid out every night, just in case. Colette opened the upstairs curtains and ran downstairs to put the kettle on, ready to fill a flask, then she hurried about, opening the downstairs curtains as well. That was one of the things you had to do, leave your curtains open so that if an incendiary should come through your roof, the flames would be seen from outside.

By the time she had the flask ready, Tony had placed their buckets of sand and water outside the front door and had switched off the gas and the water. This was a man's job, apparently, though Colette had done it enough times when she had been in the house on her own.

Tony locked up and they went to the Anderson shelter in their small back garden. They had hardly settled themselves inside before the all-clear sounded.

Tony made an impatient noise. Colette wanted to point out that this brief interruption was preferable to an all-out air raid, but she held her tongue.

They returned to the house. Tony tossed and turned in bed as if Colette deserved to be punished for the scramble down to the Andy, but finally he slept. Colette remained awake for a long time before she too settled down.

She was tired the next day, but she knew she mustn't let it show. She mustn't provide even the smallest excuse for Tony to pull out of the visit to Wilton Close.

She cooked and served their meal and cleared away afterwards, longing to throw on her hat and jacket but recognising the importance of waiting for Tony to make the first move – he would make the first move, wouldn't he? He wouldn't play an elaborate game?

No, she was safe. He was as cheerful about going as if Wilton Close were his favourite place and Mrs Cooper a second mother to him.

When they arrived, he broke away from her to take a look at the green beans scrambling up the wigwam of sticks and Colette made use of this opportunity to hurry to the front door and ring the bell. When Mrs Cooper answered, Colette threw a glance over her shoulder to make sure Tony hadn't come up behind her, then she stepped into the house, catching hold of Mrs Cooper's hand and drawing her close.

'Please – I have to speak to you – privately. You know what about.'

Mrs Cooper looked startled but only for a second. She nodded, then stood back, saying, 'We've got a full house today. Aren't Mrs Grayson and I lucky to have such good friends who come to see us? Everyone is so kind.' She looked over Colette's shoulder. 'We even have a friend who does our garden for us.'

As Tony entered the house, Colette made a bit of a fuss out of taking off her hat and jacket so as not to look at him, fearful of what he might see in her eyes. But if she failed to look at him, would that strike him as unusual? Might it arouse his suspicions? A cold feeling fluttered inside her chest. She couldn't afford to make mistakes. But then – didn't that describe her entire marriage? Don't make mistakes.

Turning to him, she said, 'Shall we see who's here?'

'Yes, come in, come in.' Mrs Cooper opened the door to the front room.

Mabel was there and so was Mrs Mitchell, the Darley Court housekeeper. As well as being Mabel's father's cousin, she had also been friends with Mrs Grayson for many years. She was the one, in fact, who had found Mabel a home with Mrs Grayson back when Mrs Grayson still lived in her own house, before Mr Grayson had demanded to have the house back so he could live there with Floozy, his bit on the side.

Joan and Bob were here too.

'There'll be two of us digging for victory this afternoon,' Bob said, shaking hands with Tony.

When the two men went outside, Joan watched them from the window before turning to Colette. 'Before I got married, I used to picture this. Our two husbands out there and you and me in here, chatting with Mrs Cooper. And now it's happening.'

'Yes.' It emerged as a whisper, as if a tiny sound was all that could creep out from beneath the edge of the great bleakness that had descended upon Colette. Joan saw herself and Bob and Colette and Tony as two happily married couples. If only she knew.

Mrs Cooper said, 'Colette dear, before you sit down, will you pop upstairs with me? I've got some fabric I'd like to show you.'

For a second or two, Colette's limbs felt weak. It was happening. It was really happening. Could she go through with it? She had to. Last week she had chickened out and then regretted it all week. She mustn't do that again.

She followed Mrs Cooper into her bedroom, which was a single room, though noticeably larger than the single in Colette's house.

Mrs Cooper sat on the bed, patting the space beside her. Colette perched on the edge. Even though she was determined to see this through, it seemed her body, of its own accord, was prepared to spring up and flee at any moment.

Mrs Cooper took her hand. 'Tell me.'

How? How to put it all into words? There was so much to say, yet it would sound silly when she said it out loud. Tony outwitted her with words, that was all. It wasn't as though he had ever hit her.

'What he said to you at the dance,' Mrs Cooper murmured after a while.

Colette's cheeks burned. 'I'm sorry you had to hear it.'

'Let's face it, chuck. If I hadn't, we wouldn't be sitting here now. Does he often speak to you like that?'

Colette nodded. She wanted to speak, she knew she had to speak, but there was a painful constriction blocking her throat.

Mrs Cooper waited. Then she said, 'Maybe you don't want to talk. Maybe you just want a hug, eh?'

The hand that held Colette's let go and started to slide around her shoulders. All Colette wanted to do was bury herself in Mrs Cooper's embrace, but she couldn't, she mustn't, she didn't deserve it. Cowards who couldn't do what they had sworn to themselves they'd do didn't deserve comfort.

Colette pulled free and stood up. She turned to face Mrs Cooper, then turned away, only to turn back again, her hands covering her mouth. She wanted, oh how she wanted to be held by this lovely lady, but she had to earn it.

Then out came the story of Bunty and their shopping trip and the way Bunty had retreated into silence when she got home.

'It made me realise that's going to be me in a few years. I'm halfway there already. I have to be so careful in everything I say and do. Tony's much cleverer than I am. He twists things and I get muddled, but I don't always see it until afterwards. He sounds reasonable and patient and I go along with it. I try so hard to do what he wants, but I'm on edge the whole time. I'm not explaining this very well.'

'I'm sorry to hear about your mother-in-law,' said Mrs Cooper.

Colette stared. *What about me?* Oh, how selfish of her. Even so, it was hurtful and disappointing to know that Mrs Cooper had latched on to Bunty instead of to Colette's situation.

'And I'm sorrier still to think of it happening to you an' all. It's not easy being stuck in a bad marriage – not that I'm speaking from personal experience, mind. I had the best of husbands. But I've heard things over the years and I'm right sorry for your trouble. I'd never have thought it of your Tony, not if I hadn't heard it with my own ears.' Standing, she held out her arms. 'Come here, my lass.'

Colette walked into her arms. Mrs Cooper was thin as a stick but being held by her was like being held by the plumpest, cuddliest person in the world. Colette clung to her and Mrs Cooper rocked her to and fro.

Mrs Cooper gently detached herself. 'My Lizzie liked you.'

'Did she?'

'Aye, and so do I. It grieves me to know you're married to a wrong 'un.'

'Thank you. Thank you for listening.'

'The thing is this, love. Ever since my Lizzie died, you've come to see me nigh on every single week. You've shown me great kindness during my darkest time and I'll be thankful to you until the day I die. The question now is what am I going to do for you in your dark time?'

CHAPTER THIRTEEN

Mum was wonderful, of course, but at the same time she was becoming increasingly annoying. If she said 'I thought your future was all sorted' just one more time, Alison might well scream the house down. The trouble with being at home was that she wasn't the only one who had lost Paul. Mum, Dad and Lydia had too. He had been part of the family. Alison struggled to cope with their shock and upset on top of her own.

Her railway friends didn't say a word, but Alison was aware that the number of meetings in the buffet had increased. The others must have got together and organised this so as to provide her with company, should she need it. She remembered how they had all rallied round Joan after Letitia died. She had never for one moment imagined that they would have to rally round her. Her relationship with Paul had been indestructible. That was how it had felt.

Confident to the point of arrogance.

In the buffet, no one pressed her to talk. They chatted about all sorts of things and she joined in or she didn't. Sometimes she felt desperate for distraction; other times she couldn't be bothered, because how could anything matter to her ever again?

'Mrs Grayson is bitterly disappointed,' said Mabel. 'She hoped against hope that this would mean America would join the war.'

'That was never going to be the outcome,' said Persephone. 'The purpose of the meeting between Mr Churchill and President Roosevelt was to look ahead to when the war is over and agree on various principles for how the world should develop.'

'When the war is over,' said Cordelia with a mirthless little laugh. 'That feels a very long way off.'

'Aye, it'll be several years yet,' said Dot, 'especially without the Yanks. Mind you, don't forget Russia. Hitler invading them puts them on our side.'

'Perhaps that's why there haven't been as many air raids recently,' Margaret suggested.

It seemed that no sooner had Margaret raised the point than the raids started up again. Alison was glad to go on first-aid duty. If she hadn't been on duty, she would have come in anyway. The damage done by high explosives and incendiaries spoke to her as never before, touching her right to the core of her own pain, almost as if her heartbreak was shaking the world around her. Ruptured gas mains from which flames leaped up through cracks in the road … Giant heaps of rubble that had once been houses, homes … Craters in the street, the air thick with the smell of smoke … Gaunt-faced civilians, broken limbs, cuts, blood – and shock, shock everywhere …

God, what was she thinking? Had she gone mad? The destruction was nothing to do with her and she was wicked to have felt, even briefly, that there was some kind of connection. A bomb fell; the ground shook; Alison's body shuddered and it was as if her fanciful notion was being shaken out of her. Good riddance, she thought, and continued offering first aid with renewed determination.

Alison sat on her bed on Saturday afternoon, using her nail scissors to unpick the name tape inside her coat. *Alison Dunaway* it said. Alison flaming Dunaway. It was important to have your name inside coats and jackets because of handing them into the cloakroom when you went to a dance or when you hung them up in a restaurant or at work. It had seemed like the right thing to do to have her name tapes made in the name of Dunaway. Right and sensible – and deeply exciting. She hadn't mentioned it to Paul. Not that she was in any way ashamed or doubtful about her decision, but she hadn't mentioned it. Alison Dunaway. Lambert was just temporary, until she got married. That was how she had seen it. That was how sure she had been.

She picked away at the tiny stitches. Alison Dunaway was dead and gone. Her identity, her perception of herself, had been stripped away. She raised her knuckles to brush away a chilly tear. She would have to order new name tapes from Ingleby's, or maybe she wouldn't bother. It wasn't as though Alison Lambert was who she wanted to be.

'What are you up to?'

Lydia walked in.

'Nothing.' Alison folded the coat over. 'That's my top you're wearing.'

'And you're a darling to lend it to me.'

'How could I refuse when you asked so nicely?' Alison replied. She was about to say, 'I do get fed up of you helping yourself to my things,' but if she did, would it sound as if she was recovering from her heartbreak and was able to bother about other things? 'Anyway,' she said, 'did you want something?'

'Not really. Just a chat. How are you, that kind of thing.'

Alison shrugged. 'So-so.'

'What are you doing with your coat? It looked like you were unpicking some stitches.'

Alison shoved the coat behind her. She wouldn't put it past Lydia to make a grab for it. She could be a nosy little beggar when she felt like it.

'I'll tell you what I do need to unpick,' said Alison, offering a distraction. 'The embroidery I did on the pillowcases in my bottom drawer.'

Lydia sighed, a sympathetic sound. 'I remember. You embroidered a little circle of forget-me-nots on the corner of each one, with a D in the centre. Oh, Alison.'

Alison refused to give in to the tears burning the backs of her eyes. 'So there's lots of unpicking to do,' she said crisply.

'You could always ... ' Lydia's voice trailed off.

'Always what?'

'Nothing. Forget I spoke.'

She ought to leave it there, but she couldn't help insisting. She knew it was going to hurt, but she still insisted. 'Always what, Lydia?' It was like picking at a scab and making it bleed all over again.

'I was going to say leave the forget-me-nots and just unpicks the D's. Then maybe one day—'

'No!' Alison was appalled. Angry too. How dare Lydia hint that one day she might meet someone else? 'Frankly, I feel like giving away my whole bottom drawer to a rest centre so that people who have lost everything can have the pick of it.'

'You mustn't do that.' Now it was Lydia's turn to be shocked. 'All those things you've collected – you can't give them away.'

'There doesn't seem much point in keeping them.'

Oh, her bottom drawer – all the items she had lovingly collected, ready for when she got married. She had the best 'bottom drawer' of anyone she knew. Bed linen, kitchen linen, towels. A set of fish knives and forks in a velvet-lined box. A milk jug and matching sugar bowl in white china decorated with pink roses; a glorious tablecloth of Irish linen edged with scallops of lace. Cushion covers, vases, a fruit bowl, a photograph frame. A wicker basket for groceries, a strong cloth bag for potatoes. There was no end to the list of things she had squirrelled away.

Releasing a huge, quivering breath, she cast her gaze up to the ceiling and shook her head. When she opened her eyes, Lydia was watching her with concern.

'If only we hadn't gone to that dance,' Alison burst out. 'He'd never have met her. I don't know what he sees in her, I really don't.'

'It was the excitement of it, I suppose,' said Lydia. 'After all ... '

'What?'

'Nothing. It doesn't matter.'

'It's obviously something. You might as well tell me. You've already dropped one clanger.'

'It might sound unkind.'

Alison laughed without humour. 'What's a bit of unkindness after what I've been through? Come on, Lydia, or else I'll think you mean that if *she's* exciting, then I'm boring.'

Lydia pressed her lips together. 'You said it. I didn't,' she said primly.

'What?' Alison's muscles went rigid and her skin prickled all over. 'You mean, that's what you were going to say? That I'm ... ' She couldn't bring herself to utter the word a second time. She had only been able to say it the first time because she wasn't being serious.

'Well, yes,' said Lydia. 'I'm not saying *I* think you're boring. It's just that ... '

'Just that what?'

Lydia huffed out a sigh. It wasn't a sympathetic sound this time. 'You're pretty middle-aged in your behaviour, aren't you?'

'I'm *what*?'

'You behave as if you've been married for donkey's years – well, you did when you were courting Paul.'

'I didn't.'

'Yes, you did.'

'Such as when?' Alison demanded.

Lydia seemed to be casting about for a reply. Ha! There weren't any examples. Lydia was talking through her hat.

'Oh, I don't know,' said Lydia. 'Yes, I do. The way you help the mums make the cricket tea when all the girls are outside chatting while they sunbathe. And you're the only person under forty to help with the church flowers and pricing things up for the jumble sales.'

Alison stared at her sister, aghast.

'I'm sorry,' cried Lydia. 'I don't mean you're dull, but you must admit you're the tiniest bit staid. And if this other girl came along and she was—'

'Exciting?' Alison said in a tight voice. 'You've made your point, Lydia.'

Her body felt as if it might collapse in on itself. Her chin trembled and her heart struggled to beat.

Arrogant and boring. Oh, dear heaven. Arrogant and boring.

There were a couple of air raids the following week on consecutive nights. Each time, the siren went off between ten thirty and eleven, the sort of time when other girls – girls with boyfriends – would be leaving the theatre, but Alison was stuck at home, fed up and miserable. Was this what the rest of her life was going to be like?

'At least it's better than having to drag yourself out of bed at three in the morning,' said Mum as she prepared the flask and Alison saw to the curtains. 'Should I make sandwiches or will the biscuit tin be enough? Raids don't seem to last as long these days.'

'Biscuits.' Alison gave her a quick kiss. She knew Mum was talking because she was worried about Lydia, who wasn't home yet. Eleven o'clock was her curfew and she always swanned in, laughing and oblivious to parental anxiety, at one minute to. Alison had always regarded her sister's breezy behaviour with a mixture of indulgence and exasperation, but now she wondered if that was a sign of her 'middle-aged' attitude.

Neither of the air raids lasted more than half an hour. No doubt, people all over Manchester, having got settled in their Anderson shelters, were now trooping back indoors to undo all the preparations so recently put in place – switching on the gas and water supplies, reinstating the blackout, putting their strongboxes of family certificates and insurance papers back into their sideboard cupboards. The routine was second nature.

'One good thing about short, early raids,' said Miss Simpson the next morning at work. 'At least we don't all come to the office bog-eyed and weary.'

Alison slid away from the chatting group. She was bog-eyed and weary all the time these days, though, oddly, she didn't feel tired. Every nerve ending felt red-raw with anguish and she seemed to be extra awake despite her lack of sleep.

As she tackled her work, she was aware of a sharp-edged chill in the pit of her stomach. She had never minded coming to work before. She had always seen it as a temporary measure, part of the prelude to getting married, which was when her real life would finally begin. But now her lovely married future had been torn from her and it was dawning on her that years of earning a living lay ahead. Truly? Was this to be her new 'real life'? She couldn't bear to contemplate it. At some point she would have to, but not yet.

She was meant to be going to the pictures that evening with Mabel and Persephone, but all at once she couldn't face it. In her dinner break, she went over to the station, where Persephone was on duty at her ticket barrier, unconsciously making her uniform look unutterably glamorous.

'Sorry, but do you mind if I duck out of this evening?' Alison asked.

There was warm concern in Persephone's violet eyes, but she didn't probe. 'That's a shame,' was all she said, 'but there'll be other times.'

Oh yes, there'd be other times, a whole lifetime of tagging along with other people's plans.

Later, she trailed home from work, feeling more fragile than usual and wondering if she'd made a mistake by not going to the flicks. It wasn't as though she had anything to do at home other than unpick the horrid D's from her pillowcases.

She walked into the house to find Lydia dancing around the kitchen. Dancing – literally. The quickstep, to be precise. She was laughing and her eyes sparkled. Mum was laughing too. The joyful atmosphere was so at odds with Alison's state of mind, with her whole life, that after a moment of being startled, what came next was a spurt of vexation. How could they be so careless of her heartbreak? Was this how her family behaved behind her back? Shouldn't they be huddled in corners, whispering about how worried they were and devising ways to support her?

'Alison.' Seeing her, Mum sobered. 'I wasn't expecting you home for tea.'

So I see were the words that sprang to mind, but she held them back. 'Change of plan.'

Mum rubbed her hand up and down Lydia's slender arm. 'Why don't you go upstairs and read your letter again and I'll tell Alison.'

Alison's skin chilled all over. 'Tell me what?'

Lydia looked at her. 'No, it's my news and I'll tell her. She'll be happy for me. I know she will. She's my sister.'

Oh, dear heaven. It couldn't be ...

Lydia waved her letter. 'It's from Alec. He wants us to get married. He's got a seventy-two-hour pass the week after next and he wants to know how quickly I can organise a wedding.'

CHAPTER FOURTEEN

'Mummy, I want to do war work – proper war work, not making the tea and putting things in alphabetical order and taking the post to the pillar box, like I do in Daddy's office. I want to do my bit.'

'Darling, you're only fifteen,' said Cordelia. 'Daddy won't think you're old enough.'

'He'd stash me away in a cave in the Outer Hebrides until the war is over, if he could.'

Cordelia smiled. 'That's true.' Kenneth was nothing if not the protective father. It was one of the better things about their marriage.

'I want to do something in the evenings or overnight,' said Emily, 'and I'm not talking about the knitting circle at St Clement's.'

'I'll think about it,' said Cordelia, holding up a warning hand when Emily was about to speak. 'I've said I'll consider it.'

Emily subsided, but she had given Cordelia a lot to think about – and not just concerning her daughter. About herself too. For months, she had felt twinges of guilt for not doing more for the war effort. Oh, she collected for the Penny a Week Fund and she knitted and helped out in jumble sales; she had poured endless energy into organising the War Weapons Week dance. But she wasn't in the WVS; she didn't help during air raids or care for the injured; she didn't work in a mobile canteen or do shifts in a rest centre.

What it came down to was that she didn't do anything that involved staying out all night. All her young friends did. Joan, Mabel and Alison were first-aiders; Persephone and Margaret did fire-watching. But Kenneth didn't want her staying out all night and, ever the loyal wife, she had fallen in with his wishes.

'You're already doing war work,' Kenneth had told her in no uncertain terms early on in the war. 'You do long hours in a God-awful, tedious job. Nobody could expect you to take up night-time duties as well.' He had taken both her hands in his, an unusually warm gesture for him. 'Besides, you'll be a lot safer at home overnight.'

She had gone along with his wishes, partly from habit but also because she was acutely aware of his distaste for the menial nature of her job, which he seemed to think reflected poorly on him.

'Do you remember wondering if you ought to volunteer for night-time war duties?' she asked Dot in the buffet during the last week in August, when it was just the two of them. Times when it was just the two of them were rare and special, because Dot's friendship was precious to her, though these days being alone with Dot had an uncomfortable edge to it. Why, oh why did Emily have to judge Dot by her friendly informality and her colloquial vocabulary?

'Aye, I remember,' said Dot. 'You were the first to point out that I'm quite busy enough with everything else, and you were right. I still feel guilty sometimes, mind, but with my sensible head on, I know you're right. What makes you bring that up?'

Cordelia smiled wryly. 'I'm experiencing a similar guilt myself. It's been growing for some time. I wonder if I should be doing more.'

'I know how that feels,' said Dot, 'but I'll say to you what you said to me. You've got a home to run and a family to look after.'

'My family is only Kenneth and Emily, and Emily's no trouble.'

'Not like some we could name, eh?' Dot chuckled lovingly. Her grandson Jimmy was always getting himself into scrapes, but there was nothing he could do that would stop his nan adoring him.

'I have the energy to do more,' said Cordelia.

'And more than enough ability,' Dot added. 'Look at how you organised that dance. That were a big event.'

'I wasn't the only organiser.' Cordelia hesitated before adding, 'I can say this to you because you'll know I'm not boasting, but I did take on the lion's share of the work.'

'Thought so.'

'You did?'

'Aye. You spent the night flitting here, there and everywhere, checking this, looking at that, talking to the hotel staff. It were obvious you felt responsible for the whole shebang.'

'I suppose I did.'

'And now you're looking for summat else to do for the war effort.'

'Yes. Not a one-off event like the dance, something regular. My husband thinks I do quite enough being a lampwoman.'

'It's only enough if it feels like enough to you.'

Cordelia looked at her friend. 'You're a wise woman, Mrs Green.'

'Thank you kindly, I'm sure, Mrs Masters.'

'I'm not the only one who wants to do something. Emily does too and I know what her father will say.'

'That she's—'

'Too young,' they chorused.

'And she is too young, of course she is,' said Dot, 'but age doesn't necessarily have much to do with it in wartime, does it? Shall I tell you what our Jimmy set his sights on the minute he turned twelve back in June?'

'What?'

'He wants to be one of them messenger boys what cycle around in air raids, taking messages between first-aid posts and ARP stations.'

'That's dangerous work.'

'You know what lads are like. Plenty of 'em want to do it and presumably their mams know what they're up to.'

'Oh, Dot, you must be so worried.'

'Fortunately, Reg put his foot down. I say "fortunately" because he seldom bothers. But he told our Jimmy he's young for his age and to ask again next year.'

'That's something,' said Cordelia.

'But you can't use that argument on your Emily. They have messenger girls as well as messenger boys, you know, and at fifteen she's old enough. If you don't watch out, she'll go and get herself a job doing that. Then you or Mr Masters will have to go down the ARP depot and refuse permission, and that'll cause ructions at home.'

Anxiety made Cordelia's skin tingle. 'I know. I have to find something for her that ... ' She smiled. 'I was going to say, something that I'd have more control over, but if there's an air raid, I shan't have much control.'

Dot laughed. 'Eh, at your Emily's age, I was getting to know Reg rather too well for my own good and ended up getting wed at sixteen.'

'Dot!'

'I'm not suggesting owt untoward about Emily. What I mean is, when I were fifteen, I thought I was grown-up and no one would have been able to convince me any different. I bet all fifteen-year-olds are the same. I bet your Emily is. You're her mam and you have to do what's best for her, but just bear in mind, she's not a little lass any more, no matter how much you want to protect her.'

As she sat in the buffet one evening, waiting for the others to arrive, Cordelia mulled over everything Dot had said. Dot's words had struck a chord deep inside her. To the parents of fifteen-year-olds, their children were just that – children. But most children left school at fourteen and started work the following day, which made them adults, albeit young ones. Cordelia knew that to Kenneth in particular, Emily would always be his precious little girl, no matter how old she was.

And never mind Emily's age – Cordelia was proud of Emily for being determined to do her bit. Perhaps she could learn first aid like Mabel and Joan; but no, Kenneth would never agree to that after what had happened to Lizzie. Moreover, he wasn't the only one to feel protective of Emily. Cordelia much preferred the thought of doing her war work side by side with her daughter.

But doing what? They could join the WVS, but they might be assigned to different units or put on different shift patterns. In any case, Emily might not be old enough to join. That was the trouble. As Dot had pointed out, Emily was old enough to be a messenger girl, but Cordelia was determined not to let her do that, so what could she do instead?

Cordelia set aside her thoughts, smiling a welcome as the others started to arrive. Alison looked especially strained, the poor girl. As soon as everyone was there, Alison said in a brittle voice that had become all too familiar recently, 'There's something I've been meaning to tell you.'

Cordelia was aware of all eyes immediately locking on Alison's face, which was white and drawn but with a touch

156

of defiance. What had happened? Had Paul changed his mind about the other girl?

'My sister's getting married.'

There was a moment of shocked silence.

'Oh, Alison,' said Mabel as sympathy rippled around the group.

Spying the gleam of tears in Alison's eyes, Cordelia spoke in a forthright voice. 'That must be hard for you to cope with. When is the big day?' Did the others think her cool and uncaring? But she didn't want Alison to be over-whelmed by kindness and concern to the point where she broke down.

'Lydia got a letter last week. I couldn't bear to say any-thing before, but … ' Alison pressed her lips together so tightly they became a white gash. 'Alec, that's her boyfriend, or her fiancé, I should say, has been granted seventy-two hours in the first week of September.'

There was a collective gasp.

'But that's—' Persephone started to say.

'Next week,' said Alison. 'You don't need to tell me, thanks all the same.'

'I didn't realise your sister was engaged.' Dot looked round the table.

'She wasn't. The letter contained the proposal and wed-ding date all in one go.'

'In other circumstances,' said Cordelia, choosing her words with care, 'we'd all be saying how exciting it is.'

'I know.' Alison gulped. 'So would I.'

'I'm sure you're pleased for her,' said Dot.

A few sounds tumbled from Alison's lips before she managed to form proper words. 'If it was just an engage-ment … ' Her eyes closed. 'If all Alec wanted was to get engaged, that would be hard enough.' Her eyes opened and they were awash with distress. 'Why did he have to suggest getting married as well? Oh, I'm not stupid. I know it happens all the time, servicemen dashing home, getting married and going away again. And I know Alec had no idea about my situation when he wrote his letter. But none of that helps me. I've just been jilted and now I've got to watch my sister get married. How am I supposed to bear it?'

The women looked at one another while Alison sniffed into her hanky, though she managed not to break down in sobs.

'You'll bear it because you have to,' Joan said quietly, 'and you'll bear it because you want the best for your sister.'

'Eh, your poor mam,' said Dot. 'She must feel torn in two, one daughter with her hopes all dashed, t'other rushing to put a wedding together.'

Alison pushed back her chair and stood up. 'I'd better go.'

'Please stay,' said Persephone.

'No. It's all a bit much. You understand.'

Alison hurried from the buffet, all of them watching her go. Then they turned to one another with shaking heads and saddened eyes.

'That poor child,' said Dot. 'As if she hasn't been through enough.'

And really, what else was there to say?

Hurrying out of the station, Alison felt shaken up and distressed. She also felt deeply, darkly furious and frustrated. Betrayed. That was how she felt. Betrayed. She couldn't blame Lydia for getting married, not really, but did Mum have to be so pleased about it? That was the kick in the teeth for Alison. It was as if her own heartbreak had been set aside as old news. Dot had said Mum must feel torn in two, but it didn't seem that way to Alison. Oh, Mum had given her a hug and shown sympathy, but as soon as Alison had done the decent thing and congratulated Lydia and given her a kiss, it was as if she had granted permission for everyone else to be happy and excited on Lydia's behalf.

She knew she was being mean, but what she wanted was for Mum and Lydia to be half-hearted about the wedding. She wanted them not to feel able to throw themselves into it because they were too concerned about her. But that was just her being horrid, she knew, only she couldn't help it. It was infuriating and humiliating to feel that her own situation had lost status now that Lydia's wedding had come along.

As for her friends in the buffet just now, with their 'You'll bear it because you have to' and 'Your poor mam' – those were the last words she needed to hear. She wasn't stupid. She knew she had to bear it. She didn't need to have it pointed out.

What she wanted, what she *needed*, was to be made a fuss of and told how dreadful her life was, and that Lydia's engagement was a terrible blow that had made things even worse. That was what she needed, not a pep talk, not advice about how to behave. She knew how to behave. What she longed for was sympathy laid on with a trowel. She needed to know that other people understood, that their hearts ached with worry and concern for her. She felt as if that was all she had left. All the dreams and devotion she had poured into her relationship with Paul had been dashed aside and his feelings for her had been wrenched away. If she didn't have other people making a fuss of her, she might as well be invisible.

Oh, being jilted was the worst thing imaginable – except that she hadn't been jilted, had she? To be jilted, you had to be engaged, but she had never got a ring on her finger. She had never been anything more than the girlfriend with hopes and dreams – with expectations. How pathetic.

When she arrived home, it was to an empty house, which came as a surprise. Ever since she had started walking home from school on her own at the age of seven, Mum had always been there to welcome her and ask her about her day. Alison hung up her things and was about to go upstairs to change into her slippers when the front door opened and Mum and Lydia burst in – it was the only way to describe it – chattering and laughing.

They sobered when they saw Alison's face and she felt a stab of shame. She didn't want to spoil things for Lydia, she honestly didn't, but – but – oh, she felt so wretched and abandoned and unwanted. The timing of Alec's proposal couldn't have been more wrong.

But if she truly didn't want to spoil things for Lydia, she had to prove it, so she smiled bravely and said, 'You both look excited.'

'We are.' Lydia returned her smile, though her eyes were wary. 'We've booked the church.'

'You're having the church?' said Alison. 'I thought – I assumed ... '

A registry-office do would have been bad enough, but to have to hold her head up throughout a church ceremony would be unendurable. Was it possible for a broken heart to shatter into even more pieces?

'No daughter of mine is making do with a registry-office wedding,' said Mum, 'no matter how short the notice.'

Alison hoisted her smile higher and hugged her sister. 'That's wonderful. I'm so pleased for you.'

Lydia angled her head to look into Alison's face. 'Do you mean that?'

'With all my heart.' Though what that declaration was worth when her heart was a quivering blob of anguish was anybody's guess.

Lydia kissed her cheek, whispering 'Thank you' in her ear.

Alison delivered a final squeeze and met Mum's approving expression. God, it was appallingly hard doing the decent thing. Wasn't being honourable supposed to make you stronger? It didn't have that effect on her. Her attempts to do right by Lydia were only on the surface. Inside, she was a seething mess of hurt and resentment. She should have been the one getting married. It should have been her and Paul.

'The church isn't the only thing we arranged,' said Mum.

'Oh?' Alison braced herself for flowers – a cake – the photographer ...

Mum smiled and nodded at Lydia. 'It's *your* news. You tell her.'

Lydia laughed. 'You won't believe it. We've found somewhere for Alec and me to live.'

Alison's stomach went stone cold and almost crashed to the floor. 'But you don't need anywhere. Alec's going straight back.'

'We have to have a married home,' said Lydia. 'Just because I'll be there on my own for the duration doesn't mean we don't need one. Alec will be able to picture it while he's away. It'll give him another reason to come home safely.'

'Of course it will,' said Mum. 'Aren't you going to ask where it is, Alison?'

'Where is it?'

'Near the cricket pitch,' Lydia burbled. 'It's a house that was converted into two flats twenty years ago. We've got the downstairs and the landlord has given permission for Dad to tart up the kitchen.'

Tears burned behind Alison's eyes. This should be happening to her, not to her little sister. And Lydia wasn't even moving in with in-laws, as Alison would have done had she married Paul, but was going to have a home of her own. Alison had planned everything so carefully and now Lydia was having it all handed to her on a plate. It was so damned unfair.

'Lovely,' she said. 'Congratulations. I must just go and – ' and what? ' – put my slippers on. I'll be down in a minute.'

She ran upstairs and into her room. Every muscle in her body urged her to slam the door hard enough to shake the house, just to make sure Mum and Lydia were in no doubt as to how bloody awful Lydia's wedding was for her. But she didn't. She clicked the door shut and leaned against it. The fight drained out of her, leaving her limbs humming with emptiness.

Did Paul have the first idea of what he had condemned her to?

CHAPTER FIFTEEN

The first of September. A new week and a new month all in one go. Cordelia always thought there was something refreshing about September. The end of the summer holidays, the start of the school year. Early September had a flavour of new beginnings. There was a crispness in the air too, or was that her imagination? August had been disappointingly dull, weather-wise. An Indian summer would be most welcome – or would it when the price to pay for it might be more air raids, thanks to the clear skies? Or was Hitler preoccupied with Russia these days? Had he removed his eye from Britain for the time being?

Cordelia was walking the line this week, climbing up the ladders to the gantries to attend to the signal lights and making sure she was well out of the way each time a train rushed by, white clouds puffing from the funnel, the long line of wagons or passenger coaches following behind, the familiar rhythm of the wheels filling her ears. Occasionally, when there was an exceptionally heavy load to pull, two locomotives would be coupled together to move the freight. It was a sight that filled Cordelia with awe every time.

Beside some of the signals stood a small hut that looked not unlike an outside lavatory, just about big enough to contain a stool and a small brazier. Some people called them fog boxes, because in thick fog, when the engine drivers wouldn't be able to see the signal lights, railway workers would be assigned to the various boxes along each length of the permanent way. It would be their job to stop the trains if necessary, by attaching a row of three tiny detonators to the track. When a train passed over the detonators, the three small explosions would give the driver the instruction to halt the train immediately.

As she walked, Cordelia mulled over various things – the fresh upset in Alison's life, Emily's determination to engage in 'real' war work, and her own desire to volunteer for something, though it had to be something she and Emily could do together. Otherwise, Kenneth would never give Emily his consent. Besides, Cordelia wouldn't feel easy if Emily was allowed to do war work on her own. She might be fifteen and old enough to have a job, but she was still entitled to all the loving protection her parents could provide.

A short air raid that night had given Cordelia food for thought. Could she really allow her daughter to tackle war work? But Emily's resolve hadn't wavered and Cordelia, remembering how Emily had left school early and arrived home unannounced, wouldn't put it past her to sort out her own war work if push came to shove.

In the morning at work, there was a distinct atmosphere in the lamp room. Cordelia got changed as normal and went outside. Mr Winton, the man who had survived the near miss in the marshalling yard early in July, was passing by.

'Morning, Mr Winton,' Cordelia greeted him, and was surprised when the normally courteous man offered no response. He couldn't have heard, though she knew he was near enough. He must be lost in thought. Come to think of it, he did have a rather fixed expression on his face.

Cordelia had just started on her way to the station to catch the train to where she would begin walking today's section of the line, when Mrs Haughtrey stopped her. The lines on her face seemed deeper than usual.

'I saw you speak to Mr Winton.'

'Yes. He seemed preoccupied.'

'I should say so. He was on fire-watching duty here last night and he dashed home at six o'clock this morning to have a shave and a bite to eat and when he got there ... ' Mrs Haughtrey stopped.

'Go on,' Cordelia said quietly. Whatever was coming had to be pretty bad.

Mrs Haughtrey jerked her head up as if forcing the words out. 'Bombed out. The house were gone and his wife and daughter and two grandchildren who were sheltering in the cellar ... ' She shook her head.

'What, all of them?'

Mrs Haughtrey nodded, then walked away quickly. Cordelia stood there for a moment or two, struggling to take it in, but standing there did no good. She had a job to do. They all had jobs to do.

She caught her train. Normally, she liked glancing at the other passengers, sizing them up while enjoying the odd impression she must give, with her dungarees and her pearls, but not today. This morning, her mind was crammed with thoughts of poor Mr Winton. How fragile the world felt. This damnable war.

As the morning drew to a close, she found herself close to a lengthmen's hut. The huts were built by the men who spent their days out on the permanent way in all weathers and temperatures. They were constructed from railway sleepers, standing up like planks, and they provided shelter from the elements during breaks from work. As a rule, Cordelia didn't like to impose unless the weather was truly filthy, but today she felt the need for company, so she knocked and opened the door to find four men inside, sitting on makeshift benches – really, stacked-up sleepers – and eating sandwiches or barm cakes, their flasks by their feet.

'Is there room for a lampwoman?' she asked and was waved to a place.

The men were discussing last night's raid and Cordelia, normally a reserved person and certainly one who wouldn't dream of speaking about someone behind their back, couldn't help saying what had befallen poor Mr Winton.

'Aye, that's a bad business,' observed one of the men. 'There are plenty that has happened to.'

'It's the train drivers and firemen that have it the worst,' said another.

'Why is it worse for them?' Cordelia asked.

'Think about it. The trains run day and night. Doesn't matter what the weather's like, doesn't matter if there's an air raid in progress. The trains keep running. The drivers and firemen get time off between shifts, a few hours, but a shift might last eighteen, twenty hours, depending on what's going on. Just imagine you're driving a loco for that length of time, maybe through fog or through sheets of rain, maybe with bombs going off around you – and railway tracks are one of the targets, you know – and at the end of all that, you head home for a rest and – well, you find what your friend Mr Winton found. And then you've got to go back and carry on with your next shift. It's highly skilled work is driving, and so is being the fireman, and they've got to carry on working regardless.'

'It happens, love,' one of the others said to Cordelia. 'Some folk think we've got it cushy – reserved occupation an' all that – but there are times when even humble lengthmen like us feel like we're working in combat conditions. It's worse for the lads doing the fighting, I know that, but it's not exactly a picnic working on the tracks when the bombs start going off.'

'Eh, come on,' said the man who had offered Cordelia a seat. 'That's enough of that. We don't want to put the wind up the lady.' He eyed his colleagues.

'That's quite all right.' Cordelia sat up straighter. 'As a matter of fact, you've helped me reach a decision.'

That same evening Cordelia met Dot in the buffet. They weren't expecting anyone else. These past weeks, since Emily had made her feelings about Dot clear to her parents, Cordelia had felt guilty in Dot's company, but that conversation the two of them had shared about Emily's desire to do war work had brought home to Cordelia how much she valued her dear friend. Dot was the salt of the earth and so what if, in former times, their paths would never have crossed. Former times were dead and gone. Here and now was what mattered – wartime, unity, endurance – and that included wartime friendships, which were real and true and lasting, no matter what Kenneth said.

So Cordelia had arranged to have a cup of tea with Dot, just the two of them. Mr Winton's personal tragedy had taken her mind off it for much of the day, but now there was no one she would rather be with.

'Have you made a decision about your Emily doing war work?' Dot wanted to know.

Cordelia felt like hugging her for asking. 'I have,' she said in her customary calm way. 'I heard some things today that helped me make up my mind.' She explained about Mr Winton and also what the lengthmen had told her.

Dot nodded, looking serious. 'Working on the trains, I hear things like that. They're heroes, these drivers – aye, and the firemen an' all. They can't see the stations or junctions or any of the landmarks in the blackout, so they had to relearn all their routes in the pitch-dark. They have to know every bend in the line, every change in the gradient; they have to know when to start slowing down for stations – and all without being able to see a damn thing, pardon my French. Sorry to witter on like that. It's hearing about your Mr Winton what's got me riled up. So what war work have you decided on for you and Emily?'

'My first idea, because I was so affected by everything I heard today, was that we could be fire-watchers in the marshalling yard.'

'Mr Masters wouldn't like that,' said Dot.

'He wouldn't like anything that took us outside on duty at night. But as I said, it was only a thought, inspired by the things I heard today. They made me want to do something specifically for the marshalling yard – but it really isn't feasible, not if I want Emily beside me. Railway tracks and marshalling yards are obvious targets for the Luftwaffe.'

'So are stations and railway bridges. I don't blame you for wanting to keep Emily away.'

'She probably wouldn't be considered old enough anyway,' said Cordelia.

'What have you settled on, then?' Dot asked.

'Fire-watching in our local area. Not as dramatic as the marshalling yard, but I don't want my daughter in the middle of any drama if I can help it. I'm going to put our names down with the local fire-watchers this evening and we'll see if they'll accept Emily. She'll have to do a good interview to be accepted at her age.'

'There's a sixteen-year-old round our way who got accepted,' said Dot, 'so I'll keep my fingers crossed for Emily.'

'Thank you. If they don't accept her, I'll look for something else for the pair of us, but if they do accept her, I'll make it a condition that we have to be put on duty together at all times. That at least will make my husband feel a bit better about it.'

'You an' all,' said Dot. 'Being there with Emily is a different prospect to her doing summat on her tod.'

'I knew I could count on you to understand.' Now Cordelia just needed Kenneth to understand as well. 'I've volunteered for something else too.'

'Blimey, there's no stopping you once you get going.'

'I've put my name down for fog-box work.'

'What's that when it's at home?'

'In fog, when signal lights can't be seen, they need people to stop the trains going through red lights by putting detonators on the tracks.'

'I know all about that,' said Dot.

'I know you do. Since I can't volunteer for the marshalling yard, this seemed like the next best thing. I'll be doing something specifically for the railways.'

'Good for you, love,' said Dot.

'Excuse me,' said a new voice and they looked round to see a well-dressed woman of a similar age to themselves. 'I think you know my daughter. The lady behind the counter pointed you out to me.'

'You're Alison's mum,' said Dot. Intuition? Or had she spotted a similarity?

'Janet Lambert.'

'I'm Mrs Dot Green and this is Mrs Cordelia Masters. Can I just say how sorry we both are about what's happened to your Alison?'

Mrs Lambert sank onto a spare chair, her features slackening for a moment as she fought emotion. 'I can't begin to describe how upset her dad and I are. We looked on Paul as one of our family. We would never have believed – well, I don't need to say it, do I? I'm sure you understand.'

'Aye, love, course we do.' Dear Dot, how easily she talked to other people, drawing them in and showing she understood. 'And then there's your Lydia getting wed an' all.'

'That must be hard for Alison,' said Cordelia.

'It's hard for all of us. My husband and I hardly know which way to turn. It seems so cruel to Alison, but how could we say no to Lydia? Supposing we said she could get engaged but not married, and then something happened to Alec. She'd never forgive us – and we wouldn't forgive ourselves. She and Alec deserve their chance. If Paul hadn't ... well, we wouldn't have thought twice about letting Lydia get married.' Mrs Lambert shook her head, her eyes suddenly desperate. 'But it feels like we're punishing Alison.'

'Whereas not to agree to the wedding would punish Lydia for Paul's actions,' said Cordelia.

'I hope this Paul lad knows what he's done,' said Dot, 'though I doubt it.'

'He's probably too busy being madly in love with this new girl.' There was a sharp edge to Mrs Lambert's voice.

'What brings you here?' asked Dot.

Mrs Lambert sighed. 'Today's Tuesday. Lydia gets married on Saturday and we still haven't got a dress. She's desperate to have a proper wedding dress and there simply isn't one to be had. She's had an offer of the loan of a couple, but neither of them suits her. Then I remembered Alison's friend who got married in the summer and I wondered ... I hope you don't think I'm wrong to ask, but ... ' She lifted her shoulders in a shrug. 'I'd do anything to give Lydia the wedding she wants. She's so keen to look like a proper bride, but she's having to face up to the disappointment of very likely getting married in a suit, like so many these days, and she hardly dares breathe a word on the subject in case it upsets Alison.'

Cordelia and Dot exchanged looks. Joan's dress – well, not Joan's, but the one she had borrowed from Margaret's friend. It was still in Joan's possession because the friend didn't want it back.

'I know it's asking a lot,' said Mrs Lambert.

'Especially of Alison,' said Cordelia.

Mrs Lambert nodded. 'I don't want to make things worse for her, but at the same time I have to do the best I can for Lydia.'

'Does Alison know you're speaking to us?' Cordelia asked.

'Lord no, and if the dress isn't available for loan, or if it is but it doesn't suit Lydia, then Alison need never know.' Mrs Lambert looked from Dot to Cordelia and back again. 'There's a part of me that hopes Alison will never know – but I still have to ask, because that's the right thing for Lydia.'

Cordelia recalled Dot's remark about Alison's mother being torn in two. How right she had been.

'Right,' Dot said decisively. 'Here's what we'll do. Joan – she's the girl with the dress – lodges with my daughter-in-law. I'll pop round there this evening and see what's what. If Joan's happy to lend it, and I'm sure she will be, I'll bring it here tomorrow. I'm on a different shift the next few days, starting at midday, so I'll be here in the buffet with or without the dress at half eleven.'

'Thank you,' said Mrs Lambert.

'If it doesn't suit, bring it back on Thursday at the same time.'

'You're most kind,' said Mrs Lambert. 'I know this can't sit easy with you, doing this for Alison's sister when Alison is so hurt.'

'If it's tricky for us,' said Dot, 'that's nowt compared to how it must be for you.'

'It certainly isn't how I envisaged being the mother of the bride. I always thought Alison would be first. We all did.'

'Including Alison, I'm sure,' said Cordelia.

'I hate what Paul has done to my daughter,' said Mrs Lambert. 'If I could take the pain off her and suffer it myself, I would.'

There was a silence as they all pondered Alison's situation.

'I mustn't keep you.' Mrs Lambert picked up her handbag and started to rise, then sat down, placing her bag on her lap. 'I'll tell you something – though I'll deny every word if you pass it on to Alison. You probably think I wish all sorts of bad things on Paul and this new girl, but I don't. I thought I would, but I don't. I hope they have a long and happy life together – because that's the only outcome that could possibly justify the way that young man has broken my daughter's heart.'

CHAPTER SIXTEEN

Alison knew something bad was about to happen when Mum sat beside her on the bed and took her hand.

'I've got something to tell you,' said Mum. 'It's to do with Lydia's wedding.'

Of course it was. Everything was to do with Lydia's wedding now. Aware of her mouth sinking into a sour line, Alison lifted its edges to form the tiniest of smiles – but when Mum quietly told her about the dress, *the* dress, the one belonging to Margaret's friend and which Joan had worn, it was all she could do not to bury her face in her hands and howl the place down.

'I know how hard this is, Alison,' said Mum, 'and my heart aches for you, it really does, but this is Lydia's wedding day we're talking about and ...'

Mum's voice trailed off, as well it might. Alison was consumed by a nasty, childish feeling that everyone was on Lydia's side and no one cared about *her*. It was like that moment when Dot had oh so kindly, yet oh so sensibly advised her to take Joan's engagement on the chin. Was that to be her life from now on? Years of taking other girls' wedding arrangements on the chin? If this was some sort of punishment for being self-satisfied about her long-standing, so-called perfect relationship with Paul, hadn't she suffered enough?

From somewhere, and goodness alone knew where, she dredged up the resolve to be gracious to Lydia and insist that she must try on the dress for Alison to see. After a moment's hesitation, Lydia was delighted to comply and the strange thing was that even though Alison's bones positively vibrated with jealousy, the tears that sprang into her eyes were those of love and pride, a spontaneous acknowledgement of how beautiful her sister looked.

Alison left Mum helping Lydia out of the dress and ran downstairs and out of the back door. She leaned against the wall of the house, slumped over, hands on her knees. Oh, it was too much.

It should have been me.

And it didn't end there, did it? She still had to face her friends – the friends who by rights ought to have told Mum to sling her hook when she asked about the dress. Mum had approached Dot and Cordelia, and Dot had asked Joan. Joan! Alison could maybe see – sort of, just about – that Dot and Cordelia would understand that the mother of the bride wanted her daughter to look beautiful, but what excuse did Joan have? Joan had known Alison and Paul as a couple and had gone out dancing with them since before she'd got together with Bob. Joan ought to be writhing with anguish at the calamity that had befallen Alison, but instead she had meekly handed over the wedding dress and Alison felt betrayed. Even though she knew that Dot, Cordelia and Joan had all acted for the best, even though she herself wanted Lydia to look lovely on her wedding day, she still felt betrayed. She was aware, too, that the dress had been smuggled into the house and that if Lydia hadn't liked it, it would have been spirited away again, with her, Alison, none the wiser. It made her feel she'd been made a fool of.

Oh, it was one wretchedness on top of another, but she had her pride and she made a point of seeking Joan out at the station, standing to one side while Joan followed two middle-aged ladies, pushing their suitcases on her sack trolley. Alison watched as Joan unloaded the trolley at the taxi rank and said goodbye to the travellers.

When Alison nabbed her, Joan looked round, startled, then smiled when she saw who it was.

'I shan't keep you a minute,' said Alison. 'I know you're on duty. I just wanted to tell you that – that the dress is beautiful on Lydia.'

Joan looked flustered. 'Good. I hope you don't mind that … What I mean is, I know this is hard for you.'

Hard? *Hard?* That didn't begin to describe it. Alison forced a smile that felt as if her face might shatter into a thousand pieces. She was sick and tired of others telling her they understood how hard it was for her.

And it was going to be harder still when she had to sit through her sister's wedding.

It should have been me.

It was over. Thank heaven it was over. Alison had spent Lydia's wedding sitting with her head up, locked in position so tightly that her neck now felt sore. All through the ceremony she had blinked to control the tears of humiliation that threatened to spill over, and had sniffed delicately every few moments as she endeavoured to prevent her nose from running. The last thing she needed was for everyone to see her honking into her handkerchief.

Feeling like death warmed up, she sat through the meal, pushing her devilled fish around her plate, then during the speeches, she fixed her gaze resolutely on each speaker while keeping what was intended to be an expression of warm interest on her face.

At last it was time for Lydia and Alec to leave.

'It's time to throw the bouquet, Lyddie,' called one of Lydia's friends.

Oh no, please no. Alison prepared to slink away. Then she heard Lydia's reply.

'I'm giving my flowers to my mum for being such an angel about organising the wedding so quickly.'

Alison almost stumbled as relief took hold of her. For one moment, her gaze and Lydia's met and she saw her sister's love for her. Poor Lydia. It couldn't have been easy for her to get married when her sister was struggling with heartbreak. A fierce hope gripped Alison that she hadn't spoiled the wedding in any way. She didn't think she had. She'd done her best to keep her chin up.

Lydia and Alec weren't going away for their brief honeymoon, but would be spending it in their new flat. The wedding party followed them home and cheered when Alec carried his bride over the threshold.

Then, with hugs and kisses all round, the group dispersed. Alison walked home with Mum and Dad. As the door shut behind them, she saw in their faces how much they wanted to tell her she had coped well today.

'I'm tired,' she said. 'D'you mind if I go up?'

There were just the three of them now, her, Dad and Mum. Lydia was a wife now with a home of her own.

It should have been me.

Alison lay in bed wide awake for a long time. Just her and Mum and Dad. The three of them. The Lamberts. Was this to be her life now – that of the spinster daughter? Would she still be here, taking care of her parents, when they grew old and grey?

She sat up in bed. All at once she knew precisely what she was going to do. There was one thing she could think of that would make her life a little better and she would sort it out tomorrow.

*

Was there a spring in her step as she left the bus terminus and walked along Beech Road in the sunshine on Sunday afternoon? Alison rather thought there was and she almost laughed. Then she remembered that she wasn't supposed to feel positive or light-hearted any more and she clamped down hard on the sensation of brightness. But why? Why turn her back on the possibility of optimism? It was almost as if – well, if she didn't know any better, she would say it was almost as if she was determined to be as unhappy as possible.

That was ridiculous ... wasn't it? Well, if it was, then she should jolly well prove it by allowing herself to revel in this moment of hope. She smiled to herself, and was that the first real smile since Paul had left her? Probably. Her life might be in ruins, but at least she had come up with a way of improving it.

Turning the corner opposite the rec, she walked along until she came to Wilton Close, where she paused before entering the pretty little cul-de-sac. This was going to be her new home. It was what she needed. A new home in the south of Manchester, well away from her old life. She would leave all that behind and come here for a fresh start.

She opened the garden gate and walked up to Mrs Cooper's house. If she remained at home, she would be the spinster daughter, getting older and older, but if – when – she came here, she would be just another young lodger, like Mabel. A girl in digs. A girl with a billet.

Tony Naylor was in the garden, sowing seeds in a line in the soil. Some glass cloches stood on the lawn, ready to be put in place to protect them. They nodded to one another, but Alison didn't stop to talk. She wanted to get her new billet sorted out. Her new billet! For a girl who had lived all her life under her father's roof, and who had expected to move from there into her mother-in-law's upon marriage, the thought of having digs with a landlady was fresh and exciting – daring, even. She felt modern and independent. Even having a wartime job had never made her feel like that.

'Alison, what a surprise,' said Mrs Cooper when she opened the door. 'A nice surprise, of course. Come in.'

She showed Alison into the front room and Alison looked round with new eyes. It was a smart room with William Morris wallpaper and dark blue curtains that hung from a brass curtain pole above the bay window. Her new home!

Mrs Grayson, busy with her knitting, sat in one of the armchairs and Colette was on the sofa. Mabel sat on the hearthrug, leaning on one hand, knees bent and her legs tucked around to the side. Soon it would be Alison sitting informally on the floor. She couldn't wait.

'Look who's come all this way to see us.' Mrs Cooper's voice rang with pleasure. 'Have a seat, chuck.' She guided Alison towards the sofa.

'I didn't know you were coming today,' said Mabel.

'Last-minute decision,' said Alison.

'Well, we're glad to see you,' said Mrs Grayson.

There was a pause and Alison, suddenly alert, looked round at the others.

'You've been talking about my sister's wedding, haven't you?'

'No, not really,' said Mrs Cooper.

'Yes, we have,' Mabel said bluntly. 'We've been gossiping like crazy, but not in a nasty way. We've been saying how vile it is for you. It's a jolly good thing you've come here today, because now we know we don't have to worry that you went into a terrible decline and died in the night.'

'Goodness, Mabel,' murmured Mrs Cooper.

Alison didn't know whether to be reassured or offended or – or what? Then she recognised the kindness beneath the offhand words. Mabel was a good sort and she would enjoy sharing a room with her.

'Thanks for being concerned.' Alison deliberately matched Mabel's breezy tone. It wasn't altogether easy, but once she got going it became easier. 'The wedding went well in all respects, including the bride's sister's behaviour, in case you were wondering. Seriously,' she added, moderating her tone, 'Lydia had a wonderful day and I just wish she and Alec could have longer together before he has to go back.' She saw the glance of approval that passed between Mrs Cooper and Mrs Grayson.

'If you don't mind my saying so,' Colette said quietly, 'I think you've been very generous about your sister's wedding.'

'Hear, hear,' said Mabel.

'Thank you,' Alison murmured.

'And today you needed to get out of the house,' Colette added and Alison looked at her with respect and gratitude. Not so long ago, she hadn't had a lot of time for Colette. Colette was the shy one, the one who was hardly ever there, the one who didn't go to the pictures with them – well, all right, maybe her husband wasn't keen on her having nights out with the girls, but Colette and Tony could have come as a couple when the others went dancing, yet they never did. Cordelia's dance had been the exception. But recently, in her quiet, unobtrusive way, Colette had shown Alison kindness and real understanding and Alison felt she might like them to be proper friends – only it couldn't possibly happen, because how could she ever bear to be close to a girl who was living the life Alison had always dreamed of?

Colette's words provided the perfect opening.

'Yes, I did,' said Alison, 'but I also have a reason for coming here specifically.' She looked at Mrs Cooper and Mrs

Grayson and half laughed, a nervous, breathy sound. 'I wondered if you'd like another lodger.'

A frisson of surprise rippled round the room.

'Are you sure you wish to leave home?' asked Mrs Grayson.

'Positive,' Alison declared stoutly. 'My parents won't like it, but I have to get away, I have to.'

'We understand, dear,' said Mrs Cooper. 'As a matter of fact, it's a subject me and Mrs Grayson have given a lot of thought to recently – oh, I don't mean you, I mean the idea of more lodgers.'

Warmth radiated through Alison. 'So I've come at the right moment.' It was meant to be.

'No time like the present,' said Mrs Grayson.

'Come upstairs and see what you think,' offered Mrs Cooper.

Alison didn't need to go upstairs. She knew what Joan and Mabel's room – soon to be Alison and Mabel's room – looked like. But she politely followed Mrs Cooper upstairs. On the landing, Alison stepped past her, opened the door and walked in, casting her eye over the matching furniture. For sharing, there was a chest of drawers, a dressing table with a triple mirror and a wardrobe with a long mirror inset in one of the doors, while beside each bed was a small cupboard. There was a fireplace, so the room would be toasty warm all winter.

She turned to Mrs Cooper. 'It's perfect. I was thinking about it all last night.'

'Oh, it wouldn't be this room, chuck. We've already made arrangements with Margaret. She's taking Joan's place. But there's the old box room. Now don't let the name put you off. It's not a bad size, considering. A little cramped, I admit, compared to the other rooms, but it's not much smaller than Lizzie's bedroom in my old house. Here we are.'

At the end of the landing, Mrs Cooper opened the door into a poky little room with a ceiling that sloped down to about four feet from the floor. There were two steps down into the room and it had a small window. A narrow bed was pushed into the corner and there was a cupboard and a chest of drawers.

'I know it doesn't look like much now,' said Mrs Cooper, 'but we can soon make it homely and there'll be your own belongings an' all. As you can see, it's been used as a bedroom before. The Morgans used to have a live-in maid and this was her room. What do you think?'

To her own astonishment, Alison burst into tears.

'Oh, sweetheart. Oh, my lass.' Mrs Cooper shepherded her to the bed and sat down with her, pulling Alison into her arms. 'What's brought this on?'

Alison sniffed and dug in her pocket for a hanky. 'I'm sorry. I don't know where that came from. What must you think of me?'

'I'm not quite sure what to think, to be honest.' Mrs Cooper rubbed her work-worn hands up and down Alison's arms.

'It's just that I've been so miserable and so dragged down and – and then I had to behave well at Lydia's wedding, and it was *exhausting*. Imagine having to be brave at a wedding.'

'I know, chuck, I know.'

'Then last night, I imagined living here. I was determined to have a fresh start and make the best of things. Only ... '

'Only you pictured yourself in the big bedroom with Mabel. Of course you did, love. You weren't to know.'

'I'm so sorry. You must think me a dreadful brat, crying because I can't have what I want.'

'Nonsense,' said Mrs Cooper. 'You cried because you're worn out with unhappiness and then you made an effort to improve things, only to find summat you never expected. It's no wonder it tipped you over the edge for a moment. Now listen. You're going to have this box room and we'll make it all snug and cosy for you. What do you bet Mrs Grayson will want to knit a patchwork quilt for you? That's better,' she added as Alison uttered a watery laugh. 'It'll be lovely for her and me, having you moving in as well as Margaret. We specially wanted to invite her because she lives in digs that I can only describe as squalid – and not through any fault of her own, I might add. It's the landlord and the other tenants. So we wanted to fetch her here.'

Now she thought of it, Alison recalled Joan mentioning that Margaret's digs were pretty awful. 'Yes, you have to bring Margaret here. It sounds as if she needs rescuing.'

Mrs Cooper smiled at her. 'So me and Mrs Grayson will have two new lasses to look after. Let's go down and tell everyone.'

As pleased as Colette was that Alison was going to move into Wilton Close, she wished Alison would now clear off and go home. How was Colette ever to have a private word with Mrs Cooper with Alison and Mabel both here?

'Show Colette your new room,' Mrs Cooper said to Alison, and Colette duly followed Alison upstairs.

Alison waved her inside. 'Welcome to my new abode.'

'I think it's charming. You'll be ever so snug.'

'When I'm not banging my head on the ceiling,' said Alison, but she laughed as she spoke.

It struck Colette that Alison was doing her best to deal with her unhappiness. A rush of feeling made Colette speak from the heart. 'I think you're brave to come here.'

'Do you?'

'You're making a fresh start. I admire that. You're in a difficult situation, but you've found a way to remove yourself from it.'

'I'm not doing anything special.'

'Yes, you are. It isn't just having the means to do it, it's having the will. Plenty of people in a bad situation let themselves get stuck there and feel they can't do anything about it, maybe because they're just too unhappy and it's dragged them down.'

'I could understand that.' Alison sounded thoughtful.

Colette waved an arm, indicating the room. 'This is the beginning of your new life, bumped head and all. You're lucky to be coming here. I can't think of anything better than living under Mrs Cooper's roof and being looked after by her and Mrs Grayson.'

It was the literal truth, did Alison but know it. Now that Colette had faced up to the truth about her marriage, she yearned every day to be in the Wilton Close house, which was the only place where she felt safe.

Shortly after they went back downstairs, Mabel stood up.

'If you'll all excuse me, I've arranged to telephone Harry's base.'

Alison got up too. 'I'd better head home and break the news to Mum and Dad.'

'I'll walk with you as far as the terminus,' said Mabel.

As the front door closed behind them, Colette's heartbeat picked up speed. Please let her have the chance to talk privately with dear Mrs Cooper again. Even five minutes would do. She desperately needed the chance to be with the one person who knew, who understood, who cared.

Mrs Cooper looked at the clock, tilting her head as if considering. 'Yes, there's just time before we put the kettle on. Would you help me deliver some leaflets, Colette dear? It won't take long.' She looked at Mrs Grayson. 'Would you care to come an' all – or would you rather stop indoors and get your knitting done? You did say you wanted to get that jumper finished today.'

'I'd better stop here,' Mrs Grayson agreed.

Colette and Mrs Cooper put on their things and Mrs Cooper picked up some leaflets from the hall table.

'Now all we've got to do is get past Tony,' she whispered. She threw open the front door and walked down the path. 'Colette has kindly offered to help me put leaflets through letter boxes.'

Tony stopped clipping the hedge and looked at them. 'Going far?'

'Just up and down a couple of roads. I've already delivered most of them. It'll take no time at all with Colette helping. You're doing a grand job there, chuck. We'll all have a cuppa when me and Colette get back.'

So saying, Mrs Cooper propelled Colette through the gate and, linking arms, bore her as far as the corner.

'There now,' Mrs Cooper said as they left Wilton Close. 'We'll get these delivered, then we'll sit in the rec for a while and have a proper talk.'

Once the leaflets had been posted through the letter boxes, the two of them entered the recreation ground, which was now mostly given over to allotments. A couple of old boys stood examining a row of bushy green potato-plant leaves, using the stems of their pipes to point. The spicy-sweet scent of their tobacco rose into the air.

Mrs Cooper sighed. 'Pipes smell much nicer than cigarettes, don't they? Lizzie's father smoked a pipe.'

'What was he like?'

'Oh, he were a good man. He always saw the funny side, though he could be serious if it was called for. He were never what you'd call a big earner, but he brought every penny home, not like some, coming home via the pub on pay day.'

'It sounds like he was a decent man,' said Colette.

'Well, he suited me and he worshipped our Lizzie. Shall we park ourselves on yon bench?'

There was nobody nearby to listen in. They settled down. Turning sideways on the seat, Mrs Cooper looked at Colette, ducking her head slightly as if expecting someone to leap out from behind one of the little sheds that the gardeners had cobbled together.

'How have you been, love?'

'Fine,' Colette said automatically. No – tell the truth. 'So-so. Nothing's changed at home, if that's what you're asking.'

'Oh, chuck. I never thought I'd hear myself say these words to anybody, but you can't stay with him. If you stop with Tony, you'll end up like his mother and you've told me what she's like, the poor love.'

Colette was shocked. You didn't leave your husband. That was a disgraceful thing to do. That was Colette's immediate, instinctive response, but it was followed by the thud of her heart telling her that it was the only way.

'I can't,' she whispered. 'He'd never let me.'

'I know.' Mrs Cooper sighed. 'But you can't stay, and it's wicked of me to say that, me being a Catholic. We believe marriage is for ever, but, eh, lass, it's all very well having rules, but the men what made them – and it will have been men, believe you me – they never had to live with the likes of your Tony.'

'It isn't just Catholics who believe marriage is for ever,' Colette whispered. 'Everyone does. If a couple separates, it's scandalous and the wife's name is blackened, even if it's not her fault. I – I couldn't face that.'

'I understand, I honestly do,' Mrs Cooper said gently, 'but if you don't leave, you've said it yourself: you'll end up turning into your mother-in-law.'

And then she really would be trapped for ever. 'I know.' A bitter taste invaded Colette's mouth. Self-disgust? 'I'm so weak.'

Mrs Cooper scooted along the bench and sat right up close. 'Weak? Nay, lass, I'm not having that. You're in a bad situation and there isn't a right way to get free of it. I know it's not in your nature to do summat wrong or break the rules, and that's to your credit. It means you're a good person. But ... ' Her voice trailed off.

'Please don't say that rules are there to be broken. That's too simplistic.'

'I would never say that, but I will say that sometimes, just sometimes, you can break a rule and maybe others think you're wrong to do it, but in your heart, you know you've done it for the right reason. Now before you say a word, just listen, because this isn't me saying "Do as I say, not as I do." There's a rule I've broken regular ever since I moved into Wilton Close.'

'Really?' Colette couldn't imagine this lovely, honest, compassionate lady ever doing anything wrong.

'Aye.' Mrs Cooper nodded. 'I'm a Catholic, but I've been in and out of St Clement's, the Protestant church, like a cuckoo in a clock. My priest told me I mustn't do it, and if I did do it, I ought to confess it as a sin every time, but I never have, because ... because it isn't wrong, and nowt that anybody says, including a priest, can tell me it is. What I've done, I've done in good heart. It's to help Mrs Grayson, you see.'

Understanding came to Colette as a feeling of warmth flowing through her. 'You take her to church and instead of leaving her at the door, you escort her inside and sit with her.'

'She's my friend and she relies on me,' Mrs Cooper said simply. 'I don't mean to set myself up as owt special, but I do try to be a good friend, and Mrs Grayson needs an extra bit of looking after … And she's not the only one. You do an' all and I want to help you. We need to think of how we can get you safely away from your Tony.'

CHAPTER SEVENTEEN

'I know you're all going to say it's far too early, this being only the second week of September,' said Dot, looking round the table in the buffet, 'but I've started thinking about Christmas.'

Christmas! Alison rejected the thought. Her first Christmas without Paul. Last Christmas she had hoped for a proposal and when it hadn't been forthcoming she had hidden her disappointment by telling her friends – sitting at that table over there, that very table – that it hadn't been appropriate to propose, not straight after the horror and destruction, the mass casualties and fatalities, of the Christmas Blitz. It had been just one in a long string of occasions when she had anticipated a proposal and had then been forced to hold her head high afterwards when the proposal hadn't happened.

Predictably, Dot's mention of Christmas brought on a few shudders as others remembered last year.

Dot said frankly to Joan, 'It'll be a hard time for you, love, I know.'

Joan had gone rather pale. 'Yes, it will. It'll be Letitia's anniversary – but it will also be my first Christmas with Bob and that's what I'm going to concentrate on.'

'Good for you,' Mabel murmured. She and Joan had grown close when they had shared a room in Mrs Cooper's house. Alison felt a spark of hope. Would living in Wilton Close enable her to form a special bond with Mabel and Margaret? She glanced at Margaret, whose dark hair, released from its work turban and combed out, had spread into pretty waves to a length between her chin and her shoulders. She looked more relaxed than Alison had previously seen her, which must be because Margaret's life was looking up now that she was leaving behind her shoddy bedsit and moving in with Mrs Cooper. Would that sort of change happen to Alison as well?

'I hope you don't mind that I mentioned Christmas,' Dot was saying to Joan.

'Not a bit,' said Joan. 'Actually, you're behind the times, because Bob and I talked about it weeks ago. Bob said – oh, he's such a thoughtful person – he said that it would be better to plan Christmas ridiculously early rather than wait until nearer the time when all the memories would have had a chance to build up.'

There were murmurs of approval.

'What have the two of you decided?' asked Persephone.

'On the Sunday before Christmas, we'll go to church and light a candle for Letitia, then visit her grave with flowers. Bob's family offered to come too, but we want it to be just us. I'll ask Gran if she wants to go with me to the cemetery the day before. Then on the night of the twenty-second into the twenty-third, which was when Letitia was killed, I'm going to work the night shift here. It's either that or lie awake all night thinking, and I'd rather be busy.'

'Letitia would approve of that,' said Alison, making an effort for her friend. 'She was fun, but she was sensible too. She wouldn't want you dwelling on it more than you need to.'

'I know,' agreed Joan.

Cordelia nodded approvingly. 'That sounds perfect, Joan. Making time to honour Letitia's memory will free you – I hope it will free you – to relax and enjoy your first married Christmas.'

'That's what Bob hopes too.' Joan smiled and her face glowed with love for her husband. For one breathless moment, it seemed that Alison's bones might crack with envy, but she didn't truly begrudge her friend the comfort she received from Bob.

Mabel turned to Dot. 'Tell us about your Christmas thoughts, Dot.'

'I want it to be a good Christmas this year, after what happened last year.'

'You'd be hard-pressed to find someone who doesn't agree wholeheartedly with that,' said Cordelia.

'I started off thinking about family and presents and goodies for the children.'

'And your Pammy's electric fairy lights,' Mabel added with a grin.

'Aye, them an' all. But then I got to thinking about last year and I knew I couldn't settle to a good old family Christmas if I didn't show that I'd learned summat from the blitz.'

Everyone drew their chairs ever so slightly closer to the table.

'What do you mean?' Margaret asked.

'I got to thinking about all them hundreds of folk what were bombed out just a couple of days before Christmas. They lost their homes, their belongings, everything, which was terrible – but they still had Christmas dinners, because hundreds of other folk got together and cooked through the night so that all the bombed-out folk could have meat pie and sultana pudding on Christmas Day.'

'Our very own Persephone was among the ranks of cooks,' said Mabel.

'So I've decided I'm going to work in one of them kitchens some nights in December. Christmas Kitchens, they're called,' said Dot, 'but they're not just for providing meals on Christmas Day. They're for the whole of December. I'll tell you straight out that I'm not spending Christmas Day doing it, because I'm spending that with my family, and you can call me selfish or hypocritical if you like, but I know that helping in one of them kitchens one or two nights each week during December will give me an easy heart over Christmas.'

'Good for you,' said Persephone. 'That sounds splendid.'

'And guess who'll be writing an article about it for *Vera's Voice*,' teased Mabel.

'I think it's a wonderful idea to have Christmas Kitchens,' said Margaret. 'Can you let me have the information, please, Dot? I'd like to be involved. My own life has taken a turn for the better and I'd like to feel I was lending a hand to others.'

'Of course, chick,' said Dot. 'There's summat else I'm going to do an' all. Last year, the evening the Christmas Blitz began, me and my family were at a carol concert. We'd just sung "Silent Night" and there was one moment of silence at the end, one moment of perfect peace – and then the Blitz started. I want to go to a carol concert this year – and I want there to be stillness and perfect peace at the end of "Silent Night". That's what I want.'

'Goodness,' murmured Persephone. 'When you raised the subject of Christmas, I thought you were going to talk about mince pies and stirring the pudding and the angel on top of the tree. I didn't realise you were going to go all profound on us.'

Dot laughed. 'Trust me, love, the next time I mention it, it'll be nowt but mince pies and presents.'

'Why don't we all go to a carol concert together?' Cordelia suggested and they all looked at her. 'Now that Alison and Margaret are moving in to Mrs Cooper's, we'll all be living fairly close together. It should be possible to find a carol concert that's reasonably central to us all.'

'I think that's a lovely idea,' said Mabel.

'So do I,' said Joan, 'but please can it be on the evening of the twenty-third or else on Christmas Eve, so it's after Letitia's anniversary?'

'Of course,' Dot agreed at once.

'There's something else we should take into account,' Margaret added, 'or rather someone: Mrs Grayson. Shall I find out if St Clement's is holding a carol service on the twenty-third or -fourth?'

'Absolutely,' said Persephone. 'If they aren't, we'll make special arrangements to take her wherever we go.'

Dot nodded, looking pleased. 'And now we've got the serious stuff sorted out, there'll be no stopping me with my mince pies and fairy lights.'

Cordelia couldn't have been prouder. Emily's interview with the fire people had gone swimmingly in spite of the attitude of the interviewers at the outset being that, at fifteen, she was too young.

'I wish you could have seen her,' Cordelia told Kenneth afterwards. 'She was so poised and unruffled.'

'It's like I've always told you, Emily,' Kenneth smiled at his daughter, 'A bit of well-mannered charm goes a long way. That's what a girl needs: charm.'

'I don't think it was my charm, Daddy. It was the fire precautions I took at Auntie Flora's house that impressed them.'

'Emily cleared the junk out of the attic,' said Cordelia.

'We've all had to do that,' said Kenneth.

'Ah, but how many people arrange to have two inches of sand spread across the attic floorboards?'

Kenneth raised his eyebrows as he asked Emily, 'You arranged that for Auntie Flora?'

His gaze met Cordelia's and she knew they were thinking the same thing: their little girl was growing up.

What would life be like when she was properly grown-up and had left home to get married? Goodness, where had that thought sprung from? But it was a fact that being Emily's mother made Cordelia's marriage worthwhile. Would that feeling live on when Emily no longer lived under her father's roof?

Cordelia found she wasn't the only one whose thoughts wandered after Emily was accepted as a fire-watcher. It happened to Kenneth too, the difference being that while Cordelia's thoughts had to remain locked away deep inside, Kenneth was free to express his and Cordelia rather thought he welcomed the opportunity to do so.

That night in bed, they finished reading, inserted their bookmarks and placed their books on their bedside cabinets before leaning towards one another for a goodnight peck. Cordelia then leaned away from Kenneth to switch off her bedside lamp, only to realise that Kenneth's lamp was still on.

He frowned at the ceiling.

'What is it?' Cordelia asked.

'Emily.'

'Being a fire-watcher,' said Cordelia. It wasn't a question. She knew exactly how Kenneth felt. Where had the years gone?

'Are you quite sure they agreed that the two of you will always be on duty together?'

Cordelia smiled. 'Positive. I'd never have consented otherwise. Even if I had, Emily would have known that you wouldn't.'

Kenneth nodded, but he didn't turn out the light. He was still frowning. 'Perhaps now that you've got this night-time commitment, you won't go to the buffet after work so much.'

'You make it sound as if I'm there every night of the week.' One thing she had learned through being married to a solicitor was to face disagreements calmly and politely. She had heard too many stories from Kenneth about how he had manipulated his client's opponent into betraying anger, which was always the beginning of the end for the opponent.

'Having assumed this new responsibility,' said Kenneth, 'it behoves you to spend as much time as you can in the home. Don't forget your duty as a wife and mother.'

'I never forget that.'

'Now is your opportunity to demonstrate that you haven't. Less buffet, more home. And less of the buffet friends, if you don't mind.'

Cordelia's heart delivered a clout that reverberated through her, but her voice was steady as she said, 'As a matter of fact, I do mind.'

'That's the trouble with the war. It's given you a skewed idea of friendships and social contacts,' said Kenneth. 'Before the war, you'd never have looked twice at the likes of Mrs Green – well, you might have if you'd interviewed her to scrub our floors, but that's as far as it would have gone. You can't deny it.'

'I've no intention of denying it. In fact, Mrs Green would be the first to agree with you.'

'Ah, so she does know her place after all, does she? Well, that makes it worse.'

'Makes what worse?'

'The way she hangs on to your coat-tails and takes advantage. You know she does. How else did I end up representing her at that disciplinary meeting?'

'You did that because I asked you to.'

'And who asked you to ask me?'

'Nobody. It was my choice. I think highly of Mrs Green and I wanted to help her.'

'You wished to help a married woman who had been publicly accused of chasing after a male colleague.'

'You're deliberately making it sound sordid. Mrs Green did nothing wrong,' said Cordelia. 'Why are we discussing this anyway? It took place months ago.'

'Indeed it did and it should have given you pause in your friendship with Mrs Green. I hoped at the time it would make you step back from the intimacy. More recently, I hoped that having our daughter at home would make you drop the woman, but once again I was disappointed. That came as a surprise, I admit. I would have expected you to have a greater regard for Emily, not to mention the question of your own self-esteem, than to let your daughter witness you consorting with that woman.'

'Don't call her "that woman". It's demeaning.'

'QED. If those are the only words you can say in her defence, it shows the rightness of my argument. Now we have reached another turning point – Emily becoming a fire-watcher. I cannot begin to express how much trust I am placing in you when you take my daughter out into the night to do that job. I'm not alone in trusting you. Emily does too, whether she realises it or not. It is important – no, it is essential that she has absolute faith in you when the two of you are on duty together.'

'You shouldn't need this assurance, Kenneth,' Cordelia said through gritted teeth, 'but I assure you that I will not simply be fire-watching. I'll be Emily-watching too, every single moment.'

'I'm not the one who requires the assurance,' Kenneth replied. 'It is Emily who needs it, even if she doesn't know it. The reason she is a confident, sunny girl is because we as her parents provided her with a feeling of safety and security. She needs that from you now more than ever. That means she can have no reservations about you.'

'And Mrs Green is a source of reservation,' Cordelia said softly, though her heart felt as if it might crack open.

'Good – you agree. I'm glad we had this talk, Cordelia.'

Kenneth leaned over and switched off his lamp.

'Miss Lambert, before you return to your desk, may I have a word with you?'

Alison looked round. It was Miss Emery, the assistant welfare supervisor for women and girls of all grades, which was one heck of a job title. As always, Miss Emery was beautifully turned out, her hair delicately waved and scooped clear of her discreetly made-up face. Her jacket and matching skirt were linen. On anybody else the linen would have been creased by this time of day, on her it was still pristine. Nail varnish and a short string of graduated pearls with matching earrings completed the look. Alison didn't see her all that often, partly because Miss Emery spent a certain amount of time travelling around the north and also because, when she was here in Hunts Bank, their paths seldom crossed. But whenever Alison did see her, she wanted to tell her to ditch the pearls and wear something less formal, less ... ageing.

When Alison stopped, the others from her office streamed around her as they returned to work following their dinner break. Miss Emery waited until they had all disappeared before she said anything else.

'I'd like you to come to my office at three o'clock, if that's convenient. I've already got permission for you to do so.'

Intrigued, Alison nodded. 'I'll be there.'

'Good.' Miss Emery smiled briefly, a professional smile rather than a friendly one, and walked away, leaving Alison looking after her before she hurried back to her desk.

Alison kept one eye on the clock as she worked. What was this about? She wished Miss Emery had given her a clue. At last it was time for her appointment. Receiving a nod of permission from Mrs Ford, Alison made her way to Miss Emery's office – though 'office' was a generous word for it. It contained a swivel chair that could be angled to face either the desk or a table with a typewriter, and a cupboard stood against the far wall. Even though she had never set foot inside it, Alison knew the exact size and layout of the office for the simple reason that it wasn't a proper room with four walls, but a large alcove with three, and anyone who walked past could see – and hear – exactly what was going on.

Miss Emery was at the cupboard at the back. It felt awkward not having a door, even an open one, to knock on. Miss Emery turned round and Alison felt silly for not having announced herself.

'Thank you for coming.' Miss Emery locked the cupboard and pocketed the key. 'I've arranged for us to meet elsewhere, so we can talk privately.' She employed a wry tone. Genuine wryness – or a professional way of hiding her annoyance at having her office in public view?

Miss Emery led the way to the office she had arranged to borrow, shutting the door behind them.

'Have a seat,' she said. 'I have something important to ask you. Forgive my bluntness, but I understand you have been let down by your young man.'

Shock clobbered Alison. She was too astonished to feel hurt.

'I can see from your face that I am correct. My reason for asking is that I know it's early days for you at present, but I wonder if you've started to consider your future.'

Alison gawped at her, eyes wide open. What the heck was this about?

'I apologise if I'm causing distress,' said Miss Emery, 'but I have a proposition to put to you and I judged it better to tell you sooner rather than later.' She paused and there was sympathy in her voice as she asked, 'Would you like a few minutes to collect yourself?'

The power of speech returned. 'No, thank you. What proposition?'

'Miss Lambert, while I can't claim to know you closely, I saw something in you when you first came to work here, but you were, or appeared to be, on the verge of getting engaged. According to the supervisors in Accounts, while your work was of a high standard, you seemed to be simply marking time until you eventually left to start a family.'

Alison gulped. She might never have actually uttered those words in the office, but anyone who had ever met her knew exactly where her ambitions lay – or where they had lain. But not any more. Her happy dreams had been wiped out.

And what did Miss Emery mean about having seen something in her?

'I imagine you're aware,' Miss Emery continued, 'of the concern felt by some of the male workers about the way that women have been placed in railway jobs.'

'Oh yes. "Concern" being a polite word for resentment and anger.'

'In some cases, yes. Why do you suppose the men feel like that?'

'Well … before the war, it could take a man years to work himself up to a certain position and now women are being trained to take on those roles in a matter of weeks.' It was no good. Alison couldn't keep her mouth shut. 'But that doesn't alter the fact that there's a war on and it's unreasonable to be vexed about women doing their bit. The railways need us.'

'As the war continues,' said Miss Emery, 'we'll need more and more women, the most experienced and capable of whom will find themselves being promoted through the ranks. This is why I wanted to see you today. You are just such a capable girl, Miss Lambert, and I'd like to see you in a more responsible position – but not if you're going to cruise along the way you've cruised along in Accounts.'

Alison stiffened. 'So you think that now I'm not getting married, I might as well be a career woman.'

Miss Emery remained calm and polite. 'I think you have a decision to make. You've suffered a deep disappointment and must feel as if you've been cast adrift.'

Cast adrift: that was precisely how she felt. The shock, the fear … the long nights of tears and regrets. Hardly daring to think because the life ahead of her seemed utterly bleak.

'I would like to offer you an opportunity,' said Miss Emery, 'assuming that you're prepared to focus on your work considerably more than you have heretofore. I'd like to prepare you for a responsible role – not in the offices, but on the railway itself. To do this, I'd arrange for you to gain a variety of knowledge and experience, which will not only help to prepare you personally for what follows, but will also make it appear to other people that you are suitable for a post higher up. What do you think?'

To her surprise, Alison was to start in her new role at once. She had assumed she would finish the week in Accounts, move into Wilton Close at the weekend and begin her new job the following Monday. But no, Miss Emery wanted her to start the very next morning.

'No sense in letting the grass grow under our feet,' she declared. Then she looked shrewdly at Alison and added, 'There are good reasons not to let the grass grow. Not everyone is best pleased with the idea of your doing this, but it'll be harder for them to raise objections if you're already doing it.'

The thought of 'not everyone' made Alison feel uncomfortable, but she felt a certain defiance too. She'd show them.

'This training I'm to have,' she said, 'is it your idea?'

'It is,' said Miss Emery, 'and there's a lot riding on it. If you make a success of it, you'll be opening the door to other girls.'

'I won't let you down,' Alison promised.

She couldn't wait to tell her friends and was delighted they were meeting in the buffet that evening. It made a change to be eager to go after the reluctance and the last-minute shall-I, shan't-I that she'd gone through every time since Paul had left her.

'How exciting,' said Persephone when Alison explained what had happened. 'Congrats.'

'Does this mean you'll do a stint as a station porter and another as a ticket collector, and so on?' asked Mabel.

'I think there'll be a certain amount of that,' said Alison, 'but not yet. Miss Emery is arranging for me to get out and about, doing what she calls information gathering. She says that's important, just to make the point that I'm receiving special training.'

'That settles it,' said Dot. 'Who can come here tomorrow to hear all about Alison's first day?'

'That suits me,' said Mabel. 'How about you, Margaret?' She turned to Alison with a smile. 'Soon you'll be able to tell Margaret and me everything at home, but for now we'll settle for hearing it here.'

Alison went home that evening pleased with the fuss that had been made of her in the buffet, but once she was there, the news of her job received a mixed reaction.

'I thought you'd be glad,' said Alison. 'I'll be doing something different that sounds interesting. I've been chosen specially.'

'And we're proud of you for that,' said Dad. He looked encouragingly at Mum.

'Mum?' Alison prompted.

'I'm sure it's a good thing,' said Mum, 'but you can't expect me to jump up and down with glee when I'm still reeling from the shock of you wanting to leave home.'

Alison smothered a sigh. 'I explained that. I need to get away. Everyone here – everyone, the neighbours, the shop-keepers – they all know about me and Paul. Everyone expected us to get married. I can't stay here.'

'But with Lydia gone, I could give you all my attention. I know how hurt you are. I want to look after you.'

'You can't blame the girl for wanting to get away,' said Dad.

'I suppose not.' Mum sounded desolate and Alison felt a complete heel.

She stood up. 'I'll go and get changed.' She hadn't even waited to change out of her smart work clothes before she shared her news – news that seemed to have gone down like a lead balloon.

As she was shutting the parlour door behind her, she heard Mum say, 'Oh, John, I feel like we've lost her,' and she almost rushed back inside with a promise to stay after all. But she didn't. She mustn't. She needed to get away. It would be good for her.

Just like this new job would be good for her. Something different. A challenge. It would give her something new to think about instead of endlessly going over and over every aspect of her relationship with Paul and the bleakness of life without him. Yes, this job would do her good.

Oh, but what a thing to set her sights on after a lifetime of looking forward to getting married.

CHAPTER EIGHTEEN

Colette placed the mock pork chops on the table. Lots of food was 'mock' these days. The so-called chops were made of sausage meat mixed with breadcrumbs and mashed potato and shaped to look like the real thing, though Colette didn't feel able to award herself many marks out of ten for appearance.

'What's this?' asked Tony. It was his pleasant voice. As recently as a month ago, she would have responded warmly, grateful for the genial note, but not any more. She had stopped being grateful.

'Mock pork chops.'

Tony tasted his. 'Well, I can tell it's not the real thing.'

A joke? Was she supposed to laugh? Or criticism? Was she a failure as a cook? She couldn't tell, but she had to respond. If she didn't, it might seem that she hadn't been listening and Tony wouldn't like that. When Tony didn't like something – anything, even things that were nothing to do with her – Colette always ended up feeling two inches tall.

When in doubt, apologise.

'I'm sorry. I know it's not as good as a real chop.'

'That's not your fault,' said Tony. 'It's rather good, actually. What have you put in it?'

'Salt and pepper. A dash of Worcestershire sauce.' Tony liked Worcestershire sauce. 'Alison's got a new job.'

'She's left the railways?'

'No,' Colette answered at once. If Tony thought that, he'd want her to leave too. 'Still with LMS, but she's not a clerk now.'

'What's she doing?'

'It isn't a job as such, not yet. It's more that she'll be gaining a variety of experience.'

'She's the one who got ditched by her boyfriend, isn't she? She probably thinks this will give her the chance to meet someone else.'

'I'm sure she doesn't think any such thing.' Colette spoke mildly, though indignation coursed through her veins, warming her skin. 'It's to stand her in good stead.'

'In good stead for what?'

'I don't know exactly. It's to show that she's capable. Maybe she'll end up as a guard on a train.'

'Well, I don't care for the sound of it,' said Tony. 'It's a good thing – what was his name?' As if he didn't remember!

'Paul.'

'I'm not surprised he dumped her, if this is what she's made of. Not very wifely.'

Colette wanted to object to each and every part of this, but she didn't say a word. So many times she had wanted to speak up, speak out, but she hadn't. And every time she didn't, she felt diminished. Was she going to end up being diminished bit by bit until there was nothing left of her but a wisp of obedience?

'What's she been up to so far?' asked Tony. He might have been asking about Jimmy Green's latest scrape.

Colette couldn't suppress the fascination she had felt in the buffet earlier on when Alison had talked about it. 'She was taken to see a fire-fighting train. They're specially adapted to carry water, and people live on them all day and all night, usually men, I suppose, but women too. The trains are kept outside the most important towns and cities, ready for air raids.'

'Interesting.'

'Yes,' breathed Colette.

'No, I mean you sound interested in it.'

'Well … ' What was wrong with that? 'Yes.'

'But not too interested, I hope.' Tony smiled. A real smile or a pretend one, a dangerous one? 'I hope Alison hasn't infected you with her unwifely ideas.'

On Saturday afternoon, Cordelia walked to Wilton Close. She hadn't been for a while and she felt guilty about it, the same way she felt guilty in Dot's company when she thought of Emily's opinion of that good lady. Added to this now was Kenneth's assessment of Dot. Although he had never approved of Cordelia's friendship with her, it was the first time he had been so outspoken, and Cordelia, deeply shocked by his ruthless opinion, wasn't sure she would be able to look Dot in the eye again.

She didn't just feel guilty; she was ashamed too. She had avoided Wilton Close because Emily didn't want to go there. Even if she could have explained away her daughter's absence a couple of times, it would gradually have become obvious that Emily had chosen not to visit. Today, when Cordelia had left the house she had informed Kenneth and Emily that she was simply popping round to Wilton Close to perform the monthly check of the property for Mr Morgan. She had employed a breezy tone of voice, but inside she had cringed. Since when had she required a reason to visit Mrs Cooper? It was like being under scrutiny the whole time, with her husband and daughter watching her every move, ready to haul her back from the brink if she looked like letting them down.

At the house, Mrs Cooper welcomed her as warmly as ever, which had the unexpected effect of making Cordelia want to throw her arms around her and hug her, though naturally she did no such thing.

'I'm here to do the check,' she said.

'Help yourself. Would you care for a cuppa now or afterwards?'

'Afterwards, please.'

'You're a creature of habit, Mrs Masters. It's always work first and pleasure second. Mrs Green is here and the girls are out, so it'll be a meeting of the mothers of the bride. Won't that be nice?'

When Cordelia had first known Mrs Cooper, she had thought her a simple soul, but now she valued that simplicity, seeing it as a kind of wisdom. Since losing her beloved only child, Mrs Cooper had looked for pleasure in small things. That was how she got by and made the best of her life. It was something to be admired. Mrs Cooper was neither educated nor cultured, but there was a fundamental goodness in her, a willingness to see the best in others, that few possessed.

Cordelia made her way round the house, smiling as she noticed evidence of the additional occupation. What did Alison's parents think of her leaving home? Cordelia remembered how empty her own house had felt when Emily first went to boarding school – but how much worse would it have been if Emily had actually chosen to go?

Downstairs, she paused outside the front room, consciously setting aside her misgivings and her guilt before opening the door and joining the other three. Dot gave her the usual warm smile and Cordelia's heart wobbled. Surely there was nothing amiss, no harm to Emily, in her friendship with Dot.

'It's the middle of September on Monday,' said Dot. 'I don't know where the year's gone.'

'You're about to discuss Christmas,' Cordelia predicted.

Dot chuckled. 'You know me so well. I've been thinking about what to get my lads. I sent them each a little box with several things in it last year: a pack of cards, a shaving stick, soap and a face flannel, and a Ronson lighter.'

'It might not seem imaginative,' said Mrs Grayson, 'but they might welcome the same again this year.'

'I know they still need the same sort of things,' said Dot, 'but I don't want to go down in family history as the mam who sent exactly the same gifts every Christmas.'

'I know summat you could do,' said Mrs Cooper. 'I read it in a magazine last Christmas, if not the Christmas before. Save each of them a mince pie and a slice of cake from the table on Christmas Day, and a joke from a cracker if you can get crackers this year, and post them straight after Christmas to show them you were thinking of them on Christmas Day.'

'The post offices are going to be open this Boxing Day,' said Cordelia.

Dot looked thoughtful. 'I might just do that.'

'Have you thought about presents yet?' Mrs Grayson asked Cordelia.

'Last year we gave war bonds. My husband said it was the patriotic thing to do. We don't normally think about Christmas this early, but he wants me to order books about the history of Russia from the bookshop.'

'The history of Russia?' Mrs Cooper repeated.

'Now that we're on the same side, he thinks we ought to know more about them.'

'Crikey,' said Dot.

All at once, Cordelia was infected by light-heartedness. 'I quite agree. It's an awful present.' She made a show of rolling her eyes and was delighted to make her friends laugh. 'I think I'll pay for subscriptions to the W.H. Smith library. I'm sure those would be far more welcome.'

'You're right about that, love,' chuckled Dot.

'While we're on the subject of Christmas,' said Mrs Grayson, 'Margaret asked me to tell you that the carol concert at St Clement's will be on Christmas Eve. She said it was your idea, Mrs Masters, that we should all go together.'

'The original idea was mine, yes,' said Cordelia, 'but it was Margaret who reminded us that we should go to St Clement's if possible, because that would be easiest for you.'

'She's a good girl, very thoughtful,' said Mrs Cooper.

'Is she settling in?' asked Dot.

'Yes,' said Mrs Grayson, sounding pleased. 'Between ourselves, I think she's grateful to live in a proper home again.'

'And Alison moves in this weekend, doesn't she?' asked Cordelia.

'It's a different set of circumstances for her, of course,' said Mrs Cooper. 'It'll take her a while to find her feet – I'm talking in general, not about living here.'

'It's nice for Mabel after being the only one for a while,' said Mrs Grayson.

Cordelia was startled by a sudden mental image of her own house full of girls. Mabel had stayed with her and Kenneth for a short time after Mrs Grayson had been forced to hand back her home to Mr Grayson and Floozy. What if Mabel had stayed on and maybe Margaret or Alison had moved in as well? But it was only a mad thought. Kenneth had been a gracious host to Mabel, but now, with Emily at home, he wouldn't have wanted lodgers.

'I hear you and Emily are going to be fire-watchers,' said Mrs Cooper. 'When do you start?'

'Tonight, and then we're on again on Tuesday night. We've done our training and learned all about stirrup pumps and ways of smothering incendiaries.'

'Let's hope you never have to put it into practice for real,' said Mrs Grayson. 'The raids have tailed off and let's hope it stays that way. Touch wood,' she added, touching her temple.

'Just take care of yourselves, that's all,' Dot urged. Was she thinking of what had befallen Mr Green when he had attempted to smother an incendiary with a dustbin lid? A chilly feeling started at the nape of Cordelia's neck and trickled all the way down her spine. As patriotic individuals, she and Emily were determined to do their bit, but as a mother, it went against her every instinct to see her daughter potentially in danger. She looked at Dot with new understanding. It must have torn Dot's heart in half when she saw Archie and Harry go off to war. At least Cordelia would have Emily by her side. That was something for which to be thankful.

Cordelia was thankful all over again when their first night passed without incident – well, without the siren going off. There was an incident, for want of a better word, of a personal and emotional nature. She and Emily had been sitting on the roof of Oswald Road School, wrapped up against the night chill. Emily had made fun of Cordelia earlier on when she had prepared a bag with biscuits, a flask and extra scarves, but well before their duty was half over, Emily had seen the value of being prepared.

'We'd have starved and frozen if it had been left to me,' she said cheerfully.

'We were warned in training that keeping warm is part of the job,' Cordelia said mildly.

'Three cheers for mothers. That's all I can say.'

And somehow or other – and afterwards Cordelia couldn't remember how – that offhand remark led to talking about how Cordelia had been one of Joan's mothers of the bride back in June.

'It was an honour to be asked,' said Cordelia, 'and I loved every moment. All four of us did.'

There was a silence before Emily said, 'I'm not sure I like you being some other girl's mother of the bride. It's as if, because I was away at school, you adopted someone else.'

Cordelia turned to Emily, shocked. The thought she'd briefly entertained earlier that day returned to her: a house filled with girls. 'Emily! I had no idea you felt that way. Of course I wasn't looking for a substitute daughter. That's plain silly.'

'I can't help my feelings,' said Emily, 'and it doesn't help to be told that they're silly.'

Cordelia proceeded with caution. 'Darling, you're my one and only child and more precious to me than life itself. Please try to understand. Joan's an orphan. Her parents died when she was a baby.'

'I know that and I know what a meanie I am. I wish I'd never said anything.'

'I'm glad you did,' said Cordelia, 'because it gives me the chance to say that your wedding day, when it comes, will be one of the most special days, if not *the* most special day, of my entire life.'

'Even more so than your own wedding?'

'Oh yes – because it will be yours. I will be the proudest mother of the bride ever. What I did for Joan came from friendship and compassion and I'm glad I helped make her day special, but what I did for her is nothing compared to what I want to do for you.'

Was this what Kenneth had meant? He had said Emily needed guidance and support from her now more than ever, and part of that was that Emily must feel no reservations whatsoever about Cordelia. Kenneth had been talking about Dot, but now Emily herself had expressed a reservation about Cordelia's friendship with Joan. Cordelia felt unsettled. She had more or less talked herself into an acceptance of Emily's dislike of Dot and Mrs Cooper by telling herself that Emily simply needed to grow up a bit and get to know them. Truthfully, though, Emily was never going to do that because she had no desire to visit Wilton Close.

Then there was Emily's opinion of Cordelia's younger friends and her belief, delivered in such a breathtakingly offhand manner, that they regarded Cordelia as a source of free legal advice, should they ever need it. That, Cordelia had put down to Emily's youth. To her, at fifteen, anyone over thirty had one foot in the grave and it was no wonder she failed to grasp that true friendships could exist between people from different age groups.

But now, Emily's response to Cordelia having acted as mother of the bride to Joan made her examine Emily's reactions to all her railways chums in a new way. Could Kenneth be right? In these dark times, was it her duty as a mother not to challenge Emily with new ideas of social fluidity, but to keep to the old ways, the class-conscious ways that Emily took for granted, because they were all she had ever known? That was what Kenneth believed.

Was he right?

Oh, how Colette wished that Tony was the man – the husband – that everybody else believed him to be. She stood gazing out of Mrs Cooper's front-room window on Sunday afternoon, watching Tony dividing the irises. Dividing the irises! What could be more normal than that? He had done a spot of bartering with the people next door. A clump of the Morgans' irises in exchange for a small pot of spring bulbs.

'That way, both gardens will benefit,' he had told Mrs Cooper and the lady next door.

It was true. With so much of every garden having been given over to growing vegetables and salad, the little bits of flower beds that remained were extra special. And yet, at the same time, what Tony had said was a socking great lie. Colette knew it was, because everything that came out of his mouth was a lie. Everything that made him sound ordinary and generous and kind was a lie, because he wasn't like that at all.

No one knows what goes on behind closed doors.

A figure appeared beside Colette in the bay window and thin fingers gave hers a gentle squeeze. Colette squeezed back, but didn't look round. They stood there like that, her and Mrs Cooper. No one outside, glancing in through the window, would have any notion they were holding hands. Not Tony, not the lady next door, not Mrs Grayson. It wasn't just plants that were being exchanged. Recipes were too.

'Have you thought any further about things?' Mrs Cooper asked quietly.

'I hardly think of anything else. I'm scared I'll say something out loud by mistake.'

'It must be a great strain on you,' said Mrs Cooper.

'It's been that way for years,' said Colette. 'It's just that I never realised it before, never allowed myself to see it.' Her fingers clung tighter to Mrs Cooper's. It had to be her fingers that did the squeezing, because if they didn't, it might be her eyes that squeezed tight shut, and if Tony should look round at that moment … 'I've got to get away. I can't live like this. But how? Tony would never let me.'

'It would have to be without his permission, love. I think we both know that.'

Colette let out a huge sigh and her body sagged in despair before she jerked it upright again lest Tony turn around.

'Come away from the window,' said Mrs Cooper. 'Let's sit down and talk, eh?'

She steered Colette towards the sofa, checking that the door was closed before joining her.

'It's impossible,' Colette said, her voice husky with desperation. She pulled herself up straight. 'I'm so sorry. I don't mean to make a fuss, but ever since I faced up to the truth, it's got harder and harder to bear. I just don't know what to do. I wake up every morning in a state of dread. I don't know how much longer I can stand it.'

'Eh, now.' Mrs Cooper spoke sharply, which was unlike her. 'You're not thinking of doing owt daft, are you?'

'What? You mean ... ?'

'I mean,' came the blunt reply, 'I hope you're not thinking of sticking your head in the gas oven.'

'No, of course not.'

'Good, because that's never the answer.' Mrs Cooper's gaze shifted slightly. Instead of looking at Colette, she looked past her and a frown cut into her brow.

'What is it?' Colette asked.

'What?' Mrs Cooper's chin gave a little jerk. She looked at Colette, then immediately looked away again. 'I'm not sure. Maybe nowt. Summat that needs thinking about, anyroad. You leave me to mull it over and we'll see if anything comes of it.'

CHAPTER NINETEEN

On Monday, Colette was sent for by Miss Emery. She went to the assistant welfare supervisor's office – if you could call it an office. She wondered whether it made Miss Emery feel the same way she felt when she was at home with Tony – always aware, always wary of what she said and how she behaved.

Miss Emery greeted her with a smile. She looked smart and well groomed, as always. Colette admired her for that. It was impossible to imagine the composed Miss Emery being ground down by someone else's personality.

'Good morning, Mrs Naylor. Thank you for coming. I've arranged for us to have the use of another office for half an hour, so we can speak privately.'

Colette accompanied her along the corridor to a small office occupied by a middle-aged lady with salt-and-pepper hair who sat at a desk that was placed at right angles to the closed door of an inner office.

'Good morning, Miss Emery.' The secretary gave Colette a nod at the same time. 'Please go through. Mr Ridley won't be back before eleven.'

'Thank you, Mrs Cartwright. We'll be long gone by then.'

Miss Emery waved Colette into the seat in front of Mr Ridley's desk, then picked up a chair that stood by the wall and set it down in front of the desk, facing Colette. Colette responded by turning her own chair.

'I must make it clear,' said Miss Emery, 'that in spite of this informal seating arrangement, this is an official interview, but I want you to feel comfortable and able to ask whatever questions you need to.'

Official but comfortable? Was there any such thing? And why 'official'? Had she done something wrong?

'I've brought you here,' said Miss Emery, 'to inform you that you are to leave Accounts and move into a new position.'

'Like Alison – Miss Lambert?' A flash of excitement was followed at once by fear.

'Not like Miss Lambert. Something different. Miss Lambert is receiving general training. You will have a specific role.'

'That's a relief – not being trained up for responsibility, I mean, like Miss Lambert.' The moment the words were uttered, Colette wanted to bite off her tongue. Yes, she was quiet and shy, but that didn't mean she was incapable. Any lack of capability had been drummed into her by five years of treading on eggshells under her own roof. *No one knows what goes on behind closed doors.*

'I'll take that remark to mean that you don't see yourself being in charge of other people,' said Miss Emery. 'The job you'll be doing won't require that of you. In fact, in the main you'll be working on your own. You'll be given instructions as to what to do, then you'll be left to get on with it.'

Colette found herself sitting slightly forward and realised she was intrigued. Yes, she had felt scared at the prospect of a new job, but before the fear, there had been that brief moment of excitement.

'Broadly speaking, you'll make train journeys dressed as a civilian and behave like an ordinary passenger. Your job will be to keep your eyes open for petty crime, though please understand, you won't be expected to tackle any wrongdoers yourself. Sometimes you might be asked to watch a particular person and on occasion that person might be a member of staff. How would you cope with that?'

Colette's mind went blank, but she was determined not to say something foolish twice in a row. 'If I were to observe a railway person, it would have to be because there were suspicions about them and it was important to gather information about what was happening. Equally,' she added, lifting her chin, 'it could be that the suspicions were mistaken, in which case it would be important to establish the person's innocence.'

Miss Emery nodded and there was real warmth in her smile. 'Well done. That's an excellent answer and it shows why you are the right person for this post. Something you must remember is that you cannot tell anyone the true nature of your job. Say that you are chaperoning passengers who aren't able to travel alone. You will actually be doing that from time to time, so it won't be an outright lie.'

A job she had to keep secret? That sounded serious and not at all what she would like or be any good at. Or did she feel like that because of being ground down by Tony? Tony. He wouldn't like this.

'I – I ... My husband won't want me travelling about.'

Miss Emery seemed to think for a moment, then she said quietly, 'I'm not asking you to consider this position. I am informing you that you have been selected. No one can pick and choose their war work – and husbands can't pick and choose for their wives.'

Colette swallowed. Tony couldn't object – well, he could and no doubt would object, but he couldn't do anything to change it. He might take it out on her at home, but ... she would have a taste of freedom each day at work.

'There's one final thing,' said Miss Emery. 'You might be asked to assist a woman or a girl who has been upset or hurt by a man, if you follow my meaning.'

Hurt by a man? Oh, she knew all about that.

*

By the time Colette reached home that evening, she was a bag of nerves. How was she to tell Tony about her new job? She had met up with Dot, Mabel and Margaret in the buffet before coming home, but she hadn't breathed a word about seeing Miss Emery. She had wanted to. If her friends had known about her supposed new role, that would have made it feel more definite, but if she had told them, Tony would then be displeased not to have been the first to know and she couldn't risk that. She needed him to accept this. It was all very well Miss Emery stating that he didn't have a say in the matter, but Miss Emery didn't have to live with him.

Oh, what a coward she was. Sometimes Colette hated herself. You were supposed to stand up to bullies, weren't you? That was what everybody said. Stand up to the bully and he'll back down because he's a coward at heart. They were easy words to say and Colette had come to the conclusion that they were said by confident people who would never be bullied in the first place. How were you supposed to stand up to someone who was cleverer than you and who only had to speak to you in a certain way, look at you in a certain way, to make you feel stupid and inferior? How were you meant to stand up to someone who hurt you in invisible ways? Someone who muddied the waters by speaking kindly and saying it was for your own good?

Gratitude sent warmth tingling through her at the thought that dear Mrs Cooper had understood and believed her. Plenty of people wouldn't.

No one knows what goes on behind closed doors.

Yesterday she had made enough fish and leek pudding to last for two days. She had served it with carrots and boiled potatoes and today it was to be with beetroot and mash. Sometimes when they had the same thing two days

217

running, Tony praised her for her housewifely skills, but other times he didn't utter a word, his uncomplaining silence making her feel like the most hopeless wife in the world. How could she offer him the same food as yesterday and then say she had been given a new job? But she had nothing else to give him. Her hands went clammy. Wait – what if she spread the mashed potato over the top of the pudding and called it fish pie? If she sprinkled a little bit of precious cheddar over the mash for the last few minutes in the oven, that would give it a golden sheen as well as additional taste. Better still, she could put the cheese only on Tony's portion so he got the full benefit. It was the best she could do.

The hastily cobbled-together fish pie was a success.

'As good as anything pre-war,' said Tony. 'What a lucky fellow I am to have married such a clever little cook.'

'Thank you,' Colette murmured. It didn't do to fail to thank Tony for a compliment. She braced herself. There would never be a better moment than this. 'Actually, I've got some news.'

'Oh yes?'

Tony looked up so quickly that for a moment she thought he had read her mind and would know that the chaperone job was a sham.

'Miss Emery sent for me today. Do you remember her? The lady who looked after the new recruits on our first morning.'

'That female – yes.'

'It's good news, Tony. I hope you'll be pleased.' Was her voice too bright? 'I've been given a new job.'

'You won't be doing the wages any more? That's probably not a bad thing. It's a big responsibility for a woman, that is. What sort of clerk are you going to be instead?'

'I won't be a clerk.'

Tony stilled. 'What, then? Come on, Colette. Don't keep me waiting.'

'I'm going to be – they want me to be a chaperone. On the trains. Looking after people who find it difficult to travel on their own. Like ... blind people. Or someone who's infirm.'

Tony shook his head. 'No. You're not a nanny. That isn't war work.'

'It is in a way. The trains are often overcrowded. Some people find it hard to manage.'

'They can go on finding it hard, because you aren't going to run around after them. I'm not having my wife gallivanting about with strangers. I take it you said no.'

Colette swallowed. 'No, I didn't.'

Tony fixed his gaze on her. 'Are you telling me you've taken on a new job without consulting your husband?'

'It wasn't like that. I'm sorry, Tony. I've made a mess of explaining. I wasn't asked if I was interested in doing it. I was – I was told it's what I'm going to do in future.'

'I'm not having it and I shall tell them so.'

'Please don't,' Colette whispered.

'I beg your pardon?' Tony's eyes narrowed.

'It wouldn't do any good. Miss Emery was quite definite about it. There's no choice.'

'We'll see about that.'

'But Miss Emery—'

'I shan't bother with her. This needs to be sorted out by men. I'll go over her head, straight to her boss.'

Was it wise to say it? On the other hand, if she didn't tell him ...

'Miss Emery is the assistant welfare supervisor for women and girls and she reports to the welfare supervisor. I think you'll find she's a woman as well.' She almost added, 'I'm sorry.' How feeble she was. No wonder he walked all over her. Determined to stand up for herself, she continued, 'Please don't make trouble, Tony.'

'What did you just say?'

'I mean, it won't make any difference. I've been given this job because they think I'm the right person.'

'You? The right person? They can't know you very well if they think that. They don't know how much you rely on me to take care of you and make decisions for you. When are you meant to start this job?'

'Not until October. I can't leave my desk in Accounts until someone has been trained to replace me.'

'October?' Tony laughed. 'That's two weeks away. More than enough time for me to sort this out. You might as well tell the new wages girl not to bother because, trust me, you won't be leaving.'

CHAPTER TWENTY

Cordelia and Emily's second night of fire-watching fell on the Tuesday. Cordelia had experienced the occasional twitch of nerves on and off all day. Working all day, then fire-watching all night, followed by another full day at work, was a tall order – but hundreds of thousands of other people did it as a matter of course and she would too.

'If Emily is washed out on Wednesday,' she murmured to Kenneth, 'you'll let her take a nap in the office, won't you?'

To her surprise, the doting father refused. 'She can't have it both ways, Cordelia. She was determined to do her bit and I gave my consent. Either she is grown-up enough to be a fire-watcher or she's still a child who needs her eight hours' sleep. Everybody's tired these days.'

As Cordelia and Emily emerged onto the flat part of the school roof between two of the gables, Cordelia wondered if tonight would see a repeat of the personal revelations that had startled her on their first night of fire-watching. But if Emily did have another emotional bombshell to drop, she didn't get the chance, because just a quarter of an hour later, the siren's wail lifted into the night air.

Cordelia heard Emily's intake of breath. For her own part, she felt a frisson of fear that focused purely on her daughter's safety. Was she mad to let Emily do this?

The drone of aircraft engines was accompanied by beams of light shining up into the sky, fastening on to the enemy planes as the ack-ack guns blazed out so loudly they might have been in the school playground. Cordelia touched her tin helmet just to make sure it was there, which was silly because of course it was, then she raised her binoculars to her eyes.

'I'll look this way and this way,' she told Emily. 'You watch there and over there.'

No one had told Emily of the resolve it took to stay out in the open during a raid, and not just that, but on a roof, feeling utterly exposed. She scoured her area for signs of fire.

'Mummy – look! Fire!'

Cordelia went to Emily's side, resisting a maternal urge to haul her towards the relative shelter of a gable. Below them on Nicolas Road was a bright flare of light, but two figures were already approaching it. One stopped and set down a bucket while the other, a length of hose trailing behind him, went closer and used a stirrup pump to extinguish the flames.

Cordelia and Emily shared a glance of triumph.

'Make a note of it, including the time,' said Cordelia, then resumed her position facing the opposite direction.

Moments later, a bomb whined its way to the ground and the school seemed to shake to its foundations. In amongst the vast, all-enveloping sound, Cordelia was amazed to be able to identify the sharp pinging sounds of shrapnel striking metal. Emily was by her side as she hurried forwards, as if that extra few feet would enable her to see more clearly. The bomb had fallen a couple of streets away, in between Nicolas Road and Wilbraham Road. Good Lord, if it had been just a bit further this way ...

Flames rose in the air. Their colour seemed to fade as a massive cloud of dust was hurled upwards, then the flames shone through as the fire took hold.

Emily started to spout out their instructions for how to report a fire, but Cordelia caught hold of her arm to silence her. Already, movement in the area showed they had no need to alert anybody.

'Make a note of it,' said Cordelia.

But Emily had other ideas. 'We can't just stay here and do nothing. Look, there's at least one house gone. People might be trapped. We have to help.'

'We mustn't leave our post.'

'You stay and I'll go.'

'Emily,' Cordelia said sharply, 'this isn't a story where the—' She just stopped herself from saying 'the children'. 'Where the characters rush in and have an adventure. We have our duty and that means manning our post, no matter what. Now make a note of what you see and the time. There might be other details to add later.'

The raid was a short one, the all-clear sounding less than an hour later.

'Now can I go and help?' Emily demanded.

'Firstly, you're not going anywhere without me; secondly, that raid might be over, but there could be another one at any minute; and thirdly, our shift doesn't finish until six o'clock tomorrow morning.' Cordelia softened her voice to add, 'I know you're keen to do your bit, darling, and I'm proud of you for it, but you have to realise that this, here, on the school roof, is where you'll be doing your bit, no matter how much you think you could do good elsewhere.'

'It's so frustrating,' seethed Emily.

'There are plenty of people down there,' said Cordelia. 'Trained people, ARP wardens, ambulance men. They'll send for Heavy Rescue, if necessary.'

'Maybe I should have volunteered for something else instead. Something on the ground.'

'And you intend to tell Daddy that, do you?' Cordelia asked drily.

Just as Cordelia had hoped would happen, Emily laughed. That was the thing about Emily. She had her little strops, but just when she seemed to have built up to the point of flouncing off in a huff, she would see the funny side and laugh at herself. She was a lovely girl in so many ways and Cordelia had adored her from the day she was born, but she had her faults. She could be obstinate and, as Cordelia had discovered in recent weeks, distinctly snobby, but what was that compared to the wonderful saving grace of being able to laugh at herself?

'I won't tell Daddy if you won't,' said Emily. 'I'm sorry, Mummy. Have I been a pain in the neck?'

As they left the school premises and set off for home at six o'clock, they passed the end of the road where the bomb had fallen. It was impossible not to pause to look. A house seemed to have lost its ability to hold itself upright and had collapsed into the road. A man lay to the side of the pile of rubble. He moved his head and – was that a rubber tube?

An ARP warden came towards Cordelia and Emily, presumably intending to shoo them away, but he noticed the armbands that showed they were fire-watchers and said, 'A bad business, that.'

'Very,' Cordelia agreed. 'What's that man doing?'

'Talking to someone who's trapped underneath. Sometimes we can push a rubber tube through.'

'And the person is all right?'

'Physically, seems to be.' The warden glanced at Emily, then looked back at Cordelia. 'But other members of the family ... '

Cordelia breathed out a soft 'Oh' of sorrow.

'Do you mean the other trapped people are dead?' asked Emily.

'Aye, love. That's why it's important to keep talking to her. She's only a nipper.'

Cordelia squeezed Emily's hand and addressed the warden. 'Is there anything we can do? Would it help for the child to hear a woman's voice? Or the voice of a girl nearer her own age?'

With a movement of his hand, the warden indicated the man speaking into the tube. 'He knows how to talk to little 'uns. He's brought up five of his own. You get on home, ladies, and remember this little lass in your prayers.'

Emily was quiet as they walked home and Cordelia left her to her thoughts.

As they walked through their empty garden gateway, Emily said, 'Thank you for making the offer for me to speak to that girl, Mummy. I'm glad you gave me that chance.'

Letting them into the house, Cordelia whispered, 'No noise. We don't want to wake Daddy.'

But Kenneth was already on his way downstairs, wrapped in his tartan dressing gown.

'Thank goodness you're safe.' He kissed them both. 'When that raid started ... '

'We're fine,' said Cordelia, 'and you have a daughter to be proud of.'

'You two go and put your heads down for half an hour,' said Kenneth.

'I'm not sure that's a good idea,' said Cordelia. 'I might not wake up again.'

They all looked round as the letter-box flap opened and the first post landed on the mat. Kenneth picked it up.

'There's one for you.' He handed it to Emily. 'It looks like Granny's writing.'

Emily opened it. 'Listen to this. Granny wanted me to go and stay with her, but I wrote back and said I couldn't, what with my new job at Daddy's firm and being a fire-watcher.' She looked up with shining eyes. 'So Granny says she's going to come here instead. Won't that be splendid?'

Cordelia smiled and then pulled the smile a little wider in the hope of making it look more sincere.

'Perfect,' she said.

Alison couldn't believe it. Colette had been given a new job. Colette! The shy one, the quiet one, had been singled out for a special role.

'You'll be perfect for it, love,' said Dot. 'You're such a kind girl. It'll be lucky folk that get looked after by you.'

Mabel laughed, saying to Dot, 'You sound like a proud mother.'

'Well, I'm plenty old enough to be mam to all you young'uns, so that makes you my honorary daughters. Daughters for the duration, that's what you are. How does that sound?'

'Lovely,' said Joan.

'Anyroad,' said Dot, 'Colette's the one we should be concentrating on. She's the one with the news.'

Colette smiled but looked self-conscious. 'Honestly, there's nothing else to tell.'

'Dot's right,' said Persephone. 'Miss Emery couldn't have found a better person to help people who feel vulnerable when they travel.'

'You're so sweet-natured,' said Mabel. 'Your charges will love you.'

Alison couldn't suppress a flash of envy. Although her friends had congratulated her over her own special role, no one had said she was perfect for it, but they were falling over themselves to heap praise on Colette. God, what a cat she was. She had never needed fulsome praise before Paul dumped her, but now that she seemed to be trying to put herself back together as a new person in a new life, she desperately wanted others to validate her and make her feel she mattered. She remembered Miss Emery saying, 'I saw something in you when you first came to work here,' and wished she had asked for details.

She leaned across to squeeze Colette's hand. 'Congratulations. You deserve it.'

And she did mean the words, she honestly did, but at the same time she couldn't help but be aware that Colette had it all – the happy marriage as well as the tailor-made new position. Talk about living a charmed life. If a little bit of Colette's good fortune would rub off on Alison, how much better her life might be.

'Thank you,' said Colette. 'What have you been doing?'

'I'm spending this week in the railway workshops.'

'That's not work I'd fancy,' said Dot. 'All them lathes and steam hammers. Give me a guard's van full of parcels any day.'

'There are plenty of women who want to be in the workshops,' said Alison.

'Who want to?' Persephone repeated. 'You mean they weren't just assigned to it, like we were all assigned to our jobs?'

'Some of them might have been,' said Alison. 'I don't know about that, but I do know that a lot of women choose to work there because it's the one place where, once you're fully trained, you can earn the same as a man, provided you need no assistance to do your job.'

Alison spent the rest of the week in the workshops and the following week she was out and about again. She was surprised to find she was interested in her work. She had never cared one way or the other about any previous job, seeing each one simply as a way of killing time until she got married. Now here she was, her marriage ripped away from her, and she was actually finding her new job worthwhile. It seemed her whole world had been turned upside down.

'It sounds fascinating, I must say,' observed Mrs Grayson when Alison explained the system by which signalmen 'offered' each train to the next signal box along the line, where the signalman had to 'accept' it, thus ensuring that there was no confusion over which stretches of line were in use.

'And you sound so interested in it yourself,' added Mrs Cooper.

Alison was about to agree that she was far more interested than she had ever expected to be, but stopped herself. How could she admit that without sounding ... well, unwomanly, for want of a better word? If she made herself sound like a career girl, would Mrs Cooper and Mrs Grayson tell one another afterwards that it was no wonder Paul had found another girl? She couldn't have that. Yet, without Paul, what was left for her except a lifetime of work? And wasn't it better to find the work enjoyable? Why couldn't she admit it?

'I'm certainly learning plenty of new things,' she said in a non-committal voice and then felt like kicking herself, because her cool tone had killed the conversation stone dead.

After a pause, Mrs Cooper said, 'I know it feels a long way off, but Christmas will be here before you know it, so when you girls know what your plans are, please tell me.' She smiled. 'Mrs Grayson needs to know how many she's catering for and I want to do a stocking for anyone who's here on Christmas morning.'

'You are a love,' said Mabel. 'It all depends on shift patterns for me. I know Mumsy would love it if I went home.'

'What about you, Alison?' asked Mrs Grayson. 'I suppose you'll go to your parents' for Christmas.'

Alison laughed. 'If I didn't, they'd turn up here and fetch me. But I'll be here first thing Christmas morning.'

'I'll be here all day,' said Margaret. 'I've nowhere else to go – oh, sorry, that sounded ungracious, didn't it? What I mean is, after the miserable time I had last Christmas all alone in that grotty bedsit, being here with you will be pure heaven.'

'Don't you have family locally?' asked Alison. She realised that Margaret never talked about herself much. Or maybe she had, but Alison had been too busy mourning her lost love to notice.

'No. My brother's overseas fighting and my sister had a baby on the way at the outbreak of war, so she was evacuated.'

'Did she give you a niece or a nephew?' asked Mrs Cooper.

'Both. She had twins.' Margaret paused. 'You may as well know that my father lives not far away, but we don't get on.'

'I'm sorry to hear that, chuck,' said Mrs Cooper.

Margaret shrugged. 'It's just how it is.'

'I don't like to think of families being on bad terms,' said Mrs Cooper, looking troubled, 'not in these uncertain times.'

'Please don't try to get us back together,' Margaret said quietly.

'Aye,' said Mrs Grayson, 'and don't get any fancy ideas about me and Mr Grayson neither.'

That closed the topic on a hearty laugh, but Alison carried on thinking about Margaret's situation. Poor girl, with no family nearby. Alison and Mabel were both lucky to come from loving families, with parents who thought the world of them. Alison decided there and then to go and see Mum and Dad on Saturday. She dropped a postcard in the pillar box, telling Mum to expect her.

Mum was thrilled when Alison arrived and gave her a big hug. There was an oniony, savoury aroma in the air.

'I managed to get some stewing steak,' said Mum.

'Have you added your secret ingredient?' Alison teased. Mum always added a dollop of HP Sauce to stew and cottage pies. It would have been Alison's secret ingredient too, had she married Paul. Her smile wobbled, but she swallowed hard and maintained her composure.

Lydia arrived soon afterwards and Mum asked the girls to set the table while she dished up.

'It's just like old times,' said Mum as they sat down, 'the four of us round the table.'

'Steady on,' said Alison. 'You make it sound as if Lydia and I left home years ago.'

'Sometimes it feels like it.'

'Now then, Janet,' Dad murmured.

'I can't help it. I've come over all emotional,' said Mum.

'Well, I've come over all hungry,' said Dad. 'Let's tuck in.'

'Grace first,' Mum reminded him.

'God bless the Merchant Navy for bringing us our food and God bless the Royal Navy for keeping them safe on the seas.'

'Amen,' chorused the three women.

Mum's stew was delicious. Alison tried not to think about all the recipes she had copied out in her best writing in a notebook – all the mouth-watering meals she had looked forward to cooking for Paul.

'Mrs Cooper asked about Christmas the other day. I said I'd be spending Christmas Day here, of course.'

'Of course,' said Dad. 'Where else would you spend it?'

'Actually,' said Mum, 'I've had an idea about that. I thought, with this being Lydia's first Christmas in her new home, we should all go round there to celebrate. What do you think? We want her to feel she's got a proper married home, don't we? Don't we, Alison?'

*

230

It was the last Sunday in September. Next Wednesday, it would be October and unless Tony put a spanner in the works at the last minute, Colette would start her new job. This afternoon they were in Wilton Close, but it was raining and so Tony sat indoors, making conversation, until Colette was ready to burst. She wanted – needed – to be alone with Mrs Cooper. They hadn't seen one another for two weeks. Last Sunday, Colette and Tony had spent the day with Tony's parents, while on the Saturday there had been a day's training for ARP wardens and fire-watchers that Tony had attended. Colette had had a few wild thoughts about dashing round to Mrs Cooper's in his absence, but the training was to take place outdoors, in the streets, and suppose he saw her climbing aboard the bus? She didn't dare take the risk.

Sunday afternoon dragged on until Tony glanced at her as a signal that it was time for them to leave.

'I'll just help Mrs Cooper take the tea things out to the kitchen,' said Colette.

In the kitchen, Mrs Cooper whispered, 'I need to talk to you. I've got an idea, but it'll have to wait until next Sunday now.'

'I can't wait that long. Please. It was bad enough not coming here last weekend. I can't wait another week.'

Mrs Cooper said in a louder voice, 'Let's get these things washed up. It's good of you to help.'

She pulled Colette into the scullery and turned on the tap. Colette started to pull the door shut, but Mrs Cooper opened it again.

'It's safer this way,' she said softly. 'We'll see if anyone comes. We can't talk about it now, but I could come into town tomorrow and meet you in your dinner break.'

Colette nodded. Her throat seemed to have closed up, preventing her from speaking.

'I'll meet you at the cathedral. There's bound to be somewhere quiet where we can sit.'

Colette pictured it, the poor, battered cathedral that had suffered so dreadfully in the Christmas Blitz – battered yet somehow still beautiful, a place that had suffered alongside its city.

The next day, as Colette approached the cathedral, Mrs Cooper came hurrying towards her and drew her to sit on the ruins of a wall away from the road.

'Right. Are you absolutely sure you're ready to leave Tony?'

The bluntness almost took Colette's breath away, but she knew they didn't have unlimited time and must get straight into the discussion. 'I don't see how—'

'Never mind not seeing how, love. Are you sure you *want* to leave him? Because if you are, it would mean me handing over things that are unspeakably precious and I can't do that if you're not sure.'

Colette gazed into Mrs Cooper's eyes. 'What things?'

'My Lizzie's identity.'

Cold air hit the back of Colette's throat as she sucked in a gasp of pure shock.

Mrs Cooper delved in her handbag, extracting an envelope from which she slipped out some papers. 'I've not got her identity card because she had that on her when she died, but I've got her birth certificate, her baptism certificate and, would you believe it, her swimming certificate. What we can do, thee and me, is go and get a new identity card. I'll be me and you can pretend to be Lizzie. We'll show 'em the certificates as proof. You'll need a photograph of yourself. You're older than my Lizzie, but you've got a young look about you. We can get you new identity papers in Lizzie's name. We'll do it at the Town Hall, where there's little chance of either of us being recognised.'

Colette made a movement, not to speak, not to do anything, just a movement of – of shock and confusion, maybe even of denial. She'd thought of leaving Tony – but she hadn't truly imagined it could ever happen.

Mrs Cooper grasped her hand, leaning closer. 'Then you'll have to cut open the lining inside your handbag and put the certificates and the new identity card inside, along with money – paper money. I'll give you as much as I can spare.'

'You can't.'

'Nay, lass, I can and I will. If it's possible for you to squirrel any money away, that would help – but you mustn't do owt that Tony would notice and ask questions about. You sew up the lining and make it good as new – and then you wait. You wait for a bad air raid that you're close enough to that folk can think you died in it.'

'But there won't be a body.'

'There isn't for everyone. That's the sad truth, chuck. The landlord of the Horse and Jockey on Chorlton Green, not five minutes' walk from Wilton Close, he was out one night in a raid and that was the end of him. Never seen again. Blown to kingdom come.'

'His poor family.'

'It's – it's what happened to my Lizzie. I'm not meant to know that, but I do. I don't want to know it. I don't want it to be true, but – well … ' Mrs Cooper fell silent, her gaze clouding over. 'I went to the park where it happened.'

'I didn't know you did that.'

'It were a while after she died. I wanted to see for myself. I knew the park-keeper's house had been destroyed and I wondered if I'd be able to find the spot where it'd been.'

'Did you find it?'

'Could hardly miss it, love. There were a ruddy great crater. Pardon my language. My mam fetched me up better than that. But honest to God – a ruddy great crater.'

233

'Oh, Mrs Cooper.'

'So you see, that were when I knew there'd been nowt left of my Lizzie. I don't know what they put in the coffin, but I'm glad they pretended – the funeral people, I'm glad they pretended. I'm glad my Lizzie got a proper funeral. That's summat to be grateful for.'

Colette squeezed her hand, but instead of comforting Mrs Cooper, it seemed to galvanise her. She sat up straight, the sombre memories switching to sharply focused ideas.

'If there's a raid and you're in the vicinity when the bombs drop, you skedaddle. You hear me? No hesitating, no looking back. Just go – and everyone will think you've been blown to smithereens.'

Colette didn't breathe, couldn't swallow. Could she really allow people to believe that? Her friends would be heartbroken. They'd already lost Lizzie – Letitia too. Letitia hadn't been a railway girl, but she was Joan's sister, and Alison and Mabel for definite, and possibly Persephone as well, had gone dancing with her. A chill rippled through Colette. It was her friends for whom she felt concerned. Not Tony. Not her husband.

That said it all, really, didn't it?

'I know how drastic it sounds,' Mrs Cooper said softly, 'but it's the only way. Otherwise, in the end you'll fetch up like your poor mother-in-law. Do you need to go home and think it over?'

'Yes,' Colette said, immediately followed by, 'No. No. It's the only way. Thank you. You've given me a plan, something to fix my hopes on.' She drew in a breath. 'Yes, let's do it.'

'Good girl, good lass.'

'You've thought of all this and all I've done is be afraid.'

'Nay, don't be hard on yourself. If you'd started having ideas, Tony might have realised. He might have seen summat in your face. It's better this way.'

234

'I can never thank you enough.'

'It were what I said about you sticking your head in the gas oven what made me put my thinking cap on. I've thought everything through again and again and I think it'll work. You'll have to keep your handbag with you at all times and the moment a bomb drops near enough to where you are, off you go and catch the next train.'

Colette pressed her hand to her chest. 'My goodness. I'm trying to picture it. Colette Naylor getting on a train in Manchester and travelling to the other end, wherever that is, and then the person who gets off the train—'

Mrs Cooper touched her arm. 'Don't, chuck. Don't say Lizzie will get off the train. Not Lizzie.'

'Of course not. I'm sorry. I should have thought. I'll call myself Elizabeth Cooper.' She tried it out. Elizabeth Cooper. Was this really happening?

'Not Elizabeth,' said Mrs Cooper. 'It's lovely, but it's a bit of a mouthful.'

'Betty?'

'Betsy,' Mrs Cooper said firmly. 'That's pretty. You deserve a pretty name.'

Betsy Cooper. Not Elizabeth but Betsy. She was going to be Betsy Cooper.

Oh, Lizzie, dear little Lizzie. You don't mind, do you?

CHAPTER TWENTY-ONE

As instructed, Colette reported to Miss Emery on her first morning in her new role. She felt fluttery with nerves, though this wasn't because of starting the job. Partly it was because she still felt numb and shocked at the thought of Mrs Cooper's plan for her escape and partly it stemmed from having to face Miss Emery, knowing that Tony had done his level best to take this position away from her. Tony hadn't wasted his time, as he put it, addressing his wishes to a woman, but that didn't mean Miss Emery was unaware of what he had attempted to do. What must she think of Colette?

But Miss Emery was her usual self, friendly in a professional sort of way.

'Good morning, Mrs Naylor. I'm pleased to see you. Are you ready for whatever today brings?'

'I hope so,' said Colette.

'Unfortunately, there isn't anywhere that we can talk privately just now, so I must ask you to join me at the back of my little office. I apologise,' Miss Emery added. 'It's far from satisfactory, I know.'

'It can't be easy for you,' said Colette.

'Not having a fourth wall and a door is deeply unsatisfactory. Still, I manage. I don't have a lot of choice.'

Colette joined Miss Emery beside her tall cupboard in the back of the alcove. Miss Emery turned her back towards the corridor, where people hurried by.

'This isn't how I wanted your first morning to start,' she said quietly. 'I'm going to tell you what you'll be doing this week. Pardon me if I sound mysterious, but I'm not going to say the names out loud.'

With a glance in the direction of the corridor, Colette nodded.

'You shall receive train tickets and petty cash. You'll be required to sign for them and at the end of the day, return any unused money. You'll catch a train to a certain place not too far away. There, you'll catch a bus to the next station along the line. Between eleven thirty and midday, you must purchase a single to Manchester Victoria. Please note the exact time of the purchase by the station clock. Then you'll catch the next train back to Victoria, but please don't use the ticket you have paid for. Use the one that will be provided before you set off. You must do this each day, Monday to Friday. I suggest you have a story ready in case you get chatting to regular travellers. You can be visiting a sick aunt, something of that nature. Behave at all times as if you're an ordinary passenger.' Miss Emery broke off and smiled. 'That's all there is to it.'

It sounded easy – but also odd.

'What's the reason for it?' Colette asked.

'Ah. I do know that, but it's not my place to tell you. My advice, Mrs Naylor, is that you simply follow your instructions. Sometimes you'll be given a reason, sometimes you won't. If you refrain from asking questions, you'll save yourself embarrassment.'

Colette nodded.

'I hope I haven't put you off.' Was that a trace of sympathy in Miss Emery's smile? 'I'll escort you across to the ticket office and introduce you to Mr Gordon. You shall report to him each morning this week and he'll provide you with tickets and petty cash.'

They went across to Victoria Station, where the long ticket office was fronted by wood panelling that gleamed with polish. At either end, the office had a graceful curve and beneath each small window was a shelf onto which the clerks pushed the tickets for passengers to pick up. Miss Emery took Colette to a side door. She knocked and waited for it to be unlocked from the inside.

As they entered, Colette formed a blurred impression of desks and uniforms and voices before Miss Emery showed her to a small office set into the corner. A handsome man, probably in his forties, with a high forehead and thinning golden-brown hair stood and shook hands as Miss Emery performed the introductions.

'I've explained to Mrs Naylor what she is to do this week,' said Miss Emery.

Nevertheless, Mr Gordon repeated the instructions, with the addition of the names of the relevant stations.

'I want to be sure you understand this is a confidential matter. You may not discuss it with anybody.'

'I won't, sir,' Colette said in what she hoped was a dignified manner.

'Good.' Mr Gordon smiled at her and it made his eyes twinkle. 'This must all seem very hush-hush, but I can assure you that you haven't been recruited as a secret agent.'

His humour broke through Colette's shyness and she smiled back.

'Here is your train ticket – and this is the money to pay for your bus fare and the train ticket back here. Please sign here to say you have received them. When you return to Victoria, come and see me and give me the ticket you bought and the money that's left over. Any questions?'

'When I leave the train and need to catch the bus, is the bus stop outside the station?'

'Mrs Naylor, as far as the world is concerned, you're an ordinary traveller making this journey for the first time. Do what anyone else would do. Ask for directions.'

Spoken in a different tone, these words would have made Colette feel that she'd been slapped down, but there was understanding beneath Mr Gordon's businesslike manner and she felt reassured.

At a nod from Miss Emery, Colette started to leave.

'Oh – and, Mrs Naylor … ' said Mr Gordon and she turned back, ' … thank you.'

A few minutes later, Colette climbed aboard the train and sat down. She heard the doors slamming, then the guard walked past, making sure each door was securely fastened. Presently, he went by again in the opposite direction, heading towards the guard's van. Colette heard him blow his whistle and a few moments later the driver blew the train whistle, which meant the guard had waved his green flag. Then came the sound of a huge puff of steam bursting out of the funnel, and the couplings that held the line of carriages together shifted and creaked as the train began to move.

It pulled out from beneath the station canopy and Colette's heart lifted as golden autumn sunshine struck the window. As amazing as it sounded, this was her job. She was being paid to make a journey. Yes, she had instructions to follow, but the only tricky bit was going to be finding the correct bus stop. Once she knew where it was, the rest of the week would be a doddle. She almost laughed, but didn't because she didn't want other passengers to look at her. But that little burst of high spirits made her realise how unusual it was for her to feel happy.

It all went according to plan. She got off at the right place and asked where to find the bus stop, arriving at her destination in plenty of time. At half past eleven, she made her way to the station and purchased a single to Victoria, taking careful note of the time as she did so. The train wasn't due for another forty minutes, so she sat in the waiting room. At midday, she ate the sandwich she had brought with her.

After she caught the train back to Victoria, she took care to hand over the correct ticket at the barrier when she left the platform. She nipped into the Ladies, then knocked on the ticket office's side door and waited for Mr Gordon to be available. He took the ticket she had bought and wrote down the time she had made the purchase, then she handed over the change from the money he had given her. She had to fill in a form, detailing how much she had spent and on what. Fortunately, she had kept her bus ticket as proof.

'That's all there is to it,' said Mr Gordon. 'Same again tomorrow, Mrs Naylor. If you see Miss Emery, I'm sure she'll find something for you to do for the remainder of the day.'

Colette returned to Hunts Bank.

'How did you get along?' asked Miss Emery.

'Fine, thank you.'

'Good. I've arranged for you to do some filing for the rest of the afternoon.'

'I hope you don't mind my asking, but could I bring my knitting tomorrow and do it while I'm waiting to come back to Victoria?'

'Of course you may. Bring your knitting. Bring a book. What matters is that you look like an ordinary passenger. Knit while you're travelling, if you like, as long as you don't miss your stop.'

'Thank you. I wouldn't want you to think I was taking advantage.'

'Mrs Naylor, I'm quite sure you are the last person in the world to do that. That's one of the qualities that makes you right for this position.'

This position – whatever it was. Would she have a greater understanding after she'd been in it for a week?

The days passed in a way Colette could only describe as agreeable – well, the job itself did, anyway. She didn't like having to lie to her friends in the buffet, making up an elderly lady with a walking stick and a blind piano-tuner as two of the folk she had supposedly chaperoned. As for telling lies to Tony, that was positively terrifying at the start of the week. What if he saw through her fibs? But he didn't and by Friday evening, somehow or other she seemed to have got used to it. That in itself came as a shock, because she had always thought of herself as an honest person.

Over the next couple of weeks, she really did act as a chaperone a couple of times, which eased her conscience, especially when talking to Mrs Cooper – it seemed extra bad to lie to her when she was facing what would have been her beloved Lizzie's nineteenth birthday.

Mr Gordon explained to her what the ticket-buying business had been about – well, up to a point.

'I can't go into detail, Mrs Naylor, but I will tell you the stationmaster was operating a clever little fiddle when he sold tickets.'

That was as far as the explanation went, but Colette appreciated being told. It gave her a sense of doing a real job and it was good to feel trusted.

Sometimes as she sat on a train, she let her mind wander. What if she changed trains, changed lines? What if she kept on travelling and didn't go back? She had her new identity tucked away inside the lining of her handbag. If she wanted to disappear from her old life, she could.

But she couldn't. She had to leave in such a way as to make Tony believe she had been killed.

'I've decided that I need to take on voluntary night-time work,' she whispered to Mrs Cooper on the last Sunday in October. 'It's the only hope I have of ever getting away.'

The two of them fell silent and Colette knew that, like her, Mrs Cooper was contemplating the destruction and loss of life that had occurred during that month. Oldham had taken a hammering and twenty-three adults and four children had been killed. It broke Colette's heart to think of children being killed. Then this week had seen four raids, which had targeted various areas, the worst damage being done in Broadheath, where, so it was said, nearly seven hundred houses had been hit. Seven hundred! Because of working on the railways, Colette knew that an aerial mine had come down on railway sidings, causing wagons some distance away to topple over even though they were weighed down with scrap iron.

'What will Tony say?' Mrs Cooper asked.

'He won't like it, but I can't see any other way.'

She was right. Tony didn't like it. Colette took the precaution of putting her name down and making sure she had been accepted before she told Tony. She thought hard about the best way to tell him – as if there could be a best way! It was tempting to blame it on Miss Emery. If she claimed that Miss Emery had told her she was expected to volunteer, it might let her off the hook – but supposing Tony then turned up at Hunts Bank, demanding to speak to someone? She couldn't allow that to happen.

When in doubt, apologise.

'I'm so sorry, Tony, but I felt I had to volunteer. This new job makes it look like I'm having a cushy time and I want to be able to hold my head up – like you do. I know how hard it is for you sometimes, being in a reserved occupation and having some people sneer at you for not being away fighting, when the truth is you're as brave as anyone – and you've got your fire-watching and your Home Guard to prove it. Can you blame me for feeling the same? I didn't want people thinking I'm having a cosy war, so I volunteered – just like you did. I followed your lead. I hoped you'd be proud of me.'

Had she laid it on too thickly? Apparently not. Tony was very sensitive about sometimes being wrongly thought of as a war dodger and it simply wasn't possible for him to have too much admiration for his nights of volunteer work. So, even though he was angry with Colette, her praise took the wind out of his sails somewhat.

And after that, frankly, Colette didn't care what he said. Whatever Tony had to say on the subject, she would swallow it. All that mattered was her hope for a new life, free from him.

CHAPTER TWENTY-TWO

After a bitterly cold day walking the line, Cordelia had to cup her hands around her mouth and blow repeatedly to warm them before sufficient life returned to her fingers for her to fasten the buttons on the silk blouse she was changing into at the end of her day's work. She pulled on a lilac jumper over the top and settled her pearls so that they peeped discreetly over the neckline. She was starting to thaw out, but she wouldn't be truly warm until she had a cup of tea inside her.

When she entered the buffet, she headed straight for the fireplace, peeling off her leather gloves and holding out her hands to the cheerful flames. God bless Mrs Jessop for having a fire going. Presently, Cordelia tore herself away from it and went to the counter, where Mrs Jessop poured her a cup of tea without being asked. God bless her for that too. She had always made the friends feel welcome in her domain.

No sooner had Cordelia settled herself at a table than Dot arrived, wearing the navy coat Cordelia had given her. She fetched herself a tea and came to sit down.

'By, it's nippy out there, isn't it? November has certainly brought a chill with it.'

Cordelia laughed, relaxing as she always did in Dot's company. 'It's nothing compared to the chill there's likely to be in my house soon. My mother-in-law is coming to stay.'

'Oh aye? Don't you get on?'

'Yes and no. On the surface, everything is calm and pleasant and quite staggeringly courteous.'

'But underneath ... ?' Dot raised her eyebrows.

'That's a different story altogether.' Cordelia knew her words would go no further. It was a relief to feel she could speak freely about Adelaide. 'She has never cared for me.'

'The old story, is it? Mothers and sons? The daughter-in-law is never good enough.'

'I wish it were that simple – that impersonal. But it's entirely personal. She doesn't think I'm right for Kenneth – not because he's her son and no woman would be good enough, but because ... because I'm me.'

'Eh, love.' Dot pressed Cordelia's hand.

'I said we're staggeringly polite to one another, and we are, but there was one exception to this. Just one. The first time she saw me, she looked me up and down and said, "Too young." Just like that. "Too young." As if I was one in a long line of girls and none of us had come up to scratch. Too fat – too thin – too tall – too young – too clever – not clever enough.'

Dot smiled. 'She sounds like Goldilocks.' Then she frowned. 'I'm trying to picture your husband and the age difference.'

'Twelve years.'

'It's not that much. Husbands are usually some years older. It's normal.'

'I was twenty-two when we married and Kenneth was thirty-four. Thirty-four seems young to me now that I'm past forty, but at the time I was aware of marrying an older man.'

An image flashed into her mind of Father, stony-faced and determined. 'It'll be good for you, Cordelia. A steadying influence.' As if she had always been a giddy little fool – but that was probably how Father had seen her, after Kit.

'Nevertheless, it came as a shock to be pronounced "too young" like that,' she continued. 'She made me sound like a gold-digger, after his money and his position in life. If I'd had my wits about me, I'd have asked her how young she was when she married Kenneth's father – but it's probably a good thing I didn't. She'd have been appalled by such rudeness.'

'But it was all right for her to be rude about *your* age,' said Dot. 'I know the sort. They can dish it out, but they can't take it.'

'I don't suppose Adelaide Masters has ever been required to "take it",' Cordelia said wryly. 'She's a very grand sort of lady. If you met her without knowing she was plain Mrs, you'd probably think you were in the presence of a duchess.'

Dot laughed. 'And did she marry young with a big age gap?'

'She did. She was only eighteen when she had Kenneth. She's in her early seventies now and as formidable as ever.'

'You know what you should do? When she arrives, throw your arms around her, give her a huge hug and say, "How lovely to see you, Ma!" That'll take her by surprise.'

Cordelia burst out laughing. She didn't often do that. 'I don't know which is more preposterous, the huge hug or calling her Ma.'

'What do you call her?'

'Mrs Masters. I called her that when I was first introduced to her, naturally. When I married, I expected to be invited to address her as Mother, but she didn't mention it, so I called her Mrs Masters on purpose to prompt her into making the invitation – but she didn't. She's been Mrs Masters ever since.'

'Eh, that's hard. I've always been Ma to our Sheila and Mother to our Pammy. Oh, look, here come the girls.'

Mabel, Persephone and Joan had all arrived together. They waved as they joined the queue. Having bought their teas, they threaded their way across the room. Mabel wore a brimless hat of green felt that went perfectly with the dark brown curls spilling over her coat collar. Persephone's coat was pure wool, the colour of caramel, her leather gloves gauntlet style. Joan's coat was nowhere near as costly as those of her friends, but it was every bit as well made. She was a skilled dressmaker.

They put down their cups of tea and Persephone dumped the shabbiest old cloth bag Cordelia had ever seen beside her chair before she sat down.

'Don't tell me that's yours,' said Dot.

Laughing, Persephone leaned down and picked it up, dangling it from her fingers for all to see. 'Don't mock it. This bag has just saved my life. I popped out to the shops in my lunch break, thinking I'd do a spot of Christmas shopping, and guess what. The shops aren't allowed to put purchases in paper bags any more, so I had to stuff a couple of silk squares in my pocket and a lipstick in my handbag, but I more or less had to juggle all the bigger bits and bobs all the way here. Fortunately for me, one of the other ticket collectors lent me this and I will be forever in her debt.'

Dot laughed. 'It doesn't do to go anywhere without your own bag these days.'

'Especially at this time of year,' Mabel added. 'You don't want your Christmas shopping on show.'

'What shall you wrap your gifts in this year?' Persephone asked. 'There's no wrapping paper to be had.'

'That isn't a problem in the Green household,' said Dot. 'I've always saved my Christmas paper from year to year until it's been folded that many times it falls to pieces.'

'I've read a couple of articles recently,' said Cordelia, 'about how all the shortages mean that this Christmas is going to be a shadow of former Christmases.'

'We'll have none of that sort of talk, thank you,' Dot said stoutly, 'not while I'm here. I don't care how difficult it is to get hold of things. This year is going to be a wonderful Christmas, because after last year's Christmas, it's what we all need.'

'You're right,' said Joan. 'A lot of it is down to attitude. This is my first Christmas with Bob and it's going to be perfect. I'm going to help in Dot's Christmas Kitchen throughout December as well.'

Dot laughed. 'It's not my Christmas Kitchen, chick. I didn't have the idea.'

'You know what I mean,' said Joan. 'You're the one who told us about it.' She added, looking at the others, 'There'll be one near where Dot and I live in Withington, so we'll be working together.'

'That'll be nice,' said Mabel.

Cordelia didn't say anything, but a sense of warm approval filled her. With Letitia's anniversary on the horizon, who better to keep an eye on Joan than kind-hearted Dot?

'Sheila and Pammy will be there an' all,' said Dot, 'and our Jimmy and his mates have built some carts to help ferry the foodstuff round to the school kitchen we'll be using.'

'They've built carts?' Persephone smiled. 'How enterprising.'

'Aye, using stuff they found on bomb sites,' said Dot, 'and when I say "found on bomb sites", I mean stuff they nicked off bomb sites, so don't get any ideas about writing an article.'

'I told Bob's mum about the Christmas Kitchens,' said Joan, 'and she found out there's going to be one in Stretford, so she and the girls will join that one.'

'I told Miss Brown and Mrs Mitchell about the Christmas Kitchens,' said Persephone, 'and they want to run one in Darley Court. Miss Brown has roped in the local WVS and the land girls.'

'You see, Dot?' said Cordelia. 'You say they aren't your Christmas Kitchens – and in the very widest sense, they aren't – but just amongst us, they *are* yours. That's how we all think of them. Because of you, Bob's family has joined one and there's going to be one at Darley Court, not to mention the friends you've roped in. You've made a difference, Dot.'

'I don't know about that,' said Dot, 'but I do believe there'll be a lot of good done by these Kitchens – and not just to the folk on the receiving end of the meals, neither, but to the women what do the cooking. We'll all be feeling glum at the thought of the blitz last Christmas and this will give us a sense of purpose.'

'Hear, hear,' said Persephone.

'Do you know yet if you'll be here for Christmas or at your mum's?' Dot asked Mabel.

'Here,' said Mabel, 'which is a shame because Mumsy and Pops would adore it if I could go home, and of course I'd love to see them too, but at the same time, there's something right about staying here.'

'After the blitz last Christmas, you mean?' asked Persephone.

'Yes.' Mabel shrugged and smiled. 'It just feels like the right place to be.'

'The Christmas Blitz affected us all deeply,' said Persephone. 'You most of all, Joan, because you lost Letitia. I think many Mancunians will feel a strong sense of home this Christmas as all the memories come sweeping back.'

'Don't forget the adopted Mancunians, like yourself and Mabel,' said Cordelia. 'You were part of what happened last year.'

Silence descended on the group and Cordelia knew that, like herself, the others were remembering. Joan was no doubt thinking of her sister, and Dot would be remembering those agonising hours when her grandson had been trapped beneath a collapsed house. As for Mabel, was she reliving the tragedy at the railway bridge? She had narrowly escaped death when, on the way to a rescue, a bridge up ahead had suffered a direct hit. A double-decker bus had taken shelter under the bridge and Mabel – dear, brave Mabel – dear, *young* Mabel – had been allotted the chilling task of searching for body parts in the ruins.

Oh, they were all so brave, these young girls. Cordelia felt a tug of regret that Emily hadn't wanted to get to know them. Having some 'big sister' figures in her life would have been good for her and Cordelia couldn't think of any young women she would rather see in that role. She thought of the words on the station's war memorial – Unity, Strength, Courage and Sacrifice. Qualities her friends embodied and lived up to every single day.

There had been a couple of air raids at the start of November, but it had been quiet since then. Colette felt as if the world was playing a gigantic trick on her. She had gone through the anguish of facing up to the truth of her life with Tony, and Mrs Cooper had helped her find a way out of it. Then Colette had eased things along by applying to do fire-watching duty at the marshalling yard, choosing it on purpose because railways in general – bridges, stations, depots, marshalling yards, not to mention the thousands of miles of permanent way – were all targets, and she needed to be in a place that was a target. She needed to be where the bombs were most likely to drop.

And now – now there were no raids. Each night she was due to go on duty, she spent all day wondering if tonight would be the night ... And so far, it hadn't been. Air raids had tailed off considerably since Hitler had turned his attention towards Russia. Had she left it too late to run away? She didn't know how much longer she could bear to live with Tony – but she had to bear it for as long as it lasted. She had no choice.

No choice – just hope.

'I've been thinking,' said Tony, lighting up a cigarette one evening and chucking the match in the fire. It fell short and landed on the hearth.

Colette cast an anxious glance. If she picked it up and put it in the fire, Tony might take that as a reprimand. On the other hand, if she left it, he might think she was being slovenly. She couldn't win. To her surprise, Tony reached down, picked it up and tossed it into the flames. She ought to be pleased, because it had saved her from getting into trouble, but instead it put her on her guard. She pretended to consult her knitting pattern, which gave her a legitimate reason not to look at him.

Tony leaned back in his armchair and stretched out his legs. Did he kick her wool basket on purpose? Inhaling on his cigarette, he tilted his chin upwards and blew a long stream of smoke into the air. Colette hated it when he did that. She imagined the smoke hitting the ceiling and bouncing down again to land on her. She had never smoked, because of Mother's tubes. Lots of people who suffered from bronchitis swore that smoking kept their tubes clear, but Mother had only needed to get a whiff of tobacco smoke and it could bring on a coughing fit.

In her first job, at the age of fourteen, Colette had worked as a packer in a small factory where a couple of the women constantly discussed their tubes. Colette, too shy to say anything, had been fascinated and baffled by the apparent connection between tubes and having, or not having, children. Was this why she was an only child? Because of Mother's iffy bronchial tubes? It hadn't been until she was nearly twenty that a conversation overheard in the doctor's waiting room enlightened her as to the existence of a completely different set of tubes elsewhere in the female body – tubes that in her case must be faulty because, after eighteen months of marriage, there was still no sign of a baby.

'Well,' Tony said affably, 'aren't you going to ask me what I'm thinking about?'

He smiled at her, so she smiled back, but she wasn't taken in. His affability might be the real thing or it might be a trap.

'What are you thinking about?' she asked.

'You and this fire-watching. I don't like it. I don't like you being out all night at the marshalling yard.'

'I'm sorry, Tony, but it's the work I was given.'

'I know, I know.' Tony spoke in his 'don't interrupt' voice. Then perhaps he remembered he was being affable because he smiled again, his voice warm and good-humoured as he went on. 'I could resign from my local fire-watching post and join you at the marshalling yard.'

Colette's heartbeat raced, but she said calmly, 'I don't think they'd let you resign – would they?'

'Don't you at least want me to try?'

No! The whole point of me working there is so I can run away from you.

'Of course,' said Colette. 'That goes without saying. But – but I wouldn't want to get my hopes up. I can't see it happening, that's all.'

'Nonsense. You said yourself that Mrs Masters was able to insist that her daughter do fire-watching with her and not on her own. This is the same as that.'

'Emily is fifteen. That's why Mrs Masters was allowed to make that condition.'

'I'll say you're not cut out for it and I want to be there to keep an eye on things. I'm responsible for you and for any blunders you make. It's worth a try, isn't it?' Tony smiled at her. 'Isn't it?'

CHAPTER TWENTY-THREE

There were times when Alison wished she had a cushy post like Colette's. Call that a job? Escorting people who needed a helping hand to get from A to B, and no doubt being thanked profusely in the process. It was all part of the charmed life Colette led. Mostly, though, Alison didn't begrudge Colette her new position. She truly liked Colette and had discovered a new respect for her because of the sensitive and gentle way she had supported Alison through her troubles.

It was when she was fed up with her own job that Alison thought wistfully of Colette's. On the whole, she was enjoying her new post and couldn't help but be interested in everything she was learning, but she had been obliged to work with a number of men who weren't at all pleased to have a girl alongside them, which she had found rather shocking – and then she'd been annoyed with herself. She should have expected it. She had known, of course, that women porters and suchlike, women with jobs on stations and on the trains, came up against this sort of attitude time and again. Dot had often regaled the girls in the buffet with the latest example of how Mr Bonner had talked down to her. He was the train guard she had worked for to start with. Earlier in the year, he had been injured and although he had made a good recovery, he was now on light duties and Dot worked for a much pleasanter guard called Mr Hill.

As silly as it sounded to her now, Alison had imagined it was the women on the trains who bore the brunt of the attitudes of those men who believed women had no place on the railways unless they worked in the canteens or as cleaners. But now that she was out and about, she was discovering there were plenty of men who took that view of any female at all who dared to work on the railways.

'Honestly!' she raged to her friends. 'Don't they realise the railway networks couldn't manage without us? Doesn't it occur to them that the country would grind to a halt?'

Dot laughed. 'The trouble is, love, that you've just asked two intelligent questions, and intelligence has nowt to do with the way these blokes are thinking. They're blinkered and set in their ways.'

'And they're not going to change,' Mabel added, 'so you'd better get used to it.'

'Never,' Alison vowed.

'Wrong choice of words,' said Mabel. 'I should have said you'll learn to live with it.'

For those first two weeks in November, Alison was in the marshalling yard, where the sight of a line of carriages being shunted together to form an express train took her breath away. Distinctly less pleasing was the dismissive attitude displayed by Mr Hastings, to whom she had been assigned. He paid her as little attention as he could get away with and more than once Alison had been tempted to slink off. Oh, how she hated Paul in those moments! It was because of him and his infidelity that she'd been lumbered with this job in the first place and for two pins she'd have packed it in.

But she didn't want to pack it in, did she? Not really. She was enjoying it and it was a big thing for her to admit that. Surely heartbroken people weren't supposed to find enjoyment. Surely they were supposed to trudge through life, getting by, feeling miserable. That was what being heartbroken was all about. But here she was, taking an interest in her job. It sometimes made her feel oddly ashamed. It was as if she was betraying her status as the jilted, heart-broken girlfriend.

And what did that say about her? Did it mean part of her wanted to be unhappy? Did she see herself as a tragic heroine? More to the point, was that how she wanted others to see her? She rejected the very idea, or tried to, but she knew in her heart that there was more than a little truth in it.

So she was feeling somewhat at odds with herself these days and Mr Hastings' patronising attitude ruffled her up completely the wrong way. She promised herself that the next time he talked down to her, or tried to overlook her in the company of men, she would ditch her good manners and fight back.

'I don't appreciate your attitude towards me, sir,' she said stoutly when the moment arose. 'I'd like you to know that I've been hand-picked to learn all about the railways.'

'Hand-picked, eh?' Mr Hastings laughed. 'That makes all the difference, doesn't it? Pardon me for breathing.'

That irked her even more. 'I think you should treat me with respect.'

'Or what, little girl? You'll run home to Mother?'

After that, when Mr Hastings had to introduce her to anybody, he made a point of saying she'd been hand-picked to learn about the railways and Alison kicked herself a dozen times for using those words. It was increasingly hard to hold her head up, especially when she saw the looks in the eyes of the men around her.

Not all the men were like that, of course. Some were real gentlemen and it was their civility and kindness that got her through.

At long last, the second Friday came round – her last day with Mr Hastings.

He was busy explaining how virtually every wagon had had to be 're-plated'.

'The war means wagons have to carry heavier loads, but they can only do that with the correct authorisation. That's what re-plating means.'

Alison was determined to acquit herself well on this final day and she tried to think of something intelligent to say. All she could come up with was, 'The extra weight must have an effect on the permanent way. An adverse effect, I mean.'

Mr Hastings looked at her and she wanted to curl up and die. She'd obviously said something superficial and shown herself up as the feather-headed little female he believed her to be.

But he said, 'Aye, that's right.' Then he surprised her by asking, 'And what d'you suppose it means for the engines?'

She thought about it. 'It must place additional strain on them, having to pull the extra weight.' Recalling something she had learned earlier in the week, she added, 'Some of the locos are old. In peacetime conditions, they'd have been scrapped, but as things are, they'll have to stay in service until the war's over.'

She pictured it, the proud old locos carrying on labouring past retirement age, working on tracks that were becoming increasingly worn. Daft as it was, in that moment she felt a surge of love, sorrow and deepest admiration for the locomotives, as if they were living, breathing creatures.

'Aye,' Mr Hastings said again. 'That's right. Huh! Maybe you've got one or two brain cells after all.'

It was a good job she was standing on solid ground. On anything else, she might have fallen over in shock at this glimmer of approval.

But it was only a glimmer and it was soon snuffed out. Her assumption that Mr Hastings would now show her respect in front of the other men was soon dashed. Once again in the company of his patronising, disdainful colleagues, Mr Hastings reverted to type and joined in the sneers and the advice to go home and get the dinner on.

Alison fumed about it in the buffet that evening.

'At least your stint there is over,' said Dot.

'I hope you'll find your next place more congenial,' said Cordelia.

All at once, Alison had the uncomfortable feeling she had been a bit of a bore this past fortnight. She'd done nothing but moan each time she saw her friends. She hadn't bothered mentioning the men who had been polite and helpful, just the ones who regarded her as fair game. Admittedly, the latter group had made her hopping mad and she had needed to let off steam, but had she turned into a grump in the process?

'You must think me a right old misery guts.'

'You've had a rotten couple of weeks,' said Margaret.

'I have, but I shouldn't have taken it to heart so much. The fact is,' Alison added as the truth opened up inside her mind, making her see things in a new way, 'if another man had been put in charge of me in the marshalling yard, say a man like our dear Mr Thirkle, and he'd been civil, the past two weeks would have been a different experience. I'll have to develop a thicker skin, that's all.'

'That's a sensible view to take,' said Cordelia.

The looks of approval on her friends' faces gave Alison a little boost. How good it felt to be held in esteem. Back in the days when she had been with Paul, she'd been far too busy feeling pleased with herself to require the approval of others. That made her pause and think, leaving the others to chat while she explored this new knowledge about herself.

When it was time to go, she and Joan nipped to the Ladies together.

'I'm sorry you had a rough time at the marshalling yard,' said Joan as they washed their hands.

'I'll cope better next time I come up against attitudes like that.'

As they emerged onto the concourse, Alison stopped, so Joan did too. Alison looked at her. Joan was the first railway girl she had met. They had bumped into one another outside Hunts Bank in February of last year when they'd been on their way to sit their railway tests. At the end of the afternoon, they had left together, along with Colette and Lizzie. Colette had hung back to wait for Tony, while the other three had said where they lived, to see who could travel home together. Alison had hoped to go on the bus with Joan, but it turned out they lived in opposite directions and it was Lizzie who had gone off with Joan. Alison remembered that now. She had always felt at a disadvantage living to the north of Manchester while her chums were in the south. She'd told herself it didn't matter because she had long-standing friends from church and the cricket club and so on, but deep inside she knew that wasn't true. All along she had dearly wanted to be more involved with the other railway girls.

'Joan, can I tell you something?'

'Of course.'

Alison pressed her lips together. It was important to find the right words. 'I've hardly known what to do with myself since Paul left me ... and then I had to be brave about Lydia's wedding. Sometimes I feel desperate and churned up. But I remember how you behaved after Letitia died.' She saw the flicker of shock in Joan's blue eyes at this unexpected reference to her sister. 'You were quiet and dignified and I'm going to try to be like that.'

'Quiet and dignified?' Joan raised her eyebrows.

'That's how you looked to me.'

'Maybe I was like that in public, but don't forget that in secret I was running around having a mad fling with Steven. There was nothing dignified about that.' Joan shut her eyes for a moment. When she opened them, she slipped her fingers around Alison's and squeezed gently. 'Grief is a terrible thing and it can make people behave in bizarre ways. I know it did with me. At the time it seemed real and I truly thought I loved him, but it was just the utter desperation of losing Letitia. What I'm saying is, grief takes us all in different ways. Just … be kind to yourself.'

'Leaving home and having this new job has at least given me something else to think about.'

'That's good,' said Joan.

'Is it?'

'It's a way of moving on.'

'I don't want to move on. I want things to go back to how they used to be.'

'So did I after Letitia died. It was the only thing I wanted – and it was the one thing I couldn't have. I'm not going to tell you to let go, because I know how hard that is.'

'Then what should I do?'

Joan shook her head, her eyes warm with concern. 'I don't know. I wish I did. You just have to live through it in the hope that one day you'll come out the other end.'

Alison spent Saturday afternoon at the Conservative Club, where two of the meeting rooms were being used for making little Christmas presents for children. There weren't enough toys in the shops this year, so this was a way of helping as many children as possible to have something in their stockings on Christmas morning. The WVS had turned out in force, as had the members of several Ladies'

Circles, as well as individuals who were eager to contribute to such an important cause.

Alison was there with Mabel, Margaret and Persephone. Joan's sisters-in-law, Maureen, Petal and Glad, waved to them from a trestle table on the other side of the room, where they were using pieces of worn-out clothing to make glove puppets and beanbags.

'Though they aren't beanbags so much as cork-sawdust-bags,' said the lady in charge, leading Alison and her friends to another table.

'I think I can manage a few beanbags,' said Mabel. 'They look easy to make.'

'You'll be over here on this table,' was the reply. 'I'll leave you in the capable hands of Mrs Sharp.'

Mrs Sharp was a middle-aged woman with faded fair hair that curled under at the back into a roll of such plumpness that it could only have been achieved by bulking it out with a rolled-up old stocking or possibly a rolled-up sanitary towel. You did hear of women doing that.

'Come and sit down, girls. You'll be making toys for the bath.' Mrs Sharp indicated pieces of rubber on a table behind them. 'Over there are inner tubes from old tyres. My daughters are cutting them up into rectangles and squares. Your job is to use these Craft Council patterns to cut out fish-shaped pieces and then stick them together with the same solution you'd use to fix a bicycle tyre. Make sure you leave a hole to push the stuffing in. We're using cork sawdust.'

It was fiddly at first, but the girls soon got into the swing of it. When everyone stopped for a cup of tea, Mabel, Margaret and Persephone went to have a chat with Bob's sisters. They all knew one another from Joan and Bob's wedding. But Alison hung back and slid into the kitchen, out of sight. She couldn't face it if the Hubble girls asked after Paul, who had been her partner at the wedding. Or maybe Joan had told them about how he had left her, in which case she didn't want to see the sympathy in their eyes.

Alison helped with the washing-up and didn't return to her table until everyone was back in their places.

'Where did you disappear to?' asked Persephone.

'Lending a hand in the kitchen.' Alison picked up a couple of paper patterns. 'Which do you want? Polly the Plaice or Monty the Mackerel?'

Constructing the rubber fish toys made Alison remember all the work she had poured into embroidering the household linen in her bottom drawer. She had left everything behind at Mum's. All those items she had collected, a mixture of the decorative and the functional – what a waste of time and money. Mum had given some of them to her as birthday presents. While other girls had received talcum powder or perfume or new gloves, she had been given a fish slice, a butter dish, even a doormat. A doormat! And she had been thrilled with it, because it was all part of the wonderful future that awaited her as Mrs Paul Dunaway. More fool her.

When the session ended, the lady in charge made a little speech, thanking everyone and assuring them that their efforts would make some children happy this Christmas, then everybody helped clear away. Alison managed to be absent when Bob's sisters said goodbye, only reappearing when she was sure they had left.

The four of them headed for Wilton Close through the dark afternoon, Persephone coming too because it was on her way to Darley Court and she wanted to pop in and see Mrs Cooper and Mrs Grayson.

'You're just in time to see Mrs Masters,' said Mrs Cooper. 'She came to do her monthly check and she's having a cup of tea with us.'

They all sat in the front room, which was comfortably warm, thanks to the fire. Mrs Cooper and Mrs Grayson both knitted as the girls talked about the various toys.

'Polly the Plaice,' chuckled Mrs Grayson. 'Polly's short for Margaret, isn't it?'

'No, Polly's short for Mary,' said Margaret, 'though I can't imagine why.'

'Has your name ever been shortened?' asked Mrs Cooper.

'No. My mum hated Maggie and Peggy, so I've always been Margaret. But she could never stop my gran calling me Maisie or Daisy Maisie.'

'My first name is Amanda,' said Mrs Grayson, 'but you call me Mandy at your peril.'

Mabel laughed. 'Pops calls me Mabs.'

Persephone joined in. 'My sister's name is Fudge.'

'Fudge?' said Alison. 'What's that short for?'

'Iphigenia.'

'Come again,' said Mrs Cooper.

'Iff-i-je-nee-a. Iphigenia.'

'By, you go in for posh names in your family, don't you?' said Mrs Cooper. 'Not that they aren't lovely names.'

'What's your name, Mrs C?' asked Persephone.

'Jessie – not Jessica. Just Jessie. That's what's on my birth certificate. That's why I wanted my Lizzie to have a proper name, a Sunday name, if you understand me. She was Elizabeth on her birth certificate, though me and her dad never called her that. She was Lizzie from the moment she was placed in my arms.' Mrs Cooper turned quickly to Cordelia. 'Where does your Emily's name come from?'

'Officially, she was named after her two grandmothers. My mother was Emma and my mother-in-law's middle name is Lily. Emma Lily – Emily.'

'That's a lovely way of combining their names,' said Margaret.

'You said "officially",' said Persephone.

'That's the reason I gave my husband and the grandparents,' said Cordelia.

'And the real reason?' asked Mabel.

'Emily Brontë, of course.'

The others laughed and Alison pretended to join in, but she was remembering being called Allie by Paul. How she had loved that pet name. How special she'd felt. Sometimes at night, she used to whisper 'Allie Dunaway' into the darkness, like a prayer. The backs of her eyes burned with sudden tears. Lord, she wasn't about to start blubbing like a baby in front of everyone, was she?

The tears vanished and she felt hot and fierce. Allie Dunaway was no more – Allie Dunaway had never existed. She was Alison Lambert, whether she liked it or not, and she had better start getting used to it. And she would begin by—

Her heart gave an almighty thump. The heat disappeared and she turned cold inside.

Tomorrow, when she went to Mum's for Sunday lunch, she would give her entire bottom drawer to Lydia.

CHAPTER TWENTY-FOUR

There was one good thing about the war, Cordelia thought grimly. It meant she wouldn't have to be with her mother-in-law the entire time. Adelaide was to arrive on the Monday afternoon and Cordelia had arranged to take Monday and Tuesday off work, using up two precious days of annual holiday.

'Then you can give Emily Wednesday, Thursday and Friday off from the office,' she said to Kenneth and didn't miss the flicker of surprise in his eyes. Did he expect the responsibility of entertaining his mother to rest exclusively with her? Of course he did, because it always had. But in the past, she hadn't worked outside the home.

'Yes,' said Kenneth. 'They'll both like that.'

'And perhaps you could take a couple of days off next week,' Cordelia suggested, keeping her tone light even though she rather felt she was prodding a caged tiger through the bars with a sharp stick.

Kenneth laughed. 'I don't know about that. I can't just drop everything.'

Oh, the temptation to enquire, 'But I can?' But it would only cause ill-feeling and good wives didn't do that. Cordelia was nothing if not a good wife. It was the very least she owed Kenneth for marrying him without loving him.

She went into town to meet Adelaide at London Road Station. Sounds echoed beneath the station canopy and the scents of steam and smoke created a spicy tang in the air. Adelaide's train was late, though only by half an hour. As it coasted beside the long platform, heading for the buffers, the brakes squealed and the train drew to a halt.

As passengers alighted and hurried along the platform to hand in their tickets, Cordelia stood to one side, watching for Adelaide, but there was no sign of her. The crowds thinned, the stream of travellers reducing to a trickle, and she still didn't appear. Was the telephone ringing in Cordelia's hall at this very moment, with Adelaide wanting to inform her that she had missed her connection?

And then – oh, why had she ever doubted it? Further along the platform, Adelaide descended from the train, preceded by a well-dressed man who turned to offer his hand to assist her. Not that Adelaide Masters required assistance. Elderly she might be, but infirm was the very last thing she was. She was followed from the train by a second man, who carried a suitcase which he placed beside her. The men glanced round and it was apparent they were offering to take Adelaide and her luggage to the taxi rank.

Cordelia hurried forward, catching the attention of a porter with a sack trolley as she went.

'Could you wait a minute for another suitcase?'

'Sorry, madam. My trolley's full. I can come back in a few minutes.'

Another porter said the same before Cordelia could even ask the question.

She arrived at Adelaide's side. Adelaide was the sort who had never been pretty when she was young, but once she had attained middle age, her strong features had earned her the label of handsome. She wasn't a tall woman, but she had both poise and presence and she had cultivated a regal air that she had long ago got down to a fine art. She still dressed in the longer lengths of the mid-thirties. Not because she was strapped for cash, but because she knew how to create the image she wished to project and she bullied her timid little dressmaker into producing it.

Adelaide presented her powdered cheek to be kissed.

'This is my daughter-in-law,' she informed the two gentlemen. 'Thank you for your assistance. We can manage now.'

Cordelia eyed the suitcase doubtfully. Was she required to heave it all the way to the taxi rank? Adelaide wasn't known for travelling light. But Adelaide, without looking round, raised one calfskin-gloved hand and waved it vaguely, whereupon a porter with an empty trolley instantly appeared by her side. Cordelia might not like her mother-in-law, but by crikey, there were times when Cordelia was overcome with admiration.

'What sort of journey did you have?' she asked once they were in a taxi on their way home.

'Fine, thank you.'

'Oh.' Cordelia had expected this topic to occupy them until their journey's end. 'People usually have a tale to tell these days – delays, overcrowding.'

'Indeed? Then these "people", whoever they are,' and Adelaide's tone suggested that Cordelia had made them up, 'shouldn't be so namby-pamby.'

Cordelia smothered a sigh. It was going to be a long visit.

When Cordelia and Kenneth had got married – or it might be more accurate to say that when Kenneth had got married – his law firm had presented him with a beautiful clock for his mantelpiece. The reason why Cordelia thought of it as a gift to mark Kenneth's marriage rather than *their* marriage, was because of the words that had been inscribed on the silver plate attached to the front of the base.

Presented by his colleagues
to Mr Kenneth Masters
on the occasion of his marriage.
24th January 1920

Strange to say, it hadn't occurred to her for quite some time that the inscription was inappropriate, offensive even, though she had no doubt it was unintentional. Fancy inscribing a wedding gift with one name, not both.

Yet somehow it didn't matter. It wasn't as though she had married Kenneth in a state of youthful adoration. It wasn't as though she deserved to have her name inscribed on the clock. In that respect, the clock might be said to symbolise her marriage. It was a handsome and expensive piece and her name was missing. But in another way, it most definitely did not symbolise her marriage, because it was a skeleton clock, with all its workings on show, and there was a great deal of Cordelia that was hidden and had been ever since Kit's death.

Then there was what the Masters family called one another. To her son, Adelaide was Mother; to Emily, she was Granny; while to Cordelia, she was always Mrs Masters. Cordelia loathed the distinction that seemed to set her apart from the others, yet at the same time she was well aware it was only what she deserved. She had been the perfect wife to Kenneth. She had entertained his colleagues and socialised with their wives. She had presented him with a beautiful, clever, funny, spirited daughter whom he adored. She had always treated him with the utmost courtesy and respect, but she had never loved him. Not even bearing his child had made her love him. Her heart had died with Kit.

Having Adelaide in the house had always had the effect of making Cordelia feel something of an outsider. Even though she knew it was going to happen, it was still disappointing and humiliating. She had never looked to Adelaide for support, so it was truly surprising when Adelaide came down heavily in favour of Cordelia's railway friends.

'Wartime friendships can be immensely important,' Adelaide declared. 'You should know, Kenneth. You were in the last war.'

'I was in the War Office for most of it and, yes, some of the acquaintances I made there have been most useful to me over the years,' said Kenneth. 'I fail to see how the people Cordelia comes across in her lamp-cleaning job can compare in any way.'

'I don't mean your War Office cronies,' Adelaide said with a touch of impatience. 'I mean before that – when you were in the trenches. Those men. You rubbed shoulders with all sorts.'

'Yes, I did. Jolly fine chaps, no matter what their background.'

'And their presence helped you to bear the unbearable,' said Adelaide. 'That's what I'm talking about. That's why you shouldn't have such a down on these women Cordelia has taken up with. It's all part of being at war and it's even more important this time round, with women engaged in war work on such a scale.'

Over the years, Cordelia had placed cool little duty kisses on Adelaide's cheek, but she had never put her arms around her. Right now, though, she could cheerfully have delivered the huge hug Dot had talked about.

Cordelia had assumed she wouldn't drop in on Mrs Cooper that weekend, but Adelaide's unexpected attitude inspired her not just to change her mind but also to invite Adelaide to accompany her. If Adelaide came home from

Mrs Cooper's and made agreeable remarks about the people she'd met, this might give Emily a nudge in the right direction and make her see that she'd been mistaken to look down her nose at Dot and Mrs Cooper. Fingers crossed.

When Sunday came round, the Masters family attended church, then Cordelia disappeared into the kitchen to prepare the meal. Some women had mothers-in-law who lent a hand in the kitchen, but Adelaide expected to be waited on; her sole contribution to meal preparation had been handing over her ration book upon arrival. Although she found Adelaide's hoity-toity ways irritating, Cordelia had to admit they had their useful side. Many a time over the years she had vanished into the kitchen to put the kettle on and taken a long time about it, knowing nobody would come to see what she was up to.

After lunch, Cordelia telephoned for a taxi to convey her and Adelaide to Mrs Cooper's. The taxi driver took one look at Adelaide swathed in her Sunday furs and leaped out of the motor to open the door for her.

As the vehicle turned into Wilton Close, Dot had almost reached the gate.

'I take it that is one of your friends,' said Adelaide when Cordelia directed the driver to pull over. 'What a well-dressed lady. You possess a coat similar to that, if I'm not mistaken.'

As they emerged from the motor, Dot beamed at them in her friendly way. Cordelia performed the introductions.

'Mrs Masters, this is my good friend Mrs Green, who works as a parcels porter on the Southport train. And this is my mother-in-law, Mrs Masters.'

'How do you do?' said Adelaide. 'I'm pleased to meet you.'

'Likewise,' Dot said cheerfully. 'It's a parky old day, isn't it?'

'It's a ... ' Adelaide repeated. Then, good manners prevailing, she replied, 'It is indeed rather cold.'

They went through Mrs Cooper's gate. As Dot headed for the front door, Adelaide hung back a little.

'When I saw that smart coat on your friend, Cordelia, I thought ... Well, I wasn't expecting the working-class voice, that's all.'

'Sorry, Mrs Masters.' Having rung the bell, Dot turned round. 'Were you speaking to me?'

'I was just admiring your coat. I believe my daughter-in-law has one very like it.'

'Not any more she doesn't,' laughed Dot. 'This is her old one. She gave it to me when mine came off worse in an argument with an incendiary.'

'Indeed?' Adelaide murmured. 'That was most generous of you, Cordelia.'

Mrs Cooper opened the front door. Cordelia introduced her and Adelaide and ushered her mother-in-law inside.

'Ah yes,' Adelaide said graciously, 'you're the Morgans' housekeeper, aren't you?'

'Just for the duration,' said Mrs Cooper. 'Shall I help you off with your coat? Oh my, isn't it soft?'

'Chinchilla,' said Adelaide.

'In here, if you please.' Mrs Cooper opened the door to the front room, looking as if she wanted to curtsey as Adelaide swanned past.

Mrs Grayson and Margaret were at home. Cordelia performed yet more introductions. Dot followed her in, carrying a cloth shopping bag, which she put on the carpet beside her chair.

'Are you enjoying your stay, Mrs Masters?' asked Mrs Grayson. 'How long are you here for?'

'I leave tomorrow to go to stay with an old friend I haven't seen for some time. After that I'll come back.'

'And how do you find your Emily?' asked Mrs Cooper. 'Is it long since you last saw her? Such a pretty girl.'

As agreeable as it was to hear Adelaide singing Emily's praises, Cordelia felt uncomfortable, as she always did when Emily's name came up among her friends.

At the first opportunity, she turned to Dot. 'What's in your bag?'

Dot reached down to pick it up. 'I've brought summat to show you.' She brought out a long stem of holly that looked as though it was covered in frost.

'How did you do that?' asked Mrs Grayson.

'Our Jenny learned it at Guides. You dip the holly in Epsom salts and let it dry.'

'It has a lovely sparkle,' said Margaret.

'Most festive,' said Adelaide. 'I'll take that idea home and tell the woman who does for me. I'm sure she could do the same with some lengths of ivy from the garden wall.'

Cordelia started to relax. Adelaide was a starchy old bird with a posh voice, but courtesy was her watchword and she would never talk down to these people. Besides, she had something to prove. She had expounded on the importance of friendship regardless of class in wartime and now she must show she meant it.

Would some of Adelaide's attitude rub off on Emily? Fingers crossed.

CHAPTER TWENTY-FIVE

Alison was among the first passengers to arrive on the platform, which meant she could be pretty sure of getting a seat. When the train pulled in, those on the platform stood back to let passengers alight, then there was a polite but determined surge towards the doors and the new set of travellers climbed aboard. It wasn't a corridor train, but one of those in which you stepped up through the door straight into the compartment, with upholstered bench seats that comfortably sat five on either side, though these days more than that often had to squeeze in. Above the seats and below the net luggage racks, a set of faded photographs of holiday destinations and a mirror in the middle were a reminder of pre-war days.

The first two people to enter had headed for the window seats on the far side, where they wouldn't be troubled by people getting on and off. Alison, third in, took the window seat beside the platform, tucking her feet out of the way of the next passengers to climb aboard. People on the platform glanced in and carried on walking, hoping to find seats further up.

Alison had a clear view of a large clock with Roman numerals hanging from the gantry and she kept an eye on the time. The train would soon be on its way. With luck, no one else would enter this compartment and she would have a comfortable journey back to Victoria. The guard walked past, checking the doors. Without needing to be asked, Alison stood up and drew down the blackout blind over the window, which prompted the man beside the other window to do the same. It was twilight now and it would soon be pitch-dark outside, with no street lamps or lights shining from windows. Inside the compartment, the single fifteen-watt bulb provided a vague glow, not sufficient to read by.

The guard's whistle shrilled, the train whistle answered, and the train slowly started on its way – at which moment the door beside Alison was wrenched open and a tall young man in a belted mackintosh flung himself aboard, yanking the door shut behind him.

'Sorry for startling you,' he said cheerfully, raising his hand to make sure he hadn't lost his hat when he ran for the train.

The people opposite Alison budged up to make room.

'No need for that, thanks all the same,' said the young man. 'I don't mind standing. I'll try not to sit on anyone's lap if we go over a bump.'

He turned round, away from Alison. Good. But then it transpired that he'd done so simply in order to say to those behind him, 'Pardon me turning my back on you,' and then he resumed his former position.

He was good-looking with blue eyes and a cheerful smile. Exertion had added a dash of colour to his cheekbones. Meeting Alison's eyes, he gave her a nod and a smile. She turned her face away. She wasn't interested in men, good-looking or otherwise. She had far more interesting things to think about. Yesterday she had been on one of the lines out of Manchester Victoria and today she'd been sent over to Leeds. Quite why they wanted her to travel all that distance, she didn't know, but she didn't mind. It was rather nice to settle back and enjoy the journey home.

Sometimes she hated and resented her new job because it was such a wretched substitute for getting married and being a happy young wife. At those times, she felt she was letting herself down by being interested in all the things she was learning. But was it really such a bad thing to be interested? Yes it was, when you compared it to leading a proper life and getting married. But it was what she was stuck with for now, so oughtn't she to make the best of it? Shouldn't she allow herself to be interested? Yet Alison knew that if this had happened to another girl, she would pity the girl for embracing her new life. 'Who does she think she's fooling?' That was what she would have said of the imaginary girl. Only she wasn't imaginary, was she? She was Alison.

She steered her thoughts away from her situation and concentrated on what she had picked up in the last couple of days. She carried a notebook with her, in which she wrote everything down so she wouldn't forget it. It would be humiliating if Miss Emery or somebody in authority asked her a question she couldn't answer. Being placed in a position of taking in so much information had given her the same feeling she'd had at school when she was cramming for exams.

With no view to look at, she glanced round the compartment. A lady was knitting without needing to look at what she was doing. A couple of men had started up a conversation. A clergyman was dozing. Without meaning to, Alison caught the eye of the man who had jumped aboard at the last moment. She looked away again. Stupid fellow, why hadn't he sat down when he'd been offered the chance instead of looming over everybody like that?

Alison decided that if she was sent on a long journey again, she'd bring her crochet with her. She had enjoyed watching the world go by this morning, but it was different travelling in the blackout.

The train slowed and came to a halt.

'Allow me,' said the young man. 'You never can tell these days.'

He opened the door and peered out. Alison glimpsed a faint blue light that was all that was permitted on station platforms these days.

'Yes – it's a station,' announced the young man. 'It isn't always.'

'This is where I get off.' The lady who had been knitting got up. 'Thank you for checking. Someone I know had an accident leaving a train.'

'Thought it was a station when it wasn't?' asked the young man.

'It was the right station, but in the dark he got off on the wrong side and fell onto the track.'

Jumping out onto the platform, the young man helped the lady out, tipping his hat to her as she walked away to be swallowed by the darkness. Climbing back aboard, the man took the free space and smiled round in a genial way. Did his bright and breezy manner make him appear younger than he was? Alison sneaked a glance. Late twenties, early thirties? It wasn't easy to tell in this dim light. Suddenly collecting herself, she twisted her face away, feeling annoyed. The last thing she wanted was to be caught looking.

The train set off again. It stopped a couple more times and on each occasion, the young man checked what was outside. Honestly, did he think he was a knight in shining armour? The next time the train stopped, Alison couldn't tolerate Sir Galahad any longer. She quickly rose and opened the door herself.

'Not a station,' she informed the others.

She was about to pull the door shut when further down, a flame flew through the air and fell to the ground, as if a burning object had been cast out of the train. In that brief

276

flash of light, Alison saw a bridge just beyond it. Everything she had learned these past two days sprang to the front of her mind.

'Someone's trying to blow up the bridge.'

She tossed the words over her shoulder while grabbing her torch from her bag and scrambling down onto the track. Even though she knew it would be a long way down, the plunge took her by surprise and she jolted her ankle. A moment later, Sir Galahad was by her side, pulling her upright.

'That way.' Alison pointed.

She and Sir Galahad weren't the only ones to have seen the flame. In the light of several torch beams, Alison could just make out a man running away and she set off after him at a sprint, or at least she tried to. Everybody seemed to be stumbling on the uneven ground in the darkness. Galahad overtook her, then turned back, catching her arm as she almost fell.

'Are you all right?' he asked.

'Go!' she insisted. A longshanks like him would be more use in the chase than she was. She followed as best she could. When she had been sitting behind a desk all day, she had enjoyed wearing heels, but once she'd started this job she'd surrendered those pretty quickly in favour of lace-up flatties and now she was glad she had.

Moments later, shouts from up ahead told her that the would-be saboteur had been caught. She came to a halt, her heart thumping from excitement, not exertion. Railway bridges were obvious targets for Jerry and she had taken part in the chase after a Jerry agent. She couldn't have felt more satisfied had she rugby-tackled him herself and brought him crashing to the ground.

A couple of soldiers, who were the ones who had actually caught the runaway, marched him along to the guard's van, the man loudly protesting his innocence all the way. Rotter! As if anyone would fall for that.

The guard and a ticket inspector spoke to everybody who had left the train, asking for details of what they'd witnessed – 'unless you're going all the way to Manchester Victoria, in which case you can give your evidence there.'

It was a devil of a job finding the right compartment to get back into. It might have had its funny side, but Alison had no intention of being friendly with Sir Galahad. When they did find their compartment, Alison wondered how on earth she was supposed to climb all that way up.

'I'll go first,' said Sir Galahad, 'then I'll help you.'

With the assistance of a couple of hands reaching down from above, he boosted himself up and through the door. Dropping to one knee, he thrust out his hand, but as she reached up to take it, he surprised her by taking not her hand but her elbow, which enabled her to boost herself far more effectively.

As the train went on its way, the others in the compartment were eager to hear what had happened and Galahad was happy to tell the story, such as it was, though Alison could see from the way he glanced at her that he considered it more her story than his.

'This lady is the one with the sharp eyes,' he said. 'I just followed.'

Everyone looked at her, so Alison described seeing the flame flying out of another compartment and falling to the ground.

'The train had just emerged from under a bridge,' she added. 'Bridges are high on the list of Jerry targets.'

There was rather a jolly atmosphere in the compartment for the remainder of the journey. Apparently, there was nothing like a Jerry saboteur for breaking the ice. When the train pulled into Victoria, the others alighted, but Sir Galahad hung back, glancing at Alison.

'I suppose we ought to wait here until everyone's gone and then find out whom we're meant to report to.'

'The transport police, I expect.'

The guard appeared at the open door. 'Excuse me. Are you the couple who helped chase the man?'

'Errol Flynn and Olivia de Havilland, at your service,' said Sir Galahad.

'If I might have your real name, sir?'

'Maitland – Dr Joel Maitland.'

'Thank you, sir. I'm pleased to tell you that the matter has been cleared up and your statements won't be required.'

'Really?' said Sir Galahad – Dr Maitland. 'Cleared up how?'

'An unfortunate incident, sir. The man concerned is an amateur photographer. A piece of celluloid film in his bag caught fire, so he chucked the bag out of the train. Then he realised everyone else thought it was a bomb and he panicked and made a run for it.'

'There's no doubt?' asked Alison. If the two men thought they were going to sort it out between them while she sat listening like a good little girlie, they were very much mistaken.

'None, madam.' The guard stepped away, touching his cap to them. 'Thank you for your brave actions. Good evening, Dr Maitland – Mrs Maitland.'

'I'm not—' Alison began, but he had already gone. Flustered, she looked at Dr Maitland. For once, his smile wasn't easy and frank; he actually looked a bit embarrassed.

He held out his right hand. 'We ought to do this properly. Dr Joel Maitland. How do you do?'

She couldn't refuse to shake hands, but she drew the line at sharing her name. 'Pleased to meet you.'

She immediately rose to her feet, picking up her bag and her gas-mask box. With a nod of farewell, she alighted and set off briskly along the platform, but Dr Maitland soon caught up with her. Had he hurried on purpose?

'If you aren't going to tell me your name, I'll have to call you Miss de Havilland.'

Alison didn't bother to reply.

'Look,' said Dr Maitland, 'I don't want to make a nuisance of myself, but would you like to go to the station buffet for a quick cup of tea?'

'No, thanks.'

'Won't you at least tell me your name? I can't keep on calling you Miss de Havilland.'

'You aren't going to keep on calling me anything.'

With that, Alison veered away, dodged around a couple of flatbed trolleys and went onto the adjoining platform, where dear Mr Thirkle was at the ticket barrier. She would chat with him for a few minutes, allowing Dr Joel Maitland ample time to leave the station and vanish from her life.

Tony hadn't been permitted to change his fire-watching commitments. Colette had braced herself to be on the receiving end of his displeasure. He never got angry with other people. He waited until he reached home and then took out his ill-humour on her. But on this occasion, he seemed to take his disappointment on the chin. In fact, he was being perfectly lovely at home, praising her cooking and complimenting her on how well she ran the house and took care of it.

'And me,' he added with an engaging grin. 'You take care of me beautifully and I want you to know how much I appreciate it.'

In former times, she would have all but melted into a puddle of gratitude and relief, but not now. Now she felt wary and disconcerted, but it was important not to let it show. She had to behave as she always had, so that Tony caught no inkling that his timid, eager-to-please wife was just waiting for her chance to fake her own death so she could escape from him.

Fake her own death. The thought of it still had the power to rob her of her breath. But Tony was being so kind, so attentive, reminding Colette of their courtship days when he had made her feel cherished and special and so very lucky. She didn't feel lucky now. She felt confused. Was he trying to win her over? Had he seen the error of his ways? Maybe he had sensed the change in her and he wanted to win her back. If that was the case, ought she to stay? What would a good wife do?

A good wife wouldn't fake her own death.

He presented her with a beautiful fringed shawl in an ivory colour patterned with a swirl of green and gold leaves.

'It's lovely,' breathed Colette as the soft, silky fabric flowed through her fingers.

'Do you like it?' asked Tony. 'It's not new, I'm afraid – well, obviously not in these days of coupons. I bought it second-hand, but you wouldn't know it wasn't new, would you?' He was eager for her approval.

'I love it. Thank you.'

'You deserve it.' Tony placed his hands on her shoulders and looked into her eyes. 'You're a wonderful girl, Colette. You work hard all day, then you come home and look after your husband and the house. Now, on top of all that, you're going out fire-watching twice a week. I'm proud of you.'

Colette dared to say, 'I thought you didn't like me doing it.'

Tony smiled warmly and his eyes crinkled. 'I wouldn't like you doing anything that possibly places you in danger.'

His expression changed and a chill ran through Colette. Then she realised he was – goodness, he was upset. Her kind heart reached out to him. He stepped away from her, and her new shawl slid along her arm as she touched him, wanting to draw him back.

Tony shook his head, tilting it away from her, but not before she had caught a gleam of – were there tears in his eyes? She didn't dare ask. Shedding a tear wasn't manly.

Clearing his throat, Tony smiled once more. 'I'm proud of you, darling.' His voice was husky. 'You're so completely selfless in everything you do. I wish I could keep you safe the whole time. It's what every husband wishes. But this is wartime and everybody has to live their life and do their duty. I understand why you want to be a fire-watcher, I honestly do, but at the same time I'm frightened silly that something might happen to you. I'm sure that the husbands of all lady fire-watchers, lady ARP wardens and lady ambulance drivers feel exactly the same, bursting with pride one minute and shaking with nerves like a jelly the next.

'I'm not saying this to talk you out of doing it. I'd hate you to think that. I didn't want you to take it on in the first place, but I've accepted it now.' He kissed her forehead, a tender gesture. 'Just be safe, that's all, my darling, my dearest darling,' he whispered. 'Just be safe.' He gently took the shawl from her and reached behind her to drape it round her shoulders. He rested his forehead against hers. 'My dearest darling.'

He drew her to him, cradling her against his body. Colette was glad of it, because it gave her the chance to hide her face, her confusion. This was the real Tony, the Tony she had fallen in love with, the man she had married.

'He'll cherish you for ever,' Mother had told her on the eve of her wedding day and happiness had blossomed inside Colette because she knew it was true.

Now here he was, cherishing her again. Her eyelids fluttered and closed as she gave herself up to the moment, unable to resist. This was the man she had married: loving, appreciative, reassuring. What bliss it had been being his wife in the early days, before she had started doing things wrong and he had oh so gently and kindly started setting her right.

But she hadn't been doing things wrong, she knew that now. Or if she had, they'd been small things, trivial things, and she hadn't deserved to have been made to feel so bad about them. All she had ever wanted was to be a good wife.

A good wife wouldn't fake her own death.

What if – what if her starting as a fire-watcher at the marshalling yard had shaken Tony out of his ways? Suppose the reason things were so bad for Bunty was that Father had never been brought up short and had therefore never questioned his own actions. Suppose that her becoming a fire-watcher had given Tony the shock he needed, so that instead of unconsciously copying his father, he was now thinking afresh about how he conducted himself as a husband. Could it be, could it really be that he had turned over a new leaf? Was their marriage now going to proceed along new lines?

All she had ever wanted was to be a good wife.

Could it be that the man she had fallen in love with was being restored to her?

CHAPTER TWENTY-SIX

It was the beginning of December. This time last year, Alison had started her own personal countdown to the Christmas proposal that had never happened. At least she'd had something to look forward to last year. What did she have to look forward to this year, other than spending Christmas Day with a fixed smile on her face while she died a little more inside each time she looked at the wedding ring on Lydia's finger? Perhaps she could duck out of spending the day with her family. But she knew she couldn't.

This week, she was dividing her time between Left Luggage and Lost Property, which wasn't exactly proving to be the most thrilling time of her life, so she was pleased to be summoned by Miss Emery, who had asked to see her at the end of the day. Perhaps something more interesting was about to come her way.

She presented herself outside Miss Emery's office, noticing how chilly it was. She knocked on the wall and Miss Emery looked round.

'Thank you for coming, Miss Lambert. How are you getting on this week?' As she spoke, Miss Emery rose and pushed her office chair towards the rear of the large alcove, placing the extra chair opposite it. 'Have a seat. I know this isn't exactly private, but we can speak quietly. It won't take long.'

Alison sat down, noticing that Miss Emery's usual professional smile had twitched into something wider and more attractive.

'I had an unusual experience today,' said Miss Emery, 'something that has never happened to me before. I think I have been asked to play Cupid. You may well look surprised,' she added with a laugh. 'I was pretty surprised myself. Do you know a Dr Joel Maitland?'

Alison's mouth dropped open. She snapped it shut at once, but there was nothing she could do to prevent the heat from flooding her cheeks. 'We've met.'

'I gather you were quite the heroine.'

'Not at all. I was one of several who took action and it turned out to have been a false alarm anyway.'

'That isn't quite how Dr Maitland tells it,' said Miss Emery, still smiling, 'but I'll take your word for it.'

Alison shook her head, baffled. 'Do you know him?'

'No. He came to see me. You were wearing your LMS badge on your lapel when he met you.'

Ah. Light was beginning to dawn. Alison glanced down at her badge with its linked emblems of an English rose and a Scottish thistle beneath a wing with the Cross of St George.

'Dr Maitland found out that there is a welfare supervisor for women. He ended up being referred to me. He hoped I could put him in touch with you.'

'You didn't—'

'Hand out personal information? Naturally not. But he is keen to see you again. The question is, would you like to see him? He said he owes you a cup of tea in the buffet.'

Alison made a tutting sound with her tongue. 'I gave him the brush-off. You'd think he would have taken the hint.'

'Maybe, but plenty of girls would be glad that he didn't. He's very good-looking and rather charming, I thought.'

Alison felt like saying, 'You have him, then.' In a politer voice than the one in her head, she said, 'I'm sorry your chance to play Cupid has turned out to be a failure.'

'It's your decision, of course, but you need to be sure, because this is your only chance – or should I say it is Dr Maitland's only chance. If you say no, I'll go and tell him and that will be the end of it.'

Alison frowned. 'You'll go and tell him? Does that mean he's here?' She looked round as if he might spring out of the cupboard.

'I've stashed him in a room on the ground floor. You needn't worry about seeing him again if you don't want to. There's something he asked me to say if you were unsure.'

'I'm completely sure,' said Alison. 'I don't want to.'

'Fair enough. I'll give you ten minutes and then I'll go and tell him.'

'What was it he asked you to say?' Alison couldn't quell her curiosity.

'He asked me to tell you that Maid Marian would never leave Robin Hood in the lurch.'

Alison laughed in spite of herself, recognising the reference to one of the films Olivia de Havilland had starred in with Errol Flynn. Dr Maitland's cheerful good humour had been agreeable rather than otherwise, now she thought about it.

Miss Emery glanced at her wristwatch. 'I'll go and see him in ten minutes.'

Rising, Alison returned her chair to its rightful position, not looking at Miss Emery as she said, 'No, don't worry about it. I'll do it. Which room is he in?'

On her way downstairs, she wondered what to do. It wasn't that she wanted to have a cup of tea with him. She definitely didn't want to do that. But it was a shame that Miss Emery hadn't come up with an alternative idea ... like Alison needn't see Dr Maitland this evening, but she could have another chance next week – or after Christmas – or in the spring. Postponing it in that way wouldn't mean she had to say yes when the time came – in fact, she had no intention of saying yes – but it would keep her options open.

Why would she be in need of options if she definitely had no intention of saying yes?

Her heart was racing and maybe that was why she threw open the door to the little room where Dr Maitland was waiting. He stood up, holding his trilby by the brim. His smile was hopeful. She had forgotten how good-looking he was.

'Hello, Miss de Havilland.'

'Please don't call me that.'

'I won't have to if you tell me your name.'

'You don't need to know it.'

Dr Maitland's face fell. 'Oh. I see. I thought when you walked in instead of the other lady … Are you sure I can't change your mind? Only I've gone to a devil of a lot of trouble to find you. I'd hate for you to slip away again.'

What harm could there be? It was only a cup of tea and a chat. It would give her something else to think about instead of endlessly remembering the hopes she'd nursed this time last year. If she was honest, wasn't it rather nice to be found attractive after having been thrown over for another girl?

'Well – just this once. Since you've gone to all that trouble.'

He smiled and his blue eyes softened. Another girl might have found them irresistible, but Alison was immune. Her experience with Paul had seen to that. She had nothing to lose by going for a cup of tea just this once, and who knew, she might claw back a bit of her self-esteem.

Forestalling him, she said, 'I don't want to go to the station buffet. Do you know the Worker Bee café?'

'Lead the way.'

'No.' She didn't want to be seen with him anywhere in the vicinity of Victoria Station. 'I'll meet you there in half an hour. Don't you want directions?' she asked as Dr Maitland put on his hat.

'I found you, didn't I? I think I can find a café.'

'It'll probably be busy.' What on earth had made her agree to this? 'If it is, I won't wait for a table. That'll be the end of it.'

Dr Maitland didn't say anything to that. Once he had left the room, Alison sank onto a chair, astonished at what she was in the middle of. She was going to meet a man – though why shouldn't she? She wasn't tied to Paul any more. But he was the only man she'd ever wanted to be tied to.

She felt like standing Dr Maitland up, but that wouldn't be fair. She would go to the Worker Bee because she'd said she would. With luck, it would be full and that would be the end of it. She would never have to think about Dr Joel Maitland again.

Alison made her way through the blackout to the Worker Bee and slipped inside, turning off her torch as she pushed aside the edge of the floor-length blackout curtains. The café's owner, who had been fined early in the war for breaking the blackout, had constructed a wooden frame a couple of feet inside the door from which hung more lengths of black cloth, so that once you were inside the door you were standing in what was effectively a black-lined cubicle, meaning that no matter how many customers came and went, there was no danger of the blackout being broken.

Alison entered the café, finding it busy, the tables full. Good. She was off the hook.

No, she wasn't. Over by the blacked-out window, a couple were getting to their feet, the girl picking up her handbag and fastening her coat. Beside them, talking to the man, was Joel Maitland. Oh no. Had he hovered over them, willing them to leave?

Alison stood aside for the couple to pass her and then made her way to the table they had quit. Dr Maitland's expression brightened at the sight of her. He made a few passes with his hands, like a conjuror presenting something to an enraptured audience.

He grinned at her. 'Your table awaits, madam.'

Aware that others were looking their way in amusement, Alison couldn't wait to sit down. To her surprise, Dr Maitland pulled out her chair for her. You didn't expect that sort of attention in an ordinary little café like this, but it was rather pleasant. She responded with a smile, then remembered that she didn't really want to be here, but it was too late. Dr Maitland had already seen her smile.

'Just the promised cup of tea?' he offered. 'Would you like something more? A sandwich, perhaps, or something on toast? They've got what look like carrot scones. Or am I breaking the rules by offering?'

'Tea, please, not too strong.'

'You won't mind if I have a bite to eat?'

Dr Maitland threaded his way between the tables to place his order at the counter, returning with a tray holding a pot of tea and a rock cake.

'You'd better pour yours at once if you like it on the weak side,' he said as he emptied the tray. 'I'll have mine after it's had a chance to brew.'

Alison poured her tea, then took the lid off the pot and stirred its contents. 'That'll brew it quicker.'

'Is that a hint? To make me drink up so you can get out of here faster?'

'It so happens I don't have a lot of time. I have to go out on first-aid duty tonight and I have things to do before then.'

'Which first-aid area do you cover?'

'I applied to Withington.'

'Is that where you live?'

'No,' she said briefly. 'I have a couple of friends attached to that group and I wanted to be with them, if possible. This will be my first night.'

'Good luck.'

'Thank you. Your tea is probably ready now. Shall I pour?'

'Yes, please. Then, if you don't want me to call you Olivia, I can call you Mother. Or you could just tell me your real name.'

'Didn't Miss Emery tell you?'

'She was highly discreet.'

Alison huffed a small sigh. To persist in not telling him would make her look daft. 'Alison Lambert.'

'How do you do, Alison Lambert? I'm Dr Joel Maitland.'

'I know.'

'I didn't exactly keep it secret, did I? I hope I wasn't too forward on the train, but – well, I didn't want you to disappear out of my life, though you've probably worked that out already.' There was uncertainty in Dr Maitland's smile, as if he didn't want to say the wrong thing.

'You certainly went to a lot of trouble to find me,' Alison said, deliberately offhand.

'Are you madly impressed? Seriously, I was the one who was impressed last week on the train. You said, "Someone's trying to blow up the bridge," and off you went in pursuit.'

'So did a number of others – you among them. I didn't do anything special.'

'I'm trying to pay you a compliment.'

Alison shrugged. 'Thanks.'

'What job do you do on the railways? I assume you're some sort of bridge expert.'

Sheer surprise made her laugh. 'A bridge expert?'

'You sounded so knowledgeable when you said someone wanted to blow up the bridge. You sounded as if you knew your stuff.'

'I do know a bit about bridges, but only a bit. Enough to know they're a target for the Luftwaffe, but I expect everyone knows that.'

'I think you're being modest.'

'Well, yes, I do know a bit more than that, but I'm no expert. It just so happens I'd spent a day or two learning about them.'

'What sort of thing?' Dr Maitland's eyes were keen with interest.

Alison stiffened. 'I'm not sure I'm allowed to talk about it.'

'I promise I'm not a spy.'

'I don't imagine you are, but you never know who's listening.' She leaned forward. 'You don't think I'm overreacting in not talking about it?'

Dr Maitland's good-natured expression settled into something more serious. 'Not at all. Loose lips sink ships, and all that.'

Oh, but it would have been good to share what she'd learned. It wasn't that she wanted to show off as such, but she would have enjoyed feeling that she had something interesting to say. Interesting? Bridges? Well, yes, actually – much to her surprise. She had learned how the bridges had been reinforced, not just against attack, but also to bear heavy wartime loads. In case they were damaged, necessary parts had been prepared and stored near the most strategically important bridges, so that they could be repaired swiftly. There were invasion plans, too, involving railway bridges, especially in the south of England and along the east coast, where, should Jerry set foot on British soil, wagons filled with pieces of concrete and old railway track stood ready to be shunted onto important bridges and have their wheels blown off.

'But there are rules about how much damage you can do to a bridge,' she'd been told. 'It's all very well stopping Jerry using our railways, but should we recapture the ground, we have to be able to make good any deliberate damage within two days.'

Dr Maitland bit into his rock cake and nodded. 'Tasty. If we can't discuss bridges, what shall we talk about? I could describe how to perform an appendectomy, if you like. It doesn't matter who overhears that, though it might put them off their barm cakes.'

'When are you going back to Leeds?'

'I'm not. What an odd question.'

'Don't you live there? Aren't you here visiting?'

'The other way round. I live and work here. I was there on a visit.' His eyes twinkled. 'You don't get rid of me that easily.' Then he sobered. 'Look, I don't want to come on too strong and put you right off, but I don't think it's a secret at this point that I'm interested in you. I hope you'll want to see me again and I'm trying not to think about how you might prefer it if I went back to Leeds. Before I make an even bigger ass of myself, just tell me if you already have a chap. A lovely girl like you seems bound to have a boy-friend – or maybe a husband.'

Had he but known it, he couldn't have asked a more difficult or hurtful question. Worst of all, though, was the colour that flooded Alison's face.

'There isn't anyone.'

She might have expected Dr Maitland to make some sort of breezy reply, but he didn't. Maybe he was trying to interpret her blushes. Alison stuck as much of her face as she could into her teacup. Having drained it, she put it down.

'Thanks for the tea. I must go now.'

'May I walk you to your bus stop?'

'No, thank you.'

'Before you go, there's something I'd like to say. For the record, I want you to know that you did something special on that train. Without a second thought, you jumped out and pursued a possible saboteur. You weren't to know that others would do the same or that the saboteur was a photographer who'd lost his head. You acted with the heart of a heroine and I'm not saying that to inveigle my way into your good graces. I'm saying it because it's true. Even if we never see one another again, I'll remember you with sincere admiration.'

Alison felt oddly breathless. It was so long since anyone had made her feel good about herself. 'Thank you.'

'Now for the all-important question before you vanish into the blackout,' said Dr Maitland. 'May I see you again? Please?'

CHAPTER TWENTY-SEVEN

For the first time in her married life, Cordelia was looking forward to having Adelaide to stay. She still felt warm and satisfied when she pictured Adelaide sticking up for her on the question of wartime friendships. She would never have expected Adelaide to understand, but as Adelaide had pointed out, she had learned from her own experience. That made her support even more valuable, because Kenneth couldn't argue with it.

He hadn't raised the subject since Adelaide had left their house to visit her friend. Cordelia sensed he was thinking about it. While he wouldn't let his mother dictate his views, he did have a lot of respect for her opinions and she had clearly given him something to think about. It was a pity Kenneth had spent most of the last war in the War Office, surrounded by high-ranking military men and upper-crust civilians. If he hadn't, maybe he would be more open to Cordelia's railway friendships now.

As it was, Cordelia had had no qualms about making firm commitments to help Dot in the Christmas Kitchen, which was making use of a school kitchen in Withington, not far from where Dot lived. The first time she went coincided with Emily being due to spend the evening with a friend, so Cordelia was spared the heartache of wondering whether to persuade her to come too. Then Emily surprised her by taking an interest.

'I'd love to have helped,' she declared. 'Our fire-watching is essential work, of course, but let's be honest, there's seldom anything for us to do. This Christmas Kitchen scheme sounds perfect for helping out in a practical way that has results.'

'Maybe you can come next time,' said Cordelia.

As she set off for Withington by taxi, she was calm and composed – and not just on the outside, in the way everybody expected of her, but inside as well, and it was thanks to Adelaide and Emily. Her sense of well-being lasted all evening. It was agreeable to spend a couple of hours with other women, preparing fish pies topped with mashed potato – no, it was more than agreeable. It was rather fun.

'What sort of fish is it?' she asked Dot.

'White.'

'I mean—'

'I know what you mean, love,' said Dot. 'You don't ask too many questions these days where fish is concerned. I don't want to be told if I'm eating summat I've never heard of and I especially don't want to be told if I'm eating whale meat.'

Joan, Sheila and Pammy were all there and Sheila started everyone singing 'We'll Meet Again', soon followed by 'Kiss Me Goodnight, Sergeant Major' and 'Run, Rabbit, Run'. Then someone started 'The Holly and the Ivy' and Cordelia thought of the carol service she and her friends were going to go to together on Christmas Eve. Just then, she couldn't think of anything that would be more special.

Pammy began the Judy Garland song 'Over the Rainbow', but this time no one else sang along. Pammy didn't have a strong voice, but it was clear and true, and Cordelia saw more than one listener brush away a tear.

Dot appeared by her side. 'That's what this is all about. Hope. Yes, it's sensible and practical and folk will benefit from it. But the Christmas Kitchens are about more than giving practical help. They're about goodwill and hope, and you can never have too much of them.'

It was the day of Adelaide's return. Cordelia would have liked to meet her at the station, but her shifts didn't permit it, so Kenneth was taking time off work to do so.

'Accompanied by the office junior,' he said at the breakfast table. 'I'll put you and Granny in a taxi outside the station, Emily, and give you the money, then I'll go back to the office.'

'I could meet her on my own, if you like,' Emily offered. 'You don't have to come.'

There was a moment of silence, then the three of them burst out laughing.

'Much as Granny loves you, darling,' said Kenneth, 'she does expect the full guard of honour.'

Cordelia had put a lot of thought into planning the menus for her mother-in-law's return visit, for the first time ever doing so out of a feeling of warmth and the desire to please rather than her usual intention of showing the old bat that her son had married a worthwhile wife. Rabbit pudding with mushrooms livened up with precious bacon promised to be a tasty dinner, and she had a recipe for beehive cake containing honey and candied peel recommended by Mrs Grayson, whose wartime cooking was second to none.

When Cordelia arrived home from work, she hardly waited to remove her outdoor things before going into the sitting room to greet her guest, not merely bending over Adelaide to give her a kiss but resting her hands on the older woman's shoulders and smiling at her. Cordelia felt a twinge of regret for the years of them not liking one another. Never mind. From now on, they would be allies. She might even drop the 'Mrs Masters' and start using 'Mother'. Wouldn't that be something?

The rabbit pudding was a success, but the real success of the evening was the sense of companionship. Wanting to befriend her mother-in-law, Cordelia displayed a warm interest in Adelaide's visit to her friend. No one could accuse Adelaide of not being happy to hold the floor and she rattled on about Lady Ogden-Kirk's committees and her Labradors, which were a lot trimmer than they had been pre-war. Cordelia smiled to herself. It seemed that all Adelaide's friends' husbands had been knighted at the end of long and distinguished careers in the law or the Civil Service, but Adelaide had been widowed before she could become Lady Masters, though that had never stopped her carrying herself as if she bore the title.

On Saturday, Cordelia asked Adelaide if she would like to come with her to Wilton Close the next day.

'To see your mixture of friends,' said Adelaide.

'I happen to know that some of my younger friends will be there and I'd like you to meet them. Perhaps Emily would like to come with us.'

Cordelia glanced at Emily, who was reading a book. Emily didn't look up.

'Thank you for inviting me,' Adelaide said in her formal way. 'I'd be pleased to accompany you.'

Satisfaction bloomed inside Cordelia. Tomorrow's visit to Wilton Close would set the seal on her new relationship with Adelaide. Adelaide making a second visit would show Kenneth and Emily the importance of reviewing their ideas. Kenneth was quick to criticise people who clung stubbornly to opinions that were shown to be mistaken and he was inclined to rub their noses in it. He would shortly have to admit his own error and Cordelia had decided to be all grace and generosity when the time came.

After lunch on Sunday, she helped Adelaide into her magnificent furs and slipped into her own wine-coloured coat on which the topstitching on the collar and the buttoned wrist straps was elegant and stylish. It was a grey day and they had walked to church that morning through fog, but that had lifted now apart from some lingering tendrils. Cordelia stood in front of the hall mirror to put on her hat, flicking the ends of her ash-blonde hair out of the woollen scarf that she wore tucked inside her coat collar.

'I'm glad you're coming with me ... Mrs Masters.'

At the last moment, she drew back from calling her Mother. She smiled to herself. What were the chances of Adelaide inviting her to use that endearing name? If it were ever to happen, surely this afternoon was the appropriate time.

'It's as I said last week,' Adelaide replied, pushing her fingers into her calfskin gloves, 'wartime friendships matter.'

'These are more than wartime friendships,' Cordelia told her, happy to discuss the subject. 'I'm sure that in my group of friends, we are forging friendships that will last a lifetime.'

She turned from the mirror to face Adelaide, her smile freezing as she took in Adelaide's narrowed eyes and tightened lips.

'A lifetime?' Adelaide repeated. 'Don't be absurd. Wartime friendships are precisely that. Friendships of the moment, friendships of convenience, if you like, and I do not say that in any way disparagingly. I say it as a statement of fact. Wartime breaks down barriers and friendships spring up accordingly. In their own way, they do a lot of good, but they're certainly not ... ' Adelaide twisted her lips as if about to utter words that were deeply distasteful to her, '... lifelong.'

'But they are,' Cordelia exclaimed. 'I know it. I can feel it. And I most definitely want them to be.'

'Preposterous.'

'No, it isn't. You said it yourself. Wartime breaks down barriers.'

'Yes – and then peace is restored and life returns to normal.'

'The rich man in his castle, the poor man at his gate?' Cordelia enquired tartly.

'Exactly. That is the natural order.'

'What about your own wartime friendships, the ones that you talked about?'

'I thought I'd made myself clear. They were *wartime* friendships – important and necessary in helping everyone do their bit, even rather pleasing in a way, but not lasting.' Adelaide spoke as if Cordelia was being silly and unreasonable. 'Definitely not lasting.'

'Well, mine are,' said Cordelia. 'Things are changing. Ideas are changing.'

'Oh, not that old chestnut.' Adelaide sighed elaborately. 'People claimed that last time and it didn't happen, or only in a very small way. Really, Cordelia, I thought better of you than to be so foolish. Lacking in duty too.'

'I beg your pardon?'

'I'm not referring to your duty to your country. I refer to your duty to your family, to your husband and daughter. How dare you indulge in this silly fantasy of lifelong friendships with the lower classes? What is Kenneth to do with you if that's how you behave? You'll make him a laughing stock. As for Emily, you're meant to set her an example of correct conduct and high moral standards. Maybe she ought to come and live with me, if your head is so full of nonsensical twaddle that you can't tell the difference between matters of the moment and those that are long-lived.' With an impressive swish, Adelaide presented her back to Cordelia. 'Kindly remove my furs. I most certainly will not indulge your idiocy by visiting your so-called friends, lifelong or otherwise.'

On Sunday afternoon, Colette took advantage of a few minutes on her own with Mrs Cooper.

'How are you bearing up?' Mrs Cooper asked.

Guilt swamped Colette. Dear Mrs Cooper had been worrying about her, but maybe there was no longer anything to worry about.

'Tony's changed. He couldn't be more agreeable. I – I feel ashamed of making such a fuss before.'

'Making a fuss?' exclaimed Mrs Cooper. Then she lowered her voice to say, 'Have you forgotten all the things you told me about the way he's treated you? Have you forgotten telling me how frightened you are of ending up like your mother-in-law?'

Tears rose behind Colette's eyes and she blinked them away. 'No, I haven't forgotten, but Tony is different now. He's kind and attentive and he appreciates everything I do. He even helps me get ready to go out fire-watching. I'll tell you something, Mrs Cooper. If he'd treated me this way for the past five years, I'd be the happiest, most adoring wife in the world.'

Mrs Cooper looked at her for a long moment. 'But he hasn't treated you that way for the past five years, has he, lovey?' Her voice was gentle. 'He's ground you down and made you scared of putting a foot wrong.'

'I know that, but now he's gone back to being the man I fell in love with. If he could always be like this ... '

Mrs Cooper hugged her. 'Oh, my dear lass.' She released Colette, smoothing her hair like a mother would.

'Do you – do you want me to give back Lizzie's certificates?' Colette asked. Had she let Mrs Cooper down?

'What? Lord, no!'

'I know how much it meant to you to hand them over. You – you said you didn't want to give them to me unless I was sure about leaving.'

'Let's see how things go, eh? You have to decide what's best for you. But it's my belief that folk are the way they are and they don't change, not deep down. Just be careful, eh?'

'I will.'

'And I'll always be here.'

On Monday, Colette was jolted out of her personal worries by all the talk of Pearl Harbor. She shared everyone's profound shock at the news of the havoc and destruction that had been wrought. But there was more than one comment of, 'They've got to enter the war now,' and she silently agreed. What had taken place at Pearl Harbor was truly terrible and she wouldn't wish it on any nation – but since it had happened, please let it benefit the Allies.

On Monday night, there was a short air raid between ten and eleven. Colette's heart hammered more or less all the way through it as she sat in the Anderson shelter. There hadn't been any raids since the beginning of November and she had spent all that month longing for one, longing for a bad one to happen wherever she was, so she could run away. Now here was a raid in progress and she was stuck in the Andy with Tony while conflicting thoughts flew around inside her head.

What should she do? Had Tony really changed? Or was Mrs Cooper right?

'Thank you, Mrs Naylor. You've done exactly the right thing in reporting this to me.'

The right thing? Had she? Yes, the men Colette had seen were breaking the rules. But who was she to judge? She – the wife who had everything in place, ready for her to disappear, leaving everyone who knew her to believe she was dead. If she went through with it. Oh, it was so confusing.

It was much easier to think about the railway men she had seen helping themselves to sugar. It had happened on a day when she'd been doing her 'official' job, something that was always a pleasure to her, because she loved helping people. She had travelled with a mother and her physically impaired son who wore calipers, and afterwards she had killed time by wandering around the station before it was time to catch the train back to Victoria. She had stood watching the arrival of a loco pulling goods wagons. Sitting on a bench out of the way, she watched as sack trolley after sack trolley piled with crates of tinned foods and sacks of flour were unloaded and borne away.

Just as she was checking her wristwatch to see if it was time to go, she had noticed that sacks of flour or sugar in an almost empty wagon were being shoved about more energetically than she had previously observed. Perhaps the men were tired and putting in an extra effort now that the end of their job was in sight. She could understand that. But then – did a sack split? And did one of the men laugh? She wasn't sure, because if he did, the sound was quickly cut off.

It seemed odd, but she dismissed it and was about to get up and walk away when a hand reached up from below, from in between the wagons, and a series of containers was passed up onto the platform – containers that were swiftly removed from the scene.

'It happens, I'm afraid,' Miss Emery said now. 'The sugar – it's sure to have been sugar – will have poured down between the boards in the base of the wagon into strategically placed containers beneath.'

'I wasn't sure whether to say anything,' Colette admitted. 'I thought maybe they were doing it just this once to help their wives make Christmas cakes.'

'It's still theft,' said Miss Emery.

'What will happen now?'

'The evidence is undoubtedly long gone, so at this point it would be your word against theirs – don't look so worried. It won't come to that. But it could be that an inspector might be on hand whenever a cargo of foodstuff arrives in future. If this pilfering is a regular thing, that will frustrate the system. Thank you for your vigilance, Mrs Naylor.'

Colette felt better about it after that. If it had been a one-off, the men wouldn't be sanctioned, but if it was more than that, they wouldn't be able to do it in the future. She hoped it was just the once. Maybe she was silly to imagine them giving their wives the wherewithal to bake perfect Christmas cakes, but this far into the war, everyone was anxious for a good Christmas.

Or was she just being foolish? She thought back to earlier in the year when her friends had worked together to catch a thief who had been helping himself to tinned goods from a secret food store. To her shame, she hadn't been able to help them because it had been at the time when Tony still didn't let her have much to do with her friends, let alone allow her to set foot outside the house at night. But she had been proud of her friends, especially Dot, when the thief had been apprehended.

There was no doubt the thief deserved the prison sentence he had been given. But what of those railwaymen who had helped themselves to the sugar? If Colette was relieved that they had got away with it, did that mean she thought that small-scale pilfering was acceptable? Or was she relieved because she was uncomfortable at having snitched on them? But why be uncomfortable about doing the right thing?

The more she dwelt on it, the more complicated it became. She would have liked the chance to discuss it and clear her thoughts, but she knew Miss Emery wouldn't want it talked about. Besides, wasn't the real reason she was concentrating on it was because she was attempting to distract herself from what was going on at home?

Tony was being kindness itself and it was impossible not to be relieved and grateful. There hadn't been a single cross word from him and not once had he made her feel all tangled up because she knew she was being outwitted. He had even made her laugh. She had forgotten how good it felt to laugh.

No wonder she had ended up focusing her thoughts on those railwaymen and their pilfering. At times she felt as if her head was crammed so full of questions and worries that there couldn't possibly be space in there for even one more idea.

No one knows what goes on behind closed doors.

When in doubt, apologise.

A good wife wouldn't fake her own death.

The three sentences that summed up her married life. All she had ever wanted was to be the best wife she could to Tony. The question was, had he truly turned over a new leaf? Had he become the husband she had always wanted?

CHAPTER TWENTY-EIGHT

Alison didn't know whether to be delighted or ashamed. She had agreed to see Dr Joel Maitland again. Never mind the confusion between pleasure and shame – what she mainly felt was surprise. No, it went deeper than that. It was honest-to-goodness amazement. She, Alison Lambert, jilted Alison, heartbroken Alison, the former future Mrs Paul Dunaway, had actually agreed to go out with another man.

She wished she hadn't put her name in the notebook to say she would be in the buffet that Friday evening. What if her friends asked what her plans were for that evening? She wasn't going to go home with Mabel and Margaret, so she was bound to be asked. She had a lie ready, about meeting up with Lydia, but what if she had a mad moment and blurted out that she was going to the pictures with a virtual stranger she'd met on a train? She knew the others would be pleased for her if they thought she felt ready to rebuild her social life, and it wasn't that she wanted to hide the truth from them – not exactly. But she didn't want them to think she was over Paul – and she certainly didn't want anyone thinking she was the type to let herself be picked up on a train. She must have been mad to say she would see Dr Maitland again. Perhaps she should stand him up.

Despite her reservations, Alison was glad to be with her friends after work. It had been an important week and sometimes you needed to be with people who mattered to you.

'Isn't it good to know that America has declared war on Germany and Italy?' said Mabel. 'It's what we've needed for a long time.'

The younger members of the group agreed whole-heartedly, but Cordelia and Dot both looked serious, even sad.

'For the second time in my life,' said Dot, 'the whole world is at war. It was never supposed to happen again, not after the last lot.'

'What's staggering is that it's happened again so soon,' said Cordelia. 'When will we ever learn?' She sat up straight and drew back her shoulders. 'Still, there's one good thing. All of you girls can be proud that you signed up to join the railways before you had to.'

Alison knew Cordelia was referring to the conscription that had been announced for single girls aged twenty to thirty. At a time when the Japanese had not only destroyed Pearl Harbor but had also sunk HMS *Repulse* and HMS *Prince of Wales*, it was more important than ever that everybody pulled their weight.

'Has anyone any good news?' asked Margaret. 'What about the Christmas Kitchen, Dot?'

Dot's smile returned to her face. 'It was Stir-up Sunday last weekend and lots of us turned out to get the Christmas puds started.'

'You're making proper Christmas puddings?' Persephone asked. 'That's impressive, with all the shortages.'

'What have you put in them?' asked Cordelia.

Dot looked rueful. 'To be honest, they're not that different to the sultana puddings that were made last year. We had some currants to add and some jars of home-made marmalade and we bulked it all out with breadcrumbs. They're not real Christmas puds, but it felt right making them on Stir-up Sunday.'

'I'm sure they'll go down well,' said Alison. 'My mother says that when you eat a meal, you can tell if someone has put special effort into cooking it for you.'

'Then I can promise you,' said Dot, 'that all the folk what have these meals right through to New Year's Day will feel like they've had a feast fit for a king.' She looked round the table. 'You've all got the dates in your diaries for when you've agreed to help, haven't you?'

Everyone else laughed and nodded. Alison realised she hadn't volunteered. Was she the only one not to? How self-absorbed she had been. She would rectify that oversight.

A little later, when the group was about to split up and go home, there were the usual questions about what everyone would be doing over the weekend. Joan and Dot were both working. Just as Alison had expected, she was asked why she wasn't heading home with Margaret and Mabel.

'I'm seeing my sister.'

Out trotted the lie and she was pleased with herself – until the others all wished her a pleasant evening and sent Lydia their good wishes. That made Alison feel rotten. She didn't like deceiving her friends. On the other hand, if she never saw Dr Joel Maitland again after tonight, there would be no more need for lies. Good. She just had to get this evening over with.

'I want to make something clear,' Alison told Dr Maitland when she met him outside the cinema. 'This isn't us going out together. Not *going out* going out. Not like a couple seeing one another. This is just meeting up as friends – not even that, really, since we barely know one another. We're just two people who might become friends. Might.' What was the matter with her? Why couldn't she shut up?

Dr Maitland nodded and was he smothering a smile? 'Understood. We're two people who happen to be in the same place at the same time, nothing more. Will you let me sit next to you during the film or shall we meet up again in the foyer afterwards?'

'Don't get clever with me,' Alison retorted, 'or I might not even agree to that much.'

They went inside. Dr Maitland purchased their tickets and they entered the auditorium. The strong smell of tobacco stung Alison's eyes and she blinked it away. The usherette showed them to their seats and they took off their coats and sat down.

'Where do you work?' Alison asked. If they talked about him, she wouldn't give away anything about herself.

'MRI.'

She nodded. Manchester Royal Infirmary. Automatically, she recalled what she knew of it from the Christmas Blitz. The nurses' home had been hit and an oil bomb had come down by parachute and destroyed the hospital's main staircase. Then there were the brave nurses who had faced fire and smoke to deal with an incendiary that had fallen down the chimney, endangering the patients in their ward.

'Are you a surgeon?' she asked.

'I am now. I did some intensive training last year. I thought that was how I could be of most use. That was when I moved to MRI. Before that I was at Withington. I started out as a paediatrician – a children's doctor.'

'Really?' Suddenly, she wasn't just making conversation. She was genuinely interested. 'What made you choose that?'

'I'm one of four children – or I used to be. I had a brother until I was twelve. He went into hospital for a routine operation and for no reason that anyone could explain, he died under the anaesthetic.'

'I'm sorry to hear that.'

'I always knew I wanted to be a doctor. Losing my brother at a young age steered me towards children's medicine, because I know what it's like when a family loses a child. I know what it's like for the other children.'

'And you wanted to save other families from that.'

'I'd like to go back into paediatrics after the war.'

The house lights went down and the Pathé News began, the principal item being the declaration of war by the United States. Alison found herself wanting to discuss the news with Dr Maitland. She would be interested in hearing his views.

Wait – no, she wouldn't. He was just someone she was here with more or less by accident.

After the film, they stood for the national anthem, then joined the crowd leaving the building. As torch beams dimmed by layers of tissue paper showed up around them on the pavement, Alison couldn't help but be aware of other couples walking close together, linking arms or holding hands, in some cases even walking with their arms around one another. Mum would have her guts for garters if she ever behaved like that in public.

It felt uncomfortable and stand-offish to walk beside Dr Maitland with no contact. She transferred her torch to the hand nearest him, as if that was the reason they were walking separately. They chatted a little about *Road to Zanzibar*, chuckling over the jokes and the lively plot.

'May I see you home?' asked Dr Maitland.

'There's no need.'

'Then if I promise not to look at the number on the front of the bus, may I walk you to your stop?'

That made her laugh, even though she didn't want to encourage him. 'You're persistent, I'll give you that.'

'But not in an unpleasant way, I hope.'

'Actually, you're rather charming.'

'I'd take that as a compliment if I didn't happen to know you're immune to my charm.'

This was becoming a bit too enjoyable. Alison blamed it on the funny, warm-hearted film. 'Let's face it. We're only here by chance, aren't we? If that couple in the Worker Bee hadn't left their table when they did, we wouldn't be here now.' When he didn't reply, she added, 'Or have you forgotten that if there hadn't been a free table, I was going to leave?'

'Believe me, it was all I could think about at the time.' Dr Maitland paused before adding, 'That's why I slipped the man the money to take his young lady to the theatre.'

'You did what?'

'If I hadn't, there wouldn't have been a table and you wouldn't be here now. When you think about it, I've done everyone a favour. That fellow got to escort his girl to the theatre and you've found out, courtesy of Bob Hope, the secret of being a human cannonball.'

'I don't know what to say.'

'You could give yourself a pat on the back for calling me persistent. It shows you're a good judge of character.' Dr Maitland waited a moment. 'I hoped that might make you laugh again. I liked hearing you laugh.'

'I'm not going to flirt with you.'

'I know, I know.' He threw up his hands, conceding defeat. 'We're just two people who happen to be in the same place at the same time.' He stopped and turned to her. 'The question is this, Miss Alison Lambert. Would you like us to be in the same place at the same time again? Because I'd like it very much.'

Alison bit the inside of her cheek. She couldn't admit it, but she did want to – yet at the same time, she couldn't bring herself to make a definite arrangement.

'How about this?' Dr Maitland said when she didn't answer. 'Let's agree on a place where we both might happen to be at a time that suits both of us. I can promise to be there, and if you turn up, you turn up, and if you don't, you don't. Is that vague enough for you?'

'Yes,' said Alison.

Alison spent Saturday morning in the office, where she was to spend the next three weeks. It was going to feel odd being back behind a desk. That made her realise afresh that she had on the whole enjoyed being out and about, doing a variety of things. Would it be dull to be office-bound once more? At least she would get to wear her pretty court shoes again.

At the end of her half-day, she caught the bus to Mum's. She had arranged to go there today instead of Sunday because of being in town this morning, but as the bus crawled through the fog, she wondered if Mum would still be expecting her.

To her surprise, Mum was waiting for her when she got off the bus. Alison hugged her. Mum was wrapped up in her overcoat with a long scarf Lydia had made her wind twice around her neck, but she still looked cold.

'You shouldn't have come to meet me,' Alison scolded her.

'I wanted to. I wanted to make sure I was the first to see you.'

'First before Dad?' Why would that matter?

'Before anyone.'

Alison laughed, tucking her arm in the crook of Mum's elbow. 'There's not much hope of other people seeing me in this fog. Let's get home.'

The grey mass of fog lay dense and cold around them and they both adjusted their scarves to cover their noses and mouths so they wouldn't have to breathe it in. The Lamberts were a family of brisk walkers, but Alison and Mum didn't walk anything like as quickly today. You didn't in the fog. Even if you knew exactly where you were going, you still had to slow down.

There was a muffled thud and a disembodied female voice exclaimed 'Oh no!' from somewhere fairly near.

'Mrs Cornwell?' Mum spoke into the fog. 'Is that you? It's Mrs Lambert.'

The neighbour from across the road appeared from the murk. 'I tripped on the kerb and dropped my shopping bag. It's a good thing it's only got a couple of tins in it.' She peered at them. 'Is that Lydia with you? Oh, it's you, Alison. Oh, my dear girl—'

'Excuse us,' Mum interrupted. 'We're in a hurry. I need to get the dinner on. Come on, Alison.'

She gave Alison a tug and they went on their way more speedily than was perhaps safe.

'What was that about?' Alison asked.

'Nothing. Let's go home and get warm.'

They arrived home with pink noses and cheeks that glowed in spite of the protection afforded by their scarves.

'Go and poke the fire,' said Mum, hanging up their coats. 'I'll put the kettle on. I'm dying for a hot drink.'

'Leave that for a minute. I want to talk to you before your father gets home.'

Alison looked at her. 'Is it to do with his birthday? That's not for weeks yet.'

'No, it's to do with ... Come and sit down.'

Suddenly, all Alison's senses were standing to attention. 'What's happened?'

Seated on the sofa, Mum looked up at her. 'Come and sit beside me.'

Alison obeyed, though she didn't want to. Something told her she would do better to stay standing so she would be ready to run away.

Mum took her hand. 'I'm so sorry, Alison. It's Paul. He's – he's got engaged.'

CHAPTER TWENTY-NINE

After Tony had gone out on fire-watching duty, Colette saw he had left his snap tin behind on the kitchen table. She always prepared a snack for him to see him through the night, a sandwich or a cold fritter and a biscuit. Tony had gone out early because the fire-watchers had to attend a talk that evening before dispersing to the various places where they would spend the night, so if Colette took his snap tin round now, she would catch him before his duty started.

She got ready to go. There had been an air raid a couple of evenings ago, a brief one that had lasted about twenty minutes. She had been on duty at the marshalling yard and, with every instinct urging her to seek safety, it had taken all her willpower to stay put. What if bombs fell? What if this was her chance to run away? Possibly the only chance she would ever have. Should she go – or should she have faith in Tony's reformed behaviour? Since he had started being kind and considerate, he hadn't once been offhand or sarcastic. He hadn't once made her feel small. Her tummy no longer felt tight when they arrived home and shut the front door behind them. She felt loved and appreciated ... and confused.

Stay or go? Stay or go? The question had coursed through her veins for the duration of the raid, which had seemed to her to last for ages instead of less than half an hour. The marshalling yard hadn't been targeted and she hadn't been required to make the decision, and she still didn't know what her decision would have been.

Warmly wrapped up, she clicked off the hall light, slid through the door and set off. The fog that had held everything in its grip during the day had lifted towards teatime.

'From fog to blackout,' Tony had said with a laugh. 'Not much difference.'

But it was different. In the blackout, the glow from a torch gave you proper guidance, whereas fog had a way of swallowing the beam that Colette found rather creepy.

It wasn't far to the school, which had been handed over to Civil Defence for the duration. She went in and looked around, following the sound of voices into what used to be the hall. Immediately inside the double doors were noticeboards with lists and street maps. The spacious room was divided into sections, each with tables and chairs, most of which were occupied.

A woman in a WVS jacket came over to her.

'It's Mrs Naylor, isn't it? I recognise you from church. How splendid to see you. Have you come to join our ranks? I'm Mrs Townsend, the butcher's wife.'

'I know you by sight,' said Colette, feeling shy, as she always did when meeting someone new.

'You get your meat from my husband, I'm pleased to say, which practically makes us in-laws these days. Do come and meet everyone. They'll be so pleased.'

'I only came to bring my husband's snap tin.'

'Left it behind, did he? What would they do without us? The fire-watchers are crammed into the babies' classroom, having a talk. You can leave the snap tin with me, if you like, but Mrs Ross and Miss Chapman are about to get the urn going. Why not stay for a cup of tea to fortify you for the walk home? It's a chilly night.'

Why not? It was nice to feel welcome. It seemed to fit in with Tony's improved conduct. Colette had always kept herself to herself because that was the way Tony liked it. When they were first married, he'd said they only needed one another. Besides, Colette seemed to be the only young wife in their road. Everyone else was Mother's generation or older. Maybe this was her chance to make friends. It would be nice to be on more than nodding terms with the local housewives if she ended up staying.

She allowed herself to imagine it, to *feel* it, to be the cherished young wife with the good-looking husband and plenty of acquaintances round and about with whom she could pass the time of day and share recipes and ideas for jazzing up old clothes and making them look new and stylish. There might even be a baby one day …

'Thank you,' she said to Mrs Townsend. 'That's kind of you.'

'Not at all. Everyone will be delighted to meet you. We feel we know you already.'

That seemed an odd remark, but there was no time to wonder about it because Mrs Townsend drew her across to the WVS table and started introducing everyone.

'Don't worry if you don't catch all the names,' an elderly lady called Miss Upton said with a smile and Colette smiled back, feeling at ease.

'Please excuse us if we finish putting dates in our diaries before the tea arrives,' said Mrs Townsend. 'Then we can chat properly. Who knows, we might even persuade you to join us.'

'What are you planning?' Colette asked.

'Sewing evenings,' said Miss Upton. 'We're cutting down worn-out adult clothing to make garments for children, so we need lots of ladies who are good with their needles.'

'Like you,' said Mrs Townsend. 'You're good at dressmaking, aren't you?'

Colette frowned and laughed at the same time. 'How do you know that?'

'Mr Naylor talks about you all the time. He's so proud of you.'

'Didn't he mention a dress the colour of bluebells?' said Miss Upton. 'You wore it to a dance in the summer and he told us you were the best-dressed girl in the room.'

Colette's thoughts froze for a moment. Tony talked about her all the time – and was proud of her? And he had praised her blue dress, the very garment he had made her feel bad about on more than one occasion? It didn't make sense – unless . . .

'Did he tell you about the dress recently – in the last week or two?' Colette asked. That would tie in with his reformed behaviour. She felt warm inside.

'No, he mentioned it ages ago, dear,' said Miss Upton, 'at the time of the dance.'

So he had done her down at home, at the same time as singing her praises behind her back. Why?

A man in his sixties, dressed in army uniform, came over. He was bald on top with white hair round the sides and he was smoking a pipe.

'Mrs Naylor? The ladies doing the tea pointed you out. Pleasure to meet you.' He thrust out a hand. 'Captain Briggs, at your service. I'm in charge of coordinating civil defence around these parts. Fire, first aid, Heavy Rescue, all the services.'

Tony had described him as something of a show-off, a civilian who enjoyed wearing the uniform. Colette smiled politely as she shook hands.

'It's good to have you here, my dear. Have you come to join our merry band?'

'My husband left something behind.'

'Did he now? And that brought you here. There's nothing like a spot of serendipity, is there? May I sit next to you for a moment? I'd like to have a word.' Captain Briggs pulled up a chair. 'Your husband is worried about you, you know. I know I wouldn't want my good lady fire-watching at the marshalling yard. So here's a suggestion. I could put in a word and get you transferred here. Close to home, don't you know.'

'My husband has already tried to get transferred and it wasn't allowed.'

'Ah, but we couldn't let him go, d'you see? He's highly experienced. Besides, it's not as though he works for the railways. They don't have a claim on him. You, on the other hand, being a woman and not having been at the marshalling yard very long ... '

Captain Briggs left the idea dangling. Was she supposed to snatch at it?

'Oh yes.' Mrs Townsend's voice rang with approval. 'If you come here, Mrs Naylor, you'll be a valuable addition – won't she, Miss Upton? And you'd be nice and close to your husband, which would lift such a burden of worry off his shoulders, as well as making things ever so much easier for you, I'm sure. It can't be easy travelling all that way to the marshalling yard. What do you think, Mrs Naylor? Do say you'll join us. We'd be so pleased to have you.'

When she arrived home in Wilton Close after church on Sunday morning, Alison could hardly keep her eyes off the clock as she watched it move ever closer to the moment that marked the time yesterday when she had heard about Paul. She was still struggling to believe it. He was engaged. Paul, her Paul, not her Paul any more ... was engaged. How many times had she convinced herself he was going to propose to her? Yet he had proposed to Katie just five months after

318

meeting her. It was astonishing. It was – actually, it was insulting. She had come home from Mum's yesterday, determined not to tell anyone, because she was so humiliated.

But when she had finally arrived in Wilton Close late yesterday afternoon after a perfectly wretched journey, she had surprised herself by announcing Paul's engagement and promptly bursting into floods of tears. It had then become a sort of competition among the others as to who could look after her the most. If she hadn't been distraught, she might have felt flattered. Mrs Cooper cuddled her and Mrs Grayson had fetched the precious remains of a bottle of sherry that was left over from Joan's wedding. They had all swigged it from the Morgans' elegant little sherry schooners, including Alison, even though she had always hated sherry. She even managed to respond to Mrs Grayson's 'Bottoms up' and Mabel's 'Cheers, m'dears' by wishing everyone good health, which was what Dad always said before he had a drink.

At bedtime, there had been a big swapping round of beds. Everyone had a single bed apart from Mrs Grayson, who had a double. At the two older ladies' insistence, the three girls had all piled into the double, with Alison in the middle.

'If I'd known I'd get made such a fuss of,' Alison had joked, 'I'd have burst into tears a lot sooner.'

She wasn't entirely kidding. She remembered the times she had ached to be fussed over, but she saw now that she had never invited it. She had kept her friends at arm's length for much of the time. Had that been because of her shame over being jilted?

Now she had a new shame. Dr Maitland. No one knew about him and now that she had been so deeply shocked and distressed over Paul's engagement, it would make it even harder to mention him. Would it seem to the others that her distress over Paul must have been at least in part put on? After all, if she could have another man in tow already ...

But she didn't have him in tow, did she? Not precisely. Not in a girlfriend–boyfriend kind of way.

Liar.

If she had truly felt no interest in Dr Maitland, she would never have gone to the Worker Bee. She wouldn't have gone to see *Road to Zanzibar*. She wouldn't have made an arrangement to see him again on Tuesday. She had told herself these things didn't really matter, finding ways of holding herself aloof from each one. Even seeing him this coming Tuesday was to be on the basis of it being a firm commitment for him but not for her.

Why was she holding back? It wasn't because she didn't really like Dr Maitland – and that was another thing. Why was she so determinedly thinking of him in that formal way when she knew his name was Joel?

So why hold back? Was it out of some kind of bizarre loyalty to her old relationship with Paul? But Paul was engaged to another girl now. *Engaged*. Alison had every right to move on. Most people would say she was lucky to have met someone else – and to have had the good fortune to meet him so soon, too.

And therein lay the problem. Alison pressed her lips together, not liking what she had just found out about herself. She didn't want others to know about Joel because ... because it might look as if her heartbreak over Paul hadn't been all that bad. And it had, oh it had. She had been desperate for everyone to recognise it. She had wanted everybody to agree that her life had been utterly shattered. But they would soon withdraw that agreement if they knew she'd already met another man.

What did that say about her? That she craved sympathy? That she wanted her friends to believe what had happened to her was the worst thing ever? If she was honest, there had been an element of that. She dropped her chin to her chest as shame engulfed her.

Well, it was time to stop all that. Did this mean she was going to tell her friends about Joel? No, not quite yet. She would meet up with him on Tuesday and see how it went. If she wanted to see him again, there wouldn't be any shilly-shallying about it, none of this 'Only if there's a table free.'

It was time to be honest – with herself as much as with anyone else.

Sunday night. Sundays seemed to be significant at the moment. Three weeks ago on Sunday, Cordelia had taken Adelaide to Wilton Close to meet her friends after Adelaide had held forth on the topic of wartime friendships. How happy and confident Cordelia had felt then – and how surprised and pleased she had been to find her mother-in-law backing her up for the first time ever. Then, on the Sunday of last week that confidence had been smashed to pieces when Adelaide had made a clear distinction between wartime friendships and lifelong friendships, refusing point-blank to accept that in some cases they could be one and the same.

What a blow it had been. Just when Cordelia had felt she had an ally, just when she had serious hopes of swaying Kenneth and Emily to her point of view. Just when her heart had dared to feel that the two parts of her life might be allowed to come together ... it had all been lost.

No – not lost. Dashed aside. Destroyed. That was a violent choice of words. Was she exaggerating? No – because it had felt violent. The injury to her feelings at the time and the battering her self-esteem had been subjected to since had been violence on an emotional level.

Adelaide hadn't kept their disagreement to herself. That would have been too much to hope for. She had flaunted it in front of Kenneth and Emily, who had both been roundly satisfied to have her on their side. They had been shocked, too, at the thought of Cordelia viewing her undesirable friendships as permanent.

'Mummy, how could you?' Emily had asked, distressed. 'It was bad enough when I thought you'd be friends with Mrs Green and the rest just for the duration, but if you want these connections to last for ever ... '

'True friendship transcends the class system,' Cordelia had tried to tell her. 'I wish you could see that.'

But Emily wouldn't have it and neither would Kenneth.

'When the war is over, do you see yourself inviting the Greens here to our dinner parties, Cordelia? That's a serious question. Please answer it.'

'Of course not.'

'Why not?' he demanded at once.

'It wouldn't be appropriate.'

'So, it is your stated intention to pursue a lifelong friendship with a woman whom you cannot invite into your husband's circle, which, I might remind you, is also *your* circle. Are you listening to me, Cordelia? Can you hear how ridiculous and inappropriate and downright wrong it sounds?'

'Put that way, of course it sounds wrong,' she had answered, summoning up every ounce of spirit she possessed. 'One can make anything sound wrong if one wishes to. Naturally the Greens aren't dinner-party company, but that doesn't mean Dot – Mrs Green and I can't meet up for a cup of tea and a chat. I value her company and her common sense.'

'Ah yes, her common sense. You're referring to the common sense she was employing when she ended up being accused of romantically pursuing a man at work. Yes, I'm sure she must have shown a great deal of common sense in that matter.'

'Don't be sarcastic, Kenneth. It's beneath you.'

'And Mrs Green is beneath *you*.' Kenneth threw up his hands in frustration, but when he spoke again, his voice was sober and the look of pain and disappointment on his face took Cordelia by surprise. 'I've lost track of the number of times I've warned you against this friendship. I don't know what else to say. Even your own daughter, a young girl who might be supposed to hold modern ideas, has warned you against it. You won't listen to me. You won't listen to her. You won't listen to my mother. We're a family, Cordelia, and you've got out of step with the rest of us. I'm at my wits' end. What is it about Mrs Green and Mrs Cooper that makes them more important to you than your own family?'

'Of course they aren't more important,' Cordelia exclaimed.

'I could say "Prove it." But I don't dare,' said Kenneth, 'because I know you see no reason why you should.'

With that, the subject had been closed – or, more accurately, it simply hadn't been discussed again – but it was all Cordelia could think about and she didn't imagine she was the only one. How could it have come to this? How had her railway friendships, which had brought her such pleasure, driven a wedge between her and her family?

Then the winter fog had descended on Manchester, its blankness as dense as clotted cream, rendering the world an indistinct place. When Cordelia had been assigned the task of manning a fog box on Sunday night, she had welcomed it. Anything to escape from the tense atmosphere at home. And here she was now, wrapped up in two over-coats, with two pairs of thick socks over her stockings, sitting over a brazier in a cramped box next to the railway line. Her job was to be ready to fix detonators to the track if the signal moved to danger, so that a train driver would know he had to halt his engine immediately.

Cordelia pulled her hat down over her ears. Braziers were meant to keep you warm, weren't they? This one seemed to be doing a feeble job. And the coke fumes were making her feel headachy. Every now and again, she opened the door and stepped outside. Not that the closely packed fog counted as fresh air.

It wasn't fresh air she needed. It was fresh thoughts, fresh ideas. What was she going to do? The situation at home had reached the stage where she had to do something. Before Emily had arrived home, Kenneth had disapproved of Dot, but Cordelia had managed to skim over that and keep going the way she wanted. But Emily's unexpected return had changed everything. Now it was more than Kenneth's huffy disapproval. Now it was her duty as a mother. It was doing what was right for Emily. It was all tied up with the kind of example she was setting.

What a shock it had been. She had turned forty-three this year. She was middle-aged. Surely she ought to be the one clinging to the old ways. But no, it was fifteen-year-old Emily whose attitudes were dominated by class and social distinctions. Moreover, Emily was resolute in her determination not to be swayed by her mother's more relaxed views. It was the first time anything had come between them and Cordelia hated it. Worse, she didn't know what to do about it. She had always known Emily had a mind of her own, but it had never brought them into conflict before. Might Emily turn against her? The thought made her heart turn over.

Cordelia pictured the friends who meant so much to her. Persephone, beautiful and cultured, but with no airs and graces, with her ambition to become a journalist. Joan and Mabel, who had both suffered shattering bereavements and who had found happiness with Bob and Harry. Brave girls, the pair of them, who had taken part in numerous rescues in the course of their first-aid duties. Mrs Grayson was brave, too, in a different way. What courage it had taken for her, after years of being confined to the house, to take her first steps outside. She left the Wilton Close house regularly now, steadied by familiar routes and a friendly arm.

Dear Colette, who was coming out of her shell now that her overprotective husband wasn't trying to wrap her in cotton wool any more, and poor Alison, heartbroken but doing well in her new job. She would come through, however hard it was. And Margaret was very much a part of their group now, especially since she'd moved in with Mrs Cooper, that dear lady, who made the best of every day. After what she had suffered, that possibly made her the bravest of them all.

And Dot. Last but decidedly not least. The friend Cordelia was closest to, ever since the middle of last year when the two of them had ganged up to deal with a dirty old man who had made Joan's life at work miserable. Dot was shrewd and funny and she had the most generous heart of anyone Cordelia had ever met. When their group first got together, Dot had been determined not to become a mother figure to the younger girls, because she reckoned she had quite enough people to look after at home, but it had happened anyway. Of course it had. With a compassionate, caring person like Dot, it had been inevitable and Cordelia honoured her for it.

All her friends were deeply special to her – but had the time come to let go? Things had reached the stage where she was being forced to choose – and there wasn't a choice. She knew exactly what to do. Emily was her life. Cordelia's heart had been destroyed by losing Kit, but Emily's birth had brought her back to life. Emily meant everything to her.

Kenneth and Adelaide were both convinced that to be the best mother she could be, she must renounce the lower-class associations that were pushing Emily's life out of kilter and making her question her mother's fitness to live in the comfortable middle-class world where the Masters family belonged. It was as simple as that. Cordelia had already upset her darling daughter by acting as mother of the bride for another girl – and while that might have been an immature reaction on Emily's part, it was symptomatic of the unease that Cordelia's new friendships had brought to the fore.

Above all else, Cordelia wanted a good relationship with her daughter, a strong, loving bond that would see them through the years ahead. She adored her only child and the possibility that Emily might decide to withdraw from her was not to be borne.

So yes, the time had come to remove herself from the group of friends she held so dear, because however much they meant to her, Emily meant a thousand times more. Cordelia might have the vision to appreciate that friendships between the classes could potentially last for ever, but her family couldn't see it and now she needed to toe the line and return wholeheartedly to the fold. It was her duty as a good wife and a loving mother. For a moment, she hesitated over the possibility of perhaps being able to remain friends with Persephone and Mabel, because of their class and backgrounds – but no. That would cause such confusion and unhappiness among the others and she couldn't bear to be responsible for that.

She had promised to spend another evening in Dot's Christmas Kitchen next Thursday. She would fulfil that commitment, but that would be her swansong – or should she attend the carol concert on Christmas Eve and let that be her final meeting with her friends? No, she didn't think she would be able to bear that. She would work for the evening in the Christmas Kitchen on Thursday and afterwards she would quietly withdraw from a circle of friendship that ought to have lasted a lifetime.

CHAPTER THIRTY

'I wasn't expecting that.' Dr Maitland – Joel – put on a spurt and came hurrying towards Alison. 'I came early so you wouldn't have to wait for me – but here you are already.' His blue eyes clouded. 'You haven't come early just to tell me to get lost, have you?'

'Absolutely not. I came because … ' Alison drew in a breath. ' … because I wanted to see you again and I wanted you to know it.'

Joel looked surprised, then his features relaxed into an expression of happiness. He was very good-looking. Alison didn't want to be shallow about it, but she liked her boyfriend to be good-looking. Her boyfriend? Well, maybe. It depended on how this evening went. Excitement radiated through her. Oh, how lovely to feel she might have something to look forward to. She had been in the depths of misery for so long.

Because Alison had some time owing to her, she had been able to leave work early this afternoon and this had happened to fit in with Joel's shift pattern. At the time they'd made the arrangement, Alison thought that maybe she could spend an hour or so with him and still get home at her normal time and no one would be any the wiser. She had also suggested they meet by the bookstall on the concourse at Exchange Station, rather than at Victoria, as it wasn't far and she didn't know anybody there.

'Where shall we go?' she asked. 'It would be nice to spend some time talking and getting to know one another.' There. She had said it.

Joel's eyes twinkled. 'We could always try the Worker Bee – as long as you promise not to run away like Cinderella if there isn't a table.'

'Shame on you, Dr Maitland, for reminding me of my bad manners. And there I was thinking maybe we could move on to first-name terms.'

He sobered instantly. 'I'd like that … Alison. And I'm Joel.'

'I know.' She smiled at him. Yes, this was exciting, but there was something comfortable about it as well.

'Before we choose where to go, would you mind if we went to the toy shop first? My sister is desperate to send a box of paints to each of her lads and I heard the shop had a delivery of goods today.'

'Of course,' said Alison. As they left the station, clicking on their torches as they went, she asked, 'Are they still living with your sister?'

'No, they were evacuated. She misses them dreadfully. They're seven and nine now. It's horrible to think of all those thousands upon thousands of children having to live away from home for all this time. It's been over two years now and this will be the third Christmas.'

Joel stopped talking as they crossed the road. You had to have your wits about you in the blackout. He held her elbow protectively until they reached the far pavement and Alison was disappointed when he let go. She would have liked to link arms with him, but she had never approved of girls being forward or clingy.

When they reached the toy shop, there was a long queue down the road. Word had evidently got round and, so close to Christmas, parents were anxious to buy presents. Joel surprised Alison by making for the front of the queue. He stopped outside the door. A thick blind covered the big window, which was criss-crossed with anti-blast tape. Joel tipped his hat to the women at the front of the line.

'Pardon me, ladies. I promise I'm not queue-jumping, but might I step inside for one moment and ask if they have any paintboxes? If they do, I'll join the end of the queue. If not, I'll be on my way with my young lady. It's the first time I've taken her out properly.'

'Oh aye?' said one of the women. 'And you think queuing outside a shop is the way to win her heart, do you?'

The women exchanged looks. There were a few grumbles behind them, but that didn't stop them from nodding their agreement.

'In you go, love. Be quick.'

'Thank you. You're angels.'

Alison and Joel slipped inside, careful to keep the blackout. The shelves were largely empty except for those on the wall behind one of the two counters, which bore some stock. There were four women inside, looking vexed – but why? They were on the verge of being served. Then Alison's attention homed in on the man at the counter. In front of him were the items he had chosen so far. Alison's eyes widened at the quantity. She stepped to the side to get a better look. Not just one box of the Bomber Command board game, but a stack of them, next to a stack of the ARP game and a pile of bows and arrows. Judging by what was left on the shelves, the man intended to buy every build-it-yourself model aeroplane and every box of Snap, Happy Families, Vacuation and Victory card games.

'Yes,' he was saying, 'them an' all.'

He pointed to the shelf where there was a display of books of cut-out dolls – *Mummy Puts On a Uniform* and *Uncle Bill Puts On a Uniform* – for children to cut out a figure in underwear and then cut out their uniform, which had tabs that folded over to hold the paper doll's clothes in place.

The young shop assistant looked flushed and embarrassed. 'I'm sorry, sir, but it isn't fair if you purchase all these things.'

'Rubbish. I've queued up and it's my turn.'

'I don't think my boss would be happy about it.'

'He won't care who buys what, as long as you sell everything.'

Joel stepped forward. 'Don't give this man another thing,' he said politely to the lad behind the counter. He picked up a wooden chair that stood beside the counter for older customers to sit on. 'Excuse me. I won't be a minute.'

Wondering what was about to happen, Alison followed Joel outside, helping to hold the blackout curtain in such a way that no light escaped. Joel planted the chair on the pavement and stood on it.

'Ladies and gentlemen, your attention, please.' He waited for the murmurs of surprise to die down. 'I believe we have a war profiteer in the toy shop, trying to get his hands on the lion's share of the stock. Please calm yourselves.' He raised his voice as anger rumbled through the queue. 'This will be dealt with, but it might take a few minutes. Please bear with me. If somebody would fetch a policeman, would the rest of the queue kindly keep their place for them?'

'I'll go.' A man with a limp emerged from the line.

'Thank you,' said Joel and he stepped down from the chair, which he carried back inside the shop, with Alison once again helping by maintaining the all-important blackout.

'I tell you I'm entitled to buy up the whole damn stock if I want to,' the man was saying in an effort to browbeat the young assistant.

'We'll have none of that language, if you please,' Joel said firmly. 'You're in mixed company, in case you've forgotten.'

The man glared at Joel, but muttered, 'Beg your pardon, ladies. Slip of the tongue.' He turned back to the assistant.

'I'll take everything that I've got on the counter and leave you with the rest. I can't say fairer than that.'

'That's your idea of fair, is it?' Joel asked.

The man ignored him, keeping his gaze fixed on the assistant. 'I'm entitled to buy what I need, same as anyone.'

'And you need all those toys and games?' Joel enquired.

'Keep your nose out. These are all gifts.'

There was the usual commotion of getting through the blackout curtain and a bobby entered the premises.

'What's going on here?' he asked, looking round.

'A clear case of war profiteering, Officer,' said Joel.

'You'd better watch what you say,' advised the man, 'or I'll have you for libel.'

'Actually, it's slander when it's the spoken word,' said Joel. 'And I'll say it again. You're a profiteer.'

'Prove it.'

The constable intervened. 'Unfortunately, sir,' he said to Joel, 'this gentleman does have a point. He isn't a profiteer unless he buys goods and then sells them on at vastly inflated prices. Buying things isn't in itself a crime.'

Alison felt frustrated. Everyone could see what was happening here, or rather what was going to happen if the man was allowed to buy so much stock, but what could they do?

She spoke to the assistant. 'Perhaps you could set a limit on how many items one person can buy. That's common these days.'

'There's no notice up to that effect.' The man made a point of peering all around.

'You said all those things are to be gifts,' said Joel. 'You must have an extensive family.'

'Aye, that's a point,' said the constable.

'Don't talk rot – not you, Officer,' the man added quickly. 'I was speaking to this man here, the one who's trying to stop me going about my lawful business. You might ask him how he ended up in this shop in the first place. I happen to know that the next dozen or so customers after me in the queue were all women.'

'Don't change the subject,' said Joel.

'Why not?' The man grinned. 'Trying to hide your own misdemeanours, are you, by making false accusations against me?'

'Certainly not,' Alison said sharply. 'You still haven't answered the question.'

'I haven't been asked one.' There was a sneer in the man's voice.

'Who are these so-called presents for?' Alison demanded.

'No one has a family that big,' said the bobby, 'not even if you've got ten brothers and sisters and they've all got half a dozen nippers.'

'A few of these are family gifts,' the man said stiffly. 'The rest are for the children's hospital.'

'Really?' said Joel. 'This has been arranged with the hospital, has it?'

'Yes,' was the bold answer.

Joel smiled. 'How strange that I know nothing of it. I'm a doctor and my particular interest is children's medicine. I work as a surgeon now, but I keep in close contact with the children's wards in several hospitals and work in some of them on a voluntary basis.' He addressed the constable. 'I assure you, Officer, I know nothing of all this bounty the children are to receive – and I would know of it, if it really were going to happen.'

'Is that so, sir?' The policeman nodded and didn't hide his satisfaction.

'Did I say it was all arranged?' said the man. 'I made a mistake. I meant to organise it ahead of time, but then my mum got bombed out last week and it slipped my mind. So

I'm just going to deliver these presents and let the nurses give them out.'

'Good idea,' Joel exclaimed and everyone looked at him in surprise. 'I'll flag down a couple of taxis and help you take everything. I'm sure the constable would be delighted to come too. After all, it's quite a haul for you to manage all by yourself. We wouldn't want you to drop anything, would we? You don't mind coming too, do you, Officer?'

'Happy to, sir.'

The man made a noise that sounded like a growl. Leaving everything on the counter, he fought his way past the blackout curtain and disappeared into the evening.

'Well done, Doctor,' said one of the women waiting to be served.

'You saw him off all right,' said the policeman.

'It's just a shame it won't stop him doing the same thing elsewhere,' said Joel.

'You stopped it happening today,' said Alison. 'That's as much as you could do.'

Joel smiled at her and for that moment it was as if they were the only two in the shop.

'We'd better join the queue,' Joel said.

'Aren't you going to ask about the paintboxes?' Alison prompted.

Joel turned to the assistant. 'I'm after a couple of paintboxes, if you have them.'

'We've got some,' said the assistant. 'A couple of dozen. You should buy them now instead of queuing up.'

'Yes, you should,' agreed the other customers.

'You're very kind,' said Joel, 'but we'll wait our turn along with everybody else.'

As they walked to the back of the queue, Alison was proud to be by Joel's side. What a decent man he was. He had handled that situation calmly and without fuss, showing quick thinking and determination. Alison light-heartedly swung her bag by her side.

But then a new idea began to creep up on her and she experienced a sense of foreboding. She couldn't help remembering her conversation with Joan, when Joan had talked about the relationship she had recklessly plunged into with Steven after Letitia died. Joan had thought at the time that she loved Steven, but really it had been grief that had made her behave like that.

Alison knew she had been decidedly iffy about Joel at first – until she'd heard about Paul's engagement. Was it the shock and upset of Paul getting engaged that had pushed her into suddenly liking Joel and wanting to get to know him?

Was this her equivalent of Joan's terrible mistake?

CHAPTER THIRTY-ONE

When Cordelia and Emily arrived at the Christmas Kitchen, everyone seemed to be saying, 'It'll be Christmas Day a week today. Fancy that,' and 'Fingers crossed we don't get a repeat of last year.' Cordelia couldn't suppress a shudder. The thought of Emily being caught up in the nightmare that had been inflicted on Manchester in the Christmas Blitz made Cordelia turn cold inside and she questioned how she could ever have allowed Emily to stay at home instead of returning her to Auntie Flora. Yet now that she had her beloved daughter at home – how could she bear to send her away? The mixture of guilt, fear and gratitude could be exhausting at times.

Cordelia was almost sorry that Emily had offered to come with her this evening. As a rule, she loved nothing more than showing Emily off in public, but this evening was different. This evening, Cordelia would make good her promise to Dot to help once more in the Christmas Kitchen ... and after that, she would, with as little fuss as possible, remove herself from her group of dear friends.

She had been considering how to do that. If she simply disappeared, her friends would seek her out, worried that something was wrong, and she couldn't have that. No. She would have to tell them something and it must sound truthful and reasonable.

All she had come up with thus far was something along the lines of: 'You know how much I value the friendships I have with all of you, but I need to spend all the time I can at home. It didn't matter so much when Emily was away, but her presence has changed things, especially now she and I are going out fire-watching two nights a week. I think it's essential I spend every moment I can under our roof, providing a stable and loving environment for my family.'

Would the others believe that? Silly question. Of course they would. It would never occur to them that she might fabricate an excuse. She drew in a deep breath and was on the verge of heaving it out in a prolonged sigh, but stopped herself. It was no use feeling mopey. She had her duty as a wife and mother. Emily was the best reason of all.

'Good. You're here,' said Dot, coming towards her, 'and you've brought your Emily. It's good to see you again, chick.'

'When Mummy explained about preparing food for those in need, I wanted to help,' said Emily.

'Have you brought aprons?' Dot asked.

'Yes,' they replied. They took off their outdoor things and hung them up, tying their aprons around their waists.

Mrs Cooper walked in, accompanied by Margaret.

'Are Alison and Mabel here yet?' Mrs Cooper asked. 'No? Well, they won't be far behind. They're cycling over, but Margaret kindly said she'd come on the bus with me, which was something of an adventure since neither of us knew exactly where we were going.'

'Especially in the blackout,' Margaret added, removing her hat and scarf and giving her hair a gentle shake. She wore it scooped back from her face, as most girls did, and the rollers she undoubtedly used in it made it curl in soft waves. She was looking happier these days, now that Mrs Cooper and Mrs Grayson had welcomed her into their home.

Cordelia glanced round, asking quietly, 'Mrs Grayson?'

Mrs Cooper shook her head. 'She'd have panicked at not knowing where we were going. To Margaret and me, finding our way here was a good laugh, but it would have been too much for Mrs Grayson.'

'It was nearly too much for us,' said Margaret with a laugh, 'but the bus had a lovely clippie who put us off at the right stop.'

'Then all we had to do was bumble about in the dark, trying to find the right street,' added Mrs Cooper. 'Look, here's Joan.'

Joan walked in, holding the door open for two more – Dot's daughters-in-law, Sheila and Pammy. Pammy peeled off her outer layers and took out a powder compact, checking her face in the little mirror. She was a lovely-looking young woman with fair hair, clear skin and doe eyes. Dark-haired Sheila had a thinner face and shrewd eyes, together with the yellow-tipped fingers of a heavy smoker. Cordelia felt a stirring of interest as she looked at Sheila. Thanks to her friendship with Dot, she knew one or two things about Sheila Green that the rest of the world didn't.

Joan hugged Mrs Cooper, who said hello to Sheila, whom she knew because of cleaning at her house, then greeted Pammy warmly even though she knew her only slightly. Mrs Cooper asked after Pammy's daughter, Jenny, whom Pammy was all too evidently delighted to talk about, especially to such an interested and sympathetic listener.

Cordelia couldn't help comparing Mrs Cooper's behaviour with Emily's earlier conduct when Dot had greeted her so pleasantly. Why couldn't Emily have said, 'It's good to see you too, Mrs Green,' instead of trotting out that deft explanation of why she was here this evening? Alas, Cordelia didn't really need to ask the question. She knew the answer only too well – painfully well, in fact. Emily was her father's daughter, that was the reason.

Mabel and Alison arrived, their faces glowing from their ride through the chilly evening.

'Look at this disreputable article we found skulking in the bike shed,' said Mabel as Persephone followed them in.

Cordelia smiled. Anyone less disreputable-looking than the Honourable Persephone would be hard to imagine, with her glorious honey-blonde hair and violet eyes. Even clad in a simple cherry-red sweater and tweed skirt, she was elegant and stylish.

Mabel looked around. 'We just need Colette and we've got a full house.'

'She can't be here,' Dot reminded them. 'She's fire-watching. Even if she wasn't, it's a bit far for her to come. You know how protective Tony is.'

A few local women arrived and there was plenty of chatting.

'I think everyone's here that's coming,' said Dot. 'Be a love, Cordelia, and close the door while I get everyone's attention.'

About to move away, Cordelia stopped, struck by the sneer that marred Emily's pretty face.

'What's that look for?' Cordelia asked quietly.

'Really, Mummy, need you ask? "Be a love, Cordelia". How can you let her speak to you like that?'

'Not now, Emily,' Cordelia retorted. 'And wipe that look off your face. If the wind changes, you'll be stuck like that.'

It was what she used to say when Emily was a child. Goodness knew why the words had popped out now. Emily was far from being the little girl whom Cordelia had striven to shape in the image of herself and Kenneth. But that was the point, wasn't it? She had succeeded in bringing up a younger version of Kenneth and herself. The trouble was that while Kenneth remained his middle-class, cultured, urbane self, Cordelia had changed. Her wartime experiences and friendships had opened her eyes and her mind – while her daughter's remained firmly closed.

Dot clapped her hands and the chatting died away.

'Thanks for coming, ladies. You all know why we're here and the good we aim to do. Tonight, thanks to donations, we're going to prepare corned-beef hash, veg casserole and sponge puddings, which will be kept in the cold store until the weekend, so let's get to it. First off, I need volunteers for potato duty.'

Cordelia was proud of her friend and glad to be here to contribute in a practical way to this good cause, but at the same time her heart was heavy. She had to make the most of this evening, because the next time she saw her friends, she must tell them she couldn't be one of their number any more.

Colette was in her fire-watcher's uniform. Tin helmet, rubber boots, a mackintosh over her warmest jumper and skirt, with the added layer of her own overcoat. Binoculars hung on a cord around her neck, and her respirator, which was what her section leader called a gas mask, was in its box, slung over her shoulder. Woe betide anybody who set the gas-mask box down for even a minute.

All the binoculars were treated as if they were made of gold. Apparently, at the beginning of the war, all the railway companies had put out urgent requests to the general public for the loan of binoculars for the duration. Colette fingered the smooth, curved edge of her pair. Not that she could feel them through her woolly gloves. Who had they belonged to? A birdwatcher, perhaps? Would every single pair eventually be restored to the correct owner?

From her post on a shed roof of corrugated iron, she looked out into the darkness of the marshalling yard. By now, she was used to the sounds of wheels on tracks and wagons being shunted. Occasionally, the dimmest lights showed for an instant. You wouldn't see anything unless you knew what to look for. It was a bit like folk having no notion what went on behind other people's front doors. They didn't know what to look for and so there was nothing to see.

She still felt shocked, numb even, when she thought of the trap that Tony had so cleverly set for her. A chill went through her at the memory of Saturday night and all those smiling faces and encouraging expressions that had surrounded her when she'd been invited to give up fire-watching in favour of joining the local WVS. Oh, Mrs Townsend, Captain Briggs and all the rest had been entirely sincere, she had no doubt of that, but neither could she doubt that Tony had used these good people in the same way he had been using her. What a clever devil he was, manipulating everybody.

He had softened her up by being all loving while telling his colleagues how desperately worried he was about her fire-watching commitments. Then, on Saturday night, he had left his snap tin on the kitchen table on purpose, knowing that she would trot round to the school to deliver it ... whereupon she would be met by well-meaning WVS ladies full of how anxious dear Mr Naylor was and what a burden it must be to poor Mrs Naylor to drag herself all the way to the marshalling yard to do her duty ... and what a good idea it would be if she would come and join them and do her voluntary work in the WVS instead. Problems leaving the marshalling yard? Not to worry. Leave it in Captain Briggs' capable hands.

Oh yes, her husband was a clever devil. And to think how she had softened, how she had begun to believe that he had truly changed towards her and that he would cherish her for ever. What a fool she had been. She had even told Mrs Cooper she might not run away after all. That was how well Tony had done his job. And if she hadn't seen through it ...

'I gather you had lots of encouragement to sign up with the local WVS,' Tony had said in a jolly voice on Sunday. 'Do you think you shall? You're guaranteed a warm welcome.' He had laughed, as if it was nothing to do with him, as if Captain Briggs and the WVS ladies had cooked it up between themselves, which, to be fair, they undoubtedly believed they had.

Colette had looked at him, at his smile. This time yesterday, she would have been taken in by that smile. She had to glance away in case he saw the truth in her eyes.

'Everyone was so kind,' she agreed. 'As you say, very welcoming.'

'So you'll give up the marshalling yard?'

'I haven't been there long,' she prevaricated. 'It would seem rather feeble to drop out so soon, as if I can't cope.'

'It's not a question of whether you can cope. It's to do with where you want to do your voluntary war work – "voluntary" being the important word here. Most women, most civilians, like to support their own community. And you could be near me.' Tony lit a cigarette, blowing out a soft puff of smoke. 'A promise to leave the marshalling yard would be the best Christmas present you could possibly give me.'

Oh, how clever he was, but she could see through him now and she knew that his recent kindness and good humour had been nothing more than a way of buttering her up so that she would do what he wanted. It would take away her one tiny piece of independence and put her firmly back under his thumb. And to think he had started off by actually making her believe ... making her want to believe ...

The hairs stood up on the back of her neck as the wail of the siren lifted into the air. Although she could barely see what was ahead of her in the vast yard, she felt the sense of urgency as the railway workers picked up the pace of their tasks. The marshalling yard had its own air-raid warning system, higher pitched than the ordinary siren and better able to be heard over the noise of the yard, but it wouldn't be sounded until the last minute. Work in the yard had to continue for as long as possible before people took cover. How brave these railwaymen and -women were. Colette's heart filled with pride. But how scared their families must be for them.

In any case, she had no business feeling proud when what she was hoping for was a direct hit that would provide her with the possibility of escape from her old life.

Cordelia was helping with some drying-up when the warning went off. Everyone froze, but only for a moment.

'Bugger!' exclaimed one of Dot's league of cooks. 'Pardon my French, girls, but honest to God – flaming Jerry! Doesn't Goering have a wife at home what needs to get the baking done? Those sponge puddings need another twenty minutes.'

'They're not going to get it until after the all-clear,' said Dot, 'because we've got to switch off the gas before we leave the building.' She looked at her friends. 'We'll see to the building, shall we?' She addressed the other women. 'You lot pike off down the public shelter and we'll see you there in ten minutes. Save us a space!'

'And let's hope them sponges don't sink,' quipped someone as the women quickly gathered their belongings and left.

'Joan and Pammy, turn the ovens off,' said Dot. 'You other young 'uns, make sure the buckets of sand and water are standing outside. Me and Mrs Cooper will open all the blackout blinds.' She turned to Cordelia. 'Will you do the switching off? The gas and electric are in that big cupboard and the main stopcock is under that counter in the corner.'

It was the work of moments, or so it seemed. They had all done this so many times that they knew exactly what was required even though this building was unfamiliar.

'Emily, you're still here,' Cordelia said and alarm tightened in her belly. 'You should have gone straight to the shelter with the others.'

'I wanted to wait for you.'

The others came hurrying back in.

'Are we all here?' Dot looked around. 'Good. Grab your stuff, girls, and let's skedaddle.'

Persephone hauled open the heavy front door and they all halted for a moment, glancing at one another as they heard the drone of aircraft engines. Then the beams of light shooting into the sky picked out the enemy planes, showing the ack-ack gunners where to aim.

Cordelia made sure she knew exactly where Emily was as the group ran in a huddle from the tarmacked playground into the street. Above them came the piercing whistles of strings of high explosives falling to earth. There was an explosion and the whole world seemed to shake. The women staggered and coughed as dust flew up all over the place.

'Which way to the shelter?' Mrs Cooper asked, her breath coming fast.

'Down there and round the corner,' said Dot. 'It's not far.'

They ran down the road, hampered somewhat by their instinctive need to stick close together so as not to leave anyone behind. Pammy missed her footing and nearly measured her length on the ground, but Mabel and Margaret grabbed her and hauled her up again.

As they rounded the corner, there came an almighty crash and the corner shop and the flat above it seemed to curtsey into the road, sending half the friends leaping aside and the other half staggering in the rubble and fighting to keep their footing. Hearing an ominous cracking sound behind her, Cordelia applied a huge shove to the back of Emily's shoulders, sending her flying forwards to safety. The next moment, Cordelia's head was crammed full of a booming sound and the ground vanished beneath her feet.

CHAPTER THIRTY-TWO

Colette watched in horror as a string of deadly incendiaries set fire to a line of wagons. For a long moment she was transfixed. Then she remembered her training and scrambled down the ladder to the ground, missing her footing and having to fling her arms around the ladder to prevent herself from falling. She hadn't taken more than a dozen steps before a railwayman grabbed her by the arm.

'Something to report?'

Colette rattled off the information – what, where and how bad. Even though she was shaken and scared, another part of her had taken over and this part was clear-headed and focused and knew precisely what to do. What, where and how bad – these were the three things she'd had drilled into her, the three things the rescue teams and the fire brigade needed to know so they could do their jobs properly. What, where and how bad.

'Righto,' said the man. 'Get back to your post. I'll report it.'

Colette climbed back onto the roof. Dazzling lights in the skies showed that Jerry was dropping flares to light up the yard. Her heart felt as if it might burst. Not the marshalling yard, not all those engines and wagons and coaches. In that moment she understood how much she had come to love the railways and everything they stood for – unity, resolve, cooperation and darned hard graft, no matter what the circumstances. All those courageous engine drivers and firemen who kept their locos moving through blackouts and air raids. The signalmen and -women who manned the signal boxes along the permanent way, heaving the levers into place even when the long bank of windows in front of them might implode at any moment in a bomb blast. The shunters in the marshalling yards, who risked their lives coupling and uncoupling the lengthy lines of wagons. And all the men and women who kept working regardless because, as every single railway employee knew as thoroughly as if it was engraved on their hearts, the mail must get through.

As Colette watched, the fire brigade lined up on the bridge above the wagons that were on fire, aiming their jets of water downwards. They hadn't a hope of reaching the wagons that were further away, but then the engine at the front of the line started to move and slowly it reversed the line, stopping and starting, so that, one by one, each wagon was halted beneath the bridge and as each individual fire was extinguished, the engine driver moved the line so that the next wagon could be saved.

Wrenching her gaze away, Colette peered all around through her binoculars, suddenly dropping to lie on the shed roof as high explosives rained down. The shed shook violently and she would have been tossed to the ground had she been upright. Even lying down, she rattled about, the breath whooshing out of her. It wasn't safe to remain up here. She must leave this post and head for another.

She crawled to the edge only to find that the ladder had fallen down. The part of Colette that seemed to be observing everything in an assessing kind of way prompted her to shift over to the rear of the roof, as the shed was built on a slope and the drop to the ground at the back wasn't as far. Hanging on to the edge of the roof, she manoeuvred herself around, ready to dangle over the edge and let go. And then – and then there was a huge booming sound and all the air was sucked from her body so violently that she all but turned inside out. The earth did not shake so much as dip down and lunge upwards again and she was hurled through the air.

This is it. This is how it's going to end.

Is this the way I'm going to leave Tony?

Twenty feet behind the shed was a brick wall. Colette hit it and crumpled to the ground behind some bushes. Every single bone in her body jolted and every joint was pulled apart and snapped back together. Her tin helmet struck the brickwork, sending waves of confusion through her head. She lay – well, not lay exactly, because that sounded like she was lying neatly on the ground, and she wasn't. She was sticking out at all sorts of angles, some of her on the ground, the rest of her inside the bushes.

She lay there, tangled up and stunned. She ought to move, report for duty at another post, but she couldn't make her body do anything. Not that she tried all that hard. Her mind was all foggy.

'Ruddy hell … ruddy hell.' A man's voice, hollow with shock. 'That Mrs Naylor were up on that shed.'

'Poor lady,' said another voice. 'Poor lass. Maybe she got away in time. Maybe she climbed down and ran for it.'

'God, let's hope so.'

Colette didn't move, couldn't have if she'd wanted to. She ought to call out, tell them she was all right, put their minds at rest. But she mustn't, must she? Those men thought she must be dead. She had never imagined it happening like this. She wasn't supposed to be caught in a real explosion. That part was meant to be pretend, with her close enough by for folk afterwards to believe she must have been caught in the blast.

Be careful what you wish for.

Colette closed her eyes and tried to drag her thoughts together. She concentrated on breathing, in, out, in, out. Then she started to move, gradually pulling herself free from the shrub until she was in a heap on the ground. Breathe, breathe. One thing at a time. Could she stand up? Oops – no. Yes, she could. She must. This was her one and only chance. Her thoughts were slow and disconnected and it would be so easy just to slump down again, but she mustn't, she mustn't.

Leaning heavily against the wall, she propped herself upright. Her head swam. Breathe, breathe. What next? One thing at a time. One foot in front of the other. Don't be seen. Hug the wall and head for the gates.

She straightened her helmet, adjusting the chinstrap. That made her head feel more like it was attached to her shoulders. Thank goodness for the cold night, which had made her leave her coat on beneath her mackintosh, thereby providing a little extra padding when she struck the wall. She didn't always wear her coat underneath. Usually she left it with her hat and shoes. Each time – Mrs Cooper's idea – she had tucked a small purse containing a few coins inside one shoe.

'It'll look like your bus fare home,' Mrs Cooper had said. 'That way, no one will question why your bag isn't with your things.'

As always on these nights, Colette's handbag with its precious contents was on her shoulder beneath her mac.

Fighting to concentrate, she made her way through the darkness, away from the flares and fires and searchlights, away from the AA fire and the aeroplane engines.

Her one and only chance.

Every time Alison breathed in, she inhaled great clouds of dust that had her choking and gasping. The others were the same. Around them, chunks of brickwork and plaster littered the ground. Alison put an arm around Mrs Cooper, who was bent double from coughing. They were all thickly coated in dust. That had been a close one.

'*Mummy!*'

The shriek made the whole group focus on the scene behind them. The corner building looked as if its corsets had burst apart and now it squatted in the road, but just where the piles of rubble ought to be thinning out, there was an extra heap – and Emily Masters was scrabbling away at it.

Cordelia! Under all that? Fear coursed through Alison's veins.

Without the need to exchange a word, she and Mabel ran to Emily and pulled her away, having to use a surprising amount of force because the girl resisted strenuously.

'What you're trying to do is dangerous,' Mabel said firmly as Emily tried to wriggle free. 'Calm down and listen.'

'Removing rubble takes time,' said Alison. 'It has to be done carefully. You don't know what might be happening underneath.'

'My mother—'

'We know, love.' Dot joined them. 'We all understand, but this has to be done proper like.' She looked round. 'Pammy and Sheila, you go to the shelter. Tell them what's happened so they don't send out a search party. Joan, you go an' all.'

'But—' Joan began.

'That's your job, the three of you,' said Dot. 'Tell the other women what's happened. Joan, you'll be able to explain about rescues. Take Emily with you.'

'No!' burst forth from Emily. 'I'm not leaving her.'

'Right,' said Dot, 'but if you stop here, you do as you're told.'

Emily nodded, her eyes huge in her dirt-caked face.

Dot addressed Pammy, Joan and Sheila. 'Off you go. The rest of us will stop here and sort this out. We'll get your mam out, Emily, never fear. Margaret and Persephone, there's an ARP station down there and round the corner by the pillar box. Get gone.'

The two girls took to their heels.

'Emily,' said Dot, 'you're going to wait over yon with Mrs Cooper. No arguments. Your mam would never forgive me if I let owt happen to you – and I wouldn't forgive myself neither.'

Mrs Cooper put an arm around Emily and bore her a short distance away.

Mabel nudged Alison. 'Our turn.' She stepped forward. 'We can't claim to be experts, but we're the ones here with the most experience.'

'They do say that as a first-aider you do more digging than first-aiding,' said Alison.

The two of them made a start on removing rubble in such a way as not to cause any miniature landslides, stopping every minute or two to press their ears to the heap and listen.

Dot tried calling through the pile. 'Cordelia! Can you hear me? Don't you fret, love. Your friends are here and we're going to get you out. Oh, and your Emily is safe and sound. I know you're more worried about her than you are about yourself. Mrs Cooper's looking after her and there's nobody better at looking after than she is. I can see her from here and she's got her arms round your lass, giving her a big cuddle. As for me, I'm stopping right here until we get you out. By, you'll be so sick of the sound of my voice, you'll be flinging aside all them bricks and whatnot so you can get free all the faster.'

Alison exchanged grins with Mabel, handing her a chunk of brickwork, which Mabel carefully bore away. Soon the rescue team arrived, with Margaret and Persephone following behind. Mabel and Alison stood back to let the experienced team assess the situation, then the two of them, plus Persephone and Margaret, joined the human chain removing the rubble.

'You need to come away from there,' an ARP warden told Dot.

'Nay, love. It's my mate under all that. If you tell me there's no way she can hear me, I'll move, but otherwise, I'm staying put.'

'It's not that simple. See the house wall that's still standing? It's not secure. It could come down at any moment. If it does, it'll land on top of this heap.'

Alison saw the distress that moved beneath the dirt covering Dot's face. Then Dot's mouth set in a line.

'You'd best get fettling then, because I for one don't fancy being squashed flat.'

The man nodded. Over his shoulder, he called, 'Rubber tubes over here, please. We'll push them down through the rubble if we can in the hope they get some air to your friend and you can use one as a speaking tube.'

Alison squeezed Mabel's hand and got back to work, listening to Dot's voice with one ear.

'That's better. I haven't got to yell now. Eh, you gave us all a fright, you did, falling through the road like that. But not to worry, love – we're going to get you out of there, because we want you with us at the carol concert on Christmas Eve. There's lots of handsome fellas up here, all working to free you, not to mention our own lovely girls. There's Mabel, Alison, Persephone and Margaret. Colette's not here because she's fire-watching, bless her. And I sent Joan off to the public shelter. I wonder how those sponge puddings are doing. We'll probably have to tell everyone they're pancakes ... '

Having escaped from the marshalling yard without bumping into anybody, Colette didn't stop walking until she reached the middle of town. She felt a jolt of fear when two ARP wardens came running towards her, but instead of yelling at her to take cover as she expected them to, they went straight past without stopping. Of course – her fire-watcher's clobber gave her a certain authority. She was allowed to be out in an air raid, because she was dressed for it.

Not far from London Road Station, she ducked into an alleyway. Resting her back against the wall, she let herself slide to the ground. Presently she removed her helmet and took off the headscarf she wore beneath it, putting it back on again in such a way that it fell over her forehead. It was the best she could manage as a disguise, ready for when she entered the station. She replaced her tin hat, securing the strap. With luck, seeing the fire-watcher's clothes, nobody would look any closer.

Taking off her mac, she unlooped her handbag from her shoulder. She would have liked to remove her own coat and carry it, but she didn't want to draw attention by having two coats. She would be fearfully hot on the train, but that couldn't be helped. She'd have to take off her tin helmet because it would look peculiar not to, but she could bury her chin and mouth in her scarf. At some point on her journey, she would have to dispose of the helmet and mackintosh and buy a pair of second-hand shoes to replace the rubber boots, but she had to get well away from Manchester first.

The moment the all-clear sounded, she jumped up and headed for the station, feeling horribly exposed and vulnerable as she looked round to get her bearings. First, she went into the Ladies and paid her penny to enter a cubicle. Here, she peeled off her gloves, stuffed them in her pockets and opened her bag, carefully tearing the lining inside which she had sewn Lizzie's documents. Leaving the certificates there, she removed her new identity card and slipped her real one into the lining. She also removed some banknotes and pushed them into her purse.

After a moment's thought, she carefully put her finger into the pocket that was sewn into the handbag's lining for keeping a powder compact easily to hand. Hers didn't contain a compact. Instead, she had tucked inside it the flower that Mrs Grayson had knitted. She had made them for the girls to wear to Joan's wedding, at which Colette had been the matron of honour. Colette gazed at the flower. It was the one keepsake she was taking with her, something special to remind her of her dear friends. From the reverse, she unfastened the safety pin and used it to fasten the lining once more.

Concentrating fiercely on what she was doing, because otherwise she would be consumed by terror, she let herself out of the cubicle and went to the ticket office. Shortly after that, she made her way through the barrier and found a seat on her train. She took off her helmet and placed it, together with her gas-mask box, her handbag and the binoculars, on her lap, then casually drew up her scarf over her mouth. Then she leaned into the corner, feigning sleep and waiting with a thudding heart for the train to leave. When she got off this train, she would catch another one.

No. *She* wouldn't.

Betsy Cooper would.

*

Above Cordelia, the noise stopped and everything went quiet and still. Even though she could guess what must be happening, it was impossible not to feel a lurch of pure terror. What if they had given up? But she knew they wouldn't. They wouldn't give up until they had found her, dead or alive.

And she was alive. Oh, thank heaven. There had been that one terrible moment when the ground had opened up and swallowed her and she'd thought she was about to meet her maker – but after that she had known it was a question of waiting. Her friends knew what had happened. She had to wait it out and ignore the pain as best she could. Emily! Was Emily safe? She had pushed Emily ahead of her at the crucial moment. Out of harm's way? Oh, she hoped so.

She had fainted and come round again. That was the pain. Well, fainting was one way of passing the time.

Then she had started hearing Dot's voice. An auditory hallucination? If it was, it was a singularly comforting one. Dear Dot, with her common sense, or her nous, as she would call it, and her sense of humour. People like Dot made the world a better place.

Now everything had gone silent. Cordelia was pinned where she was, so she couldn't do anything useful like tap out an SOS.

'Cordelia! Cordelia, can you hear me down there?' Dot's voice was significantly louder this time. 'Can you answer me, love?'

'Yes.' Her voice seemed rusty. She spat out some dirt and tried again. 'I'm here.'

'Oh, Cordelia,' came Dot's reply. 'There's a young lady up here who'll be so happy that I heard your voice. Don't fret. I shan't let Emily anywhere near the rescue, but I'll go and tell her. The men want me to shove off out of the way, anyroad. They'll soon have you out. Just a little longer.'

Emotion swelled inside Cordelia and her eyes filled. She blinked away the tears and sniffed hard. A few minutes later, something above her shifted and cold air poured in. Gradually, the hole got bigger and the weights that had held her locked in place eased and vanished.

Alison appeared beside her. 'Let's have a look at you before they lift you out. Where does it hurt?'

A broken collarbone. A significant quantity of a house had been dumped on top of her and all she had to show for it was a broken collarbone.

Alison spoke to Mabel up above and Mabel passed something down to her.

'I'm afraid this might hurt a little,' said Alison.

'It doesn't matter,' Cordelia whispered. It had hurt like billy-o all this time and even if the first aid briefly added to the pain, it would be worth it to know the correct treatment had begun.

Alison and Mabel strapped her to a stretcher and she was lifted out. There were a few jolts as the ambulance men took her down the side of the rubble heap and then Cordelia had a vague sense of a small whirlwind and Emily appeared at her side. She had pushed Emily out of harm's way and the girl was unhurt, which was the only thing that mattered. She would willingly have suffered every bone in her body being snapped in two if it would have saved her daughter.

'Mummy, I'm so relieved,' breathed Emily through her tears.

'Step aside, sweetheart,' one of the ambulance men said kindly. 'We have to get your mum to hospital.'

When Cordelia was inside the ambulance, there was a bit of commotion and Dot plonked herself down on a canvas stool beside her.

'They've given me a minute to talk to you. Don't worry about a thing. Between us, we'll fetch your Emily home and tell Mr Masters what's happened. We might even save some of them wretched sponge puddings, if we're lucky.'

'Time's up,' called an ambulance man.

'It's all right, love. I'm coming an' all.'

'Oh, Dot,' said Cordelia. 'Are you coming with me to hospital?'

'Let them try and stop me.'

CHAPTER THIRTY-THREE

After a night in hospital, Cordelia felt much stronger, even though her collarbone was painful.

'We can't set collarbones, I'm afraid,' the doctor told her. 'You'll just have to take care while it heals. The sling will help. Make sure it doesn't come loose. The fingertips of this hand should be up here, touching the opposite shoulder. That will give the bone the support it needs.'

Cordelia was discharged that afternoon and Kenneth took her home in a taxi. The journey left her feeling a bit ropy, but she was glad to be home.

'I'll stay on until you're better,' said Adelaide.

'Lovely. Thank you,' said Cordelia, keeping her feelings to herself. She was going to need help and she ought to be grateful.

'Those two women from Wilton Close turned up earlier,' said Adelaide. 'They brought vegetable stew and a syrup pudding.'

'Those two women have names,' said Cordelia.

'Of course they do. Mrs Cooper and Mrs Grayson. I'd find it easier to be gracious about them if it weren't for your intention to grub about in the gutter with them after the war.'

'Mother.' Kenneth spoke in a warning tone. 'That's enough. We have to do everything we can to make Cordelia comfortable, so she can start recovering.'

'All I need to help me recover,' said Cordelia, 'is the knowledge that Emily is safe.'

'Exactly so,' said Kenneth. A look passed between him and Adelaide. 'Please excuse us. I'd better tell her now.'

Cordelia felt cold in spite of sitting by the fire with a blanket tucked around her. 'Tell me what?'

Kenneth didn't say anything until Adelaide and Emily had left the room.

'I'm sorry, Cordelia. There's no easy way to say this. I'm afraid that last night, your friend Mrs Naylor – she ... '

'Colette? No! What happened?'

'The marshalling yard was targeted.'

'Oh, poor Colette.' Cordelia's breaths were coming too quickly. She made an effort to steady herself. 'Are you telling me she's – she's dead?'

Kenneth nodded.

Cordelia slumped in disbelief, then had to sit up straight because her collarbone sent discomfort pouring through her. When she had been lying in that hole under the rubble, with all those people working to free her, Colette had died all alone, doing her duty.

'I can't believe it,' she whispered.

But she could and she did. This was wartime. These things happened. Even when you desperately didn't want something to be true, you had to accept that it was.

Kenneth produced a bottle of brandy.

'Where did you get that?' asked Cordelia. 'No one can get hold of alcohol these days. You didn't ... ?'

'Use the black market? Certainly not. I've been saving it. I set it aside in case we were invaded. I thought we'd all need a jolly good swig.'

'It'll knock me sideways. I'm full of aspirin.'

'It's good for shock,' said Kenneth. 'And it'll fortify us for my mother's extended visit.'

*

That evening, Cordelia moved in the armchair, trying to resettle herself in such a way as to reduce the deep ache in her collarbone. She didn't want to make a fuss, partly because she'd been brought up not to, but mainly because she couldn't whine over such a triviality when dear Colette ...

'Are you all right, Mummy?' Emily asked anxiously. 'Are you comfortable?'

'I'm fine, thank you, darling. I was remembering my friend who was killed.'

'I keep thinking about her husband.' Kenneth looked up from his book. 'Poor devil. What must he be feeling?'

'It could have been our family, not his,' said Emily.

'I know,' said Cordelia. 'Sometimes it's a lot to take in, isn't it?'

The doorbell rang.

'I'll go.' Adelaide stood up. 'I was about to fetch my knitting anyway.'

She disappeared. Cordelia heard the muffled sounds of voices at the door. Presently, Adelaide returned with her knitting bag.

'Who was it?' Kenneth asked.

'Who was what?' replied Adelaide.

'Who was at the door?'

'No one.' After a moment, with three pairs of eyes looking at her, Adelaide said, 'It was two of Cordelia's ... friends. They wanted to know how she's getting on. I said she's doing well – which you are, aren't you, Cordelia?'

'Didn't you invite them in?' asked Cordelia. 'Who was it?'

'Mrs Green and Mrs Cooper.'

Cordelia waited, but Adelaide said no more. 'And you didn't ask them in.'

'No, I didn't,' said Adelaide in what might be described as a bold way for anybody else, but which for Adelaide was her usual manner. 'I'm sorry,' she went on in a voice that expressed no sorrow at all. 'I know this is your house and it's not up to me to make the rules, but in this case I judged my intervention to be essential. It's bad enough that you intend to spend the rest of your life being intimate with these women, but I draw the line at their being invited into this house.'

'It isn't up to you to make those decisions, Mother,' Kenneth said quietly, 'but it so happens I consider you did the right thing. Cordelia's fondness for these women is unfortunate all round and as she is well aware of my opinion on this subject, no one else need take her to task.'

'As a matter of fact ... ' Cordelia began, but had to stop to compose herself before she could continue. 'I've decided it would be better to withdraw from those friendships. It will upset me to do so, but I have reached the conclusion that it's the appropriate thing to do. Kenneth has been critical of my friendships all along, and then Emily came home and made her opinion clear, and then you weighed in, Mrs Masters. If the three of you think one thing, and you think it so strongly, it would be unreasonable to set myself against you. However much my friends mean to me, I want above all to be the best wife and mother I can be, and so I have decided ... ' Her voice failed her for a moment. 'I've decided to drop my friends.'

'Oh, Cordelia,' Kenneth said gruffly.

'Just imagine if I'd died last night and one of your final memories of me was that I hadn't been the wife and mother I should have been.'

'Thank you, Cordelia,' said Kenneth. 'I've waited a long time for this. You've reached the correct decision and it does you credit.'

Emily jumped up. 'No, it doesn't, Daddy. You weren't there last night and I was. I saw what Mrs Green did – I heard every word she said. She lay on that rubble heap calling to Mummy, even though she was warned how dangerous it was. She kept me safe too. She wouldn't let me anywhere near. Mrs Cooper stayed with me. She hugged me and comforted me. I've no idea what she said because I was straining to hear Mrs Green, but I know that Mrs Cooper was being as kind as she could, because she wanted to help me through. They might not be educated and they might not speak with plums in their mouths, but last night they were kind and brave and steadfast. Mummy's other friends, the young ones, they knew what to do and they got on with it. They didn't think about themselves. They didn't run away to the shelter. They wanted to save her.'

With that, Emily rushed from the room. The front door opened and shut again.

'Well!' said Adelaide. 'Whatever brought that on? The poor child is overwrought from last night.'

A few minutes later, the front door opened again and there were voices in the hall. Then the sitting-room door opened and Emily appeared, her eyes bright and her mouth determined.

'Come in, please,' she said, turning to smile at the ladies behind her. 'Mummy will be so happy to see you. You're her friends and she thinks highly of you – and so do I after what you did for her. I'm so pleased you're here.'

CHAPTER THIRTY-FOUR

Alison still hadn't taken it in. Colette had died on Thursday night and it was still hard to believe what had happened. Thinking of it made Alison feel numb, as if her thoughts had come adrift and couldn't find the right place to be. Her body felt numb too. That would be the shock, she supposed. Poor Colette. First Lizzie – then Letitia – now Colette. She'd only recently started fire-watching, too, whereas Alison had done her first-aid training in the spring of last year and had been out in any number of air raids, including all through the Christmas Blitz. Yet she had come through unscathed while Colette had barely had time to get started. There was no justice – no sense – no understanding it.

She had been supposed to go out with Joel on Friday evening, but she telephoned him at the hospital and had been lucky enough to speak to him personally instead of having to leave a message. She had cancelled their arrangements and explained about Colette. Joel had been kind and understanding, but she was too choked up to stay on the line for long.

She'd cancelled going to Mum and Dad's for Sunday lunch as well. She had started to write a message on one of those postcards that were blank on both sides. That was what Mum had always told her and Lydia to do.

'If you're not coming home for your evening meal, pop a postcard in the pillar box before midday and I'll get it by the afternoon post.'

That was what Alison had intended to do, but when she had tried to write about Colette, she just couldn't put the words on paper, certainly not on a postcard. Instead, she'd rung Lydia at work and sent the message that way.

Sunday lunch in Wilton Close was a subdued affair even though there were five of them round the table. Afterwards, they sat in the front room, drinking cups of tea.

'When I think of all the Sunday afternoons Colette used to come here,' said Mrs Grayson.

'We'll all miss her,' said Mrs Cooper.

'Things had got so much better for her this year,' said Mabel. 'Tony stopped being silly about whisking her off home instead of spending time with us, and she'd just started her new job as a railway chaperone.'

'I can't think of anyone more suited to taking care of passengers who need help,' said Margaret. 'She was such a thoughtful person.'

'She went out of her way to be kind to me,' recalled Alison.

'It just goes to show,' said Mabel. 'You have to make the most of every good thing that comes your way, because you never know what's going to happen.'

The doorbell rang.

Alison stood up. 'I'll go.'

It was Tony. Alison caught her breath, not knowing what to say. He looked awful, as if he hadn't slept in weeks. There were huge shadows under his eyes, and his face, which had always been thin, was now gaunt, his cheeks hollow. He hadn't bothered with an overcoat and the tweed jacket that normally fitted him well now hung off him.

'Come in,' said Alison. She went quickly to the front room and opened the door, wanting to give everyone a moment's warning. 'It's Tony Naylor.'

'Tony, my dear boy.' Mrs Grayson stood up and took his hands. 'I'm so dreadfully sorry. We all are. Come and sit down. We can squeeze another cup out of the pot, I'm sure.'

'I don't want one, thanks.'

'You might not want it, but you need it. You're freezing cold.'

Alison listened in awe as Mrs Grayson said all the right things.

'I'm sorry to turn up like this,' said Tony. 'I didn't know what else to do.'

'It's normal for you to come here on a Sunday,' said Margaret.

'Nothing will ever be normal again.' Tony swallowed, blinked, seemed to fight for control, then shook his head. 'I can't believe it. Only last weekend, she was on the verge of packing in her duty at the marshalling yard, I know she was. Our local WVS wanted her to join. She would have been much happier doing her volunteer work near home. But now – now ...'

'I know,' said Mrs Cooper. 'It's so hard.'

Tony swung round and stared at her. 'How did you do it?' he demanded with sudden energy.

Mrs Cooper pressed a hand to her chest. 'Do what?'

'How did you manage, how did you cope, when you lost your daughter? How did you get through the days? I feel as if I might go mad.'

'You've got your job,' said Margaret. 'You have to concentrate on that. I'm sorry if that sounds heartless, but jobs are good like that.'

'But I've still got to go home at the end of the day. I've still got to go back to that house without her. She was a quiet girl, but the place feels so empty without her in it. I can't bear it. I just want her back. I kept thinking – when they

365

told me, I kept thinking it would be all right, that they would find her unconscious somewhere. I kept giving myself deadlines. They'll find her by midday on Friday. They'll find her by teatime. They'll find her before midnight – they're bound to, because she can't be missing for a whole twenty-four hours. But they didn't find her on Friday and they didn't find her yesterday.'

'Are they … still looking?' Mrs Cooper asked.

'No.' Tony's mouth set in a hard line. 'They looked for her in case she'd been knocked unconscious and had then woken up and wandered off, but it turned out they didn't really expect that to have happened. They knew where she was – and that place took a hit. I went down there and raised merry heck. I said to them, "I won't believe she's gone until you give me her body." And that was when they told me that … with her caught in the explosion, there – there wouldn't be a body. So you see, there's no body, no funeral, just an empty house with her clothes and her hairbrush and her knitting that she was in the middle of.' Closing his eyes, Tony shook his head. 'And I don't know what I'm supposed to do.'

After tea, Alison and Margaret did the washing-up.

'You don't mind if I bunk off, do you?' asked Mabel. 'Harry's expecting a telephone call from me and I need to get to the telephone box.'

'We'll let you off this once,' said Alison.

'Wrap up warm,' said Margaret.

'It's a shame the Morgans never had a line put in,' said Mabel.

'If they had, you'd never be off it,' said Alison.

Mabel disappeared upstairs. When Alison and Margaret had finished, Margaret went to join Mrs Cooper and Mrs Grayson in the front room.

'I'll pop upstairs and fetch my book,' said Alison.

At the top of the stairs, she hesitated, then knocked on the door of the room Mabel and Margaret shared and went in. Mabel was fastening the buttons on her velvet-rayon dress in two shades of green.

'Come in,' she said. 'You're going to think I'm daft, but I always dress up to telephone Harry at his base. We don't see anything like as much of one another as we'd wish to, so I try to make a little occasion out of our telephone calls.'

'If that's daft, it's nice daft.'

Mabel tilted her head to the side and brushed her hair. She had the most glorious hair, full and wavy. Alison could feel her own hair getting straighter by the moment.

'Have you got a minute before you go out?' Alison asked. 'I've got something to ask you, but it can wait until you come back, if you'd rather.'

'How much time do you need?' Mabel glanced at her wristwatch. Then she came and took Alison's hands and drew her further into the room. 'You look serious. Tell me.'

'I don't want to make you late.'

'I usually have to queue at the telephone box. Harry knows that. He won't worry if I keep him waiting. On the other hand, I'll definitely worry if you keep me waiting when I can see something is bothering you.'

Mabel sat on the side of her bed, indicating for Alison to sit opposite her on Margaret's bed.

'It's what you said earlier about Colette,' said Alison, 'about making the most of every chance that comes your way.' She plunged in. 'It's made me wonder about the situation I'm in.'

'You mean, with Paul getting engaged? Lord, you're not going to hurl yourself to the ground, clasp him round the knees and beg him to come back, are you?'

Alison laughed in surprise at Mabel's bluntness. 'No, it's not that at all. It's ... ' She leaned forward, dropping her voice to a whisper. 'Can you keep a secret?'

'Cross my heart.' Mabel moved across to sit beside her, putting an arm round her. 'You can tell me. I know I lark around sometimes, but if you confide in me, I won't let you down.'

They both looked round as the door opened. Margaret appeared. She took one look at them and stopped.

'Oh – sorry. I just popped upstairs to fetch a hanky. I'll leave you to it.'

She started to withdraw and Alison was about to let her, then she changed her mind. She had kept her distance from her friends for so long. Now it was time to change all that. She remembered how kind both Margaret and Mabel had been when she had come home after hearing of Paul's engagement. They had looked after her then and she wanted them to look after her now.

'Don't go,' she said quickly. 'Come and sit with us – please. I was about to tell Mabel something important and I want you to hear it too.'

Margaret looked uncertain. 'Only if you're sure. I don't want to intrude.'

'I'm sure.' And she was.

Margaret perched on Mabel's bed, facing the other two.

'The thing is,' Alison said to Margaret, 'it's a secret for the time being. I'd like you to keep it to yourselves.'

She saw the glance that passed between Mabel and Margaret.

Mabel nodded. 'Go on.'

'I've – I've met another man.'

'Oh, Alison, that's – '

Please don't say it's too soon.

' – that's wonderful,' said Margaret.

'Is it?'

'Of course it is, you duffer,' said Mabel. 'You've been through the most horrible time and we've all been worried about you.'

'You deserve something good to happen,' Margaret said quietly.

'You dark horse,' Mabel added with a laugh. 'Fancy keeping it to yourself. Come on – spill! We want to hear everything. What's his name?'

'Joel.'

'I knew a Joel once.' Mabel pulled a face. 'He was the brother of a school friend of mine and a real spotty herbert.'

Alison laughed. 'Well, this Joel is definitely not one of those, I assure you.'

She poured it all out, how she and Joel had jumped off the train to chase the supposed saboteur; how he had tracked her down and she had grudgingly met him at the Worker Bee; and the way he had tackled the war profiteer in the toy shop.

'And is he good-looking as well?' Mabel asked.

'Very.'

'Crikey. If it weren't for the fact that he's obviously so keen on you, I'd be asking if you might like to swap him for Harry.'

'The trouble is,' said Alison, 'it's not as straightforward as it might sound.'

'What's the matter?' asked Margaret.

'I held back to start with. I wouldn't let myself like him. When I said I'd meet him at the Worker Bee, I told him that if there were no free tables, I wouldn't wait.'

'It's a good job there was one free, then,' said Mabel.

Alison lowered her voice. 'Only because Joel gave a chap the money to take his girl to the theatre.'

'You're kidding.'

'Seriously. Then the next time I saw him, he'd have liked to take me for a meal, but I insisted on going to the pictures.'

'So you didn't have to talk,' Mabel finished.

'It makes me sound horrid, doesn't it? And there's worse to come. We made another arrangement to meet, and it was definite on his side and loose on mine.'

'Ouch,' said Mabel. 'You've kept him dangling, haven't you?'

'I know, but after that – well, I realised how much I liked him.'

'So he likes you and you like him,' said Mabel. 'Are we building up to a happy ending?'

Alison shook her head, tears stinging her eyes. 'I'm scared I'm making a mistake. I keep thinking of Joan and Steven and what a mess she nearly made of things with Bob. It was before you were friends with us, Margaret, but Mabel knows what I'm talking about. What if I don't truly like Joel? What if I just think I do because it's all tied up with Paul getting engaged? What if I'm just kidding myself? But then you talked earlier on, Mabel, about how important it is to make the most of chances – and I think of Colette – and I just don't know what to do. I want to be with Joel, but not if it turns out to be a hideous mistake.'

Mabel nodded slowly. 'Getting involved is a risk. It doesn't matter who you are or what your situation is. It's always a risk. I'll tell you something that only one or two others know. Early this year, I found out something about Harry and I was dreadfully hurt and let down.'

'I had no idea,' breathed Alison.

'I came close to never seeing him again. That's how bad it was. But I thought hard about what I wanted and in the end, we sorted things out. Just like Joan had to decide what she really wanted. Now you have to decide.'

'That's just it,' said Alison. 'I don't want to make a mistake.'

'Nobody sets out to do that,' Mabel said kindly. 'Mistakes just happen. You can only do what feels right at the time. It would be very handy if you could put all the Paul stuff neatly into a box and slam the lid and never open it again. Then you could walk hand in hand into the sunset with Joel. But life isn't that tidy. Believe me, I've learned the hard way.'

'I thought I knew what I wanted,' said Alison. 'I thought I wanted to get to know Joel until I saw the similarities between my situation with him and Joan's with Steven.'

'I can understand that,' said Mabel. 'But try thinking of it the other way round.'

'What do you mean?'

'What if you were to stop seeing him – only your situation is nothing like Joan's and leaving Joel was a mistake? Then you'd have given him up for nothing.'

Alison tilted back her head and blew out a long breath upwards. Margaret moved across and sat on her other side, squeezing her shoulder and making her look round to meet Margaret's gaze.

'What do you want?' asked Margaret. 'In a wonderful world where everything was straightforward, what would you choose to do?'

'Carry on seeing Joel – as long as he doesn't get hurt if I let him down.'

'It all comes back to what Mabel said about risk and it sounds to me, judging by how he has persevered, that it's a risk he's willing to take. This could be your chance to be happy, Alison. For what it's worth, I hope you'll take it.'

'Truly?'

'Good grief, girl!' Mabel grinned at her. 'He chased after a suspected saboteur, so he's brave. He tackled a war profiteer, so he's principled. And on top of that, he's handsome. What are you waiting for?'

CHAPTER THIRTY-FIVE

Christmas Eve

Inside St Clement's Church, the lights were low and there were some candles, though nowhere near as many as there would have been pre-war. With Kenneth to one side of her, looking prosperous and distinguished in his wool overcoat and polished shoes, and Emily on the other, adorable in a nicely fitted coat and a jaunty beret, Cordelia was filled with gratitude. Against all her expectations, her family had changed their minds about her friends. It was all thanks to Emily, whose impassioned acceptance of Dot and Mrs Cooper had made Kenneth realise the full extent of what all her friends had done for her when she was trapped under the rubble. Dot's courage, Mrs Cooper's compassion, together with the skill and efficiency of the others, had finally been brought home to him. Cordelia closed her eyes in silent thankfulness that never again would she be torn between friends and family.

Adelaide had said to her in private, 'I shan't give in as easily as Kenneth and Emily.'

'They haven't given in,' Cordelia had replied. 'They've opened their eyes. If you prefer to keep your own eyes firmly shut, that's up to you.'

'Well, really!' snorted Adelaide.

Cordelia found she didn't care what Adelaide thought. She was older and set in her ways. It was Kenneth and Emily who mattered and their change of heart was the best and most meaningful gift she could possibly receive this Christmas. It was almost a shame she couldn't tell her friends of her happiness, but they must never know the reservations Cordelia's family had held against them.

It was the one good thing to have come out of this time of grief. Dear Colette had been taken from them, suddenly, violently – like Lizzie. War was unspeakably cruel. A young woman, a wife. There was no sense in it, but that was true of all civilian deaths. There wouldn't even be the comfort of a funeral. After Tony had been told there was no body to bury, he had refused to hold a service of any description. The poor man must be beside himself with grief.

Sitting on the hard wooden pew, Cordelia leaned forward a little so she could see across the aisle to where Joan was sitting, surrounded by the Hubble family. Not only had Joan had to face Colette's loss, she had also had to go through Letitia's first anniversary. It warmed Cordelia's heart to see her now with her Hubble family all around her, lending her their support. Joan had said from the first that they had welcomed her into their midst, accepting her not simply as Bob's girlfriend but as someone they cared about in her own right, and that was the best possible foundation for her life now as a Hubble.

In the pew in front of the Hubbles sat Mrs Cooper and Mrs Grayson, squeezed in with Mabel, Margaret, Alison and Persephone. Cordelia's heart gave a little tug of sympathy for Mabel, separated from her darling Harry at this special time of year. She and Margaret were to spend Christmas Day with Mrs Cooper and Mrs Grayson while Alison went to her family. Persephone would be at Darley Court with Miss Brown, Mrs Mitchell and the land girls. After Christmas, Mabel and Persephone were each due to go home for a couple of days to see their families, Mabel to

Annerby in the north of Lancashire and Persephone to Surrey, was it, or Sussex?

Pain stabbed the site of Cordelia's injury when she looked over her shoulder, but that wasn't going to stop her setting eyes on Dot. Was it because of losing Colette that Cordelia felt the need to make sure her friends were close by? Dot had brought her husband, daughters-in-law and grandchildren to this service, even though it would have been much easier for them to attend a local one in Withington.

Silently, Cordelia gave thanks that her friends had arranged to come to this carol service together. They had done so never imagining the bereavement that lay ahead. Being here now didn't just feel like something they were doing in honour of Christmas. It was in Colette's honour too. Cordelia quietly moved her hand and took hold of Emily's.

The service began and the Christmas story was told through a series of readings and familiar carols. When it came to 'Silent Night', Cordelia recalled Dot's description of hearing that beloved carol this time last year, followed a moment later by the siren that had signalled the start of the Christmas Blitz. Now, as the carol finished, in the moment of silence that followed, Cordelia turned to meet Dot's gaze.

Dot gave her a watery smile and bowed her head to hide her tears.

Outside the church, the friends all hugged one another, gently squeezing Cordelia's hand.

'The service was lovely,' said Mrs Grayson, 'but it made me dreadfully sad.'

The younger girls were wiping away tears.

'It felt like we were there for Colette,' said Persephone.

Kenneth appeared. 'Our taxi is here, Cordelia. You mustn't overdo things. You need rest.'

'Yes, you must look after yourself,' said Margaret.

But Cordelia couldn't bear to part from the friends she had come so close to losing. 'I've a better idea. Mrs Cooper, forgive my cheek, but would you mind if we all went to your house? Not absolutely everyone,' she added. 'Not the families. Just us friends.'

'Oh, yes, please,' said other voices.

'Of course,' said Mrs Cooper. 'It'll be my pleasure.'

Kenneth looked irritated, then his expression softened. 'You must promise to come home by taxi afterwards.'

'I will,' said Cordelia, 'and be prepared for a hefty taxi bill, Kenneth, because I'll be taking others home first – Mrs Green and Joan to Withington, Persephone to Darley Court.'

'There's no need,' Dot said quickly, with a glance at Kenneth.

'There's every need,' said Cordelia. 'You're my friends and I want to look after you. Please let me.'

'I'll book the taxi for ten o'clock,' said Kenneth. 'You'll be exhausted if you stay out longer than that.'

'Mummy,' said a small voice at Cordelia's side, 'please may I come with you? I'd like to spend the evening with you and your friends.'

A warm sense of rightness flowed through Cordelia. This was what she'd wanted all along. Emily's initial rejection of her friends had been hurtful and shocking, but now Emily had come round to a new way of thinking and Cordelia's wish had come true.

'You're not going to Edge Lane after all,' Kenneth was saying to the taxi driver. 'It's Wilton Close instead, please. Who is travelling with you, Cordelia?'

'Mrs Cooper ought to,' said Margaret with a laugh. 'She's the one with the front-door key.'

'And Mrs Grayson,' Alison added.

Cordelia looked at Dot. 'I expect we can squeeze in one more.'

'Nay, love. You need space.'

Cordelia slid into the vehicle, trying to hide the wince of pain, but the pain vanished the moment she looked out and saw Emily in between Mabel and Alison, both of whom had linked up with her for the walk.

It wasn't long before the taxi reached Wilton Close.

'Let me take your coat,' said Mrs Cooper, easing it away from the arm in the sling and sliding the other sleeve from Cordelia's arm. 'I'll see to the fire and put the kettle on.'

Presently the front door opened and the others spilled inside, complete with muffled exclamations and giggles as they bumped into one another in the dark before the door was shut and they could switch the light on.

Soon they were all in the sitting room, which was crowded but in a comfortable way. Cordelia and Mrs Grayson had the armchairs, with Mrs Cooper and Dot on the sofa.

'You come and sit with us, love,' Dot said to Joan, patting the place beside her.

Persephone perched on the arm of Mrs Grayson's chair. Margaret sat on the floor, leaning against the sofa, her back between Mrs Cooper's and Dot's legs. Mabel sat on the footstool and Alison was on the hearthrug. And Emily – oh, Emily sat at Cordelia's feet, leaning against her legs.

'I'm sorry the tea isn't stronger,' said Mrs Cooper, 'but you know how it is. You have to squeeze all the taste you can out of the leaves.'

'It's kind of you to share,' said Dot. 'We all keep turning up here like bad pennies and you always put the kettle on.'

Cordelia looked round the room, wanting to compliment their hostess on her Christmas decorations, but there weren't any apart from a small wooden Nativity scene and some stems of laurel coated in pretend frost.

That made her smile. 'I see you made use of the idea with the Epsom salts.'

That then needed to be explained to those who hadn't been present at the time and everyone admired the results.

'Don't you have any other decorations?' asked Persephone.

'Sadly not,' said Mrs Cooper. 'My box of tinsel and coloured stars was lost when I was bombed out. The Nativity scene over there is Mrs Grayson's.'

'It was my mother's' said Mrs Grayson. 'When you rely on others to do your shopping for you, you can't ask them to buy frivolous things like decorations.'

'Christmas decorations aren't frivolous,' Persephone declared. 'They're essential, especially these days.'

'There are no trees to be had this year,' said Mrs Cooper, 'real or artificial.'

'What about the Morgans' decorations?' asked Emily. 'Have they taken them to Wales?'

'There's a box upstairs,' said Mrs Cooper, 'but I would never presume ... '

'Mrs Masters is here to give permission, if you need it,' said Dot.

'Go and fetch them,' said Cordelia. 'We all need cheering up.'

A stout cardboard box was brought downstairs. Mabel removed the lid to reveal a mishmash of tinsel, paper garlands and coloured glass baubles.

'Was there a tree up there?' asked Alison.

'The Morgans always had a real one,' said Cordelia.

'Then we'll decorate the room,' said Persephone. 'We can pin up the garlands and hang the baubles from the gas lamps and the picture rail. We could put some in a fruit bowl on the hearth, then they'd twinkle in the firelight.'

The four older ladies sat back and watched as the younger ones set about decorating the room.

'Come on, Emily,' said Alison, picking up a garland. 'Help me with this.'

There were two garlands, old and faded, but that didn't matter. Mabel fetched the stepladder from the garden shed and they strung the garlands from two corners to meet at the ceiling rose of the central light.

'This tinsel has seen better days,' Alison commented.

'That doesn't matter,' said Persephone. 'The point of Christmas decorations is that you keep them for years and years and they get more memories attached to them with each Christmas that passes.'

'These decorations will be yours for the duration,' Mabel said to Mrs Cooper. 'We'll use them again next year and we'll look back and remember Colette and how we lost her the week before Christmas.'

'I know there can't be a proper funeral,' said Joan, 'but I wish there was going to be a memorial service. It's Tony's choice, of course, but … ' She looked troubled.

'Let's hold our own service,' suggested Persephone. 'Here – now. We're all here together and Colette is fresh in our minds. What better time? And what better place? We all love this house and Colette came here virtually every week.'

'That's a lovely thought,' said Alison, 'but how would we set about it? These things need to be planned.'

'When my grandmother died,' said Persephone, 'we were children and my father took the view that children shouldn't attend funerals. Up in the nursery, Nanny got each of us to choose a special word that applied to Grandma and we all talked about her.' She smiled. 'We wrote the words down and afterwards we burned them, because my brothers wanted a funeral pyre.'

'Have you some bits of paper we could use?' Dot asked Mrs Cooper.

Soon everyone except Emily had a scrap of paper. Mrs Cooper produced two pencils and they passed them round. Cordelia thought, then wrote *shy*.

'Now put all the papers into this saucer,' said Mabel, 'and Emily can pick one out.'

Emily swished the scraps about, then chose one. 'It says *kind*.'

'Who wrote that?' asked Persephone.

'I did,' said Joan. 'She never had a bad word to say about anyone and she cared about all of us.'

Everybody agreed. Emily looked at Cordelia, who nodded, and Emily picked out another bit of paper.

'*Sweet-natured.*'

'That's mine,' said Mrs Grayson. 'Colette was such a lovely girl, just as Joan described her. There wasn't a shred of temper or malice in her.'

'*Good listener,*' said Emily.

Alison moved her hand. 'I don't just mean she never talked as much as the rest of us. I mean, she paid attention to other people.' She paused. 'She made me feel she really understood when I told her a bit about what it was like for me after Paul left me.'

Mabel squeezed Alison's arm. Emily reached for the next word. It was Cordelia's.

'I found her shyness appealing, though it made me wish I could give her more social confidence. These past few months, she started to lose her shyness.' Cordelia shook her head. 'What a waste of a life. It seemed to me she was becoming more assured and even more lovely and now that's all gone.'

'What's next?' Alison asked Emily.

'*Brave.*'

'That's mine.'

Mrs Cooper and Mabel spoke at the same time, then looked at one another.

'You first, dear,' said Mrs Cooper.

'It was so brave of her to volunteer for fire-watching duty in the marshalling yard,' said Mabel. 'With her being quiet and gentle, you might not have expected her to do that. It made me think there was more to her than I'd realised.'

Taking the next one out, Emily read, '*Right thing.*'

'That's all there was room for,' said Dot. 'She were always one to do the right thing. She had a sense of responsibility. It wasn't just that she had a kind nature. She did something with her kindness, something positive. I bet you any money that it's what made her good at her chaperone job. She would have done everything she could to make her charges' journeys comfortable and pleasant, because that was the best way to do it.'

There were murmurs of agreement all round.

'*Reliable.*'

Persephone spoke up. 'I wrote that because of how she came here regularly, because she wanted to be a good friend to Mrs Cooper and Mrs Grayson. There was something steadfast in her.'

'And *brave*,' finished Emily and they all looked at Mrs Cooper.

'I were thinking of a different kind of bravery to Mabel,' said Mrs Cooper. 'I meant the courage it took to come knocking on my door after Lizzie died. Colette had never met me, but that didn't stop her, for all that she was quiet and shy. It's like Mrs Green said – she would do the right thing. I'll never forget that. When you have a serious bereavement, there are folk you've known for years who can't think what to say to you. One or two even cross the road so they don't have to speak to you. But that young lass came to see me because … ' Her voice hitched and vanished.

'Because it were the right thing to do,' Dot finished for her.

'What a dear girl,' said Mrs Grayson.

'She was,' said Mabel. She wiped away a tear and she wasn't the only one.

As filled with sorrow as she was, Cordelia also experienced a sense of release. Who would have thought that sharing their feelings about Colette would feel so special and meaningful? It had been exactly what they had all needed, their own small and deeply personal memorial for their lost friend.

Mrs Grayson tucked her hanky up her sleeve and cleared her throat. 'After that, I think we need something to lift our spirits. Has anyone got anything good to share?'

There was silence, then Joan spoke up.

'Well … I have, but it doesn't feel quite right to say it after what happened to Colette.'

'All the more reason to say it,' said Alison.

Beside Joan on the sofa, Dot took her hand. 'It's always the right time for good news, chick. We don't want to end Christmas Eve on a sad note if we can help it.'

Joan laughed and blushed. 'I'm having a baby. I'm going to be a mum.'

The swell of sorrow in the room changed into a burst of delight and Joan was showered with congratulations and good wishes.

'This baby is going to have so many godmothers,' Mabel declared.

'When is it due?' asked Margaret.

'June.'

'An anniversary baby,' Persephone exclaimed and they all laughed.

'I'm that chuffed for you, love,' said Dot.

Joan turned to her. 'You knew, didn't you? You could tell.'

'I did wonder,' said Dot. 'You had a certain look about you.'

'That's why you sent me to the air-raid shelter the night of the bombing.'

'I couldn't take any chances with everybody's future godchild, could I?' said Dot.

'It's been a strange time,' said Joan. 'Letitia's anniversary and Colette's death ... and me expecting.'

'Now you can relax and be truly happy about it,' said Cordelia.

'I think this calls for mince pies,' said Mrs Grayson, getting up.

Alison and Margaret followed her out, the three of them soon reappearing with plates and sweet-smelling mince pies.

'In the absence of alcohol,' said Cordelia, 'I think we should raise our mince pies in a toast. To Colette, whom we'll always remember, and to Joan, who has given us something wonderful to look forward to.'

'Colette and Joan,' said the rest as they lifted their mince pies and then laughed because it was such a daft thing to do.

'That's the way we'll remember this Christmas,' said Dot. 'A time of grief, but also a time of hope. You've given us all a very special present, Joan.' She kissed Joan's cheek. 'None of us will ever forget it.'

Emily looked up at Cordelia and said quietly, 'You look tired, Mummy. Are you all right?'

Cordelia leaned forward. 'I'm fine,' she whispered. 'A bit achy, that's all. Are you glad you came this evening?'

Emily nodded.

'Thank you, darling,' Cordelia said softly. 'That's the best Christmas present I could have wished for.'

EPILOGUE

Mrs Cooper slipped out of the back door and stood in the garden. It was a cold night and the ink-black sky was dotted with stars.

That impromptu memorial to Colette had nearly been her undoing. Listening to the sorrow-filled tributes had torn at her heart. These friends didn't deserve to lose Colette, didn't deserve to suffer the grief they now had to endure. But it was the only way. The truth of Colette's life and her disappearance had to remain a secret for ever.

The news of the bomb blast at the marshalling yard had come as a terrific shock. She had lain awake night after night, dreading that Colette truly had been killed. Had their careful plans for taking advantage of an air raid turned into a horrible reality? Had her own idea for Colette's escape ended up sending Colette to her death?

But a Christmas card had arrived that very morning, a flimsy one compared to those from before the war, but the most precious she had ever received. The words *Love from Betsy* had almost robbed her of the ability to breathe.

Love from Betsy.

She had tucked it safely away under her pillow.

'Are you all right, love?'

Mrs Green appeared, arms wrapped around herself against the cold.

'Just getting a bit of air.'

'Aye, it's sweltering in there with all them people.' Mrs Green looked up at the stars and then at her. 'Having a moment with your Lizzie, are you?'

What could she do but nod? Thinking of Colette – Betsy – was all tied up now with thoughts of Lizzie.

'Losing Colette must have brought it all back,' said Mrs Green. 'I know Colette were special to you. You were special to her an' all. I could see that. She didn't come round here just because it were the right thing. She came because she liked you. She cared about you.'

'Thank you.' It came out as a whisper.

'I'll go back in. Don't stop out here too long. You don't want to catch cold.'

'I'll be indoors in a minute.'

Mrs Green left her.

Oh, Lizzie, you don't mind that I gave away your name, do you? Lizzie wouldn't mind, she was sure. Lizzie was a good girl, a kind girl. She would understand.

Mrs Cooper looked up at the stars for a final time.

'God bless you, Betsy Cooper,' she whispered, and went back indoors.

Welcome to

Penny Street

where your favourite authors and stories live.

Meet casts of characters you'll never forget,
create memories you'll treasure forever,
and discover places that will stay with
you long after the last page.

Turn the page to step into the home of

MAISIE THOMAS

and discover more about

Christmas with the Railway Girls

Dear Readers,

Have you heard of 'bread-and-butter letters'? In times gone by, if you went to stay with someone as their guest, afterwards, when you got home, you would write to thank them for their hospitality – for sharing their bread and butter with you – thus, a bread-and-butter letter. This letter I'm writing today is a bread-and-butter letter of sorts, because I want to say a huge thank you to all my lovely readers for welcoming the Railway Girls characters into your hearts and onto your bookshelves and e-readers. When I started writing the series, I was asked to write three books; and because of their success, I have been asked to write three more – and that is thanks to each and every one of you.

While I am busy with my thank-yous, I'd like to say a special thanks to Jennie Rothwell. Jennie has been my editor through *Secrets of the Railway Girls*, *The Railway Girls in Love* and *Christmas with the Railway Girls*, but now she is leaving to move onto other things. The relationship between an author and their editor is a special one. Being required to work with an editor with whom you don't get on with must be an absolute nightmare, because the editor has significant influence over each book. All I can say about Jennie is that she and I hit it off straight away, both professionally and personally, and I have complete trust in her judgement. You may have noticed that I like to put my characters in sticky situations and then make things even worse for them – well, Jennie is the person who makes sure there is a happy ending!

In fact, when I was asked to write a second set of three Railway Girls books, it wasn't just a matter of saying 'I'd love to' and signing on the dotted line. What happens in that situation is that the author has to write a series proposal, which means coming up with plot outlines for each book, which the editor has to be happy with. When it came to one particular outline, Jennie was very concerned about what I had in mind and said firmly, 'You can only do that if it has a happy ending.' Because of this, the words 'Jennie and I have agreed that the outcome of this plot will be entirely happy and positive' were subsequently immortalised in the proposal that was put forward to the powers that be in the acquisitions meeting. Which plot was it? Not telling! All I'll say is that it isn't in *Christmas with the Railway Girls*.

What a pleasure it has been to write this book for you. I know from many of the reviews of previous books that lots of you have been intrigued by Colette's marriage – well, now the truth comes out. And I loved writing a plot from Cordelia's point of view. She is the calm, composed one of the group, but, as you'll see, there is a lot going on under the surface. As for Alison and her urgent wish to get engaged … Well, it's no secret that I like making things difficult for my girls! But one of the reasons why I am able to do that is because, no matter how tough life is for any of them, they always have one another to rely on. That feeling of friendship is the basis of every story.

I hope you enjoy this book.

Much love,
Maisie xx

The Fine Line between Fiction & Reality

Like many of my fellow authors, a question I'm often asked is, 'Of all the books you've written, which is your favourite?' And my usual response is, 'The one I'm writing at the moment.' I can't speak for anyone else, but for me, this is because the current WIP (work in progress) is the one that fills my mind most as I live through all my characters' experiences, sharing their triumphs and their woes as their story unfolds on the page. Being so immersed in their world makes it feel like the most important one ... until it's time to start work on the next one, of course!

I'm sure you can understand how an author becomes so deeply absorbed in their WIP, but it might surprise you to know that there can be times when the world of the story and that of reality merge. For example, do you remember the Christmas Blitz scenes in *Secrets of the Railway Girls*? It was summertime when I wrote them, yet inside my head, the recollection I have of writing those chapters is that it was winter and pitch-dark outside – just the way it would have been during the Christmas Blitz itself. Even with the knowledge that the memory is false, it still doesn't make me remember writing those scenes in broad daylight. Isn't that strange?

Another example – and this might make you smile – is to do with another scene in *Secrets of the Railway Girls*. I was working on the copy-edits early in the spring lockdown of 2020 when I came across these lines early in Chapter 38: 'Arriving in Wilton Close, she and Joan wheeled their bicycles up the passage and through the gate into the back garden. The kitchen door opened and Mrs Cooper looked out.'. . . And a cold thrill passed through me, a feeling of genuine alarm, because *Mrs Cooper wasn't social distancing!*

The Challenge of Writing *The Railway Girls in Love*

Christmas with the Railway Girls was my winter 2020–2021 lockdown novel, but the book I wrote in the first lockdown, in the spring of 2020, was *The Railway Girls in Love*. For those of you who take an interest in the writing process, I thought you would like to read this short piece that I originally wrote, at Jane Cable's request, for *Frost*, the online books and lifestyle magazine. You can find Frost at www.frostmagazine.com

* * * *

'What was the most challenging aspect of writing *The Railway Girls in Love*?' That's what Jane Cable asked me. I imagine she – and you – suppose it was difficulties with the plot. But no. The plot had been sorted out eighteen months previously. The book is part of a series, you see, and I have to be on top of the plot at all times, and that includes knowing what is going to happen in future books.

Maybe, then, you're wondering if there was a particular character I found tricky to put on the page? Again, no. Having already written two books about my Railway Girls, I feel I know them inside out.

What, then, was the most challenging thing? Was it when my editor mistakenly sent me the wrong version of the track-changed document for editing? Nope. That ended up meaning that I had two track-changed documents open side by side, but it couldn't be described as a challenge.

The most challenging thing – and I can't begin to describe how I struggled to cope – was that *The Railway Girls in Love* was my spring 2020 lockdown novel, meaning and the public library was shut. If I tell you that all but a few scenes of both *The Railway Girls* and *Secrets of the Railway Girls* were

written in the local library, you'll perhaps start to understand why the library closure posed a problem. For me,
writing is about discipline, and discipline is about routine –
and my routine was to go to the library every morning and
knuckle down to work. So when my usual plans were scup-
pered by its closure, I was astonished by how hard I found
it to work at home. It's not as though I live in a madcap
household full of noise and disruption – quite the opposite.
I can't explain it. All I can say is I found it remarkably tough
to work at home instead of tucked away in my little corner
of the library.

Turn the page for an exclusive
extract from my new novel

Hope for the
Railway Girls

Coming April 2022
Available to pre-order now

1

Friday, January 2nd, 1942

With the oily smell of the rag making her nostrils itch, Margaret rubbed hard at her allocated section of the locomotive's enormous body. Polishing the loco sounded like an easy job, but it wasn't, not if you did it properly. It called for loads of elbow grease, but she had discovered the effort was more than worth it.

It was funny how things worked out. She had sat the tests in English, maths and geography to work on the railways simply as a means of escaping from her old job, a job she had loved ever since she had started at Ingleby's the day after she left school, aged fourteen. But she had ended up dreading going to work in case one of her old neighbours appeared. You couldn't run away and hide, not when you were an assistant in a successful and highly regarded shop.

Margaret smiled to herself. You were supposed to run away and join the circus, weren't you? Well, she had run away and joined the London Midland and Scottish Railway. She had even been desperate enough to write a letter, asking if she could please have a job that didn't involve working with the public. She had no idea whether her request had been paid attention to, or whether she would have been assigned to engine-cleaning anyway, but it didn't matter. She was here now and she loved it. There was something deeply satisfying about giving a loco a jolly good clean. Everyone depended on the railways. They were an essential part of the war effort and Margaret believed all the way down to her toes that the war couldn't be won without them. Troops, munitions, food and fuel were all transported around the country by rail.

As a railway worker, Margaret was aware that dummy tanks were moved about on the back of huge flat-bed wagons, just to keep Jerry guessing when he flew over in his spy-planes. And then there were the ordinary passengers, of course, who put up with all sorts of delays because they were at the bottom of the pecking order these days when it came to deciding which trains were given priority. But folk took it on the chin, because everybody knew the importance of transporting soldiers, coal, weapons, foodstuff and other essentials.

Margaret stopped for a moment to roll her shoulders inside her boiler suit. All the women in the engine sheds wore boiler suits or else heavy-duty dungarees with old blouses underneath and in some cases, old shirts that had previously belonged to their husbands. Although Margaret preferred dungarees in warm weather, she was in a boiler suit now, because this January was proving to be colder than usual.

'Let's hope it's even colder in Russia,' Alison said a couple of evenings ago at home in Wilton Close, when Mrs Cooper was busy preparing hot water bottles for her, Margaret and Mabel. 'That'd freeze Jerry in his tracks.'

Wilton Close. A warm feeling crept into Margaret's heart as she pictured it. Even now, after living there for a few weeks, she still felt like pinching herself to make sure it was real. Imagine her, Margaret Darrell, having such good luck. It wasn't just that she appreciated having a billet somewhere clean and comfy after the frankly shoddy bedsit she had lived in previously. It was the *feeling* of home that permeated the house, thanks to the good nature of Mrs Cooper, her landlady, and also of Mrs Grayson, who was really another lodger but who did all the cooking and was a wizard at producing tasty meals in spite of shortages and rationing. Mabel joked that Mrs Grayson possessed a magic wooden spoon, and she wasn't far wrong.

'Forget Elsie and Doris Waters and Freddie Grisewood and 'The Kitchen Front',' Mabel had declared. 'Mrs Grayson should have her own programme on the wireless. It could be called 'Meals by Magic'.'

'Get away with you,' Mrs Grayson had said, but she hadn't been able to hide how pleased she was.

Margaret shared a bedroom with Mabel, and Alison lived in Wilton Close too, which had helped Margaret to feel very much a part of the group of friends she had been drawn into last summer. It had been daunting, to say the least, to join a group of such established friends. Margaret had Joan to thank for her inclusion. They had known one another back at Ingleby's, though it hadn't been until they were put on fire-watching duty together that they had become friendly. Truth to tell, it had been because Joan had left Ingleby's in a state of such pride and excitement to join the railways that Margaret had decided to do the same when she had been in need of a bolt-hole.

And how glad she was that she'd done it. Thanks to that decision, she now had a cosy billet with the loveliest landlady in the kingdom, and she had a group of chums to whom she felt closer than she had to anybody else in a long time.

Life was looking up and the past didn't matter quite so much anymore.

Sometimes.

At the end of her shift, Margaret hurried to the changing room, which, in spite of the staggered shift patterns, wasn't big enough for the number of women needing to get changed at any one time. Peeling off her boiler suit, Margaret put on an oyster-coloured faux-silk blouse and a tartan wool skirt, which, along with some other items, had been given to her by the women running the local rest centre after her house had been bombed and she had lost just about everything. Back when she had worked at Ingleby's, she had always dressed nicely with everything properly coordinated, thanks to her staff discount, though when you'd been bombed out, swish clothes never seemed as important afterwards. You weren't supposed to use your staff discount for anyone other than yourself, but sometimes Margaret had been unable to resist treating her sister to something special. Anna was kind-hearted and generous, as well as being pretty and she deserved to have lovely things.

A pang smote Margaret. She hadn't seen Anna for such a long time. Anna had had a baby on the way – twins, as it had turned out – when war broke out, so she had been evacuated along with all the children and the other mothers-to-be. That had been in the September of 1939 and now it was the start of 1942 – and the country was still at war. To think she hadn't seen the older sister she had always looked up to in all that time. It would have been unthinkable before the war, but now these things, these separations, were normal. Anna's twins, one of each, would be two this month. Two! 'Strewth, but war was a cruel business.

Over the top of her blouse, Margaret put on her new jumper, which was mainly a warm russet-brown with a three-inch stripe in cream about four inches above the waist. Anna had knitted it for her for Christmas and she was dying to show it off to those of her friends who hadn't yet seen it. It might not be the best match for her blouse, but Margaret didn't have so many clothes that she could afford to be choosy. Besides, she would have loved anything her sister made for her and worn it as much as she could.

She removed the turban she wore all day long to protect her hair and keep it out of the way. Lots of the girls and women wore curlers under their turbans, though Margaret hadn't to begin with, because she had seemed to hear her dear late Mum's voice inside her head. Mum would have seen it as setting foot out of doors improperly dressed, but she had passed away several years ago and things were different now. It was normal for women in factories and other mucky jobs to wear curlers under their turbans. Margaret, declining to do so when she started in the engine sheds, had ended each shift with flattened hair while all the others had been busy fluffing up their curls and waves. These days, Margaret was very much part of the fluffing up brigade. As for Mum – well, Margaret had done a lot worse than wear her curlers outdoors.

When her dark brown page-boy cut hung lose and uncurled, they sat on Margaret's shoulders. She styled it so that full curls waved away from her face and she had let the fringe grow long so that it too could be curled and sat in a froth at her temples. She shrugged into her coat, winding her scarf round her neck, paying attention to her brimless felt hat and making sure it didn't muss up her hair.

Calling cheerful goodbyes, she set off to walk to Victoria Station, where she was going to meet up with her friends in the buffet. As she entered the station, she was greeted by the mingled aromas of smoke and steam. The sound of a train pulling in lifted up into the arched canopy that covered the station platforms and echoed around the enormous building.

The concourse was packed, as always at this time of day, with people going home after work. It was a bit early for the 'funk express' crowd, those folk who legged it out of Manchester to spend the night elsewhere in case the city was bombed. One or two people looked impatient as they made their way through all the passengers standing about smoking, chatting or reading newspapers as they waited, but Margaret didn't care how busy it was. She enjoyed feeling that she was a part of it. She loved her position as a railway girl and loved the thought of joining her friends for a cuppa and a good natter before heading for home. It was to be their first get-together since Christmas Eve. Margaret's heart delivered a bump. Christmas Eve. Oh, Colette. They had all shared their memories and feelings about their dear friend. It had been a deeply emotional experience, but also the beginning of healing.

The buffet was busy, but Dot had already bagged a table near the fireplace – and with her was Cordelia, one arm in her coat-sleeve, the other hidden beneath her coat. Margaret went straight to them.

'Cordelia!' she exclaimed, only to become aware of eyebrows raised in surprise and disapproval at neighbouring tables at her use of her friend's first name. 'I mean, Mrs Masters,' she corrected herself, feeling heat in her cheeks. For a girl in her twenties to address a lady in her forties by her first name simply wasn't the done thing and the group of friends were flouting convention by allowing it, so it was important to maintain the proprieties in front of outsiders.

Margaret sank onto a chair, leaning towards Cordelia, her delight at seeing her washing away her moment of embarrassment. 'I wasn't expecting to see you today.'

Cordelia smiled. 'I wasn't going to miss the chance of seeing you all.'

'How's the collar-bone?' asked Margaret.

'Mending, thank you. It doesn't ache anything like so much as it did. I'll be back at work in no time.'

'Well, it's lovely to see you,' said Margaret.

She went to join the queue, her gaze drawn back to her friends as she waited. Cordelia wore her wine-coloured coat with the fancy top-stitched collar and her grey hat with the upswept brim that showed off her fine features, ash-blonde hair and discreet pearl earrings. Dot wore a rather good navy coat with patch pockets and wide lapels – the reason it was rather good being that it had once been Cordelia's; and that was a mark of their friendship, if anything was. Cordelia had passed on the coat out of pure friendship, not out of concern or charity, as might have been expected by anybody who didn't know them, given their social differences.

Those two were great friends. Margaret knew that Mum would have been baffled by their friendship, but that was the war for you. Pre-war, Mrs Kenneth Masters, wife of a solicitor and not just middle-class but upper-middle-class, would never have crossed paths with working-class, Dot Green, but thanks to their work on the railways, they had met and become firm friends.

In fact, so Margaret had been told, it had been Miss Emery, the assistant welfare supervisor for women and girls, who had advised her friends to stick together and overlook all the things, such as background and class, which would normally have separated them in society. Margaret hadn't been there on everyone else's first day, but even so, she was grateful to Miss Emery, because she had benefited from the advice as much as any of them.

When Margaret reached the front of the queue, Mrs Jessop poured her a cup of tea without her needing to ask. Picking up the teaspoon that was tied to a block of wood, Margaret stirred her drink. With cutlery now being in short supply, and certain to remain so for the duration, it was normal for cafés and such like to take precautions so that their precious items stayed put.

Margaret made her way to the table and sat down. Soon they were joined by the others – Mabel, Joan, Persephone and Alison.

After the first smiling greetings, they all fell silent, looking at one another.

'We're all thinking it,' said Dot, 'so I'm going to say it. Colette.'

Margaret swallowed a lump in her throat. Colette, their dear friend, had been killed doing fire-watching duty one night the week before Christmas. It was still hard to believe. Being all together like this made it both harder to believe and yet at the same time more real.

'It must have been a pretty awful Christmas for her husband,' said Persephone.

'He must be lost without her,' said Mabel. 'He could hardly bear to let her out of his sight.'

'I've been wondering,' said Dot. 'Ought we to do something for him, like we did for Mrs Cooper after Lizzie died?'

'That was before your time, Margaret,' said Alison. 'We gave Mrs Cooper the notebook we all write in to make arrangements to meet here, and we all wrote our memories of Lizzie in the back.'

'Do you mean us to do that for Tony?' Joan asked Dot.

Glances were exchanged around the table.

'It's one thing to do it for Mrs Cooper,' said Cordelia, 'but she's a woman and a mother. It's different for a man.'

'It was just a thought,' said Dot,' but happen you're right.' She laughed. 'If I cop it, I can tell you now that my Reg wouldn't thank you for giving him our notebook.'

'It was a kind thought, Dot,' said Persephone, 'but perhaps not appropriate in this instance.'

'Tony needs to rely on his family and friends to see him through,' said Mabel.

'Does he have family?' asked Joan. 'I know Colette was an only child and she'd lost both her parents.'

'I know Tony still has his mum and dad,' said Mabel, 'because Colette occasionally mentioned going to her in-laws' for Sunday lunch, but I don't know if Tony has brothers and sisters.'

'He's in the Home Guard as well as being a fire-watcher,' Margaret added, 'so he'll know a lot of people. I'm sure they'll all be keeping an eye on him.'

Cordelia shook her head. 'Such a tragedy.'

'Aye, well, there are plenty of tragedies about these days,' said Dot, 'though perhaps not as many as there used to be, since the raids have tailed off. Let's hope they fade away altogether.'

'America's in the war now,' Mabel reminded them, 'and that's good news. The first American troops should arrive at the end of the month.'

'That's summat to look forward to.' Dot pressed Joan's hand. 'Talking of things to look forward to, how are you keeping, our little mother-to-be?'

'I'm fine, thanks,' said Joan. 'The morning sickness seems to have passed now.'

'Bad, was it?' asked Dot.

'To put it bluntly, I practically heaved my heart out every morning. Jimmy heard me a time or two, so Bob told him I have a sensitive tummy and it wouldn't be polite to mention it to anyone.'

'I bet that kept him quiet,' said Mabel. 'From what I gather, Jimmy thinks the world of Bob.'

'Aye, he does,' confirmed Dot.

Margaret looked at Dot. Was it hard for her to have her young grandson hero-worshipping Joan's husband in the absence of his father, who was away fighting? Joan and Bob lodged with Dot's daughter-in-law, Sheila, near where Dot lived in Withington, and young Jimmy Green, Sheila's son, sounded like a bit of a handful.

'I need to see Miss Emery about my condition,' said Joan.

'Shouldn't you tell the head porter?' asked Alison.

'I'd rather speak to a woman.'

'Are you going to arrange to be evacuated?' asked Margaret, thinking of Anna.

'No. I don't want to leave home.'

'I can understand that,' said Cordelia.

'And it means you'll have all of us buzzing about, keeping an eye on you,' said Mabel.

The conversation turned to descriptions of everyone's Christmas.

'I saved each of my lads a mince pie and a slice of Christmas cake,' said Dot, 'and posted them on Boxing Day.'

'So they know you were thinking of them on Christmas Day,' said Cordelia.

'I must thank Mrs Cooper,' said Dot. 'She was the one who suggested it. It was a lovely thing to do.'

'Sad, though, I should think,' said Cordelia.

'Very sad,' Dot admitted, 'but in a meaningful way.'

'I'm sure Harry and Archie will appreciate the parcels,' said Persephone.

Dot laughed. 'As long as the pastry hasn't gone mouldy by the time they receive them. What about you, Persephone? You went to see your folks after Christmas, didn't you?'

'It was wonderful,' said Persephone. 'Of course, it's all very different at home now, because it's become an Air Force billet, so the family has been relegated to a few rooms.'

'A few rooms?' said Dot with a wry smile.

'I know.' Persephone took the teasing on her perfectly sculptured chin. 'Shocking, isn't it? When I say "family" Daddy isn't there most of the time, because he's in London at the War Office.'

'Your mother must miss him,' said Alison.

A thoughtful look came into Persephone's beautiful violet eyes. 'I'm honestly not sure. That is, I'm certain she must, but she's just so frightfully busy all the time. I don't know if you're aware, but at the outbreak of war, every village had to appoint a head man. With Daddy due to be away so much, Mummy decided she would be the head man and she's … well, embraced the role, shall we say? The first thing she decided was that if the invasion happened, she would plunder the gun-room to help arm the village. She said she would personally die with a shot-gun in her hands.'

'Crikey,' said Dot.

'I think I'd like to meet your mother,' said Cordelia.

'She says the war is a lot more interesting than taking my sister and me to London in search of suitable husbands ever was.' Persephone turned to Mabel. 'You went to see your family too, didn't you?'

'Yes, I did and it was perfect. I hadn't seen Mumsy and Pops for ages. My mother organised a dance for everyone who works in Pops' factory and their families.'

'What a shame Harry couldn't have gone with you,' said Joan.

'Yes, it was, but Mumsy said that didn't let me off the hook. As the boss's daughter, it was my duty to dance with whoever asked me – and I did.'

Margaret quickly moved the subject along. She unfastened her coat. 'Do you mind if I show off my new jumper? My sister knitted it for me for Christmas.'

'Let's see,' said Dot. 'Oh, isn't it lovely?'

'She wrote in her card to me that the cream stripe is a patriotic stripe, because she couldn't get hold of enough of this reddy-brown.'

Everyone admired her jumper and Margaret lapped up the praise on Anna's behalf, but she had also wanted to divert the conversation from visiting family and she had succeeded in that. All she had done in that line was put a card for Dad through the letterbox of the house where he had been billeted since their own house had taken a direct hit. It sounded such a simple thing to do, to walk down the road where she used to live and pop a card in, but her stomach had started churning the moment she stepped off the bus and didn't stop until after she'd posted the card and walked rapidly to the corner to make her escape. Even in the blackout, she had been frightened of being seen by the neighbours.

At Wilton Close, she had made it clear quite early on after moving in that she didn't want to talk about her family and everyone respected her wishes. Even so, part of her deep inside ached to talk and be understood, but that was just her being silly and unrealistic. Some things could never be discussed, especially not when you were clinging to the remnants of your self-respect.

But hearing Persephone and Mabel talk about their mothers had made her miss Mum more than ever. Mum was long gone, but Anna wasn't and suddenly Margaret's heart ached with the need to see her beloved sister.

Hear more from

MAISIE THOMAS